D0385393

ROBIN HOOD

Tilman Röhrig

ROBIN HOOD

The SHADOWS of SHERWOOD FOREST

Translation by Oliver Latsch

Arctis

This is a work of fiction. Names, characters, places, and incidents are from the author's imagination or are used fictitiously.

Arctis US

W1-Media, Inc.
Arctis
Stamford, CT, USA

Robin Hood. Solange es Unrecht gibt first published in Germany by Dressler Verlag, 1994
First English language edition published by W1-Media Inc./Arctis, 2021

Visit our website at www.arctis-books.com
Author website at www.tilman-roehrig.de

1 3 5 7 9 8 6 4 2

Library of Congress Control Number: 2021937642
ISBN 978-1-64690-007-7
eBook ISBN 978-1-64690-607-9
Translation by Oliver Latsch
English translation edited by Carol Klio Burrell
Jacket design by Alexander Kopainski

Printed in Germany, the European Union

I

WEST OF FRANCE. CHINON CASTLE.

"The king is dead."

Whispers were spreading through long corridors, past chambers and halls. They quickly descended to the kitchen, and from there they leapt into the quarters of the maids, servants, and valets. Even before the news had left the palace courtyard on this sixth day of July, year of Our Lord 1189, the servants were already raiding the manor's contents. Candlesticks, furniture, velvet, the silver tableware, whatever they could carry was seized by greedy hands and carried away. The servants entered the royal bedchamber and robbed the deceased of his rings and chains. And they tore off his clothes.

Then silence.

Hours later, some of the vassals who were still loyal to their lord finally arrived. They stormed through the looted halls and stared in horror at the deathbed. Henry Plantagenet, King of England and ruler of the western provinces of France, Henry II, the Norman prince, so powerful in life, lay half dragged from his bed, naked and motionless before them.

The loyal ones brought new robes, clothed the dead man, and folded his hands on his chest. Only then did they cry out, "The king is dead!"

ENGLAND. LONDON.

"Long live the King!"

Two months later, the great city on the River Thames was garlanded. Shoulder to shoulder, the crowds swayed through the streets between St Paul's Cathedral and Westminster. Not just the citizens of London had left their shacks and houses to attend. They had come from all parts of England, on horseback, in carriages and carts, or on foot. Merchants and beggars, freemen and bonded men, they had all been waiting for the grand event since the early morning hours of the thirteenth of September, 1189.

The villagers from the shire of Nottingham stood close together. They were hardly more than a handful: the tinker, some women, and two children. They had sold well yesterday and the day before—carved ladles, spoons, jars, and woolens.

In the crush, the weaver woman practiced with her little son. "Say it: Long live the King!" The child struggled. The mother repeated it patiently. Suddenly, she paused. Her gaze grew stern. Her nine-year-old daughter wiped her dirty hands on her gown again. "Stop it, Marian! And stand up straight!" The mother sighed. "And please, when the king comes, shout as loud as you can!"

"I'll shout what I want." Marian ducked away and shook her head, sending untamed blond curls flying.

Armed men in chain mail pushed the people aside to form a wide passageway to the open portal of Westminster Abbey.

Fanfares! The ceremony was beginning.

Barons, earls, bishops, the noblest of the island, led the coronation procession. They were not met with applause or cheers. The citizens stretched their necks in silence. With closed faces, they watched as chosen knights and nobles carried the symbols of royal power past them: the scepter, the golden spurs, the purple cloak emblazoned with heraldic lions.

Restlessness. Suppressed curses. Here and there, artisans, fishermen, and grocers hid clenched fists behind their backs.

"Prince John," the tinker hissed to the women of Nottingham. "So, that's him."

Rumors were circulating about the younger brother of the new king, terrible rumors. And yet he was allowed to carry one of the three golden swords the long distance from the cathedral to the Coronation Church at Westminster.

Many who saw him for the first time that day shuddered.

A splendid garment hung over his slight bent shoulders. The small head turned left and right. The eyes scrutinized the crowd from under half-closed lids. Whoever happened to meet that icy gaze quickly turned away in fright.

"By St. William," the tinker muttered. "Better I stay in London for now. He has no authority *here*."

The prince who used to be known only as John Lackland had been in England for two weeks, and for two weeks, his servants had been pressed in the taverns every night. *"Tell us about him!"*

And for a jug of ale, a pitcher of wine, the grooms and footmen and bellboys quickly forgot all caution. "He is false and wrathful. No one is safe from his knife." They showed scars on their faces, their necks, their arms.

The prince was ruthless to everyone. John had always looked for an advantage. He betrayed his father, betrayed his brother, then shortly after begged them on his knees for forgiveness. John played friend and foe against each other, and now he had finally succeeded. He could shed the nickname Lackland. To keep the peace, the future king had bestowed upon his brother several counties, including sole dominion over Nottingham's castle and city, with its fertile fields and vast forests.

The tinker's glance followed the Prince. How the little head twitched to the right and left! "No, no," he reaffirmed. "Best not to go back home for a while." He scratched his bearded chin. Back home up in Nottingham, and farther north to York, the poor people would now have even more reason to be afraid. Greed, unbridled cruelty, and lust for power were truly the only qualities the twenty-three-year-old prince was known for.

Solemnly and slowly, the procession moved through the crowds.

"Over there. Do you see?" The weaver carefully turned her son's head. "There goes our old queen."

"Long live—"

She quickly covered his little mouth. "Not yet."

Queen Eleanor, the mother of these unequal sons, smiled openly and warmly to the people at the roadside, and it was returned with equal warmth.

At last—here came Richard, walking under a silken canopy. He was tall, broad-shouldered, with red hair and a red beard, and his gray eyes were set firmly forward.

The weaver lifted her son above her head. "Now."

"Long live the king," her son crowed in a bright voice.

Marian watched the tall man, her eyes shining. She supported her little brother at the top of her voice. "Long live the king!"

"Hurrah! Hail!" the bystanders shouted.

The new king radiated such strength. Even the tinker extended his arms to him and was not ashamed to do it.

True, Richard Plantagenet was a Norman, like his father. A Frenchman, a stranger to this island. For more than a hundred years, since the great battle of Hastings, Norman kings had ruled over the English people from a distance. However, their liegemen and bishops had settled here, had taken the best lands, built castles, and extended the monasteries' power. The fancied-up nobles turned up their noses at the people—*they're just barbarians,* the nobles said, *without courtly manners or culture.* They parlayed in French and laughed at the language of the oppressed. They were more ruthless than the marauding knights of old, and pressed more and more taxes from the defeated.

Who could break the tyranny of the almighty lord sheriffs, the barons, and the merciless bishops? What good were law and order if they were not applied equally to the rich and to the poorest of the poor? Up to now, the Norman kings had been too weak, or they had come to England only rarely and far too briefly. Thus the Norman nobility had ruled over the Saxons without restraint.

And yet, the people rejoiced today. Richard was strong—strong enough. His heart possessed the strength of a lion, and he had given his word: "Before me and before the law, there is no difference between Normans and Saxons." Perhaps soon they would know a life without fear? Perhaps peace and justice had really returned to the land?

"Richard the Lionheart! Long live King Richard!" All the hope of the oppressed lay in his name.

Countless candles lit up the church. The Archbishop of Canterbury daubed the head, chest, and arms of the thirty-two-year-old prince with holy oil. "Do you solemnly swear to uphold your oath?"

"Yes. With God's help."

Richard Plantagenet knelt before the altar. The archbishop slowly placed the glittering, gem-encrusted crown on his head.

Queen Eleanor looked proudly at her beloved son. Next to her, his head slightly turned away, John rubbed the white knuckles of his fingers against his teeth. His gaunt frame trembled.

"Long live the King!" Fanfares sounded from all the towers of London. "King Richard invites you to feast!"

The smells of roasted meat and fresh bread filled the streets. Foaming ale spilled out of overflowing pitchers. The weaver's son held a honeyed bun in each hand and did not know which one to tuck into first. Marian stood beside her mother with glowing cheeks, amazed and laughing.

Drums rolled. Jugglers performed daredevil tricks. Bonfires blazed until late into the night.

"Long live . . ." the tinker murmured drunkenly as he curled up against a wall.

And not a thing got better. Richard the Lionheart had no time for England, nor for the plight of his subjects.

Queen Eleanor confronted her son. "You gave your word. Your people are being tormented and enslaved. You are their hope. Do not disappoint them!"

"First, I must go to the Holy Land. My Crusade pledge is older than the oath I swore to the English people." Gently, the great man put his arm around the now-elderly dowager. "Do not worry, Mother. In two years at the most, we will have driven the infidels out of Jerusalem. When I return, I will—"

"And what happens until then?" The queen angrily freed herself from his embrace. "Who shall be your representative? Your brother John? He has the right." She sighed and quietly continued, "He also is my son. But even I am afraid of him."

"Do not worry. I appointed one of my closest friends as high judge. He will represent me during my absence. John must bow to *him*."

With a bitter smile, Eleanor looked at the king. "How little you know your brother."

Heavy clouds gathered. Rain. At the first gray light of December eleventh, Richard's ship weighed anchor.

"Safe homecoming!" On the shore, the king's courtiers and lieges shouted and waved. "We wish you safe return!"

Prince John waited motionlessly for the wide Norman ship to turn into the wind and set course for France with a billowing sail. "You shall never return," he whispered. He pressed his narrow lips together. You gave me six counties. That is not enough. I want England, your throne, and everything you own." His eyes gleamed icily. "And I wish you death, brother dear!"

II

The latest dispatch from the Crusade: *In June and July of 1191, Richard the Lionheart and the Crusader army besiege the coastal city of Acre. Sultan Saladin cannot hold the gateway to the Holy Land.*

NOTTINGHAM SHIRE. SHERWOOD FOREST.

He cut the struggling animal's neck. Still crouched in hiding, he rubbed his blood-smudged hands with earth and cleaned them on the dewy grass. It was early, just graying, a chilly October day. The smell of steaming blood and intestines hung in the air.

The giant man slipped out of the undergrowth with a brief glance back. No one would discover the spot, and by tomorrow, foxes and crows would have dispersed the bloody remains. He quickly walked away with his load. The bushes were still. No twig snapped to the right or left of the path. With the gray hood of his thick, tightly woven wool cloak pulled down to his forehead, John Little carried the dead deer draped over his shoulders and neck.

He had had good hunting. His lips stretched into a smile under his thick black mustache and beard. Forbidden hunting. He had to bring the game safely to the village before the forest rangers or the mounted soldiers of the Lord Sheriff of Nottingham started their daily patrols through Sherwood.

A jay sprang high, its warning cry audible far and wide.

"Be quiet," John growled. His fists tightened their grip on the deer's legs. He had slung the longbow on his left shoulder, and the bowstring pulled his short cloak tight against his worn leather jerkin. Antlers down, the mighty deer head hung in the crook of his right arm. John looked up and narrowed his eyes. Here and there, the first rays of sunlight flashed through the crowns of the trees. "I'm late." He quickened his pace. No sign of danger yet. "And may it stay that way." He would check the rabbit snares later.

The giant carried his heavy prey without effort. "There will be enough meat today." He pictured the wide eyes of the children, the grateful look of the women, and smiled. "Enough for us all."

His village—five huts, the stable, and fourteen people, children included—belonged to Newstead monastery. The men and women worked hard for the monks' welfare, and the peasants hardly had time to cultivate their own narrow strip of land. And this past wet summer, the fruits in the fields had rotted. Hunger loomed. The pious brothers would give nothing of their wealth, neither now in autumn, nor during the winter months.

Marian's mother always clenched her fists when she mentioned the monks. "The prior fawns over his sheep and pigs. He doesn't care what happens to us, John. While we must slave away for those black-robed vultures . . ." After a while, she added bitterly: "Until we are dead. Oh, John, it was supposed to get better for us, King Richard promised. I heard it myself. But it is worse . . ."

"Hush! I'll take care of it," he had assured her. It was no comfort to her, John Little knew that. He had lived with the weaver and her two children ever since her husband had been killed by a falling tree the previous spring. His wife had died in the harsh winter three years before. He had learned to live with the loss, but her own wound was still too fresh for Marian's mother. He did not pressure her. He gave her, her little boy, and her girl Marian his bear-strong protection, and waited.

Cattle were more valuable to the prior than the serfs who guarded them! What was left for the bondsmen of the Augustinian monastery? *Someone* had to supply them with meat.

All game in Sherwood was King's game. Such was the law. Before the coronation feast, Richard the Lionheart had granted the shire to his brother. From that day on, hares, roe deer, wild boar, and every animal of the forest belonged to the hard-hearted John. His governor and judge, the Lord Sheriff of Nottingham, had no mercy. Pity the man who was found poaching an animal. His trial would be short. Mutilation, dungeon, or death awaited him after the verdict—and woe to the village where royal game meat was found. The inhabitants were at the mercy of the judge's cruel whim.

John Little knew every trail, every deer passage in Sherwood. His fists were hard, his arrows always struck, even at a hundred paces. And so he went hunting for everyone.

Luck of the hunt, this morning he returned with great spoils. He stopped still in the shelter of the woods and peered through the leaves into the wide clearing.

Children were fighting over a wooden ball. The sod-covered huts stood together in a circle. Thin columns of smoke rose from the roof openings. There was the familiar smell of hearth fire. Two women were already sitting outside on the village yard, plucking sheep's wool from the distaff, making the spindle dance as they wound the yarn. Across the yard, next to the stable, the blacksmith and the three other men of the village were plastering the new barn's wood-post walls with clay.

"Not too late." John Little saw no black robe anywhere. The monk who supervised the day's work was not yet there.

Satisfied, he released his breath. With a swaying step, he carried his prey toward the huts. As soon as the children spotted him, they forgot their game and let the ball roll carelessly away.

"John!" They ran toward the hunter, cheering. The giant man made a frightening grimace for them, clawing back and forth like a bear in front of the giggling pack.

"Turn around! Turn around!"

"That's enough, now," he growled after a moment.

The little mouths shut immediately. The children silently ran from door to door. "A deer," they whispered. "Come quickly." Their spread arms were not long enough to show the size of the animal.

Marian stormed into the open. Her little brother followed right after. In his eagerness, he stumbled, miserably shouting after his sister. Marian did not care. She laughed at the bearded hunter, examined the prey, and took in the sight of the large antlers. "How many did it take? Say it!"

"One arrow. Straight through the heart."

"On your honor?"

"It is as I said, girl."

"Someday, I'll be able to do that, too." She whirled around in circles, blond curls flying.

The weaver woman was waiting for him outside his hut. "I'm glad you're back."

John paused a moment to give her a loving gaze, and reassure her. "It's all right." He smiled.

Behind the stable, the men of the village had already erected a wooden frame. John heaved the carcass from his shoulder, and together they hooked the game by its hind legs to the crossbar.

"We share." The giant pushed his woolen hood back around his neck. "But this time, I want all of the hide." Almost embarrassed, he wiped the sweat from his forehead up into his black mane. "I need a new jacket. There won't be much left after."

"And the antlers!" Marian reached for them.

"Let it go, girl," mumbled John. As he walked away, the neighbors carefully began to peel the deer out of its hide. What a day! Anticipation lit up their faces. There would be a feast, and everyone would be able to eat their fill!

In the hut, the hunter loosened his longbow and put it down next to the quiver. "Be right back. Just quickly checking the snares."

Marian's mother looked up from her loom. "Take care of yourself! We need you, John."

"Yes, yes." He briefly checked the hunting dagger in its sheath and reached for his oaken staff. In his hand, the man-tall, arm-thick trunk became a dangerous weapon. He could bring down rabid boars with a single blow. Push and strike: in a fight, he let the stick whirl and feared neither sword nor battle-ax.

Marian was waiting for him outside the hut. "Take me with you!" She had girded her wool frock with a leather strap, at her narrow hip she carried a knife. In her hand, she weighed the stick John had carved for her.

"I can't, girl. It is too dangerous now. Go help your mother!"

"To weave? I don't feel like it today."

"Mind what I say . . . It's getting late. You'll slow me down." Gently but firmly, he pushed her aside and left the circle of huts.

Marian ran along beside him. "Just because I'm not a boy? Is that why?" Her blue eyes sparked. "You are a coward."

He gave her no answer.

"Yes, a coward and a fool."

John walked faster toward the edge of the clearing.

"You probably needed more than one arrow for the stag." Fury drove her on. "Yes! You lied!"

The giant suddenly stopped. The scar though his beard on his right cheek flamed red. He bent down to the furious girl. "No." His voice became dark. "I will never lie to you, you know that. Or to your mother."

With that, he left Marian and plunged into the brush at the edge of the clearing. No sound of rustling marked his passage as he disappeared from her view. Not a twig snapped.

Marian looked after him and stamped her foot. "Vile man!"

Only when she had reached the village yard did her shoulders sink. The day was spoiled. And it was that big oaf's fault. Marian wiped her eyes. Should she help her mother now? No. Maybe later.

Unnoticed, she crept her way around the cottage. Right behind the henhouse, she crouched down, pushed the reed-woven lid a little to the side, and climbed into an underground chamber. She closed the hatch again, but just enough to allow a slit of daylight to enter. John and her mother stored their supplies here in the coolness. There was not much this year: two loaves of bread. A trough half-filled with grain. Next to it, some apples, pears, and nuts. And pots full to the brim with honey-sweetened berries.

Marian loved the smell of the bread and fruit. When she had been in a fight, when she was unhappy, this is where she fled. Nowhere else could her thoughts be put in order again and her heart be calmed. Marian closed her eyes. *Oh, John, I was mean to you. You never lie to me, I know that. But a girl can be just as fast as a boy. Why can't you understand that?*

Horses! Marian flinched. The thunder of hooves came closer, had already reached the village. Orders. Shouting.

Now children were crying. The women called out loudly for them. Marian pressed her hand to her mouth and pushed her face up close to the gap of light. No, her mother was not among them. She was in the hut with Marian's brother, for sure.

"King's game!"

The raw roar of strangers was everywhere.

"You stole a deer from Prince John!" one cried out over the noise. "Round them all up!"

Marian closed her eyes. Her heart was pounding. Armed men, the soldiers of the Lord Sheriff, had discovered their stag. *Holy Mother of God, do not abandon us!*

Only fragments of sentences reached her hiding place.

"Have mercy . . ."

"Spare us . . ."

"Thieves must be punished, you know that . . ." Laughter, terrible laughter. "Chop off their hands."

"Stop! Wait."

That's the blacksmith, Marian thought.

"You must not do this without the judge. Wait—" His voice broke off with a gurgling sound. Silence.

Into the silence shot a sharp cry: "Murderer! You murderers!"

"M-mother," stammered Marian. "Please don't. Please!"

But the weaver fearlessly hurled her indignation toward the henchmen. "We belong to Newstead Abbey. You can take us to court, that's all you can do. But now you are murderers, a murdering gang, nothing more. Now the father prior himself will bring charges against you with the sheriff. And we will all bear witness to what you did to our blacksmith."

Again the squad leader laughed and laughed. Suddenly he stopped. "No one will say anything."

Marian heard her mother's horrified cry. "Spare my child!" Then Mother screamed and sobbed.

Again and again, Marian shook her head. "Don't! Don't! It's not true." Tears flowed down the girl's cheeks.

"Kill them! No survivors." The leader of the troop laughed. "And you, woman, will watch. I'll kill you last."

Stomping hooves. The villagers cried out in terror, whimpering until their moans died away.

I must help Mother. "Must help." Marian opened the hatch and climbed outside. She pushed herself along the hut wall. Frozen, she stopped. Her neighbors lay in the square. Children, women, and men. Four riders rode back and forth over the dead, still stabbing them with their spears.

"Must help." There was Mother.

The troop leader had wrapped his left arm around her mother's neck from behind and pulled her pressed against his chain mail. "Open your eyes!" He shook her.

Marian whispered: "Must help. Must help." She could not move. She saw her brother, lying at their mother's feet. The cloth over his chest was dark red. "Must help."

Now the leader raised his right fist. A dagger! Marian tore open her mouth to scream. But no sound came. In her head, she kept screaming, shrill.

The man carelessly pushed his victim away.

The loud scream inside of Marian died away, but a steady muffled echo remained and filled her up. Almost gently, the world shifted away from her a little. She watched her mother fall.

The girl stood there but not there, her eyes wide.

As if from far away, she heard another roar.

The iron men spurred their horses around and formed a line. Ready for battle, their leader drew his sword. John Little was already upon him. His oak staff struck the Lord Sheriff's man right in the face. The man's head snapped back. Another roar—circling, the giant knocked two riders out of their saddles. Another roar—his blows tore through the chain mail. The fourth man stabbed with his spear at the raging giant. John repelled it, pulled the fellow down, and killed him before he reached the ground. In wild haste, the last of the murderous gang spurred his horse. The mare leaped over the corpses and rushed toward the forest.

John Little did not pursue him. Breathing heavily, he scanned the village square. His eyes found the woman slumped next to her son. John staggered over. The oak staff slipped from his hand. His mighty shoulders trembled. Silently, he dropped to both knees. As if he was afraid to wake her up, he leaned gingerly over the dead woman, lifted her long hair, and pressed it to his eyes.

The bell of the monastery rang out. The chime tore John out of his pain. He had to flee before the monk reached the village.

No matter what the mounted men had done to the peasants, the man who had escaped would blame John. The Lord Sheriff believed his own men over any serf. John knew that. And if the prior went to Nottingham to give witness? No, that would not change a thing. There would be no tedious investigating; only one man would be blamed for the slaughter. "They will hunt me down like a wild beast, like the outlaws who live in the woods," he murmured.

John Little placed the boy's body in his mother's arms. One last look. He hastily grabbed the staff and stood. No one must find him here. Longbow, quiver, flint and sponge, some bread, especially the leather water bag! In the hut, John gathered up the essentials and hurried outside again.

There he found the girl. She stood motionless next to the entrance.

"Marian." Despite his misery, he felt joy. "You're alive. You were waiting for me."

Her pale eyes looked at him, blankly.

"Marian? It's me."

She did not answer. John gently took her hot hand, touched the ashen face. "Say something!" She was silent.

"There's no time. Come on, now. I'll take you with me." She did not move a muscle. The bell of Newstead Abbey rang hard. With no further hesitation, he picked up the girl and draped her body around his broad neck. "Fear not, little one! I'll take care of you."

He left the clearing at a run. Northward, but not via the great trade road along the forest's eastern edge, not along the cart tracks that ran from village to village through Sherwood. John knew the old, almost overgrown craftsmen's trails. But quickly now—he would have to cross the forest before the pursuers could cordon off the area. There was not much time, perhaps only until the next noon, and at night it would be too dangerous to run, and the limp girl only further slowed his progress.

Not too much haste; he must not tire himself out too quickly! John slowed his speed. His mind forced his muscles to rest. From there on, his steady, measured breaths determined the steady, persistent pace of his steps. Now and then, he spoke to Marian but received no answer. So the giant only made sure that no branch, no thorny vine hurt the girl. They would not be safe until they had crossed the border to Yorkshire. Alone and in dry weather, the route usually took him a day via the trade road. "Two days this time," he estimated.

The night fell far too quickly over Sherwood. The outlines of the trees turned black. Before darkness descended completely, John Little sought a sheltered campsite.

"Have a drink, child." He squatted next to Marian in the moss, held her curly head, and placed the leather bag's horn mouthpiece against her cracked lips. At first, the water ran down her chin, but then Marian opened her mouth. A first sip, a second.

"That's the way." John smiled. When he felt her hand on his arm, he murmured, "I will hold the bag. You just drink."

Next, he took the horn between his teeth. Without stopping, he quenched his great thirst.

"Do you want bread?"

The girl shook her head slowly.

"Say something," he asked and waited.

Marian was silent. Suddenly she trembled all over her body. Helplessly, she opened her mouth, and tears ran down her cheeks.

"Don't. Leave it, then. Let it be!" He stroked her skinny back. "No more crying!"

Later, John cleared the hiding place of rotten branches. On top of the moss, he piled more moss, so that his charge would be comfortable. "Sleep now, little one!"

She stared at him.

"We must rest. Tomorrow will be hard."

Marian curled up.

"That's right," he murmured. Lying on his side, he moved the girl closer to him so that she could sleep on the mossy bed, protected in the crook of his giant body.

III

NOTTINGHAM SHIRE.
SHERWOOD FOREST.

Visible from far across the plain, the castle stood high above the River Trent on a hilltop. Extending close to the edges of the steep cliffs, the defensive walls, towers, and buildings enclosed a courtyard. The only way up or down was through the gate and drawbridge to the northeast. To the right and left of the sloping road, the poorest peasants had built their huts and stables. A little farther down by the market, beside the smoky taverns, stood the houses of the court servants and merchants, substantial houses with carved doors. The most splendid one, only a few steps away from the church, belonged to the Lord Sheriff.

In case of an imminent attack, the inhabitants fled up to the castle fortress. Its walls could withstand any assault, and Nottingham Castle was well equipped for a siege.

The mountain's sandstone was riddled with countless caves, back and forth and up and down, ancient, carefully closed tunnels and newly excavated passages. Almost all the entrances into them were located in the city. And the more recent shafts had been expanded into chambers by stonemasons. There, grain and salted meat and dried stockfish were stored, enough to hold out until a besieging enemy ran out of supplies.

However, the citizens were careful not to open their ancestors' tunnels and penetrate deeper into the dark labyrinth of caves. They were often startled from their sleep. *Wasn't that a scream? Can't you hear the whimpering?* Mothers pressed their children to their breasts. *Hush! Herne the Hunter is driving the souls of the damned through the mountain. Hush! We are safe here in bed.*

The largest cave belonged to the castle. Those who knew its secret could travel the tunnel through many turns all the way down to the cliff directly above the banks of the River Trent. The tunnel's upper, spacious niches served as wine and ale cellars, and the lower side tunnels were lined with iron grates embedded in the rock. How many of the sheriff's prisoners had perished miserably in those dungeon cells, tortured, tormented by rats? Up in the castle hall, daylight fell through high slit windows and spread like a shining jewel directly upon the elevated dais at one end. This bright area, surrounded on three sides by tapestries of hunting scenes, was reserved for the count and his guests of honor. The rest of the room remained in a gloomy twilight even during the day, sparsely lit by the glow of the fireplace.

When Prince John was not in Nottingham, his governor and Lord Sheriff took advantage of the freedom. He claimed the stately dais for himself and loved to conduct his official business there instead of in his own house. It gave him pleasure to look down on the accused on court day.

Small in stature, Thom de Fitz dressed according to the latest French fashion. On each hand, he wore three artfully forged rings. In a tournament bout with sharp weapons, the Lord Sheriff had lost the tip of his nose. Since this defeat, he had covered the scarred stump with a false nose of chalk paste every day. Despite his pleas and then his threats, his wife Beatrice had never gotten used to this sight. But no stranger dared to scoff, especially when anger darkened the sheriff's face and made the mark of his shame stand out even more.

Thom de Fitz was on his guard this morning. As a precaution, he had taken a seat in his master's high armchair behind a massive oak table. His visitor sat directly opposite him, eye to eye. More than an hour had passed, and again and again, the Lord Sheriff had tried to outsmart the prior of Newstead Abbey.

"He is the only witness!" With an outstretched finger, Thom de Fitz pointed toward his man-at-arms somewhere deep in the hall's semidarkness. "And he is telling the truth."

"The truth?" The prior mockingly raised his brows. "Pardon me. Since Prince John appointed you judge here, the truth has become a rare commodity. Hardly anyone has seen it lately."

"Hold your tongue!"

Unimpressed, the prior smoothed a wrinkle on his dark travel cloak. "The fact is, *cher ami*: My monk, who supervises the peasants, went over to the village yesterday after the morning bell. There he found all the inhabitants slain. Slaughtered most horribly, if I may say so." A slight indignant shake of the head. "Even the children!" The pious gentleman continued: "These people belonged to my abbey. I have lost property!"

"*Diable!* My men were lying just beside them. I am less four armed men. We are even."

Tense silence. The sheriff pressed his hands against each other, an angry blush spreading over his angular face. Only the white spot on his nose did not change.

They eyed each other. A conciliatory word spoken too soon would cost money, pieces of silver coins.

"The fact is, *cher ami,* none of the villagers would have dared to attack your henchmen."

The Lord Sheriff thumped his fists on the table. *"Diable!"*

"Do not curse in my presence," the prior admonished him softly. "It will get us nowhere. We are negotiating a transaction, nothing more."

"Very well. By St. Dunstan, then! Let's start at the beginning. for the last time." Thom de Fitz snapped his fingers at his armory sergeant. "What happened yesterday in this village?"

"It was like this ..." Under cover of the semidarkness, the sergeant repeated his memorized story. They had discovered the stag. As ordered, they had rounded up the people in the village square. "Our squad leader was just about to start the interrogation. Then the monster came out of the forest. Not with a staff, he came at us with a tree trunk. Nothing could be done against the savage. My comrades were dead. I barely escaped."

"And the villagers? Were they still alive?" the sheriff pressed on.

"When I left, everyone was well." A long pause.

"Go on, lad!"

"That's what happened. I heard the screams behind me. That's what happened. Everyone was screaming, including the children." The servant fell silent.

"*Bien*. Are you finally convinced, venerable father?" Thom de Fitz pulled out a small cloth with the ringed fingers of his right hand and wiped his face, carefully dabbing around the stump of his nose. He then ordered his sergeant: "Get out! Wait outside!"

No sooner had the armed man left the hall than the prior added, in the witness's tone of voice: "And then, the monster mauled the peasants. Yes, it was just like that." He laughed dryly. "Excuse me. Even the third time doesn't make the story any more credible. No, *cher ami*. This is not going well for you. Consider that it is not just some Saxon chief who has had valuable serfs slaughtered like cattle, but I, a Norman and prior of an Augustinian monastery. And this act was not committed by forest rangers, but by Nottingham castle guards. No law gives armed men the right to do this. They only undertake such raids on your express orders. And don't they have a far greater nuisance to deal with in Sherwood?"

The Lord Sheriff froze, struck to the core ...

Before Thom de Fitz could compose himself, the pious prior lifted his finger. "Is it not so? Your men are hunting those outlaws in vain. They stalk through the forest like blind sheep. There are rumors everywhere that the vagabonds have become more and more organized during your time as sheriff. They are even said to have a leader. What was the name?" The prior tapped his fingers on his forehead. "*Capuchon? Capeline?* That they wear over their heads, it's supposed to be green. I cannot think of the word in the language of these uncouth Saxons."

"Hood!" Thom de Fitz grunted. "Robin Hood is what this fellow calls himself. *Par saint Fontin!*"

"No swearing in my presence!" The prior glared, menacingly.

The sheriff bit his lips.

"*Bien, mon cher.* It's no secret: Because you neglect your duties, the savages run free. Instead, you let the villagers be terrorized. You alone are responsible for the killing and plundering. Pitiable Thom de Fitz, you know your master well enough. Prince John wants his shield to look unblemished ... on the outside. And you must see to it!"

The sheriff's face had lost all its color.

Coolly, the prior dealt him the final blow: "What will happen if I report the matter higher up and bring charges before England's highest judge, King Richard's deputy? No one in the kingdom will dare to challenge the influential Order of Augustinians, not even Prince John. *Mon Dieu,* I cannot imagine how he will deal with you in his rage!"

"Enough. No more!" The sheriff leaned far over the table. "What do you want?"

The pious prior modestly folded his hands over his bulging belly. "For each woman and each man twenty shillings. Ten for each child."

"*Bien.* This time I will be generous." Thom de Fitz had already pulled out his coin purse, but suddenly he hesitated. "What do we say if inquiries are made at your monastery or here in the city?"

"*Nom de Dieu*, my dear sheriff, did your man not mention a monster? Just between us, there *was* a man of unusual size in the village. I do not know his name, but I have often been told of his amazing strength. It would appear that he killed your men. He has become worthless to me. Let us make use of him: We have our monster. The fact is this: A rabid peasant caused the bloodbath and is on the run."

"You are a sly fox, my lord." The sheriff smiled. "You came to me to report this terrible incident. I have ordered a hunt for the killer, as is my duty. When he is caught, he will resist and be killed. No more witnesses. And on top of that, I shall have satisfied the law. *Parbleu, mes compliments!*"

"If you compensate my loss with coin, I will confirm your story."

The ringed fingers tugged at the string of the pouch. "How many there were?"

"Four men and three women, and five children. That's seven pounds and another two pounds and ten shillings."

Thom de Fitz walked his guest out. High up on the battlement, carpenters were mending damaged planks. As usual, the courtyard of the castle was bustling with maids, manservants, and armed men. The iron-reinforced gate stood wide open, the drawbridge was lowered, and the cries of merchants echoed up from the market.

"One more word of advice, in parting." The prior took the sheriff's arm. With a sideways glance at the obediently waiting man-at-arms, he whispered: "Only when there is no one, and I emphasize *no witness*, left, only then can this *affaire funeste* no longer harm you. May God be with you!" With this, the prior went over to the two friars of his abbey. One of them held his mule's bridle, the other helped the corpulent prior into the saddle.

Thom de Fitz watched the Augustinian until he had ridden through the archway. "It is not just your robe that is dark, you cunning cutthroat!"

With a snap of his fingers, he ordered the sergeants of the castle guard to come to him. "The murderer of your comrades is still at large. He is probably trying to head north." The orders were brief. Five men and a pack of dogs were to follow the trail. "And no mercy, Baldwin. Bring him to me, dead!" He pulled the sergeant down by his beard. "But before that ..." His thumb pointed to the waiting man-at-arms who had given testimony. "As I have just learned, your mates would still be alive if that bastard had not cowardly abandoned them. Therefore ..." The ringed hand made a tight horizontal cut across his throat. "You understand, Baldwin? And right away. Nothing should be left of him."

The man's hatred was inflamed as intended. "To the kennel with him!"

"No, no. Leave him to the rats! The dogs must not eat now. They must be starving when they chase the killer through Sherwood."

The sergeant straightened and turned to the man-at-arms. "Hey, you! Before we set off to hunt your monster, we'd better have a drink. The sheriff is treating us to a pitcher of ale. Come along!"

The soldier was only too happy to obey and was already licking his lips. With a broad grin, Baldwin closed the gate down into the cave behind them. "Take the torch and go ahead!"

Before they reached the ale cellar, he rammed his knife into the unsuspecting man's neck. "Shame. If it had been up to me, I would have let you die slowly." The sergeant spat and raised the torch. With one hand, he dragged the dead man by his iron collar deeper into the mountain. He left the body below the dungeon cells, in a blind corridor. In time, nothing would remain of it but a skeleton. And who in Nottingham cared about bones and rusty chain mail?

When he returned to the courtyard, Baldwin nodded to his master.

"Bien. Très bien," murmured Thom de Fitz. "Now there is only one witness left. And he will not escape me." Elated, he returned to the hall to attend to his official business.

A short time later, five men-at-arms mounted their horses. Each had a crossbow, sword, and lance. Their helmets' iron nose guards gave their faces a rigid cruelty. The high-legged gray hounds were panting, baring their teeth, impatiently yanking at their long leather leashes.

Sergeant Baldwin raised his fist to the sky. "Fooor-ward!"

The hunt for the monster, for the murderer of his comrades, had begun.

IV

SHERWOOD FOREST

In the morning, Marian ate some of the bread. She had tried to walk, a few steps, unsteady, much too slow for an escape.

"You'll be all right." John Little was confident, although the child still did not speak. "You'll be all right if you eat and drink."

Before they left, Marian had made it clear to him by signs that she wanted to sit on his shoulders, rather than be draped across them like a carcass.

"Then show me you can!" The giant slung the taut bow on his left shoulder and the fighting staff beside his right leg. Marian hesitated.

"Come on, little one! You can do it all by yourself."

She finally clambered up over his knee and arm and sat astride his neck. She wrapped her arms around the giant and leaned her face into his black mane.

John snorted and pranced. But there was no laughter, not even a giggle in response. Only a faint tug at his chin beard signaled that his ward felt safe.

Hills and valleys, thick-stemmed oaks, beeches, ash trees, then thick bushes again. They had made good progress through Sherwood. Around noon they reached the rise above the River Meden. "If these fellows are fast, they'll be waiting for us down there," John figured. From his shoulder, Marian had clambered onto the broad branches of a beech tree. "Wait here."

John carefully surveyed the riverbank below. Then, roaring like a bull, he suddenly stormed through the ford to the opposite side. He stopped, waited.

Nothing moved. No ambush. The hunters had not entered Sherwood from the main road along the Meden River. "Then they'll be trying farther north at the River Poulter. Otherwise, they'll never catch me."

And on they went. They bypassed two settlements. No dog barked, nobody noticed them. In the early afternoon, rain set in. At first, they heard the patter high above them, in the leafy canopy. Eventually, the water came through, and soon the path was sodden. John let Marian get down. Her curls hung in limp strands, the wet frock stuck to her. She stared past him absently.

"You shall not freeze." He loosened the neck strap of his gray wool cloak, and wrapped the cloak around the girl, pulling the hood over her wet head.

In the vast, jagged valley of the Poulter, they waited. The only way to cross over was between the upper and lower lakes, where the water flowed past the village of Carburton and through a narrow riverbed for a good two miles.

And from there, John already heard the hoarse barks of a pack of hounds and the horn signals of the Lord Sheriff's men-at-arms.

"We can't get past them that way," he whispered to his rider. "Hold on tight! It's going to get rough." Marian tugged at the beard hairs. She had understood.

John left the path and entered Sherwood to the west. Gradually the barking of the dogs faded away. The cloudy sky covered the sun. In order not to lose his bearings, John wandered within sight of the upper lake. He knew that the shore would eventually lead him north again. His progress was laborious. On paths torn into by the storm, he was blocked by giant fallen trees. And rain, ever more rain. The hidden gullies were dangerous. Often, he groped with his staff like a blind man across heights covered with thickets and moss. The giant lost time, valuable time.

At dusk, rocks rose up on their left. "We mustn't go any farther, girl. Creswell lies beyond that." The village was in the shire of Derby. The Sheriff of Nottingham also ruled Derby.

John found a dry cave, built a fire, and persuaded Marian to eat some bread. She took only two bites. "We'll make it across tomorrow," he promised. The girl had closed her eyes and sank forward. Gently John caught the slumping body and leaned her head against his side.

The space was too narrow for him. He tried to sleep, but terrible images rose through his dreams. John groaned and pressed his fist against his forehead. He wanted to get some rest, at the least.

Dense wafts of mist hung in the treetops. The rain had stopped.

John gathered some mushrooms to strengthen them. "They won't find us in the fog. What do you think?" Tense, he waited, hoped. In vain. Marian remained silent.

"Well, never mind. You'll see, one day, everything will be good."

She refused to climb onto John's shoulders, paced up and down the cave to prove to him how strong she was again. John clapped his hands. "That's it, girl."

He gave her time. For a grueling mile, Marian bravely kept up. After she had stumbled the third time, she yanked at his leather jacket and pointed to his shoulders.

"Well, come on up! I have plenty of room."

They crossed the upper reaches of the Poulter. In a wide arc, John returned to a path that tradesmen had once used on their way north.

The fog lifted. The trees stood far apart, with more bushes and shrubs instead. They had almost reached the edge of Sherwood when the smell of roasting meat warned John. He stopped at once and held the fighting staff tighter.

It was too late. A voice from behind commanded, "Move on, man! Nice and slow . . . or you'll have my arrow in your back."

John obeyed. With Marian on his shoulder, he could not let himself fall, nor could he suddenly jump to the side and turn to attack the enemy behind him.

"Now, go left!" the voice ordered.

John obeyed. "Don't be afraid!" he whispered to Marian. They came through the bushes to a clearing. Three men sat around a fire. Each of them was roasting a hare on a stick.

Forester rangers! The silver emblems on the dark leather caps and the almost-black leather jerkins were unmistakable.

They had hardly spotted the giant when each one threw his roast into the grass and reached for a bow—three arrowheads were aimed at John's mighty chest.

"Quiet, people!" came the voice with another order. "He won't risk anything." With that, the fourth forest ranger slipped past John. He stood there, standing broad-legged, and mocked, "He is obedient as a lamb."

I could crush you. John conquered his rage. His opponents had the advantage, and he could not fight them. *Just as well,* he thought.

The forester had to tip his head back to look face-to-face with his prisoner.

"Where are you from?"

"From back that way."

"What's your name?"

"John."

"What are you doing in Sherwood?"

"Goin' up that way."

The woodsman shouted over his shoulder to his comrades. "A bit dimwitted, this one. What do you fellows think?"

"I don't know," said one.

"Be careful," said another.

The leader narrowed his eyes. "You're under arrest."

"I'm not."

"Any man caught with a bow and arrow in Sherwood will be arrested," the leader announced. "We'll take him over to Worksop. He stays in jail until court day."

With both fists, John deliberately clutched the man-size, arm-thick oak staff and put one foot forward.

The forester jumped back. The others stood ready to shoot.

John did not seem to notice the danger. He sniffed, stared at the roast hare, and licked his lips. "I'm hungry."

"Yes, he *is* dim."

"Ask him about the brat," someone demanded.

The forester pointed at Marian.

John was silent.

"Well, come on."

"What?"

"Who's that?"

"Daughter."

"Drop the girl. But before that, hand over your bow and quiver."

The giant obeyed only when one of them aimed the arrow at his ward.

Marian stood still. Her blue eyes showed no fear, but stared blankly through the men. The forester asked her name, but she did not answer. He shouted at her. He grabbed the girl by the shoulders. He shook her. No reaction. Upset, he raised his fist.

A rumble made the guy spin around.

"She's got the awful fever."

Horrified, the royal forest rangers stepped back. John grinned stupidly, babbling, "The Master has cast us out." He let his big head dangle back and forth, stepped from one foot to the other, and uttered strange sounds.

"Both have it. By St. Godrick. Both of them!" Fear seized the troop. "Chase them away," one of them demanded hastily.

"Don't move!" The forester ducked and crept closer, picked up longbow and quiver from the ground, and hurriedly threw the weapons into the fire. "There. And now grab your brat! Get lost!"

John shouldered the oak staff, shook his head, and nodded to Marian. He pushed her closer to the fire. The men's drawn arrows followed every move of the giant.

"I'm hungry." Calmly John bent down and took a wooden skewer together with a brown-roasted hare and laid it on his shoulder with the fighting staff.

"Away with you," cried the forester.

Without haste, without turning around again, John led the girl from the clearing. No sooner were they out of sight than he lifted Marian on his arm. "Hold on, little one!" He made off at a run.

Soon, Sherwood opened. John stopped running. At a safe distance, he walked west past the town of Worksop, breathing with relief. A vast sunny landscape opened up in front of them: villages, rolling hills, fields and meadows, scattered small copses of trees. "We'll be down there by evening."

They rested in a sheltered grassy hollow. John enjoyed the smell of roast hare. "King's quarry." He winked at Marian. "No one has ever voluntarily given one to me." Happily, he cut a tender piece from the back for her. "Here. This is the best."

Marian took it. For a moment, she looked at him clearly and openly.

John leaned over to her. "Yes. Come on, say something. Yes, try!"

Marian clenched her fingers into the meat. She moved her lips, struggled. Tears rose.

John quickly stroked her head. "Never you mind! If that's how it is, that's how it is."

They ate the rabbit. The girl took only a little, John ate the rest, nibbled every bone clean.

As they headed along the edge of a cart track, Marian sat on his shoulders again. After an hour, John tugged her foot. "I don't understand, little one. Before I ate the rabbit, my hunger was not nearly as bad as it is now. Do you understand that?"

She grabbed his mane of hair and shook his head.

Then he laughed.

Farmers' wives passed them. A wagon overtook them. Nobody paid much mind to the man who carried a child on his shoulders and greeted them politely. John was convinced: "The men-at-arms won't look for me this far north." And if they did, if he was stopped? Very well. He was merely a father taking his sick daughter to the next town. Who would be suspicious? Unless . . . ? John thought of the sole one of those murderers who had escaped. No. He brushed the thought aside. *They won't look for me that far north.*

At last they crossed into Yorkshire, late in the afternoon. Like a big wheel, the giant let the staff whirl around his right hand, then grabbed it again firmly. "Tonight, little one, we sleep well. I promise."

He spotted a mill by a stream and knocked. With a bland expression, the miller listened to the father's story about the sick daughter and asked no questions. It was fine with him. They could sleep in the hay.

His wife brought a cup of milk over to the barn. She had pity on the exhausted, mute girl. Uncertain, the woman stood there, staring John in the face and then turning her back to him. Falteringly she asked, "Might you know my son?"

"What is his name?"

"Much. Yellow-haired boy."

"No, I've never met him."

"He's on the run, too."

John sucked in his breath. “What are you talking about? I’m taking my daughter—”

“Stop! I saw it in your eyes. They change, I’ve seen it.” The miller’s wife turned around again. “Don’t be afraid! We won’t say anything. We never say anything.” Her lips trembled. “When you meet my son . . . Tell him we are thinking of him. But he must not come here, tell him. Tell him it was the Baron’s own servants. They killed the steward. And Sir Roger ordered it. Tell him that!” And she raised her hands in despair. “But Sir Roger blames my boy. Because he needs someone to blame.”

She began to hurry away. After a few more steps, she stopped again. “Much. That’s his name. Much. Remember that!”

John scratched his beard, staring after her until she disappeared into the cottage. “Fine, then,” he murmured. “I’ll remember.”

Later, he lay stretched out on his back. Marian had curled up next to him. “You know, girl, we are going over to Doncaster. That’s a real town. I’ll ask at the blacksmith. I bet he could do with another pair of strong hands. We’ll stay there through the winter.” John paused and listened. In short, regular pace, Marian breathed in and out. “Poor thing. At least I can hear that much from you.”

Before he fell asleep, he thought, *Next time, I’ll take* all *their rabbits.*

V

YORKSHIRE. DONCASTER AND FARTHER NORTH.

John had asked twice. And for the second time, the blacksmith had shaken his head. With sharp hammer blows, he stretched the red-hot iron on the anvil, thrust it into the water, until he was satisfied. Only then did the blacksmith look at the tall man and say, "Look! I won't feed two mouths." He pointed to Marian. "The mute there is worth nothing." In a mollifying gesture, he offered the giant a sip of ale. John refused.

"I can do the work of three."

"You must understand . . ." The blacksmith drank until the brownish ale ran down his chin and neck. "I could use you. But first, you have to get rid of that one. Mutes in the house bring bad luck. You best leave her outside a convent."

John breathed heavily. The scar through his beard turned dark.

The blacksmith didn't notice. He carried on. "Or better still, sell her to a beggar. They like to have mutes with them because mutes make good thieves."

"I'll shut you up!" John grabbed the man by the leather apron with his left fist and lifted him up to his face. "By Dunstan! I'll—"

Marian tugged at the giant's coat and shook her head pleadingly. Her fear brought John to his senses. He eased his anger. "It's all right, little one."

No sooner was the blacksmith safely back on the ground than the man puffed himself up. "Out! Or I'll call the guards. Get out!"

He gasped for breath. "Everyone here knows me. Even our Sir Roger. Because I am the Baron's blacksmith. You'll find no work in Doncaster, I'll see to that. You understand me?"

Without a word, John turned around. Marian was already waiting at the wide-open door of the workshop.

"Get out! Don't you dare come here again," cried the blacksmith. In the street, John could still hear him cursing. "Damned scum! Where are you from anyway? You come here with a mute? Miserable vermin!"

Without a look left or right, they left Doncaster. Marian walked beside the giant. Since the day before, since the miller's barn, he had not had to carry the girl. Her gaze was now mostly clear and alert.

John was silent. Now and then, Marian poked him on the arm. He smiled briefly but said nothing. Anger and powerlessness kept their grip on him.

In the afternoon, the walls of a monastery appeared beyond green pastures. Marian crouched down in the grass. She pointed to the bag of provisions the miller's wife had slipped to them when they left.

"Good eating, little one." John sat with her.

Cheese and apples. Marian ate her fill, then she got up.

"Not so fast. No one will look for us here."

Their faces were at the same level. She lightly tugged his beard, turned around, and walked away across the pasture toward the monastery.

It took a while before John realized what she was planning to do.

With one motion he leaped up, was beside her in giant strides, obstructed Marian's path. "Don't, girl. Don't!"

Her eyes were determined. She pointed over to the monastery wall and tried to pass him.

"No. I won't give you away."

Her eyes remained fixed on the wall.

"Your mother would ..." John faltered. For the first time, he'd spoken of the weaver, and he could not speak any further. He wiped his eyes. "You know, Marian. I, too, have ... you know ..." With his big hands, he gently enclosed her outstretched hand. "You know, Marian ... I need you. You can't leave me alone!"

Her narrow shoulders sank.

Although no sound came out of her open mouth, she shook with sobs. "We'll stay together," he comforted her. "We stay together," he consoled himself.

They were lucky. A wagoner let them sit in the back. John talked a lot during the ride. He made plans. "We head north. I ask for work in every town and village. And if there isn't any ... Fine. Then we go on." Marian just watched him. Sometimes she smiled. "And if we can't find a place to stay ... I'll build us a hut for the winter, where no one will find us. I just need a new bow. An elm—no, better still, I'll find a yew. We won't starve."

At Wrangbrook, John helped the wagoner unload the barrels and was paid three pennies. "Well, there you are, little one."

They saved their money and lay down to sleep in an abandoned cattle shelter outside the village. The day had been unusually warm for early October. The night would not be too cold. Nevertheless, John had piled up some stones and lit a fire.

As it burned down, he returned to his plans, reading the pictures from the flames, hope for Marian, and for himself. "You know, far in the north, the highlands begin." He had never been there before, and he could not remember a place name. There was surely a piece of land somewhere that belonged to no one, no monastery, no prince. Surely there must be something like that. He promised Marian such a small patch. That would be enough for a home. "And just beyond, you know, where the sky almost touches the earth, that's where I think the old gods live. And somewhere in the middle, King Arthur has a castle, too. Remember, dearheart, how the tinker told us about it? And King Arthur's bailiff, he must need a guy like me." He listened. Marian had long since fallen asleep. "Even if you never say another word," he whispered, "so be it. I will speak for you."

In the morning, before the girl woke, John stood up quietly, found some embers under the ashes, and built a new fire. The morning sun had already dried the dew and opened the autumn flowers.

They had no more bread. For a moment, he thought of the blacksmith of Doncaster. No, no stealing. Marian could ... certainly anybody would give to a mute ... John slapped his forehead violently. "One of these days, I'm going to shut that fellow up," he said to himself. Their misery was not all that great. After all, they had three pennies, more than enough to buy bread. But it would be better if they put the money aside for the winter. "Don't worry, girl, I'll take care of it!"

In the nearby forest, John refilled the empty bag with tasty mushrooms, enough for the day. On the way back, he heard a buzzing. It passed by him again, and again. The hunter narrowed his eyes and followed the bees' flight to a withered, man-high tree stump nearby. "This is going to be quite the surprise, little one."

He quickly brought the mushrooms to the campground, pulled a charred branch out of the fire, and turned back. With the hood of his cloak pulled over his head, and bent low, without sudden movements, John crept behind the tree trunk.

The guards had not spotted the enemy.

He drilled an opening at knee height with his knife and pushed the smoldering branch into the hollow tree. As smoke began to billow out of the hole, John struck at the roots with his flat hands and then kept striking higher and higher toward the trunk. At the base of the tree, he clenched his hands into fists. Blow after blow, the beats became stronger.

The honey fortress trembled and smoked. Inside, the excitement grew. Alarm! Highest alarm! The escape route was not yet blocked. Her Majesty the Queen dared to flee under the guard of the whole swarm.

The raider waited until the buzzing and humming faded into a distance. A mighty fist punch widened the hole. With both hands, John broke the trunk apart and retrieved the waxy treasure.

What a meal! John laughed when he saw Marian's round eyes. He and Marian squeezed out the honeycombs. The honey melted on their tongues. Marian left her hands sticky.

Soon they were wandering north again on the main road. Marian put one after the other of her sweet fingers in her mouth and licked.

"You will see," John said with a smile, "the two of us will get by." Even without begging! He was ashamed of his thoughts from the morning. He stopped abruptly. Had he just seen rooftops on the left? John slowly went back. After the fifth step, he saw them. After the sixth, they were out of sight again. "Over there, little one." Only a trained eye could make out the dark thatched roofs in the dense, rising forest while passing by. Finally, Marian nodded.

The village seemed very close, barely a mile away. "I'll ask for work there."

There were no crossroads. John took note of the direction and left the road with Marian. After an arduous stretch across the woods, they suddenly came upon a path. "People rarely walk here." John thoughtfully examined the tracks. "Well, little one. We've come this far now. It can't be much farther," he promised.

John was wrong. The winding path broke off abruptly and descended between boulders into a ravine. The settlement had to lie somewhere on the hill opposite.

From the depths they heard dull roaring and rustling. The descent lasted a good hour. Nearby, water plunged from high above into a lake, which poured it into a broad riverbed. Water droplets flickered, weaving colorful, iridescent veils over the valley.

Before the last bend, John pulled the girl into a bush. Crouching, they pushed on and peered through the leaves. The path ended at the river. A thick, long tree trunk led across. At its top, wide notches were hewn in like stairs. Below, the water rushed, splashing and swirling. John scratched his beard. If hardly anyone used the path, why was the tree hewn into a footbridge?

"I don't know, little one," he whispered. On the other side, the terrain remained level for a while, with shrubs and bushes at the water's edge. Behind it, mighty oaks and beeches stretched up the hill.

Immediately after the crossing, the path lost itself in the thicket. The big man felt uneasiness all the way down his neck. Determined, he put down their provisions and the water bag. "Wait here," he whispered. "Don't move! I'll get you in a moment." Marian nodded and crouched down on the soft forest floor.

With the fighting staff in his fist, John returned to the spot where they had left the path.

Humming a song, he stepped around the bend. Like a thirsty wanderer, the giant knelt down by the water, drank and cooled his bearded face, and from the corner of his eye he checked the opposite bank. Nothing. Nowhere did branches twitch, no leaf turned differently than the others.

But the uneasiness remained.

"Fine, then," he murmured and climbed over the stones that formed steps up to the tree footbridge. The notches in the bridge had been hewn to match the strides of a normal-sized man. For John they were much too close together. He quickly reached almost the middle.

"Hey! Get away!"

John jumped to attention. He had looked down for only the briefest of moments at his feet. Just a second ago the footbridge had been empty. As if from nowhere, a stranger had appeared. He was coming toward John, had already come as close as ten paces. Now he stopped, his left foot braced in front of him. "Are you deaf? Go back!"

The top of the man's head almost reached the top of John's chest. A tall fellow compared to anyone else. He had strength. Tensely, John assessed the danger. A quiver sat high and slightly slanted at the man's back, the arrow shafts were quickly at hand, as good archers kept them. But the longbow was still shouldered. John breathed out. *Until you grab it, I have you.* He took his time. Everything on this fellow was green except his belt, hunting horn, and dagger. The trousers, the doublet—nothing ragged and everything dark green. *Maybe that's why I didn't spot you.* Even the short cowl was green, the hood pulled far over the man's forehead. John saw nothing of the man's eyes, only the narrow nose, mouth, and chin. No beard. A smooth face. *So, you are a nobleman.*

"How much longer do I have to wait?"

The giant knew that tone. He grinned in reply and spat in the water. *I'm not taking orders from anyone here. He's no reckless youngster, but he's got a big mouth.*

"Come to your senses, dwarf, and get off the bridge!" The stranger spoke to him now as if to a child. "Don't make me have to get cross with you!"

Anger rose in John. "You pompous . . . frog," he growled at the man dressed all in green.

"Now, that's what I like to hear. I was afraid you were mute."

Marian! She was waiting behind John. *No matter what happens, that man must not get to the other side.* "No more talking!" John gripped the fighting staff tighter and crouched to attack.

The stranger flexed his shoulder, his bow jumped into his left hand, his right hand shot up and grabbed an arrow. In one smooth movement, the feathered shaft sat on the string, already pulled back to his ear. "Try it! And you are dead."

John had only managed two steps forward. He faltered and shook his head in disbelief. Never before had he seen such speed with a bow. "All right." Very slowly, he stood upright again and lifted the staff in front of him.

"Back! I will not tolerate strangers in my territory." The voice had become sharp, cutting. "Walk backward. And then get out of the ravine! Before I change my mind."

John did not move. *You're not an earl, nor one of the royal foresters.* Beads of sweat ran down the giant's forehead. Yesterday it was *get out of town!* And today it was *get off the road!*

Marian and I are not street dogs. Everyone we meet can't give us a kick.

But the braggart on the bridge had the advantage. John had to buy time, had to stop the scoundrel somehow. He forced his face into a grin. "All I've got is my walking stick. What about you?" He spat at the green man's feet. "You're gonna shoot me off the bridge just for trying to cross it? You're a coward. You're nothing without your bow."

The stranger laughed gleefully but kept the string taut by his ear. "The dwarf has wit. Nice."

John snorted and tightened his grip on the staff again.

"Now, now. I wouldn't do that." The green man clicked his tongue. "Coward? No one's ever gotten away with calling me that."

"You've also not met me yet."

"That's enough. I could shoot you like a dumb ox, just like that. But it's no fun. I've already wasted too much time on you. So I'm giving you a chance." He lowered his bow. "Don't move. I'll cut a young oak . . . and come back without my bow. Then I'll teach you a thing or two." The green man laughed again. "A fair game."

"This is no joke," growled John.

"I make the rules here," the stranger barked at him. "And you will be sorry if you do not follow them."

John nodded. *I'm going to crack your skull,* he thought.

The green man turned around nimbly, ran back the way he had come, jumped off the tree-bridge with a giant leap, and disappeared into the bushes.

He is quick, like a marten. John wiped his brow. "By St. Dunstan. If only I had stayed on the big road." He didn't fear the fight, but he had unnecessarily endangered Marian. Should he just go back now and get her out of this valley as fast as he could? Why brawl with that fellow first? *No, when I turn around, I'll end up with an arrow in my back.*

"Hey, dwarf!" The green man returned, without bow and quiver, armed only with a roughly smoothed oak staff. Ready for battle, John pulled his tightly woven hood over his head. The stranger jumped onto the walkway and came closer, playfully twirling the stick, throwing it from one hand to the other. "If you fall into the water and aren't dead, I will give you time to disappear. I promise I'll stand by my word."

The stranger had come close enough. "Shut up!" John gave him no time to prepare. His heavy staff jerked forward like a snake's head and struck the stranger in the chest. His big-mouthed opponent staggered. John pushed on. The green man repelled the first blow. But the next one got past his guard. John used both ends of his thick tree trunk. Neck. Head. Neck again, and a terrible blow against the man's heart. The stranger was lifted off his feet and thrown back, found his footing on the bridge again, panting. His jacket was torn apart. Blood ran from under his hood.

"Enough?" John weighed the fighting staff in his fists.

The green man shook his head, dazed. Blood ran down his cheeks.

"Jump in the water, and I'll let you live," John offered. "You may hop along the river like a frog. Until I never see you again."

His opponent had regained his composure. Suddenly, he bent his head to the side as if he saw something behind the giant. "Now, that's unexpected," he gasped.

Marian! Had she come out of hiding? John looked back over his shoulder. That moment was enough. The man took two leaps, thrust the end of his stick into a notch in the tree bridge, lifted himself up, and flew, legs first, like a bolt toward the giant. Both feet hit the mighty chest. The force of the impact sent John staggering. He stumbled, crashed backward onto the footbridge, slipped, clung on with his legs, did not slip off, and quickly held the staff up in defense.

No attack followed. Nothing happened. Where was the green man? John sat up and stared down the tree bridge but could not see his opponent. Then he saw the hands, right in front of his sandals. The fingers clawed into the bark. John pulled his legs up.

On his knees, he crawled closer and bent his head down. There the stranger hung, paddling his feet above the water. The hood had slipped off. Clear, gray eyes looked up at John from a bloodstained face. They showed not a trace of fear.

"Let go," John demanded.

"If I had landed on my feet," the green man hissed through clenched teeth, "I'd have you now, you runt."

"Still got that sharp mouth?" The giant rose to full height. From high above, he stared down at his opponent. "I'll shut it forever if you don't let go."

"I just had a bit of bad luck. But otherwise, it was a fine bout, don't you think?

John couldn't figure this stranger out. This was serious, deadly serious, and yet this frog kept croaking. "For the last time . . . let go."

He raised his staff like he was trying to churn butter in a barrel.

"You won't kill a defenseless man." The gray eyes looked calm and steady.

Right he was. John was annoyed, even more so because the frog knew it. "You're not worth it. But you deserve this." He slowly moved the heel of his sandal forward and rolled it over the man's clawed fingers.

"Damn bastard!" With that curse, the green man dropped into the swirling water. John nodded with satisfaction.

The stranger was carried along a bit, paddled out of the current, and waded into shallower water. He hopped from stone to stone toward the shore. John rushed over the tree bridge, jumped, and awaited his opponent, ready to strike.

"I give up. You win." Laughing, the man raised his hands. "I surrender."

John was silent.

"You are on the other side," the man pointed out. "What more do you want?"

Marian was still lying in hiding. John needed to make sure the stranger stayed where he was until he could get away with the girl. "Stay in the water. And shut up!" John hissed. *Now what? The best thing would be I smash his skull in.* He dismissed the idea in an instant. The stranger no longer had a weapon.

"Hey! You, giant! Until you figure things out, may I at least play something on my hunting horn for you?"

"Blow all you want! As long as you keep your mouth shut."

The stranger put the horn to his lips. A long, bright tone, then two fast ones, followed by a long, deep tone rolled through the valley and came back as an echo.

No sooner had the sound faded away than arrows struck the

ground to the right and left of John. "A trap," he gasped as he spun around.

Two men with raised bows broke free from the riverbank shrubs. They were dressed in green like the stranger. Shouts! John leapt back. From the nearby oaks and beeches, four green figures came flying toward him. They swung on long ropes, landed on the riverbank simultaneously, and were already drawing back the feathered arrow shafts on their bows.

"Well, Robin," one of them shouted to the stranger in the river, without letting John out of his sight, "were you at the blacksmith's? Did he heat you up and stretch you thin?"

John narrowed his eyes. Was the man grinning? He could not tell. Both corners of his mouth ended in scars that stretched up to his ears.

"By Willick," another declared, "then he doused you, as any proper blacksmith would." That man's head was almost bare, the skin over his skull shriveled like old tree bark. Only at the back of the head did hair grow, into a long braid tied at the back of his neck.

"What now, Robin?" a third man asked. John saw that the man's bow hand was as white as snow.

What are these people? There was no time to figure it out. John was not deceived by the cheerful chatter. The men's eyes all gleamed with the same hard determination. *Oh, Marian. I tried to protect you.*

"Wait, friends!" their leader called back. "No one shoots without my order. But keep this bear well in check!" He stomped to the shore. He shook himself like a wet wolf in front of John. He dabbed at the wound under his reddish-blond hair and then looked at the traces of blood on his fingertips. "You've got a fine punch, mate. I thought my head was going to burst."

"I wish I had smashed my staff into your mouth earlier."

"Be glad you didn't! You'd have been dead before it struck. None of my friends would've missed you." The gray gaze scrutinized the prisoner. "Tell me your name."

"John."

"John what?"

The giant swallowed and poked at the soft ground with his staff. "Little. John Little."

Laughter. The green man silenced his men. "Who sent you? Sir Roger of Doncaster?"

John shook his head. *Nobody.* He told them he was headed north, wanted to go move along, nothing more. *Oh, Marian, hold on! As long as they let me talk, they won't shoot. Maybe I can still get us out of here.*

"Who's your master?"

"Nobody."

"You lie."

No. It was the truth. John told them about the village near Newstead Abbey, down in Nottingham shire, about the stag, about the raid by the Lord Sheriff's men-at-arms. He reported the murders with faltering words.

The green figures lowered their bows, one by one.

"And what next, John?" the leader asked softly. "I must know everything."

"I took care of four of the murderers. One escaped. He fled as soon as the fight turned. And this damn sheriff believes his hired killer more than an innocent man."

"But I believe you." The leader clenched his fist. "We all know of this miserable Norman scoundrel, this Thom de Fitz. But after the winter, I swear, he will know *us* well." His people nodded.

"One more thing." The gray eyes froze to ice. "And you'd better not lie." He came closer, his left hand slowly grasping the giant's heavy fighting staff. John let it happen. "How did you find our valley? Why did you come from that direction? Only the initiated know the path."

John looked first at the leader, then at the faces of the others. What was suddenly so important? Suddenly the valley seemed to fall silent, despite the roaring waterfall, despite the rushing river. "Coincidence. Because I have good eyes, I saw the roofs of the village somewhere up there. And the path? Well, because I'm a hunter."

The leader let go of John's staff and walked thoughtfully up and down in front of the giant. Finally, he turned to his men. "What do you think, friends?"

The man with the shriveled scalp was first to respond. He took the arrow from his bowstring and lifted it in the air. The others followed suit.

The leader laughed. All tension had disappeared from his face. "John Little," he shouted loudly, like a herald, smoothing his wet, torn jacket. Finally, he tilted his head back, overdoing it, to look up into the giant's face. "Before you stands Robert Loxley, called Robin Hood. And these—" his arm swung with a flourish toward the men "—are some of my brave friends. There are more, and by next spring, we will be even more."

"I do not understand." John remained cautious. "Another game?"

"By the Virgin Mary, this is no game. In short, we are all outlaws. Outlaws, convicts, hunted down, you know how quickly it happens. I know of no judge in the whole of England who protects us simple, Godfearing Saxons from those Norman high-and-mighties. When it suits them, they crush us like beetles between their fingers. Those who are lucky enough to escape flee into the woods. Where else? There is no other choice. Until now, many of them lived alone or in small groups, hunting royal game, robbing a merchant here and there, or plundering a priest. Out of necessity, out of fear, they have become vagabonds. But I want more. I want an army—a brotherhood of outlaws. No lumbering, iron-clad men! Instead, we are quick, invisible, and honed like the tip of an arrow." Inspired by his own enthusiasm, Robin Hood ran his hand through his hair, forgetting the wound, and winced. "By the Virgin!"

"Sorry for that . . ."

"It's all right, John—old William's spearwort will heal it quickly. I want you to know one more thing: We're not bandits. I declared us free men, and I gave us this territory as a gift. We're free men! And we no longer bow down to greedy Normans, bow to no abbot, no earl, and no lord sheriff. We bow only to our king. And when Richard the Lionheart returns, let him judge us. But until then, by the Blessed Virgin, we shall fight for ourselves." Robin Hood took a deep breath. After a while, he crossed his arms in front of his chest. "Well, what do you say?"

John again poked his stick into the soft ground. No one had ever given him such a long speech before. Some of it sounded good, some he had even understood. But Marian was waiting. "You mean, I can go?"

Robin Hood openly laughed at him. "I'm not holding you any longer. You are free."

"Good. Then—"

"Stop, wait! I ask you as a free man: John Little, will you stay with us? I offer you twenty pounds a year. Enough meat. Ale and wine, all you want. Plus, free battle gear for summer and winter. And a dry roof, such as it is. If you join us, you will *truly* be a free man."

"Never been free," muttered John.

"Very well." Robin Hood showed him the hunting horn. "Then follow my signal, take up our green garb, and become my friend!"

Where else can I go? It's better than fleeing, John supposed, *better than being chased away. And Marian needs a roof for winter.* Where did he expect her to go? *No, little one, don't be afraid!* He had made his decision. "Fine, then. I am your man. On one condition."

“Whatever it may be, John Little, I give you my hand on it. It’s already done.”

And the giant smiled and took his hand. The handshake was firm. The deal was struck. The outlaws rushed to the two of them. Everyone wanted to shake the hand of their new companion.

Robin Hood sounded the horn. “To the camp!”

“Wait!” Astonished, they all turned back to John. “Over on the other side of the river, there’s . . . something else, something I must carry with me always.” He scratched the scar in his beard and grinned. “That’s my condition.”

Generously, Robin clapped his hands. “Go on. Go get it, and then we’ll celebrate!”

As a sign of his trust, John left the fighting staff behind, jumped onto the tree bridge, and ran to the other side. Beyond the bend, he pushed himself into the bushes.

Marian was crouched on the ground.

“It took a long time, girl.” John looked at her and faltered. “What’s the matter?”

The ground in front of her was dug into a shallow hollow. Her face was covered with earth, dirt all over her. Streaks of tears ran down her cheeks. Marian bravely shook her curls and smiled. She stretched out her dirt-covered hands to him.

“You waited for me and hid yourself, that’s good.” John reached for the waterskin and the food sack. “Come on! These men are good people, I think. We’ll stay there if they want us. Both of us.”

He looked hard into her eyes. “And if they don’t, that’s fine, too. We’ll just move on.”

He crouched down on the path. “Come on, let’s go. Don’t want you to slip.” Marian climbed up over his knee and arm and sat astride the neck of the giant.

Again John hummed his song, as he walked to the riverbank. Humming, he climbed the tree bridge and walked onward slowly.

On the other side of the river, all laughter and talking ceased. Robin Hood and his companions crowded to the end of the bridge. Jaws dropped.

Step by step, John approached with his ward. He stopped, still on the trunk. "Marian is her name. She must stay with me. That is my condition." Scanning their faces, he looked from one to the other and added, "I'll tell you right away: She is mute. Ever since the sheriff's men killed the woman who . . ." He breathed heavily. "I am not her father. They stabbed her brother and mother. Damn it, don't look at me like that! What is it? Yes or no?"

Robin Hood caught himself and asked quietly, "But where is the girl going to live?"

"With me. I'll build her something."

"Nobody is sending her away. But wouldn't it be better if she lived in the village?" Robin pointed up the hill, "In Barnsdale Top." Some of the outlaws' wives and children were already living there. "The village is under our protection. No one will betray us. Nothing will happen to your Marian up there."

John felt the girl pull his beard violently. "I believe you. But for now, she stays with me."

Robin Hood looked at John, looked upward to a higher power, and frowned. "I can't see much of your little 'condition' underneath all that dirt." He laughed. "I gave my promise. All right, men, to the camp! We have double reason to celebrate today."

As they followed the outlaws downstream through the dense brushwood, John pulled his ward's foot. "Well, little one?" She pressed her face into his hair.

The valley became narrower, darker. Hills moved in on both sides of the riverbank, and soon there were only smooth cliffs to the right and left of the riverbed. The water shot through them, and at the banks it surged and foamed over large boulders.

John felt his ward tense up. "It's all right. They know their way."

At the front, Robin Hood sounded the hunting horn: deep and long, high and short. Immediately another horn responded with two quick deep notes.

The man in green jumped up to a slab protruding far above the water and disappeared around the sharp rock nose. One after another his men followed. The last one waved to their new companion, and then he was gone.

"Another one of those tests?" John hesitated. The man who had just waved him on—with the white hand. It was still as white as before? *And I thought it was because he was pulling hard on the bow . . .*

"Fine." He had to keep up with the others. He carefully climbed up the stone slab, made sure his feet stood secure, and bent his upper body forward. Marian peered around the rocky outcrop. "Can we make it?" he asked her.

Her body relaxed, and she spurred him on with her heels—two more steps to the farther edge. The water roared beneath him. John turned sideways as the slab narrowed and skirted the rock like a high castle battlement. Iron wedges were driven into the stone as handholds.

Onward. A path now meandered close to the bank, between ten-foot-high boulders and directly toward a cliff face. There was no sight of the men. John followed their noises. All at once, the voices changed, echoing dully, and then they became quieter.

There was a cave! The last of the troop was again waiting for John at the entrance, waving his pale hand briefly, grinning before diving into the darkness.

"We're much too big for this." The giant let the girl down. He ducked his head and went forward. Before the darkness swallowed them completely, they made a turn, and the end of the tunnel gleamed before them like an eye.

They stepped outside.

Marian took his hand. John breathed in deeply. A valley spread before them. More than that—it was a garden, bordered by high cliffs, and stretching down to the riverbank. On the other side of the river, the cliff rose directly out of the water. Mighty groups of trees lined the edges of the valley all around. Under their protection, solidly built huts crouched between the trunks. To the front, all was meadow! Flowers, blue and red, dotted it all the way to the river. And in the middle of this colorful carpet rose an ancient, sprawling linden tree. "Nice, isn't it?"

Marian squeezed his big hand more firmly.

The man with the white hand waved to them again and again. What was the matter? He pointed impatiently to the firepit behind the linden tree. There Robin Hood and two cooks were loudly defending the soup pot and the roast game on the spit from attack. "If you don't hurry, they will start without us."

Only now did John smell the scent. His stomach clenched. In a flash, the smell became more intoxicating than the sight of the valley. Food! There was nothing more wonderful.

And there was meat, indeed—for the giant a whole deer leg, and broth, which he scooped from the pot with a tin bowl. The fatty broth dripped into John's bushy beard.

Marian had long since eaten her fill, Robin Hood and the outlaws had long since stretched out in the grass, the ale jug wandered from hand to hand. The men watched their new comrade speechlessly. No one dared to interrupt him. The afternoon sun sank behind the western hill. With knife in hand, John circled the deer carcass. He scraped every last bit of meat from the bones. Finally, he patted his belly soundly, and a loud belch answered.

"Hey, John Little!" Robin Hood sat up. "Now I know why you would *have* to be a good hunter." It took a moment for everyone to catch his meaning; then, they laughed and slapped each other on the shoulders.

Even John understood. "Fine, then." His gaze found Marian. She sat upright, a bit away from the men. Gray dirt stuck to her cheeks. She stared at the sky above the cliffs.

"I need a place for the night," John told the men. "For us."

Without hesitation, each of the freemen offered their own lodgings. No, no one was to vacate their hut, Robin Hood decreed. "We have room enough." The guards who were assigned for the night or the day would be away from their huts anyway. They were positioned in Barnsdale Top, and up at the post by the stables and the caves, and one each on the rock walls to guard the three paths down to the main camp. "Until you have built your own, you and the girl can use one of the huts that are currently vacant."

"Thank you," said John.

The man with the scars up to his ears led John and Marian over to the trees. He stopped in front of one of the shelters and lifted the crossbeam from the door. "In there. The boy won't come back until morning."

John could not tell if it was really a smile, but he grinned himself. "Thank you. Go on back."

A block of wood, a straw bed upon it, and a blanket of sheepskin—what riches! "We haven't had anything like this for a long time. Lie down, little one!" Marian obeyed and moved close to the wall. Carefully John pulled the sheepskin up to her chin. Suddenly her fingers clawed into his sleeve.

"Don't worry! I won't be far."

She held him tight. Her eyes were glistening wet.

"Understand, girl! It will be all right now. I'm just a little thirsty." She reluctantly let him go. He straightened up. He could only stand hunched over in the little hut. At the door, he looked back into the semidarkness. "I'll take care of you. I promise. I'll never leave you."

And John drank. Only after he was handed the overflowing pitcher to empty for a second time did he pass it on, after a deep draught. The past days and nights fell off his shoulders. But neither the ale nor the stories of his new friends could banish all of the pain and misery from his chest. But it became easier. As the logs collapsed into embers, John spoke about Sherwood's foresters and how he and Marian had escaped them. "And then, I took one of the rabbits with me."

Robin Hood interrupted. In excitement, he cried, "John Little! What kind of a name is that?"

The laughter around them quieted.

The giant wiped his sleeve over his mouth. "Don't, Robin! Don't start. I like—"

"Calm yourself!" The leader of the band smiled slightly, adjusting the dagger in his belt. "No, no truly, I don't think I like your name."

The anger in John drove away the ale haze. He growled low.

Robin seemed not to notice. "Friends. I think it's time to rename the giant. So that he truly belongs to us. What name comes to mind?"

The two men next to John stealthily moved out of reach of the giant's mighty arms. Only then did they nod their heads in agreement and laugh expectantly like the others.

John breathed heavily against the drunkenness. *I don't want to fight. He can insult me. I can bear that easily. But he should stop this.*

Robin Hood pulled out the hunting dagger, laid his left hand on the ground, and spread his fingers. "Friends, you know the game. Watch out, John! I ask four times. The fourth time, the name fits."

John clenched his fists, struggling to hold back. *I don't want to argue, but this ...*

The tip of Robin's blade floated between thumb and index finger.

"John Little?" The leader looked around.

"No!" the choir determined in a deep voice.

The tip of the blade shifted and stopped over the next gap between fingers.

"Dwarf?

"No!

"Giant?

"No!

The shining blade hovered, aimed between the last two fingers of Robin's left hand. "Little John?

"Yes!" was the solemn answer.

Robin Hood plunged the dagger into the ground right up to the hilt. "So be it."

With roars and applause, everyone rose and approached John. He sat there, trembling. The outlaw leader shouted, "I baptize you with the name of Little John," and emptied the ale jug over the newly baptized man's enormous head.

With one wild blow, John smashed the jug. "No more of these games!" As quickly as he could, he scrambled up, groped for his own dagger, searched for it, fumbled around, and finally shook his head. The sheath was empty.

"I borrowed it," Robin explained, menacingly and softly, as he turned John's weapon back and forth in his hand. "Little John. You are an idiot. Don't spoil our fun!"

"You call this fun—"

"Quiet! I make the rules." The Robin laughed. "Nobody means to insult you here. You belong with us, and that's that." He handed the dagger back.

Speechless, John slipped it into his belt. His thoughts came together. "It's always been like this. I've always been irritable. Maybe it's because I'm so big and my name is so small. That's why."

A new pitcher of fresh ale was brought.

"You know, John." Robin sat down beside him and pointed to the companion whose mouth was disfigured by scars. "The executioner slashed this one's mouth open. We call him Pete Smiling. He says, if he pulls his lips up so you can see his teeth, only then is he actually smiling—otherwise not. But nobody makes fun of Pete. You should see him with his sword. *Nobody* makes fun of Pete. We laugh with him, yes, but no one mocks him."

Robin pointed again. "And our Gilbert over there. The Sheriff of Nottingham had him tortured. See his right hand? He can still move it, but he feels no pain, and the blood no longer flows properly to his fingers. It's always pale. That is why we call him Whitehand." Robin pointed to a man whose sole plait of hair dangled from the back of his head. In the glow of the embers, the shriveled bare skin of the top of his head seemed itself to glow. "This is Tom Toad. Because he looks like a toad. Hey, Tom, what happened to your head? But make it short."

The outlaw stroked his naked skull. "In Doncaster, in the harsh winter of three years ago. I needed money for herbs and a health powder. So I cut some of the Baron's wood. My twins were only little boys. Both boys were sick. Sir Roger's forest rangers got me. The Baron laughed when they cut off my Beth's ear. And then they heated up some oil. Well. Hair won't grow where they dashed me with it anymore."

John felt as if stabbed in the chest. "And your twins?"

Tom Toad went silent and shook his naked head.

"Still upset?" Robin asked the giant quietly.

"All right." John felt at the scar in his beard. How small it was, far too unimportant to be pointed out, told of in a story. From the corner of his eye, he looked at the leader. A smooth face, and a fine-featured, handsome one. The man had a good laugh. "And you?"

With a quick flick of the wrist, Robin pulled the hood over his head. "Hood, very simple. You can tell at once who it is. Because everybody's special. You'll soon know each of us by name." He nodded with a smile to the two old men who had turned the stag on the spit. "Neither of them is named Cook, because they can't always get it to taste as good as tonight. But our William Herbghost there knows about herbs. And the other, Paul Storyteller with the stiff leg, he can tell stories better than he can cook."

John was not satisfied. "And you?" he asked again. "What about you?"

A steep wrinkle appeared on the leader's forehead. His features became hard. Robin pulled up his green doublet and turned his back to John. Wide dark scars crossed one over the other from his neck to his hips. "That was fifteen years ago. I was twelve, then, when the bishop's servants came to Loxley." He pulled the doublet back down. "I couldn't get away from them. I was too young to escape."

"I see." John had a hard time standing up. "I'm tired . . . and . . ." He found no words, just stood there and stared into the faces of his new friends.

Robin measured the shape of the giant from bottom to top with his gaze and marveled exaggeratedly: "Truly: our Little John!"

A grin crept onto John's bearded face. "Whatever. *Frog*." As he stomped over to the trees, he heard amused laughter behind him. "Little John," he muttered. "I'll get used to it."

Muffled blows. Still mostly asleep, John growled, reluctant to stir. He felt his shoulder pushed, his beard pulled. John opened his lids and was looking into the girl's frightened face. "What is it?"

Marian pointed to the door.

Thumping, jiggling at the door. "Open up! By Satan! Who's in there?" A male outline was faintly visible through the cracks between the willow trunks, which were firmly tied together with hemp ropes. "Open up!"

Danger. Sheriff's men-at-arms! Not quite awake yet, John pushed the girl behind him into the farthest corner. *Danger!* He jumped up, hit his head hard on the ceiling beam, ducked again, and grabbed his fighting staff. Not enough space to swing it. "Get away from here," he thundered. "Or should I come make you?"

Immediately the demanding knocking stopped. Silence. After a while, a boyish voice stammered: "This ... this is my... That's where I live."

Now John remembered where he was, and he eased his breath. Since yesterday they had been safe with friends. The men who had been on guard were returning from the night watch. No enemy was waiting outside. But did the person outside also know that John was no enemy, lurking in his hut? John peered through the viewing hole in the closed door. A slim lad, barely a grown man, with flaxen hair, a bit of fuzz on his upper lip. The fellow held a bare sword in his fist. "It's all good, boy," he shouted. "Take a few steps back and put the toy away!"

The young man did not move.

As you wish. John sighed and put the staff aside. Quietly he lifted the inside locking bar off its iron hooks. He grabbed the door at its middle and pushed it through the opening, held on and hefted the willow door like a shield, and stormed out roaring. There was no time for the boy to react. He hit the ground backward. Immediately he started to jump up again., but when he saw the massive figure above him, he stayed down.

"I am John Lit—I mean, Little John. Why didn't you listen to me?"

Laughter all around. Some of the band of men came up from behind tree trunks, around the corners of the neighboring huts, and applauded John. Pete Smiling placed himself next to John with his legs apart, his head reaching barely up to the giant's shoulder. "We were all looking forward to this. And, by St. Wilfred, you're even better than I thought. The other sentries have already gone to bed. You'll get to know them later. But this here is Much, our youngest. Full eighteen years, he says, but I think sixteen." Pete Smiling finally addressed the young man. “Hey, Much! This little one is our newest.”

“Why . . . why . . .” the lad’s voice faltered “. . . didn’t you . . . you idiots . . . tell me?”

Pete nudged the giant in the side. “Our Much stutters. Sometimes. When he is excited.”

“Fine.” John bent down and reached out his hand to the young man. “Come on!” He pulled him up. “No offense. Didn’t know what else to do. And thank you . . .”

Incredulous, Much stared past him. “And who . . . who is this?”

The girl stood in the entrance of the hut. Her curls were shaggy, her face as dirty as her gown. John waved her over. Marian approached reluctantly.

“She belongs to me. Marian is her name. She’s mute. But was a time she could speak faster than you or I, believe me!”

Much had recovered from the shock. He clasped his hands behind his back. “She’s not too clean,” he said with a grin. “And that’s what was sleeping under my sheepskin.”

Before John could say anything back, Marian suddenly clenched her fist and waved it threateningly at the young boy.

“Well, look at that.” Pete Smiling nodded approvingly. “She’s just fine. She won’t be told what to do.”

John scratched his scar. Since that day in the village, Marian had communicated only to him, silently. Strangers had gotten nothing but apathetic stares. And now? All that was missing was if she had screamed, “Shut up!” John sighed at the thought. That would have been something. Then all would have been right again.

“We won’t sleep in your hut anymore,” he said dismissively. “It’s much too low for me. The bed is too short. But for you, boy, it’s enough. Get some sleep!”

Marian nodded, satisfied. John smiled at her approval of what he told the runt.

Robin and some men had left very early in the morning to go hunting. With the enormous appetite of their new man, more meat had to be provided. They would be back in the evening, or tomorrow morning at the latest, Pete explained; until then, Pete was in command. John was supposed to build a shelter. "We've already chosen the place. Come!" The current commander walked on ahead. The place was marked out between two mighty, smooth-stemmed beech trees right at the edge of the meadow. "We'll give you a hand. We have wood enough, even for a giant like you."

They rammed sharpened stakes into the earth, dragged rocks from the river, and skillfully carved the crossbars.

Marian stole to the water, returned with a freshly washed face and wet hair. She helped to cut flexible willow rods to the right length. She smiled when John looked at her.

Much stumbled out of his hut in the late afternoon, yawned, and strolled over to the construction site. Marian's eyes flashed angrily.

"She's clean," the young lad mocked.

She turned away and continued working.

"Leave her alone," growled John.

"Why . . . are you . . ."

The giant hefted his ax. Annoyed, Pete Smiling ordered: "Much, get your provisions and go up to the sentry. Bill Threefinger and the others have already left. You're always last."

"All I did was . . ."

"Much Miller's-son! Get on with you!"

Reluctantly, the lad obeyed. John watched him go. "That Much . . ." With a sudden realization, he slapped his forehead. "What did you say? His father is a miller?"

"As I said. His parents have a mill outside Doncaster."

John tossed the tool aside and went after the boy. He reached him by the firepit. "Hey, boy. Wait!"

Guiltily, Much ducked his head.

"Don't worry. I have a message for you. From your mother."

"From? For? Where?" He couldn't say another word. By the time John was done speaking, tears rolled down Much's cheeks.

John put his hand on his shoulder. "It's all right, boy."

Much wiped his nose on his green sleeve. "I'll be all right." He tried to smile. "And . . . and if you want, you can sleep in my bed for now. You and Marian."

"We will."

By noon the next day, the roof of the new hut was weighted down with earth and stones. The men brought furs. Robin Hood contributed two candles. And to celebrate, John was given the ale mug. "You get the first sip."

"Wait!" cried Much. He had forsaken sleep, had walked over to the village right after guard duty, and returned with a pot under his arm. Now he brought from his hut a drinking horn filled to the brim with milk and held it out to Marian. "This is for you."

The girl crossed her hands behind her back. She shook her head.

"Go on." John winked at her.

Marian stretched her chin forward and raised both fists. Only just before she reached the drinking horn did she open her fingers and snatch it from Much's hand. The milk spilled over. The celebration could begin.

VI

Yorkshire. Winter Camp in Barnsdale.

In mid-October, the sun lost its power. The nights became cold, and the morning fog only rose very slowly from the narrow valley. The big linden tree in the middle of the meadow turned yellow. The colorful splendor of the beeches and oaks intensified with every passing day. In the autumn breeze, the first leaves drifted to the ground. The outlaws exchanged their green summer outfits for brownish-black winter jackets and brown hooded cloaks.

John could not fit into any of their uniforms, and Marian had drowned in all the fabric of each one.

Tom Toad accompanied them to Barnsdale Top. "Bread. Ale. What we need, we get from there. There are also workshops there. Ropers. Bowmakers. Blacksmith. Quite normal." Tom reached around to the back of his head and pulled the leather strap tighter around his pigtail. "In reality, these are all our people. Even the farmers, because we protect them, and Robin always pays double for their crops. No stranger would know. They work for us in secret, sometimes even at night. My Beth sews. And there are plenty of bales of cloth."

Marian trembled when she noticed the scar on the left side of the woman's head. Beth patted the girl's hand. "I would have given both ears, princess, if only it had saved the boys. You would be their big sister now."

Tears flowed down Marian's cheeks. She tried to speak, to explain, could only gasp.

"I understand you." Beth smiled. "You are my little princess now. Yes? And I'm going to make you something very special."

For the past two weeks, John had been instructed by Robin Hood. Three trails climbed up the gorge from the main camp below. One carefully carved out with long switchback turns. It was the only way to transport supplies and loads into the valley. The other two were steep, leading over crevices and protruding boulders. The freemen used them daily for quick ascent and descent. And if an enemy ever succeeded in finding his way down to the main camp, these paths served as escape routes.

Robin crossed his arms in front of his chest. "Well, what do you say?"

"Safe as a fox in a hole." John peered down from the edge of the escarpment and pursed his lips. "No sight of the valley. Only the river. By St. Dunstan, nothing else."

"And you, out of all people passing by, found our fourth path." Robin took the giant's arm, smiling lightly. "Threefinger had already spotted you above the waterfall. He raised the alarm because the branches were moving. His eyes are the best. But we didn't *see* you until you came to shore."

"That was just by accident," mumbled John.

Robin laughed. "Not accident. Good luck, I hope. And we both really needed it."

In the dense forest, he led John to another compound in their sprawling hideout. "Anyone who finds this place will stop here and look no farther."

Huts surrounded a fireplace. They were larger and not as solidly built as the shelters in the main camp. "Whenever we stay up here, they'll do for the night."

Ten horses grazed in the paddock outside the stables. Almost in awe, Robin pointed to three white stallions. "The knights of the Round Table rode such stallions, I believe. I would be sorry to lose my white horse, but it wouldn't bother us if the others were discovered. We'd just get new ones." The corners of his mouth twitched. "John, you wouldn't believe how many nags are there for the taking over on the great trade road—hardly any white ones, but black, brown, and spotted ones. And all of them free, and they come with saddlecloths and bridles."

Via another path, they reached the carefully cleared training grounds. "This is what we built this year. Courage alone is not enough. I want fighters. Do you understand, John?"

This was where daily exercises were to take place throughout the fall and winter. Sword, lance, knife, and above all, archery skills had to be improved. "You'll teach us what you can do with your stick." Robin tapped the healed wound on his head. "You won't be able to do this again."

John looked straight into the gray eyes. "There won't be a next time, believe me!"

Robin laughed again. Then he showed John the well-camouflaged caverns. In the first were barrels of ale and wine. "The monks up at Fountain Abbey will have to cut back a little this winter."

At the sight of the armory, John took a deep breath. More than fifty bows were arranged according to size. Unbreakable bowstrings twisted from linen. The quivers were filled with the best arrows: gray goose feathers, needle-sharp iron tips. Astonished, the giant took in the swords and shields, enough to arm more than twenty men. "And all new!"

"Luck, Little John." The leader grinned broadly. "By luck, on the road from Wakefield to York, we met a cart with only two chain mail shirts for protection. The delivery was meant for the Abbot of St. Mary's Abbey. Well, we managed to persuade them, and in the end, they were kind enough to leave the whole load to us. And here—" Robin picked up a crossbow. "We took six of these from the sheriff's iron puppets down at Sherwood last summer."

The next cave contained three large chests that stood side by side like coffins. Robin lifted the first lid. Cloaks—some almost white like those worn by Cistercian monks, others black like those worn by Benedictines and Dominicans. John shook his head. "That's enough for a whole monastery." The second chest contained splendid clothing—silk trousers, coats of the finest velvet trimmed with fur. Pointed leather boots. Artfully forged spurs. And hats! Pearl embroidered, feathered, round, peaked, even a tall bishop's mitre. In the third, piles of leather aprons, tunic shirts, caps, and coarse sandals—clothing worn by craftsmen of diverse professions.

Deeper in the cavern were baskets filled with silver and gold cups, plates and bowls, and the finest tableware. "That's better." John nodded. "At least this stuff here is worth something." He returned to the chests. "But what do you want with these?"

"The simpler things here, we bought from the people who made them. But monk robes and all the expensive clothes, well, they're . . . gifts."

"Naked? You sent the people you robbed on their way naked?" John enjoyed the thought.

"Not quite. The gentlemen were allowed to keep their dirty undershirts."

"I like it! But why do you need—"

Robin Hood tugged John's hood. "This is our battle dress. None of us can be seen in this in Nottingham or Doncaster or any other city. Now do you understand?"

The giant shook his head.

"Actors dress up, too. Sometimes they're monks, sometimes dukes, sometimes potters. That's how we do it." Robin slammed shut the lid of the robe chest and sat on top of it. His eyes were sparkling. "Ruse, John! That is the name of the game. And cunning is a dangerous weapon."

"When I hunt, I know what I'm doing. And when there is danger, I can handle it. I don't know anything about dressing up."

"You'll learn from me." Robin hopped off. His face changed, and he gave the giant a serious look. "You're not like me, but I like that. I'll make you my lieutenant. Just hold on till I've talked to Smiling, Toad, and Whitehand. So there'll be no jealousy."

John froze in disbelief. Finally, he said, "So fast. You've only known me—"

"But I know you. When I was swinging from that bridge, I already knew you." He lightly thumped the giant man's chest with his fist. "I want you not just as a lieutenant. I want you as a friend."

John wiped his eyes and muttered, "Fine, then." That would have to do for an oath.

In the hut that evening, John checked the string of his new longbow. Marian crouched in front of him, skillfully straightening the feathered shafts of the arrows. Beth had kept her word. The girl was now also wearing the brown-black winter outlaw outfit. The individual pieces of cloth were not roughly joined together with leather threads like on the men's garb. Marian's seams were turned under and covered over with soft leather strips. Beth had even lined the hood with fox fur for her princess.

"Are you all right, little one?"

Marian nodded, curls falling into her face.

We are home, he thought as he flicked the bowstring with his thumbnail and listened to it sing.

Two days later, John and the girl were woken up early in the morning by unusual noise. No one had sounded the alarm, and yet all the men were on their feet. Some carried their weapons rolled up in fur blankets.

"What's happening?"

The answer came in the form of a cheerful wink from one of them.

"Damn it!" John straightened his belt. Yesterday, he had been named a lieutenant in the Brotherhood in front of everyone. And today, he already had no idea what was going on.

The voice of old William Herbghost kept nagging through the camp. Pots, crucibles, ladles, all necessary kitchen utensils were to be brought up to the base camp.

On the riverbank, Paul Storyteller was enthroned on a boulder like a grizzled commander. A wicker basket next to his stiff leg, he ordered three fellows around. The three men were wading naked in the water despite the cold and drizzle, hunting for fish with spears, nets, and hooks.

"Don't just stand there!" William waved to John and Marian. "Not you. The little one. She can help." The old man presented her with five small, tightly closed leather pouches strung together on a strap. "Would you tie them under your jacket and carry them up? In them are the finest spices, crushed and dried. You keep them close until I am up! I'm counting on you."

Marian nodded seriously. She glanced at John, then followed the heavily laden men to the supply path. "By all the saints, don't lose them, child," William Herbghost cried after her. "Otherwise, it won't taste of anything."

"Will you tell me what's going on here?" asked John.

"Don't interfere! I've got enough to do until you get back." And with that, the old man turned and harangued a comrade who had forgotten the skewers for the roast.

Laughter! John whirled around. Robin Hood was laughing at him. "Move along, sir lieutenant. Today is your day, Little John. You will bring a guest to my base. There'll be no food before that." His voice sounded clear and determined, as usual, a tone of voice that each of his men trusted and obeyed unconditionally.

"What did you say?" John scratched the scar in his beard. "Is everything all right?"

At once, the gray eyes became hard. "I've decided . . ." Robin broke off. "Oh, no matter. Nothing about you." Smiling, he reached for the giant's arm. "Come on. It's an easy game."

As they climbed the steep path, one behind the other, John learned his task. Everything was thought out down to the last detail. He was to lie in ambush above the bridge over the River Went. "From there, you can see everyone coming up the main road. If it's a team, then the horses will be foaming at the mouth when they reach the top. They must rest. The coachman won't be able to drive them onward even with a whip. Any rider will be in the same situation. His horse will be so tired that you could keep pace walking beside him.

John was ready. Not really a game, then. It was serious. Robin wanted him to prove himself today. He had to bring in some loot. Good. But why all the effort, the move to the upper camp? "And who am I to grab?"

Robin stopped on a ledge and looked down at the giant. "Not a farmer or a freeman! They have it hard enough. John, we're not ruffians, never forget that! My men and I are polite as long as someone does exactly what we ask in a friendly manner. Nothing is taken from anyone except the puppets in chain mail. Not from merchants, royal messengers, not even from Norman squires, goodly knights, or simple priests. We merely unburden the liars."

"I do not understand. How can I—"

"Wait and see. You shall learn the gentlemanly way from me." The outlaw touched the hilt of his sword. "But there are exceptions to civility. You can always give the Lord Sheriff or one of those bishops a good thrashing first. And if he's still alive, you will bring him safely tied up to the base."

Robin continued on with light feet. John silently stayed at his heels. *I am supposed to be a robber and yet not a robber, that much I know now.*

Near the huts, Robin brushed the strands of wet hair from his forehead. "Just hope the weather clears up by tonight. Otherwise, we'll have to go into the stables." The men would not care. They would sit under the trees with their bowls. "I, you, and my three other lieutenants will dine with our guest. Do you understand, John? Only the best."

"And we need a stranger here? If we eat alone, everyone will have more."

"Don't be a fool." Robin quickly raised his hand. "Now, now, I don't mean it like that. Calm down! But I learned from William how our old King Arthur did it. The king would not eat until a stranger sat at the table, and the guest had to tell him new stories. I like that. I'm going to do that and a little better."

"That's fine," said John, thinking: *I'll learn his ways.* After a sigh, he grinned broadly. "So, you want a fat, tied-up bishop, and before I slap him in the mouth, I'll ask him if he has any new stories to tell."

John stayed serious until the last word. When he saw Robin's astonished face, he couldn't hold it back any longer. He snorted and slapped his thighs. Robin joined in.

Startled by the booming laughter from both of them, some of the men curiously abandoned their work. Robin wiped his eyes. "Enough now. Get out of here, little man! Much and Threefinger are with you." The two were already waiting impatiently at the edge of the dwellings. The miller's son waved and flailed his arms in the air. "Much is as fast as a hound, and Bill can see what is not even there yet."

John shouldered his staff. Where was his ward? Marian waited silently amid the kitchen utensils, clutching the treasure of herbs with both hands. She wasn't looking at John. She was watching Much and seemed determined not to laugh at his shenanigans. What was that about? *Ah, never mind.* John stomped away with broad steps.

Robin's voice was clear and strong. "And remember. Everyone is hungry tonight. But we wait. We will not eat until you bring a guest! And be polite. Remember that."

They had taken position on the hill between hazel bushes two hours ago. And for those two hours, they had been watching the wide main road. John stared northward down to the bridge. He had the straight section of road directly in front of him firmly in view. Further below, the paved lanes could only be seen at the three hairpin bends. With their backs to him, Much and Bill peered intently to the south. Nothing so far. A potter had cursed and dragged his mule and cart behind him. A craftsman's apprentice. A knife grinder. Nothing else. And it had been raining for two hours. Their hair was sticky, and moisture seeped through to their skin, despite the tightly woven brown-black cloth of their clothing.

John asked over his shoulder: "Tell me, Bill. Who did that to your fingers?"

Much giggled. "Nobody. It was he himself."

"Shut up, boy! I didn't ask you."

"He's right, though," admitted Bill. "It was me. Butchering. A long time ago."

"And why are you with Robin?"

"Couldn't get a proper grip anymore. And it was always festering. They chased me out of the kitchen. So I just moved around." His eyes became bright. "Then, I met Robin. First, he took me to Kirklees Abbey. To his aunt. She's a nun there. She knows all about healing and stuff."

Much rubbed his thumb and forefinger together. "Costs a lot. But Robin pays for us. If someone gets something bad, he sends them to Kirklees to Sister Mathilda. Once, when I was—"

"Shut up, boy! Keep talking, Bill!"

"And afterward, Robin looked at my hand and said I only needed three fingers to pull a bowstring. That's the way it is now. I can shoot an arrow. And I've got good eyes."

Silence.

The rain became heavier.

All of a sudden, John's back tensed. "There. Down there on the bridge."

Immediately, the two companions stood beside him.

It was a rider in a black rain cape. He seemed to be in no hurry. The horse trotted calmly across the river.

"What is he?" John rammed the staff into the ground before him. *I'm tired of this. Whoever you are, I'm gonna get you. You eat, don't you?*

"That's a shield hanging off the side of the horse," Threefinger said. "Must be a sword under the cloak." They waited until the next turn. "Two boxes, right and left, not big, but who knows." The rider took his time. "All I can see is a speck of the face." Finally, the rider reappeared. "We're in luck. He's wearing chain mail under his cloak."

No sooner had the horse disappeared behind the last bend than Much took the bow from his shoulder. "A knight, clearly."

"By St. Dunstan," John said. "About time." He tapped the miller's son. "Go on to the other side. Hide. Wait for my signal!" The boy rushed across the road. "Bill, you stay here!" Threefinger put an arrow on his bowstring and nodded.

The rider appeared in the straight section of road. He had almost reached the highest point when John, the hood low over his forehead, broke cover and positioned himself in the mud of the cobbled lane with his legs set wide apart.

The horse trotted on toward him. The knight seemed not to have noticed the giant in the middle of the road. John narrowed his eyes. The man seemed to have closed his own eyes. *Is he asleep, or . . . What is he doing?* Just as well. John was alert and ready for anything. The horse was close enough. "My lord!

All in one moment, the rider's eyes opened, his left hand threw back the cloak, his right hand shot to the sword's hilt. Fast. Not fast enough. John's staff swung forward and pinned the rider's right arm against his armor breastplate. In the same instant, John had grabbed the horse's bridle tightly. "All right, sir." He grinned as politely as he could. "I have something to tell you. If you listen, I won't push you off your horse."

Silently and calmly, the knight looked at the giant figure.

"How about it?"

No answer. The rain poured down on them.

"If you won't say anything, then at least nod your head," John suggested. "Or do you not understand my language?"

"I understand every word you say, man. I respect honest Saxons as I respect honest Normans." A full, dark voice. "But I'm not sure about you. I don't know who or what you are. I didn't expect anyone here in such weather. You've torn me from my thoughts. Yet I am ready to hear what you have to say."

He is a gentleman, the way he speaks. Carefully, John drew back the staff. The knight did not move his sword hand.

Now came the hardest part. John pulled back his hood and bowed his head in greeting. "My friends and I . . ." He solemnly waved to the right and left. No sooner did his companions step out of the bushes than the knight made to reach for his weapon again. "Easy, easy," John placated him. "So: My friends and I, we would like to invite you, Sir Knight, in the name of our master, to a meal. A wild boar, nice and fat and crispy. And fish." John let out a breath. That had to be enough of politeness.

"Who is your master?"

"Robin Hood. He owns all the land around here. What of our offer?"

"So, he does exist." The knight raised his brows. "I suppose I have no choice."

"No, damn it," the giant blurted out before he could stop himself.

"Well, then . . . I am delighted and accept your invitation."

The torches on the walls of the stable were half burnt down. On the tabletop, the melted wax of the candles pooled between the silver bowls and plates. The spicy fish had really whetted everyone's appetite. No sooner had the head and bones been discarded onto the clay floor than Robin Hood and his lieutenants had plunged their knives simultaneously into the browned rind of the wild boar's back, cutting out steaming pieces. Paul Storyteller limped around the table and poured dark red wine into the silver goblets. Sweet wine and sauce dripped from the outlaws' chins. Marian sat next to the knight with both elbows propped on the table, gnawing dark, savory flesh from a bone.

Except for the men's noisy chewing and swallowing, silence prevailed at the table. No laughter. No conversation wanted to arise. From beneath half-lowered eyelids, Robin watched his guest at the other end of the table, glanced at Tom Toad now and then, shrugged his shoulders, and continued to watch the taciturn, stiff man.

As soon as he arrived, the freemen's leader had formally welcomed the knight and offered him hospitality.

"Baron Sir Richard at the Lea, lord of Fenwick Castle and loyal servant of his king, Richard the Lionheart." After introducing himself, the knight had thanked Robin formally and as was customary, had taken off his cloak, chain mail, sword, and armor. Astonished, the outlaws had gawked at his tattered tunic. No gold chain, no ornate spurs on the boots?

This was supposed to be a baron, a Norman? By St. Cedric, what kind of pathetic figure had Little John dragged up there? But the elegant gestures! That fine voice! Yes, he had to be of noble birth. "It is long since I have been asked to sit at such a richly set table," the man announced. "And, if I may say so, I would not have expected such refined courtesy here in the wilderness."

"So they say, sir." Robin had led the guest to the seat of honor. "Many claim to know me. But who among these babblers has ever fired Robin Hood's bow!"

"Very well parried."

That was all. Since then, the knight had not spoken. A small filet of fish, only three bites of wild boar, that was all he had eaten so far, and so far Storyteller hadn't had to refill his glass. Richard at the Lea stared absentmindedly into the flickering light of the candles. A slender head, a high forehead, the beard trimmed to a wedge on his chin, and gray hair that fell down to his robe's worn velvet collar.

Only Little John was pleased. He noticed nothing of the discomfort of his companions. He enjoyed the reward of his first kidnapping more and more with every bite and every sip. He had no time to talk, anyway. Just before the feast, Robin had told him that ridiculous rule. And before the signal came, he wanted to at least have eliminated the worst of his hunger.

Paul Storyteller bent down briefly to Marian. "Come with me for a moment! It won't take long."

Outside the entrance to the stables, old Herbghost grabbed the girl's hands. "What's wrong? Does the fellow not like the food?"

Marian moved her lips, nodded, and shook her head.

"By St. William, why doesn't he eat? As lean as he is? I seasoned everything. Twice."

Marian waited silently.

"Listen, child!" Herbghost turned her around. "Go in and shove the fish in front of his nose again. He has to eat at least one."

Marian nodded her understanding.

The two old men did not let her out of their sight. "You know, Paul, if Robin complains again this time, I'll chuck it in."

Storyteller stretched a stiff leg forward. "You're right. Let him cook for himself! And he can tell stories to himself while he's at it."

The girl bent over the table and pulled the silver plate through the grease and wax to the place of honor. With both hands, Marian grabbed one of the remaining fish. Her blue eyes shone up at the guest.

Returning from his thoughts, Richard at the Lea looked at the girl's face. "How pretty you are."

Marian lifted the fish to just below his chin and smiled pleadingly.

"No. Thank you, my child. But I do not feel like eating today." With that, the knight dipped his hands into the silver water bowl.

The signal! Robin and the other men let their knives lower. John quickly stuffed a last piece of roast into his mouth, chewed, swallowed, and wiped his fingers on his doublet. The feast was over.

Richard at the Lea raised his silver chalice. "A toast would be insufficient to praise this generosity. Therefore, gentlemen, I ask you from the bottom of my heart to accept my gratitude!"

Robin never touched his goblet. "I would like to, Sir Knight, but the picture is upside down." His lieutenants nodded approvingly. Only John's jaw dropped in surprise.

"I'm afraid I don't follow." Slowly, Richard at the Lea put down the chalice.

Robin frowned. "The bondsman gives to the lord? The yeoman entertains the baron? It's against every custom." He put his hands together over his chest. "Therefore, I beseech you, sir, turn the picture right side up and pay us for the meal, for all the trouble we have taken."

John shut his mouth. *You're a sly fox, Robin; I finally understand the game.* John stared intently at the knight.

Suddenly, the composure of the knight's expression faded, his face looked sunken, his eyes seemed exhausted. "I have nothing in my saddle chests. Nothing I could offer without shame."

"Now, now." A thin smile played around the outlaw chief's mouth. "Sir, don't be modest."

"I have no more than one silver mark."

"You don't say?" Robin shook his head slightly, his tongue clicking regretfully.

"By God, this is the truth," the knight replied with indignation. "Thirteen shillings. Barely more than half a pound, that's all."

The gray eyes turned to ice. "Good. I will believe you. But too often, the trust of the Saxons has been shamelessly exploited by you Normans. Therefore, sir, forgive the scrutiny. If there is only that much silver in these boxes, I ask nothing of you. But if there is a penny more, I will take it all. Horse, armor, boots, everything you own."

Robin snapped his fingers at John. "The gentleman's luggage!"

Neither Robin nor the three other outlaws moved. Richard at the Lea sat stiff and composed. Next to him, Marian had put her head on her arm; she was tired and seemed to be unaware of the tension.

The giant spread the knight's coat on the floor of the stable His fingers ran over the finely crafted chests. The dark wood was sanded and polished, and a coat of arms decorated the sides. John pulled the pin from the first lock and lifted the lid. The chest was empty. He opened the second one and reached in. He held up a silver coin between thumb and forefinger. "This would be a lot for me. For a knight, it is not much." He threw the coin back into the chest again and grinned. "Fine, then. The man is honest."

Robin laughed. He called out for Paul Storyteller and had him fill his goblet to the brim. "Sir!" Robin got up from his seat. "I am a man of my word. I'll take your thanks in payment."

Together with their guest, the outlaws drained their goblets down to the last drop. Richard at the Lea drank and agreed to a refill, but he still did not respond to his hosts' exuberant cheerfulness. With every sip, his mood became darker.

"Stop!" Robin Hood slammed the cup hard onto the tabletop. The others fell silent.

"Sir Richard . . . though it may not seem fitting for a freeman to ask: What kind of knight are you? Your chests are empty. Your clothes are worn out. And you barely touched the food." A quick glance fell on old Storyteller. "And my cooks really outdid themselves today."

Paul sighed and hobbled quickly outside.

"Tell me—what's the matter with you?" Robin asked.

The knight remained silent, staring into the goblet, and then furrowing his brows. "With the end of this day, all is lost. I see no way out."

Despite the grief in his voice, he set forth his words carefully. Not quite three years before, his son Edward had killed a knight and a nobleman during the tournament in Ashby. "It was a fair fight. That was the unanimous verdict of the marshal and all the heralds. But scarcely had the tournament ended, when my neighbor, Sir Roger of Doncaster, brought an action against my son before the High Court." The knight turned to Little John. "My castle, Fenwick, lies southeast of the River Went. Barely ten miles from where we met."

"I did not know . . ."

"No, I do not regret being brought here. I never expected to spend my last evening in such decent company."

"Go on," Robin prompted him quietly. "Everything about Sir Roger is of interest to us. And especially to my friend Tom." With the flat of his hand, Toad wiped his gray, shriveled scalp and stared straight ahead.

"The dead nobleman was a distant relative of Baron Roger. Yet it was not for the sake of justice that he brought his case. But out of greed and vindictiveness. The tragic accident served as his pretext. He had always envied me my land, the yield of my fields. At the same time, he dislikes me because I am steadfastly loyal to King Richard the Lionheart."

He recounted bitterly how Sir Roger and, with him, many feudal lords from the counties of Nottingham, Derby, and York had sided with Prince John in recent years. "They support the plans of the cruel prince. During the absence of his brother, Prince John plans to seize power and throne of England, and anyone who offers him his shield has the ear of John's hired judges. So it was with the trial of my son. Life imprisonment or payment of an outrageous sum, that was the verdict. What was else left for me to do as a father?" The knight's shoulders sank. He had mortgaged the castle, goods, and everything he owned and paid off his son's bounty.

"We agreed to pay off the debts together. My Edward immediately took the Crusader's vow and followed our king to the Holy Land to try his luck. I stayed and worked hard." But the harvest last summer had been so poor, and he had not wanted to burden his hardworking peasants with higher levies. "I was able to repay a large part of it. For the rest, I lack the means."

That morning he had been in Pontefract, hoping to borrow the much-needed sum from a friend of his, a landowner. "Alas, in times of need, it is rare to find a friend. I had to leave with empty saddle chests. And the deadline is tomorrow at sunset. The bond expires." He gently stroked the sleeping Marian's hair. "My daughter is barely older than she is." He straightened his back. "I will take my child and her mother to relatives and set out for Jerusalem across the sea myself. Perhaps if my son is still alive and we return with King Richard, I will be able to find hope again."

John muttered into the silence: "By St. Dunstan, I didn't know the Normans also stabbed each other in the back."

Richard at the Lea raised his brows. "Politics and greed are treacherous sisters. No one is immune to their venom."

"Well." John scratched the scar in his beard. "Just wanted to say I'm sorry about all this."

"Quiet, John!" Robin Hood admonished him. Thoughtfully, the outlaw rubbed his fingertips together. "I have some questions, sir. And on your honor, answer them openly and truthfully! Who has the bond?"

"The Abbot of St. Mary's Abbey in York. A lackey of my neighbor, Sir Roger."

"What is the balance of your debt to the abbey?"

"Four hundred pounds."

Robin's men were startled. Robin whistled through his teeth. "For such a sum, even a bishop would walk to church on foot." He looked calmly from one to the other. "Tom? Pete? Gilbert? I won't ask you, John. You got us into this mess. But you others? What do you think?"

Pete Smiling pursed his lips and nodded. Gilbert Whitehand agreed. Tom Toad agreed as well.

"Sir," said Robin, "I am prepared to advance you the sum."

Richard at the Lea closed his eyes. His chin trembled for a moment. Then, once again in control, he opened his eyes. "The offer alone touches me deeply and shows me your compassion. Thank you. However—"

"I stand by my word," the outlaw chief interrupted him curtly. He winked at his friends and continued: "Sir, at least imagine it could be so. Play along. Don't let the evening end in grief and tears."

"Forgive me that my troubles have made me … All right, a make-believe. Very well, then: I am ready."

Robin laughed. “If I lend you the four hundred pounds. What guarantor can you bring me? Who will repay if you cannot?”

Richard at the Lea answered with great earnestness. “By all the saints, I know of no one who would stand surety for me.”

“By the saints? Who have we here? St. Dunstan, St. Dubric, St. Winibald, St. Willick, St. John, St. Catherine . . .” Robin paused for breath. With both hands, he clutched at his red-blond hair. “And I am to trust all of them? Shall I run to all of them to get my beautiful gold back? No, you cannot expect that. Name a better guarantor!”

“Don’t torture me!” The knight knitted his brows. “I cannot offer any security. I swear this by the Virgin Mary. My fate is entirely in her gracious hands.”

Robin’s gray eyes lit up. “The pure Virgin. In all England, there is no better security in these times. A pledge by the Virgin Mary is enough for me. She has never let me down. Sir Richard! I shall advance the money for exactly one year. Tomorrow you can pluck your bond from the jaws of that pious leech in York.”

For the first time that night, the knight smiled. “If the circumstances were not as they are, and if you and your friends were guests at my table, then, believe me, I would reward you for this entertaining game. But now I am tired and ask for a place to sleep. A hard day awaits me tomorrow.”

“Patience. Since it is my game, we will play it to the end according to my rules.” Robin turned to the others. “I will give the gold. And what about you? What do you give?”

“The way he looks,” John blurted out, “he needs a new robe. To make him look like a knight again.”

“All right, little man. Although I’ll have to have a word with you later.” The leader pointed to Tom Toad. “Now, you?”

“He needs a stallion and a good saddle. He should use his own beast for a packhorse.”

Whitehand was willing to give away the best boots in the garment chest. Pete Smiling added gold spurs.

"And a squire?" Robin smiled. "A knight without a squire is no knight. Therefore, sir, I lend you not only four hundred pounds, but also my smallest lieutenant. You already know him. Our Little John. He will accompany you to York as your squire."

"Good idea," the giant growled when he saw the smirking faces of his companions. "Nothing will happen to him, then."

"Thank you." Richard at the Lea propped up his forehead with his hand. "A beautiful dream. But now, let me rest!"

Robin led the guest to an adjoining hut. "Sleep, sir—but do not dream, sir. Otherwise, reality may fade."

When he returned, John left the stables with Marian. He carried the sleeping girl in his arms, her head leaning on his shoulder.

"Hey, you runt!" Robin called. "I have some advice for you."

"Keep your voice down, or you'll wake her up."

Robin came close to the giant. "Next time," he whispered, punching his fist against the broad chest, "next time take a closer look before choosing your victim! Understand? Otherwise, this is going to be too expensive for us."

It took a moment, then John smiled. "Fine, then."

The fog rose slowly. It still shrouded the raven nests in the treetops. They croaked down to those below: *The day! Day! The day!*

Robin Hood only woke his lieutenants. He gave out orders in a low voice. "And no dallying, John. Hurry!" Everyone knew what they had to do.

Loaded with robe, boots, and spurs, Whitehand entered the knight's hut.

"Don't let him out until I call," Robin had instructed him.

In the clothing cave, Little John had to take off his brown-and-black clothes. Accompanied by the rumbling laughter of Pete Smiling, he tried to squeeze his huge legs into light blue, finely knitted stockings. They had already burst at the knee. Also, none of the embroidered velvet robes could be laced closed over his chest. "Stop laughing, or I'll shut your mouth," he scolded and threw the expensive pieces back into the trunk. "Damn it! I am not a doll."

"Orders are orders." Smiling bared his teeth. He handed John a livid green, yellow-striped travel cloak with an oversize hood. "Then put your own stockings and tunic back on! This fine piece here will at least reach over your bottom, and this tent is just right for your fat little head.

No, he could not take his staff with him. He had to strap on a sword and tuck a long-handled hammer next to it. Smiling was finally satisfied. "What a squire," he mocked. "Stand in a field, and no bird would dare eat even one grain!"

"I'll knock your teeth out . . ." Anger and laughter struggled for control of his face. John drew his sword. He was much too slow for Smiling. Pete had already drawn his own weapon, and he let the blade bob up and down in front of the giant's chest. "Wouldn't it be a pity to spoil his beautiful coat?" His blood-red scar twitched, then he bared his teeth again. "Forward, Squire John! Your lord knight calls for you."

"All right. Just wanted to see if this pointy thing wouldn't get stuck in its scabbard." Growling, John put the weapon back.

Three horses waited outside the stable—including a strong brown one for John. The guest's skinny nag carried the empty chests. Both lids were open. Robin had chosen the white stallion himself, had saddled and bridled him. "Where is Tom?" he whispered. Toad was to go down to the camp, get the gold from the treasury, and immediately bring it up. Why was it taking so long? "That toad-head. He better not spoil our fun!"

His impatience was contagious. Pete and John paced back and forth in front of the knight's hut. As soon as the conversation broke off inside, the giant blocked the exit with his sheer size. "Not yet, Gilbert. Keep him talking."

The fog had lifted—a clear sky. The croaking ravens circled around the bare treetops, dropped into their nests, and rose again.

At last, Tom Toad approached with heavy strides. No sooner did he spot the giant in his new disguise than he stumbled. Only with great difficulty did he manage to keep his balance. He put down his leather bag, laughing and gasping: "If my Beth sees you like this, I think—"

"You're having a go at me as well now?" John snorted. "One more word, and I'll cut off your braid!"

"Hush!" Robin whispered. He sounded the hunting horn. Before the long-drawn-out alarm signal had faded away, the few men who had stayed overnight at the base stormed out of their quarters, half-dressed but each one holding his weapon in his hand. "Line up!" Their leader gestured for them to form a semicircle.

All but Marian obeyed, even the two cooks. The girl ran to John and tugged violently at the hem of the bright green travel cloak with the yellow stripes. Questioningly, almost anxiously, she looked up at him.

"Everything is all right, little one," he rumbled. "It's only a game." Marian cowered on the ground near him and never let him out of her sight.

Robin put both hands on his hips. "Sir Richard at the Lea! The Brotherhood of Freemen wishes to bid you farewell."

Whitehand was the first to leave the hut. He threw the weathered coat and the discarded, tattered clothes onto the packhorse and quickly joined the others.

The knight stepped outside. He cut a dignified, tall figure, the ermine collar of the scarlet overgarment draped softly over his shoulders. The breastplate shimmered softly. His pale, tired face appeared even more angular. He looked calmly at Robin Hood. "I thank you and your friends. You have given me a rich gift with this robe. Though this outward splendor is not . . ."

"I beg you, sir, be silent," Robin curtly interrupted. "Grief paralyzes the mind."

The knight raised his brows.

Robin laughed. "We are partners because you have given me the best surety. Now it is up to you to fulfill the contract. And for that, you need to show the strength and determination of a bold man. Whining and complaining only sours the transaction."

Richard at the Lea tensed his back in indignation. Only now did he notice the horses and the giant, all ready to leave. His gaze stopped on the open empty saddle chests. "You dare to reprimand me? Well then, I forgive you, considering the hospitality I have enjoyed. Thank you for your generous gifts! They help, yet they do not save me. Therefore, on my honor, I ask you to stop playing this game with my misery!"

Robin replied calmly: "Thank the Blessed Virgin! The sudden anger in your eyes, sir, convinces me. Yes, you will pay me back my gold in time." He waved at Toad and Whitehand. "Count it! And do it loud and clear."

Tom lifted one bar of gold after the other out of the leather sack, placed it in Gilbert's white hand, who placed the shiny pieces in the saddle chests, the first bar in one, the second in the other, and so on to distribute the weight evenly. None of the freemen dared to grumble. Robin Hood's orders had to be followed, and they always had a purpose. Their heads moved back and forth in the same rhythm. In silence, the men escorted their beautiful gold on its short journey to the chests.

At the sight of the first bar, Richard at the Lea had groaned loudly, and since then, he kept stroking his beard.

Gilbert locked the two chests. "Fourteen there, and fourteen here. Together that amounts to exactly four hundred pounds."

Robin stepped before the knight and crossed his arms. "Well, what do you say?"

"I've never met a man like you before." The knight's lips trembled. "You barely know who I am, and you entrust me with this fortune?"

"I have known you since yesterday, sir. And that is long enough. Besides, I have the surety of the pure Virgin. And furthermore . . ." Robin smiled crookedly. "Me and my men, we are hunters. We can track any game, no matter where it hides."

"You know where to find me. By our gracious Virgin, do not worry! Now that I have my reputation, my castle, and my goods, I will repay you in full over the year."

The knight held out his hand to the leader of the freemen. "Take my thanks. That's all I can give you now! Overnight my fate has miraculously turned for the better. I firmly believe that England's fate will also turn to the best with the return of our king. If you or any of your men ever need my help or my intercession, I swear on my honor I will receive you and defend you."

Robin took the offered hand. "I never would have believed a Norman could ally himself with an outlawed Saxon. This is all very upside-down. But I like it."

It was time to leave. Time was short. The bond had to be redeemed at St.t Mary's Abbey by sunset. Richard at the Lea sat up straight on the horse and stroked the mane of the magnificent white steed admiringly. "I'll fly to York."

"I shall not ever find such a fine beast . . ." Robin stopped himself. "Yes, a beautiful horse." And he glanced at John with a stern look. "Why are you dawdling, squire?"

Marian clung to the giant's cloak. Tears were rolling down her cheeks.

"I'll be back, little one. I will. Believe me, I won't abandon you!" John gently loosened her clasped hands. "Tomorrow, or the day after tomorrow at the latest, I'll be back. In the meantime, go over to the village. Beth will be happy to see you."

Marian wiped her eyes with her fists. She opened her mouth, formed words, but only wheezing and gargling escaped her throat.

"It's all right, little one. Go to Beth and wait for me." John abruptly turned and mounted the brown horse.

Pete Smiling had attached the knight's shield to the saddle horn. "If he calls for it, you pass it to him, nice and polite like a good squire." John gave a strained grin. Pete bared his teeth and pointed to the feet hanging down below the horse's belly. "And if your steed isn't fast enough, just put your feet on the ground and give him some help!"

Before John could think of a suitable response, Robin Hood ordered, "Forward!"

The knight spurred the white horse on. He sat upright in the saddle. John put the hood of his coat over his head and snatched the packhorse's reins from Pete's hand. "I'll be back," he threatened.

I'll be back, his gaze promised the girl. He clicked his tongue and followed his new master.

Marian's shoulders sank. Even when horse and rider had long since been swallowed by the forest, she stood motionless.

"Hey, little condition!" Robin Hood waved his hand up and down in front of her eyes. "Hey, here I am!" He crouched down. "You were John's one condition, and I gave my word. At first, nobody knew what we should do with a girl amongst us boys." He continued in earnest: "But now you no longer belong just to that giant. You belong to us. We are your family."

For a long time, Marian searched the gray eyes of the leader. Then she nodded.

Robin straightened up. Looking dubious, he asked, "How fast are you?"

The girl put one foot forward and set her chin.

"Very well. Whoever gets to the village first. The rules are, if I win, I give you a knife. If you win, I owe you a knife."

Marian frowned. Finally, she sneered contemptuously.

"Not a good game, is it?"

She shook her head.

"Very well. We'll walk to the village together. You'll stay with Beth. And you can pick out a good dagger from the blacksmith. Deal?"

That was when Marian finally smiled at him.

VII

The latest dispatch from the Crusade: *Sultan Saladin's prisoner exchange does not fully meet the demands of the victor of the battle of Acre. In a rage, Lionheart has 3000 Muslim prisoners—women, children, and men—slaughtered on August 20, 1191, outside the city walls. Lionheart marches on toward Jerusalem with his army.*

ST. MARY'S ABBEY IN YORK.

An oak crucifix was affixed to the front wall of the hall with iron wedges. The spear wound on the Savior's body had been renewed with fresh red paint only a few days earlier. In painful devotion, the suffering Christ looked down on the richly laid table. The sound of the noon bell had long since died away. "He will not come. *Deo gratias!* Not if he hasn't by now." The well-padded cheeks of the abbot were flushed. "Be seated! Let's enjoy the meal." He waved his guests and the monks to the table.

The abbot submissively led Baron Roger of Doncaster to his seat. The mighty patron of St. Mary's Abbey had kept his word. All the costs for the restoration of the crucifix and the refectory had been paid by him. "A modest meal will fill our stomachs till sundown. And after the deadline, the knight's possessions will fill our purses. What a day for the Lord!"

Sir Roger swiped the Benedictine's hand off his black velvet sleeve. "*Prudemment, abbé,* I detest being touched. Even by a man of the cloth!" The thin lips of the gaunt, hollow-cheeked man barely moved when he spoke, thrusting the words from his mouth and nose. The pale green eyes showed annoyance. "Not a day for the Lord. It is my money that you lent out. It is my day."

"*C'est vrai.* Pardon me. *C'est vrai.*" Bowing low, the abbot held the chair for the Baron and waited for Sir Roger to settle down. Then he gestured to the next of his guests. "And you, my dear judge, will take your seat right here!"

"With pleasure. Gladly." The stout man pulled in the high-backed chair for himself. "Hunger and thirst are gnawing away at me." His eyes were already eating into the fragrant hare pie.

As a royal judge and tax collector, he traveled from castle to castle, from monastery to monastery. He cared little about robbery and murder. He calculated the sums that had to be paid to London, imposed fines, and threatened delinquent lords with property seizure. So, one was kind to him and more than kind. Everyone knew about his sticky open hands, his insatiable greed. He gratefully accepted generous gifts. In exchange, he reduced one's tax debt. He gladly delayed his journeys for lucrative side deals.

"It should be done lawful and proper," the royal judge said. "If the knight lets the deadline expire, you shall bear witness to it with your seal." For this small service, the abbot had given him an advance of fifty silver pieces from the monastery coffer that morning. The debtor still had a few hours left. The judge licked his lips with gusto; he intended to use this time to enjoy the wine and good food.

"For the emissary of the Lord Sheriff of Nottingham," said the abbot, "I have reserved the place on my right."

The squire sat down. With his knife upright in his fist, he waited for the meal to begin. He had only been sent as a witness. It was puzzling to him. He did not understand the whys and hows of it all, but he did know that he had rarely seen Thom de Fitz so outraged: "*Diable!* That pathetic knight has actually repaid all his debts in our shire. *Sang de Dieu!* All that remains is the bond in York." The lord sheriff's face had been red, except for the white stump on his nose, at the idea that this long-prepared plan could fail at the last moment. Thom de Fitz had received a splendid gold necklace from his friend Sir Roger after his testimony at the knight's son's trial.

The Lord Sheriff had chosen the simplest squire in Nottingham to represent him today. "You swear to everything that you are asked!" had been the instructions. "For this, my noble and valiant warrior, you may kill a stag at the next hunt. You sign anything and everything, do you understand?"

"Sign? As in write?" the squire had replied.

"*Par tous les diables.* Then just put an X!"

So far, the day had gone without a hitch. No one had asked him anything. No one had asked him to read or write anything. The squire was pleased with himself.

"Brother Prior, come to me." With his finger, the abbot ordered a slender, somewhat misshapen monk to the seat to his left. "Brother Cellar Master, sit down to his other side! Just to be safe." The large-headed cellar master thanked him piously, and as he sat down, he almost knocked the prior off his stool with his well-fed bulk.

The abbot looked over his shoulder up to the Redeemer, muttered a short prayer of thanksgiving, made the sign of the cross, and cried out: "God save Prince John! Enjoy whatever your heart desires!"

And the round table did enjoy. Over the course of an hour, meat pies, ham, and hot wheat cakes were devoured and finally washed down with wine. The abbot snapped a finger at Brother Food Master. "Well, why are you dawdling?" He pointed to the baron's place.

With a blank face, Sir Roger of Doncaster first poured the rest of his wine at the monk's feet before he had the cup refilled with fresh drink. His green eyes looked scornfully at the abbot. "Was that it?" he sniffed through his crooked nose. "Is that all the food you have to offer me?"

“Wait, wait. A delicacy will crown our meal. Uh . . . *une délicatesse excellente*.” The abbot clapped his hands. At once, the food master rushed back out.

“Have a little patience, Sir Roger! These taste best freshly prepared, crispy. They sweeten our estate. I may have the peasants tithe more, for the benefit of my humble monastery.”

Next to him, the little prior shook his head. “It’s not right,” he said softly.

“Quiet!” hissed the abbot

“Forgive my disobedience, Father!” The prior stared straight ahead. “It is not right to deprive the knight of all his fortune. His debt is only—”

“Brother Prior! I forbid you to speak!”

The monk ducked his head. His hump bulged higher under his black robe. “Forgive me! But I am your deputy.”

The royal judge frowned with uncertainty. “I wash my hands of it. But if there is anything amiss in this transaction . . .”

“No!” cried the abbot. “The law is on our side. If the knight does not appear and pay his debt, then, *par la Vierge*, he loses all his property, no matter how much his property is worth.”

Relieved, the judge nodded. “Right. Right. That’s a fair way to look at it.” He leaned back.

“Forgive me,” began the prior again, “but it’s cruel to treat a human being—”

In a flash, the cellar master stamped the pommel of his knife on the back of the prior’s hand—the prior broke off in a stifled scream.

“Forgive me, dearest Brother Prior,” said the cellar master. “But with all due humility, it’s none of your concern.” The cellar master shook his head. “I’m responsible for the monastery’s operations, the cellar, and the barns. And I am in accord with our gracious Father Abbot.”

Sir Roger had listened in silence. “It amazes me,” he began and waited until everyone turned to him. "Yes, for a long time, I have wondered how a crippled man could have succeeded in obtaining such an elevated office. Are there no straight-backed men of faith in the order of the Benedictines?"

The hunched monk let his chin sink to his chest.

The abbot eagerly agreed with his patron: "On reflection, yes, it seems necessary, yes, that we may have to make a new choice for the monastery."

"I have so decided," Sir Roger of Doncaster declared nasally.

The two tapestries hung as curtains at the entry were parted. Led by the food master, three friars carried in the delicacies.

They lowered the platters next to the Baron's seat. Larks, warblers, and nightingales! Plucked, rolled in honey, and roasted brown on long, thin wooden skewers!

Sir Roger helped himself with both hands. He did not wait for the others to be served. He bit the heads off the crispy birds, spat them across the table, then he tore the first nightingale from the skewer with his teeth.

No more talking. The gentlemen of the table chewed the delicacies with relish. Alone among them the prior ate nothing. He sat slumped down on his stool.

Forest, fields, pastures, and again forest. Not galloping, but at an easy trot, so they would not tire the horses. As the trees and shrubs moved in closer to the road, the foliage dampened the hoofbeats.

Sir Richard at the Lea reined in the white horse at the top of a hill and waited until Little John caught up with the packhorse. "Just under an hour. Then we will reach our destination."

The road cut down through a narrow, straight gorge. Only when it reached the plain did it leave the forest for good and wind its way between brown-black fields to York's city gates. No roofs could be seen beyond the powerful ring of walls. Still, there were plenty of church towers to be seen, close together, all dominated by the cathedral's blunt tower.

"About time." John pushed the hood off his head. He looked up at the sun. "It's all right, sir. There's still time."

Sir Richard stretched out his arm. "There. Left side. Outside the city walls. There's St. Mary's Abbey. That's where I'm expected."

"Or not." John grinned.

The knight turned grim. "Yes, perhaps. The abbot just wants a quick profit. But my neighbor, Sir Roger, would surely be disappointed. He has prevented anyone from lending me the final four hundred pounds with threats and promises. He would enjoy seeing my final humiliation."

"Well, then he will be disappointed." The giant pulled up his bright-green and yellow hood again. "I can't get it into my head how you fine Normans peck each other's eyes out. Not even a crow will do that to its own."

"Silence! Remember one thing: Not all Normans are greedy." Sir Richard drove on the horse with a light touch of his spurs. He let the animal gallop, quickly increasing the distance.

"Very well, sir!" The squire gripped the leather strap of the packhorse tighter, snapped the reins on his brown steed, and trotted after.

They had almost reached the plain. The path was still narrow. Trees and dense woods still lined the roadside. Richard at the Lea rode twenty horse lengths ahead.

Suddenly, just in front of John, a ragged figure appeared from behind a tree trunk, a huge club in his fists. The face was dirty. The eyes glared. "I am Robin Hood. Get off that horse!"

In John's mind, the journey had been as good as over, he had as good as reached the comfort and shelter of the monastery. "Hey, what the—? Who the—? Who are you?" The giant was slow to process this unexpected turn. An ambush. *How dare he! Calls himself Robin Hood!* "Get out of here before I show you who's who!"

The man leapt closer and swung his weapon with both hands. John barely managed to pull himself back away from the blow, then the club crashed into his mount's skull. The horse's front hooves buckled.

"By Satan!" The giant did not fall down. He stood with both his feet on the ground, the wounded horse gurgling between his legs. "Don't tangle with me, lad!" Everything in John tensed.

As the animal tipped to the side, John grabbed the shield off its saddle. Roaring, he pushed himself off and rushed toward the highwayman. The club swung in for a second strike. John dodged. The gnarled wood grazed his left arm, and he stumbled and hit the ground. Above him, the man took his time. He drew back wide to swing the third blow.

That moment was enough for John to squat down and grab the shield with both hands. He jumped into the blow and rammed the attacker. The highwayman was thrown backward off the road. "You rat! Robin Hood, my ass. You're a damned rat!" John made to throw himself over him.

The packhorse was neighing behind him. John spun around. A second man was dragging the horse and the saddle chests into the bushes. "Miserable scum!" John dropped the shield and ran at him, but the first attacker was on him again. He fell, grabbed a foot, and clung on. "Not with me!" John let out a roar and slammed both fists into the man's back.

Richard at the Lea heard the squire's roar. He turned the white horse about and galloped to help. Before he reached John, the highwayman hand already collapsed.

John pushed the motionless body aside. "You damn idiot! Didn't I tell you? Not with me!" He rushed across the road, plowed into the undergrowth. The second man hadn't made it far with the bucking packhorse. When he saw the monster roaring up behind him, he forgot his prey and fled, screaming.

John let him go. "That's fine by me," he panted. He slowly approached the frightened animal. "Shush!" He reached for the bridle. "Steady. It's all right."

From the road, Richard at the Lea anxiously called his name.

"All is well, sir. I got the gold."

The giant brought the packhorse safely back to the road.

"He's dead." The knight had dismounted and turned the highwayman on his back.

"Warned him." John wiped his brow. "Couldn't help it. It happened too fast for me to get to the sword or the hammer. Had I had my staff, I'd have taken care of him right away. He'd have had a limp all his life, but he'd still be alive." John knocked the dirt off his traveling cloak. "Trash!"

Richard at the Lea pointed to the brown horse. It lay on its side, twitching and wheezing. "Help him," he demanded.

John looked at the knight, then lowered his eyes. "He's suffered enough," he murmured. Richard at the Lea understood, and he drew the sword himself.

Silence. John adjusted the saddle chests, moved them back and forth, slapped the bundle of clothes. After a while, he paused, thoughtfully scratching the scar in the beard. "Sir? The robe. I think the new robe was to blame. The fellows saw it and thought, *Here comes a rich man.*" John took the knight's old bad-weather cloak off the packhorse. "Put this back on! It's better, I think. That won't be attracting anybody's attention."

"Good. Give it to me. We have to go." Sir Richard followed the advice without hesitation. But then he paused, smiling softly: "Your idea is better than you think." As he climbed into the saddle, he added: "This tattered garment will fool robbers like those, but also the other kind. But now . . . we've lost time."

"Don't worry, sir. I'll keep that packhorse moving. I've got good feet. It's gonna be close, but we'll make it."

As the giant ran after the knight in great strides, he kept on ranting. "Those rats! They just take and use Robin's name. The vermin! Lurking behind the trees like that. The mangy, lousy vermin!"

Finally, Sir Richard turned to him and said, "Who do you mean, Little John?"

The giant fell silent. He pulled the large hood down over his forehead. "It's all right, sir. Well, I mean, there are such foul robbers in the woods. That's what I mean."

Red and golden sunlight flooded through the west windows of the abbey's dining hall. Candied apples and nuts had rounded off the meal. Once again, the abbot had a refill of his cup. Slightly drunk, he lifted the goblet: "A toast to the sun. In another little while it will sink away. Hello, night. Farewell, knight!"

"Stop your babbling!" Sir Roger of Doncaster thumped his fist on the table. "Even if the bond expires, the knight still must sign the deed. We need certified confirmation."

"Just a formality," the judge reassured him immediately. "However, it will cost—"

Voices. Noise. Hoofbeats outside the hall. The porter monk slipped through the door hangings, hurried to the table, and bowed. "Forgive me, Father Abbot! The knight and his squire. They are waiting just outside. I could not stop them. They even refused to take the horses into the stable."

The abbot stared at the sun. The glowing red orb still stood above the horizon in the west. All color disappeared from his face.

Sir Roger's lips stretched into a smile. "There. At last! Let him enter! And you, dear father, you lead the performance. And . . . *par la Vierge*, woe unto you if you fail now." With that, he leaned back and crossed his arms. Obediently, the porter grabbed the two door curtains, tied them to the side, bowed, and quickly withdrew.

The knight at the door carried his helmet in his hand. His chain mail hood fitted tightly around his head. The weathered cloak was pulled closed and enveloped his tall figure. Thus Sir Richard at the Lea entered the hall. Behind him, his squire stopped in the doorway, his massive body filling the entrance, his large hood hiding his eyes and nose. He held the packhorse's rein in his left hand.

After a few steps, the knight bent to his knees before the assembled gentlemen. "I offer you all my greetings. I greet you, Reverend Father."

The abbot just nodded. He did not ask the guest to get up and come sit down, as politeness dictated, nor did he offer him a welcoming drink.

Richard remained on his knees. "After twelve months, I am come exactly to the day and hour—"

"You have my money?" the abbot interrupted.

"The harvest was poor. The yield was not enough to raise the sum."

The abbot shot up from his seat. But he regained his calm and lowered himself back into the chair. His eyes roved across the faces of his dinner companions. "Did everyone hear?" He pulled the deed from where was tucked into his rope belt, lovingly laid it down before him. "*Deo Gratias!* He does not have it. He really doesn't have it. What a—"

"Carry on," Sir Roger said. From narrowed eyes, he watched the humbly kneeling knight.

The judge leaned across the table. "Reverend Father?" he murmured. "What do you offer me if I see to it that he signs the deed of transfer today?"

"You want more? You already have—"

"That was for my seal."

"No more haggling!" the baron snapped.

"Very well," the abbot huffed. "Fifty."

The judge held out his hand. "Now, if you please!"

"Au Dieu!" The abbot pulled a pouch from the sleeve of his black robe. "There's fifty in there, trust me."

Opening the coin pouch, checking its contents, and weighing it in his hand took the royal judge hardly longer than a breath. "*Bien.* You have my deepest trust, Father."

A vein pulsed across the Benedictine's forehead. The flabby skin hung pale from his cheekbones. He had already lost a hundred pounds from the monastery's purse. His rage found a target in the kneeling knight: "You come here empty-handed! And still dare to enter my sight? You are worthless! What a pitiful figure you are!"

"Mercy!" Sir Richard entreated. "That is why I dared to come here. Have mercy! Don't take my land away from me! Don't push my family and myself deeper into misery!" Richard at the Lea clasped his hands together. "By the pure Virgin, I beg you, extend the due date for the debt!"

"Ungrateful wretch! It was out of pity and charity that I gave you the money a year ago at all. You've lost your chance to repay it." The abbot was fortified by a quick glance at Sir Roger. "Given the other beneficent duties of my monastery, I am forced to be mercilessly strict."

Except for the prior, all the gentlemen at the table nodded.

Richard at the Lea did not relent. "And you, honorable judge? Never have I owed our king a penny in taxes. Help me out of my misery and advance me the sum."

"A pity, it's a pity." The judge heaved a long sigh. "I am but an officer of the Crown. And as the king's servant . . ." He let the word trail away and shrugged his shoulders.

The knight looked at the emissary of the lord sheriff. Who was grinning stupidly. Richard at the Lea turned to the baron. "Sir Roger of Doncaster. Neighbor!" He fell silent and seemed to be searching for words.

At the entrance, Little John flinched. Sir Roger of Doncaster! Under the hood, his eyes turned to ice. *So, it is you. Our Much's parents tremble before you. You had Tom's head doused with boiling oil. You had poor Beth's ear cut off.* John breathed heavily. *You let her children die. I have seen your face, you bastard. I will know it forever now.*

Richard at the Lea began with a firm voice: "We both come from old and noble lineages. Our grandfathers came to this island together with the victorious King William more than a hundred years ago. We are both Normans. Forget your hatred. Do not leave me here on the ground!"

The baron's nostrils flared. "You dare to compare yourself to me? I'd rather give a sausage to a stray dog than give you a single penny." He pointed to the west. The sun almost touched the horizon. "When it sets, you too will go down. And I will watch."

John stared anxiously at the window. Why was the knight dawdling?

"I've been saving some coins," the prior feebly inserted. "I would be ready to—"

His words cut off in a choked whimper as the cellar master stuck his knife blade through the back of the monk's hand. Blood poured from the gaping wound.

"Oh, pardon, dearest brother!" The cellar master's grin grew wide. "What did I hear? You keep personal property? Did you steal from the abbey? Or did I mishear?"

Once again, the large-headed cellar master set the tip of the blade against the prior's hand. The prior stammered pleadingly: "M-misheard. Y-yes, misheard!"

Sir Roger snapped his fingers at the crown official. "Finish the last formality and then throw the beggar out the door!"

Richard at the Lea, with painstaking self-control, closed his eyes and remained silent.

"Be generous, venerable Father!" the judge put in. "And pay him a little something for the land. It will make our business go more smoothly!" The judge winked at the abbot. "Give him another hundred pounds . . . and in exchange, he will sign the deed."

"A hundred pounds?" The Benedictine monk put a hand to his throat. "I am to shove one hundred pounds down the purse of a knight who has broken his word?"

"Broken my word?!" Sir Richard at the Lea rose. "Never! Never will I allow anyone to accuse me of breaking my word. On my honor, if you were a knight—!" He shook a fist. "You would face this! And if you offered me a thousand pounds, I would never put my signature on such a shameful document."

"I represent the law," the judge began. "And it seems to me that you have—"

"Silence!" demanded Sir Richard. "I am ashamed to see you wearing the colors of our king." His wedge-trimmed goatee trembled. "And you, Father Abbot. What a travesty to have to call you holy father. I came to stir your heart, but you are false and greedy. You confirm everything that the tortured, exploited Saxons accuse you servants of the church of being. And the only one who shows mercy, you torture with a knife." Anger flared in the knight's face. "And you, my neighbor! You are the head of this? Yes, outwardly, you are the great patron of all! But in reality, you sneak around like a greedy wolf. One monastery, one aristocratic hall after the other, you force all into your control with your money and influence. Power is your lust. You never soil your hands in the process. To whom have *you* sworn allegiance? I ask you. Is it really Richard the Lionheart? Oh yes, I know all too well why you want to destroy me."

"Strong words," Sir Roger drawled. "You are right. I won't soil my hands on worms. I stomp on them."

Sir Richard at the Lea rose to his feet. He pointed to the window.

The glowing red ball was still half visible. "A year ago, I gave my word of honor. And today, to the hour, I repay my debt."

For a moment, he enjoyed the incredulous looks around the table. Then he ordered, "Squire!"

Relieved, John obeyed. He dragged the packhorse right through the doorway into the hall. With a saddle chest under each arm, the giant stepped toward the assembly. He tipped the gold bars over the empty platters.

"That should do it," he growled.

With practiced skill, the judge assessed the dully shining pieces. "It's true. That's four hundred pounds' worth."

Sir Roger swiped his goblet from the table. "Who dared give you this? Who helped you? *Enfer et damnation!* Who?" He reached out and caught John's green-and-yellow striped cloak. "And who is this monster with no manners? He's no servant. Show me your face, man!"

John grabbed the hand, pulled it up and off him, and crushed the fingers in his fist. The baron pressed his lips together in pain but made not a sound.

"Do not wish to see my face. You'll see it just before I break your neck."

"Squire!" admonished Richard at the Lea.

John released the baron's fingers.

"With this, all debts are paid." The knight demanded return of the deed.

Hurriedly, the abbot gathered up the parchment document protectively. "No, wait! First, I want my hundred pieces of silver back. Judge, give them to me!"

"I have done what I could. I have earned my reward fair and square."

"Then I demand them from you, knight! I must have my expenses back. Or I will not give up the deed.

Sir Richard shook his head in disbelief. "A den of thieves. Not monks, but robbers dwell within these sacred walls."

"Well." John urged the knight aside. "I can handle thieves," he growled. With that, the giant spun around, as he pulled the hammer from his belt. He let it whirl once, then the massive iron head crashed onto the table. The tabletop splintered. Cups, plates, gold, bones, and bowls flew up. Pie scraps, sauce, and wine scattered everywhere. The shock paralyzed the thoroughly splattered men. John leapt upon the table and, kicking table debris aside, cleared a straight path toward the abbot.

"My son. Please! *Par la Vierge*, do not sin," the abbot stammered. "Don't sin, my son."

"It's all good, Father. Just give me that paper."

The parchment was willingly handed over. The squire asked his knight: "What now? We paid on time. We have the deed of debt."

"Those present must bear witness. Only then shall we depart."

"You heard him." John let the hammer dangle in front of the gentlemen. "Hurry!

The prior smiled and raised his bleeding hand. "I testify before God that Sir Richard at the Lea has paid all his debt, that our monastery at St. Mary's Abbey has no more claims on him."

The judge made an effort at dignity. "By the power of my office, I confirm that Sir Richard at the Lea has fulfilled his duties according to law and order. He is debt free and remains in possession of his castle and all his lands. Whoever says otherwise, whoever slanders him or persecutes him, shall himself be subject to severe judgment."

"Well said. I like that," John growled under his hood. "And what about you other fellows?" The hammer swung ominously.

Baron Roger of Doncaster confirmed with a quick hand signal, as did the abbot and the cellar master.

"What shall I do?" asked the lord sheriff's emissary.

"Fingers up, you idiot, if you value your knees." The squire raised both hands, even stretched them above his head. "Good boy. Now that's the way I like it." John put the hammer back in his belt. "Lead the way, sire!"

Sir Richard at the Lea eyed the baron with cold contempt. "England is threatened by a wolf and his pack. Only yesterday did I learn that the real danger does not lurk in the woods. It's not the outlaws and their dreaded leader. I met rough but upright men there in the wilderness. Yes, they are rebelling. Yes, they are breaking the law because they feel betrayed by us Normans. But their loyalty to the king is such as can hardly be found in our counties. In the castles, in the monasteries, that is where the real danger for England lurks. God save King Richard in the Holy Land! May the Lord safeguard his speedy return!" With this, the knight pulled off his worn cloak, threw it over the ruins of the table, and stepped out of the hall in his fur-trimmed robe, his head held high.

"That's that," growled John. He grabbed the packhorse's halter and followed his knight.

The knight and his squire safely exited the gate of St. Mary's Abbey. The sun had set. The western sky was still glowing.

"Thank you," said Sir Richard. "Thank you, and Robin Hood!"

John jogged beside the white stallion. "It's all good. Now I know, sir. About the Normans, I mean. There is one kind, and there are the other kind."

In the dining hall of the monastery, Sir Roger was still sitting in his armchair. "Where did he get the gold? *Sacre Dieu.*" His hollow-cheeked face was ashen. Except for the abbot, the others had quickly melted away. The baron carefully opened and closed his bruised right hand. "So, our plan failed. Now I must be a good neighbor to this Richard at the Lea. He triumphs over me, and my hands are tied. But at the next opportunity . . ." The pale green eyes stared at the window. "Outlaws! He defended that filth!" His nostrils flared. "No Norman, no landowner, not even—" his voice sank into additional contempt "—one of the wealthy Jews of our shire would dare to thwart my plans. *Sacre Dieu!* I can guess who lent him the gold. Yes, I know. What does he call himself?"

The abbot shrugged. Sir Roger threatened him: "You should know his name, if you want to remain in my favor. Robin Hood! That self-declared freeman. I have had reports from all over that he and his cohorts want to take revenge on me. How careless I have been!"

The knight had only been the tool. Today, *Robin Hood* had skillfully struck a first blow against him, Baron Sir Roger of Doncaster. Such humiliation! The woods no longer harbored mere rabble-rousing creatures who would eventually end up on the gallows. This Robin Hood had welded the outlaws together and turned them into his army. And the stolen gold and silver was not just used to fill their bellies. And weapons! For three years, the robber had seized wagonloads of weapons! Roger of Doncaster slapped his forehead. "And I paid no attention to the Lord Sheriff of Nottingham's request for help! I laughed because I thought this yapping mutt could do no more than lift his leg on a few trees. Now I know better. I will never forget this shame. But Robin Hood poses a danger not only to me but to all our plans. And I want him. From this day forward, I will not rest, I swear it! I will stand by the lord sheriff with everything I have at my disposal. I will convince Prince John that this pestilence must be burned out of our forests. And woe to anyone who dares . . ." He broke off. The corners of his mouth twitched. "At Kirklees. In the convent of Kirklees. Those pious sisters also live off my generosity. Father Abbot? Think on it!"

"They live well. I know nothing more about them."

"One of the nuns is an expert in the art of healing. People come from far away when they have serious wounds."

"This is well known. I don't follow."

Revived, Sir Roger nodded. "Sister Mathilda. A capable, honorable woman. Whoever pays is treated well. Norman or Saxon, honorable or bad, no matter, she helps everyone, because pieces of silver don't stink. I always liked that about her. And one day, yes, she told me that her family is related to this Loxley, this Robin Hood. We laughed about it, then." Sir Roger of Doncaster stood up. "Right," he said, dangerously soft. "I think it's time we paid a visit to Kirklees Abbey."

VIII

The latest dispatch from the Crusade: *Richard the Lionheart wins the Battle of Arsuf on September 7, 1191. Sultan Saladin is forced to retreat. Richard does not attack Jerusalem, even though it is barely defended! He digs in his heels in Jaffa with the Crusader army. In November, the rainy season begins. Still, Lionheart hesitates. The allied military leaders grumble.*

YORKSHIRE. BARNSDALE WINTER CAMP.

The first snowflakes fell in early December. They remained on the frozen ground.

"It's getting too cold for you at my place, little one." Little John was determined.

Marian had fought back, had threatened the giant with her fists, had put three sheepskins over her shoulders. It was no use. John took her to Beth. "You'll be comfortable by the fire. And you can crawl under her blanket to sleep. And you'll be warm."

"My little princess!" The seamstress's happy smile had wiped the anger from Marian's eyes. She squeezed John's hand. She finally consented.

Just before Christmas, a snowstorm howled over the ridges and bare forests. It also snowed on the first nights of the twelve holy days. Every morning the peasants and craftsmen in Barnsdale Top had to dig out their huts' doors and the path to the stables.

Below, in the storm-protected main camp, the snow fell soft and silent. The linden tree stretched out rigidly in the middle of the whitened meadow. The river piled ice floes over each other against the bank.

Robin had allowed his troop a break to rest. No weapons training. Only the guards took their posts day and night as usual. Only after Twelfth Night was the hard combat training to be resumed again. The few who had family had wandered home.

"Not you, Much!" Robin had ordered. "You stay here."

"Why ... why not?" the boy babbled. "I ... I want to. Only for Christmas ... Christmas. Please." His chin trembled.

"It's too dangerous, boy. For your parents and for you. Do you think that damn Baron Roger has forgotten you? His spies are just waiting to get their hands on you." Robin put his arm around the unfortunate lad's shoulders. "But soon. In the spring, we'll go to the mill together. When we move down to Sherwood, we'll go past your mother's house. I promise you that."

While the others enjoyed the feast days, Much had been carving. He carved faces into wood, then he cut them away until only broken shavings remained scattered around him.

Idleness defined their days. The remaining freemen slept through the mornings. Only around noon did they trudge over to the long supply and kitchen shed. To the blazing fire. Hot soup. Dice games. Ale.

In the evening, they crouched around Paul Storyteller. "The Christmas feast was just over," he began. "At the castle at Camelot, King Arthur sits with his head propped on his fists. A bad mood darkens his face. 'I will not celebrate the New Year until I see a miracle.' The Knights of the Round Table are tearing their hair. A miracle? Who can conjure up a miracle just like that?" Paul looked at the tense faces and grinned. He held his silence.

"You'd better know how the story continues," Robin threatened. "Or I'll stick your head in the snow with my own hands."

Paul smirked. He laboriously straightened his stiff leg. Suddenly, his eyes grew wide and he stared at the door. "Do you hear it? Outside, hooves are clattering. A knight rides into the hall. He is green."

"Oh, *I* see. That's fine, then." With a look at Robin, John gleefully rubbed the scar in his beard.

"Don't break my flow," Storyteller scolded. Again he widened his eyes. "So: A knight rides thundering into the hall. Everything about the stranger is green: face, hair, armor, shield, sword, everything. Even his stallion is green. Only just before he reaches the big round table does the knight pull on the reins. The horse rears up, its front hooves whirling, then it stands still, snorting."

Old Paul painted the story not just with his voice but with his hands and arms. He turned the kitchen shed into the royal hall at Camelot. Suddenly, the freemen themselves became part of the round table. Everyone saw the stranger.

"The Green Knight stays in the saddle. At first, he mocks Arthur and his brave knights. Finally, he pulls out a giant ax. One of those present must strike him with this weapon—no matter where. There is one condition. After one year, exactly to the day, he will demand satisfaction. Then the brave knight must face him in a fight.

"Angered by the arrogant challenge, Arthur wants to grab the weapon himself. His nephew, Sir Gawain, catches hold of his arm. He will face the challenge for his king.

"Already the brave Gawain stands beside the green warhorse. The stranger smiles." Paul Storyteller swung his arm in a circle. "Then Gawain cuts off his head with a mighty stroke. 'Good work, nephew,' praises the king."

The audience in the kitchen shed also nodded approvingly. Warningly, Paul Storyteller raised his finger. "But look! Slowly, the Green Knight, just as he is, dismounts his horse. He goes to his head, lifts it up, and sets it back on his neck.

"Horror paralyzes the Round Table. As if nothing had happened, the stranger clasps hands with the king. Then he turns to Gawain and speaks . . ."

Paul slowly bent forward, bringing his lips close to Little John's ear, and stage-whispered: "'So, in one year, warrior! We'll meet at the Green Chapel.'" The old storyteller sat back and uttered a frightening laugh. "Yes, that's how the stranger laughed. The walls tremble. He climbs into the saddle, waves his hand again. The Green Knight gives his stallion the spurs and gallops out of the hall. Outside, the hooves thunder across the drawbridge. Then he is gone."

Silence. The freemen stared breathlessly at their Storyteller.

"And then what?" Robin Hood filled Paul's ale mug to the brim. "Did Gawain go to the chapel?"

"I'm done for today." The old man drank. He wiped the foam off his beard with his sleeve. "Arthur asked for a miracle. The spirit world had to obey. Yes, that is how it was at Camelot. Now the New Year could be celebrated."

On the penultimate day of the twelve, the day before Epiphany, water was heated over the fireplace. Outside, the freemen stood in the snow. Sun. Blue sky. Their breath froze in the clear air. One by one, they undressed. Each carried over hot water for another. "Tomorrow is Epiphany. Wash yourselves," Robin had ordered. "Our pure Virgin and the saints have keen noses. We must not frighten them tomorrow." He had led by example.

Three times Little John asked for another bucket. He scrubbed himself all over with grease, salt, sand, and ashes until his skin glowed. He held up the fourth bucket with outstretched arms and let the water run slowly over his head and shoulders, grunting in satisfaction. Away in Barnsdale Top, Beth and Marian had been cleaning the house since the early morning.

"When the Three Kings come, princess, everything must be

clean and tidy," Toad's wife had explained to the girl. "Otherwise, they get angry, and then we'll have bad luck all year long."

Marian was not convinced of that. With her lower lip pushed out, she had waggled her finger and shook her head.

"Everyone in the village is cleaning today. That's the way it is. Come help me, princess! And when everything is clean, then there's a delicious surprise for you." It was only this prospect that had convinced the girl.

Soon the bales of cloth lay tightly rolled on top of each other in the pantry, the pieces of leather piled up in order of size, precious and costly needles stuck in the pincushion, strings and threads hanging from the nails like combed strands of silken hair.

At dusk, Beth stirred up the embers. "Stay close to me now," she whispered to Marian and put small bundles of consecrated juniper on the fire. The fragrance rose, almost taking away her breath. The smoke filled the hut, every nook and cranny. Both sank to their knees. Quietly, Beth said a prayer, imploring a blessing for house and yard, and asked the Blessed Virgin to look after her two boys in heaven every now and then.

Marian trembled. Timidly she pulled Beth's sleeve. She pointed to her heart, pointed upward. Pleadingly, she put her hands together. Her lips formed only one word over and over again.

"What do you mean, princess?"

Tears rolled down Marian's cheeks. She pointed to herself, pressed both hands against the woman's lap, pointed to herself again, and again to the ceiling. Silently she mouthed the one word.

At last, Beth understood. Both bent their heads over their hands. "And also look after Marian's mother and little brother! Please. For my children and for the mother and brother of my little princess. Because we are alone here."

Later, apples sizzled on the grill. They were served with honey-sweet bread baked with nuts and hot milk. Marian ate. Her eyes were shining.

Even before daybreak on the Epiphany, Robin Hood and the troop reached Barnsdale Top, in long dark cloaks, black wide-brimmed caps, torches blazing in their hands.

John retrieved Marian up from Beth. "I'll bring her back to you," he promised.

"Come on now," Robin urged. "Wrangbrook is a long way. We can't be late."

Little John took the lead, closely followed by Marian. One after another, the men tramped through the snow, following in his tracks. His strides were too long. Soon the girl was panting.

"Wait!" John called out to his companions. "Come on," he said with a smile, bent his knee, and let Marian climb up. "Is that better?" She took hold of his beard with both hands and nodded his head.

Silently, the men marched through the forest and across vast white fields, fourteen night-black figures.

The stars faded. The sun rose red, and soon its light glittered on the snow. Just before Wrangbrook, Robin stopped. He pointed over to the small church. "Gilbert, it's your turn at the first mass. Take four people." While Whitehand ran ahead with the outlaws, Robin assigned the next set. "Tom, you take the second mass! And you, Pete, the third. That way, every man can hear at least two masses. John and I will hear all three."

His gaze stayed on Marian. "Let the little one help. She will hold the offering plate."

John frowned. "You didn't tell me about this. We are going to mass, you said because we need it. No games today. Why—"

"Don't get upset. Nothing will happen to our little condition," Robin reassured John. "Just you wait! Let her help. Nothing more."

Marian looked up at the giant and winked one eye.

"Fine, then."

The church bell rang out. Bright and inviting, the ringing sounded across the low roofs. Almost simultaneously, the doors of all the huts and houses opened. In their Sunday best, women, children, and men hurried through the snow toward the center, toward their church.

"Only go when the villagers are all inside. Only then."

The bell fell silent. Standing just before the portal, Robin Hood whistled. Whistles replied. The churchyard wall was lined with his guards. Thus secured, the leader, his first set of chosen men, and Marian entered the dark interior.

"In Nomine Patris et Filii et Spiritus Sancti," the priest sang while making the sign of the cross on his forehead, shoulders, and chest.

"Amen."

The outlaws quietly pushed themselves forward through the kneeling congregation. Here and there, one of the villagers lifted his head, recognized the men in the long cloaks, and nudged his neighbor. Whispers. Eyes lit up. Soon all the congregants knew who was attending mass as a guest today.

"Dominus vobiscum."

"Et cum spiritu tuo," Robin sang, and his full voice resonating over the murmuring of his companions.

The companions stood side by side, upright in front of the altar step. The priest paused and turned around. He raised his brows. Robin took off his cap; his men followed suit. Still dissatisfied, the Cistercian monk waited. As one, the outlaws sank to their knees. Marian moved close to John and folded her hands in prayer. The light of the candles shone in her eyes.

Now the priest nodded, and loudly and solemnly, he celebrated mass. Together with the congregation, the companions confessed their guilt and asked for mercy and intercession.

The monk lifted the host. He drank from the chalice. He turned to the congregation.

"Ite, missa est."

"Deo Gratias."

The mass was over. But none of the faithful stood up. Even the Cistercian waited in silence at the altar.

Robin showed him three fingers. The pious man agreed. Slowly the outlaws rose and left the church. Just before the exit, Robin tapped Marian on the head. "Stand here by the side." He reached for the wooden offering plate, wiped the depression with his sleeve, and handed it to Marian.

Little John watched the leader like a hawk. A game after all? He snorted.

From under his cloak, Robin extracted a bulging pouch and piled a mountain of silver pennies on the plate. "Stay like that and just hold it," he whispered, smiling at John. "Come on, we'll wait outside!"

"I'll wait here." The giant never took his eyes off his Marian.

"Don't be silly, Little John," whispered Robin. "Well, suit yourself." He waved and followed his men into the churchyard.

From the altar, the monk gave the signal. The faithful rose. Orderly, they walked toward the bright exit. No one pushed or shoved. The first man reached Marian. His hand jumped forward. Ready to defend her, John clenched his fist. But the man's clumsy fingers reached for a coin. He nodded gratefully and went outside. A woman took the next piece of silver. Men, women, they all grabbed one. Nods and curtsies. Marian beamed and stretched out the plate. Children pecked out pennies with pointed fingers from the silver mountain. Some pecked twice. Marian laughed silently.

"That's all right," hummed John. His ward was not in danger. And to give silver away? He didn't understand it. But if this was Robin's game, then fine.

The priest was the last to step to the offering plate. With both hands, he reached for the silver pennies. But there were too many. Without further ado, he lifted his light-colored robe and swiped the remaining coins into it. With a happy step, he turned and hurried back to the altar. John watched and marveled.

The bell rang, bright and inviting. With a devout look on their faces, the people of Wrangbrook entered the church again, followed by the freemen. This time Gilbert Whitehand was there, but Tom Toad and four others were missing. They had been ordered to stand guard. Robin stroked Marian's hair. She was supposed to put the plate down again. He winked at John. "Well, what do you say?" he whispered as they walked side by side to the altar step.

The giant shook his head. "It's all right."

"In Nomine Patris," sang the priest. And together, they ended the second mass with the praise of *Deo Gratias*.

The new silver mountain was cleared away. The bell rang. This time Pete Smiling was sent off to guard. *"In Nomine . . ."* And what a resounding *Deo Gratias* there was to finish the third mass in the small church of Wrangbrook!

Outside, the mothers held their children, collected all their pennies, and hurried home with their men, rich. The little ones threw snowballs, laughing, cheering.

In silence, the freemen put on their wide-brimmed caps and trudged to the gate in the churchyard wall. A snowball hit Robin Hood's back. Slowly he turned around. The daring attacker retreated. With a grim face, the outlaw bent down, reached into the snow, and formed a thick, hard ball. He weighed it in his hand. Screaming and giggling, one child ducked behind the back of the other. Robin weighed the bolt, pulled his arm back, and hurled the ball high above the church tower, into the sunlight.

The wide pairs of eyes followed its flight, blinded.

"He hit the sun," the children marveled. "Definitely."

A little one crowed: "I know his name."

Immediately his sister covered his mouth. "You must not say his name. Mother has forbidden it. Otherwise, he'll never come back."

They left Wrangbrook far behind them. Robin Hood stomped to the front. He nudged John's side. "What do you say?"

"Well, it's good for the poor folks."

"And nobody's going to tell on us." Robin clapped his hands. "But it's for more than that, John. We help them. Two or three silver pennies will keep the misery at bay. You see, people must not be afraid of us. That's what I want. And who knows. Someday they may protect us, someday they will help us. To these people, we are not criminals."

Little John walked silently beside his leader. Suddenly, he grinned broadly. "That'd be ridiculous. I mean, who would rob poor people?"

Robin laughed. He tore the cap off his head and whirled it up into the frosty air. "Oh, John, my friend. I'm glad you're with me." The reddish-blond hair glowed. "You know what else we need? A priest of our own."

"What?"

"No, wait. A monk, who lives with us, who belongs with us. He could say mass before every fight, but at least once a week. You know, like King Arthur had." Robin earnestly added, "Everyone has a priest along with them, the good and the bad. Why shouldn't we?"

John stretched. "But, Robin. Would the priest hide with us in the bushes? There's no order of green-robed monks."

"There could be. Why not?" Robin's voice became soft. "And one more thing, but it's between us. Know what my dream is? You know, everyone builds churches, or even cathedrals in their own town. Someday I'll build us a chapel. In Barnsdale Top. And an altar for the statue of our pure Virgin."

John stopped. "And where will you steal that?"

"You don't steal a Virgin, giant. I'm having it carved. I want it to be at home in our chapel." Robin held up his chin.

Home! Little John thought. *Marian, me, we've found one with Robin. And if he thinks the Blessed Virgin should be with us . . .* "Why not?" he rumbled.

Robin Hood grabbed the giant's arm. "'Tis a good day today. It will also be a good year. What do you think?"

"Sure."

A horn signal sounded, breaking into the silence of Epiphany in the late afternoon. High and long, it echoed down to the main camp. Not an alarm, but: *Attention! An urgent message is about to be delivered.*

In the outlaw leader's spacious hut, Robin Hood and his lieutenants interrupted their discussion. "It's is the Barnsdale Top guard post." They stepped outside and listened for more, and everyone in the camp also paused. They waited tensely.

At last, a long note followed by two short blows at the same pitch: *Strangers in the village.*

Robin raised his horn. Before he put it to his lips, he asked curtly, "Is everyone else back?"

Gilbert Whitehand shook his head, holding up his white thumb. *One.* "Of those who went home, one is still missing. But that one also has the longest way to travel. His sister lives in Blidworth, down near Nottingham."

Robin sounded the horn. Deep and long, then high, then short: *We're coming.*

Orders were given. Tom Toad was to take command of the camp. Gilbert and Smiling were to stand by with ten fully armed companions until Robin blew the all clear. The assigned men ran to their quarters. "Bring your staff, John, also your bow and arrows! We'll both go look."

The sentry awaited them outside the village in the snowy darkness. "Our Vincent from Blidworth. He brought three new people with him. They want to join us, he said. Sent them to the cobbler."

Robin's face relaxed. Two long low calls from his horn announced the all clear through the forest.

"While we're up here—" John pointed to Beth's cottage. "I'm going to check on the girl."

"No," said Robin. "These newcomers, John," he warned. "Are they lice and scoundrels? Or are they men we can use? You're my right hand. We decide together."

Very well. The giant shrugged.

The cobbler had divided up his house. Half of it was a workshop and living space; the other half was a tavern. When John and Robin entered, Vincent and his companions put their mugs down. As agreed, John waited at the door. From the semidarkness, he kept an eye on the strangers.

Robin stepped into the light of the lamp, the brown hood low over his forehead. He nodded briefly to his companion from Blidworth. His gaze fastened on the newcomers. Took in their faces. Eyes. Hands. Clothes. Two quiet men, unarmed, waiting. Only the third, a young, muscular man, returned the leader's gaze, demanding. He struck a flat hand against the sword at his side. "I thought you might need a little help. What is this place, anyway?"

Robin was silent.

"Aren't you Robin Hood? Huh?"

"Perhaps." A smile twitched in the corner of his mouth. He turned to his comrade. "You're late getting back, Vincent. Why so?"

The harvest had been poor the previous year. And the lord sheriff's men-at-arms had plundered the village three times. Hunger was rampant in Blidworth. There was only enough food for his sister and her child. That was why his brother-in-law and brother had come back with him. "I'd give my right hand for them." Vincent pointed to the impatient fellow. "We met this one on the way. He says he was with the Nottingham City Watch. But the sheriff chased him away. He is strong and has no fear. So, that's why so."

The fellow reached out his hand to Robin. "I am Charles. Think I'll be the best man you have."

Robin ignored the hand. "Slow down." He gestured at Vincent to come with him. At the door, he murmured, "Well, Vincent, from which direction did you come?"

"Nobody knows where we are. I took a turn, then I came back this way from the west. That's why I'm so late." He looked at his leader plainly. "And another thing. Charles has money ... but he won't say where from."

"Vincent, what did you tell him?"

"Not anything. Because you told me not to. I didn't even tell my family."

A hard, searching look held Vincent's eyes. After a moment: "Good." Robin trusted him. "You go down to the camp. Tell Tom we'll postpone training. Not until noon tomorrow, then all are to come up to the base. I don't want to see anyone there before then." Without a word, Vincent Blidworth left the tavern.

"Well, what do you say, John?" Robin crossed his arms.

"The brother and the brother-in-law are fine by me. The young fellow? I don't know. He's wild tempered. I'd guess he can fight. On the outside, he looks all right. But ... I don't know."

"All right, John. I feel the same. That's why we're going to spend the night with these three here at the cobbler's. And tomorrow we're going to have a real thorough go at them." Robin grew serious. He squeezed his friend's arm. "You've learned quickly, John. That's what I need. You know: if you don't use your head, your eyes stay blind."

By dawn, Robin and John had left with the new men. They had first equipped the three of them with protection for their hands, and bows, and arrows. "There's a clearing in the forest. That's our camp." The strangers were not allowed to know more. Only after careful consideration was Robin going to initiate them. They were led to the training area by a detour, without passing the hideout's stables and huts.

The lad, Charles, saw the two makeshift sheds and slapped his forehead. "That's all?" The other two men also looked confusedly across the flat terrain. Clearly nobody had been there for a long time. Animal tracks ran crisscross on a thin, hardened blanket of snow. In the center, facing north, stood a wooden wall, thickly padded with straw. Nothing more. Ravens fluttered up sluggishly from the shed roofs and withdrew into the treetops at the edge of the wide field. "Thought there was more going on at your hideout," moaned Charles.

"What do you mean?" Astonished, the leader raised his brows. His eyes remained cold.

"Oh, well, I thought—an army. Armory. Horses. And women and stuff. Just all the things you hear about."

"Things you hear about." Robin Hood waved it off and sighed a heavy sigh. "No, my friend. So far, we are little more than a handful. But they are brave, bold men."

"What's the use?" Charles struck his forehead again. "And to think you are feared by all. Especially the sheriff..."

"Stop whining, lad!" mumbled John.

The lad spun around. "What did you call me? I could knock any of you in the—"

"Enough." Robin cut him off sharply. "In a moment, you'll be able to prove everything you want." To cool the lad's temper, he asked Charles to get the target cloth from the shed and fasten it to the wooden wall.

"How about you?" Robin looked at the other two. "Can you handle a bow?"

Yes, they had shot before, as anyone would have, but not enough even to be good at hunting, they confessed openly. They preferred to set traps—much easier.

Robin nodded agreeably. "Don't be ashamed. Archery is an art. You will learn it from me."

Charles returned at a light trot. "Learn?" he mocked, bending and stretching his legs, loosely waving his arms, and testing the bow. "No need." He pointed to the target cloth a good seventy paces away—three white rings and the small black center dot. "I think I'll go ahead and earn a few coins now. I'll bet three pennies against each of you. Well, how about it?"

Robin swayed in shock. "That much money?" He looked to Little John as if for advice. Twice he winked at him.

At last, the giant understood. Game time. That braggart deserved no better. With an embarrassed tone, John scratched his beard. "That is really a lot. It's too much for me."

"What are you, cowards?" exclaimed Charles. "I thought I was with Robin Hood!"

Robin took Charles aside. "Later, you can shoot against us. I'll convince the giant. But first, I'll practice with these two from Blidworth. Meanwhile, you show this meat pie what you can do with a sword."

Battle lust flashed in the young man's eyes. He confidentially nudged his elbow into Robin's side. "But, the fool has no sword."

"Nor should he. What are you thinking? A blade is too sharp. He might get hurt. That's why he has the stick." With great seriousness, Robin put his hands together in supplication. "I beg of you, let this be only a game. Attack him hard, but do not hurt him."

Charles couldn't hold back any longer. He drew his sword. "Hey, big guy, come on! Between the sheds where the sun won't blind you. And where you won't be able to run away from me."

John growled and lumbered after the boy like a bear.

"By St. Cedric," sighed Robin. When he saw the uncomprehending faces of the two men from Blidworth, he laughed. "Do not worry. It is really only a game. Come, let us begin."

They slipped the leather guards over the fingers of their right hands. First, they learned the correct posture. No, not square on, they were to keep their body sideways to the target, legs slightly spread, and feet firmly flat on the ground. "Very good," praised their teacher. Clasp the bow with the left hand, not in the middle, a little below. Place the arrow with the notch on the string. "Turn it! The fletching must not touch the bow when the arrow is fired. Otherwise, the arrow will spin away. Yes. Very good." No reproach—Robin encouraged the clumsy men, guiding them painstakingly and with praise until they made their first shots.

Now and then, he stopped and listened over to the sheds. Iron and wood clashed, mixed in with gasps and angry shouts from the lad. Robin smiled. "Let us continue. Look closely here!" Robin took one of the short bows himself, nocked the arrow, straightened the weapon vertically, lifted it, and pulled back his arm. Slowly, his right hand drew back the sinew. "But not all the way to your ear, you understand? This is not a longbow." Effortlessly he pulled the string until it touched his nose, lips, and chin at the same time. He did not shoot. Gently and slowly, he released the tension of the bow. "That's how it works."

The trainees made an effort. What seemed so easy for Robin Hood took all their strength. "Not so fast. Speed comes naturally with practice. With your eye, align the shadow of the string precisely with the point and the target. And now!" The arrows whizzed out. They flew high above the wall. "Not bad," Robin cheered the shooters on. "Once more. Lower!" Only on the fourth shot did the arrows hit the straw. "And now try to hit the cloth. Think about the center! Only the black circle, nothing else."

The men had beads of sweat on their foreheads. They pulled back their bow arms, they drew the bowstring.

A scream! A painful roar from between the sheds!

In shock, the men from Blidworth let the arrows fly. None hit the target. They didn't even hit the straw. Despondent, the men lowered their bows. "You will learn, in time, from me." Robin laughed. "Just wait and see! Soon nothing will distract you from the shot."

Another scream! Even more shrill! Like a discarded doll, Charles flew into view from between the sheds and crashed backward into the snow. John clomped after him calmly, using the fighting club like a walking stick. "I didn't hurt him," he reassured Robin and the men. "I was just getting bored."

Charles pulled himself up. "He's a monster!" He spat in the snow. "But if I hadn't lost hold of my sword—"

"I'd have broken it for you, boy." John had a big grin.

The taunt stung. Charles limped to the men. "I'll show you." He reached for his short bow and shook it menacingly. "With this. With this, I am the best in our city guard. And better than any of you. Now it won't be for just three pennies. I want five pennies."

A quick glance between the leader and his lieutenant was enough. Wordlessly Robin took the cap off one of his trainees' heads and held it out to Charles. "I find the wager unfair. But I keep my word. Place your stake."

Charles threw five coins into the cap. "I'll take everything you have off your hands. Five is just the beginning."

Robin sighed deeply and counted his pennies. John frowned, ever so sadly. He picked one coin after another out of his pouch. "A good man should not compete with a bad one. That's what I think."

Charles looked like he already felt like a winner. Without waiting, he set the rules. Robin let him. Only one shot each. The best one was to receive the full prize money. The choice of bows? The lad patted the wood of the short bow. "I think this one will do."

Patronizingly, he allowed his opponents to use their larger weapons. "You begin!"

Robin fired. His arrow struck the white of the outer ring. The boy laughed. "That's very poor. That's too bad. Too bad."

"Why did you . . . ?" the giant blurted out. At a warning look, he fell silent.

Robin whistled happily and tapped his nose with two fingers.

Don't worry, Robin, I'll play along. Cumbersomely, John pulled back the arrow, took aim. His shot landed in the second ring. "That's fine." He sighed. To hit the second ring exactly was an art too.

"You're not bad." Charles let loose his bow. His arrow whizzed off and hit the edge of the black dot. "But not better than me." He snapped up the cap and emptied the silver into his coin purse.

"I want my money back." Robin knit his brows.

"Sure. Gladly." The lad jeered and capered happily around the losers. "But now . . ." He stopped. "Now the shot costs fifteen pennies."

Robin groaned loudly. John moaned, "That's everything I have."

"What is it? Yes or no." Charles made the coins tinkle. Reluctantly, his companions agreed. The boy won the prize, again.

"It's not fair," cried John.

"Hah, we shoot better than you!" In his triumph, he did not notice the quick glance between the two outlaw friends. "For thirty coins, you may try again."

The men from Blidworth flinched. "I didn't earn that much all summer," whispered one.

Some ravens landed on the roof of the nearest shed. They flapped their wings and watched the men with interest.

"All right." Agitatedly, Robin pulled a well-filled pouch from his belt. "I need to know what will happen. Here are ten pounds. I'll bet you ten pounds, for my friend and me."

The poor peasants pressed their hand against their chests. Filled with greed, the lad felt the bulging contents of the pouch. "Ten pounds," he tasted the sum on his tongue. But then he lowered his hand. "But I only have four pounds."

"That's enough for me. When do we ever get to compete against such a marksman?" cried Robin as if in a fever of competitiveness. "Well, then, our ten pounds against everything you own."

"If that's how you want it." Charles chuckled, flattered. "By St. Swibert. It's a deal." Quickly, he emptied his pouch into the cap. Robin put set his pouch on top.

"I think I'll go first this time." The lad chose his arrow, fired, and hit the edge of the black center spot again. "Yield! Then you won't have to bother shooting."

He bent to pick up the silver. John looked at Robin, who gave him a quick thumbs-up. Finally! With the tip of his arrow, the giant tapped the young man's behind. "Wait a minute, little fellow!"

"Don't call me that," yelled the lad.

"Fine, then." John waited patiently for Charles to stand up. Then John calmly raised his longbow and pulled the feathered shaft back to his right ear. The string whistled. An instant later, the bright feathers shone from the center of the black dot. "Not too bad. What do you think?" With difficulty, the giant tried to suppress a grin.

The boy stood frozen.

Robin reached into the quiver. Draw, aim, a single gliding movement, the shot! The arrow bore itself into the eye of the target right next to his lieutenant's arrow's feathers. "Not bad either," John remarked.

Charles slapped both hands against his forehead. "Luck. That was nothing but luck."

"That luck cost you everything you own." Ice hardened in Robin's voice. "And maybe your neck, too."

Charles did not listen. Angrily, he puffed himself up in front of the freemen. “That wasn’t fair. Your weapons are better. I want to redo my shot. But with a good bow. Give me one of yours.”

“That’s all right, lad,” John replied with threatening calm. “I’ll let you shoot with mine … but only if you can draw it all the way.”

“Give it to me!”

The bow stood a good three inches taller than the lad’s head. He pulled, pulled again, tugged at the string. He didn’t have the strength. The arrow was barely drawn back. Charles could not even bend his right arm.

“Let me show you.” John took the bow from his hand. Without effort, he stretched the hemp-twisted string up to his ear and slowly guided it back again. “This is not a toy. Do you understand?”

“I can shoot! Better than anyone.” Charles did not give up. He had already raised his light bow again. He swung it toward the sheds and fired. The arrow went through a raven. The other birds fled, screaming in rage. The raven fell lifeless from the roof. “Try that!” Charles’ laugh sounded like bleating.

When he saw the faces of the freemen, he fell silent.

“Are you hungry?” John stretched and rolled his shoulders.

“Why?”

“Around here, we only shoot an animal when we’re hungry.” The giant hand reached out and grabbed him by the neck. John lifted the lad off his feet. Charles fidgeted, struggled against the grip. It was no use. Wordlessly the giant dragged him over to the shed and pushed him into the snow in front of the raven. “Pluck him!”

“You can’t ask that of me.”

Robin Hood placed himself wide-legged next to his lieutenant, sword in his hand. “Do as he says, or I’ll chop off your head!”

Black feathers scattered. Soon the naked bird lay before the kneeling lad.

"Good." Robin sheathed his sword. "And now, boy, tell the truth! You have already given yourself away twice, so no lies! Who sent you?"

"Nobody."

With his foot, John pushed the plucked raven closer to Charles's knees. "Eat it!"

Charles shook his head. "Nobody." Crying, he raised his hands. "By St. Swibert. I beg you, believe me!"

"Eat it!"

"No. I'll tell you. I'll tell you. Yes, the lord sheriff sent me. He sent me to look around your hideout." The words bubbled up. He was a sergeant of the City Watch of Nottingham. The money he carried was the first half of his pay. The second half he was to receive on his return.

"I want to know one more thing." Robin pulled back his hood. His red-blond hair shone in the sunlight. "What does the Sheriff intend to do with Robin Hood if he gets hold of him?"

Charles faltered. "Please don't. Please let me live!"

"Answer me!"

"A trial in front of all the townspeople. And then the gallows. You are to hang until . . ." Charles faltered again and stared at the corpse of the bird in front of him. He choked. Finally, he blurted out: "Until the ravens eat you."

Robin took John aside. "That's no mere little louse, my friend. By the Virgin! A full-grown spy almost planted himself in our midst." He clenched his fist. "The penalty has to be death."

"What did he see? Our faces. Nothing more." John scratched the scar in the thicket of his beard. "He knows nothing of the camp. He doesn't even know where he is. So why . . . ?"

Robin stared steadfastly at the target wall, chin up, jaw muscles clenched. "I make the rules. Never forget that, my friend." All of a sudden, his face softened. He nodded. "But you're right. We do not kill defenseless people. Right. Take him away. Quickly. He cannot harm us."

Charles was made to strip down to his boots and undergarments. He was allowed to put his belt back on. John stuffed the plucked raven into the collar of the trembling man's undertunic. "So you won't starve."

The giant shoved him across the wide field. At the forest line, he urged him to hurry: "And now run. So you won't freeze."

Noon was long gone by the time John returned. He had chased the spy halfway across the forest. Charles was never allowed to turn around, never allowed to rest, no matter how much his sore legs hurt him. Moaning, he had had to hobble in front of the giant. Near the trade route, John had quietly fallen behind and had waited until the boy disappeared between the trees.

Sharp commands now rang across the training field. John set his fists on his hips. "Nobody knows how strong we are. And that's good."

Weapons clanged everywhere. At short intervals, swarms of arrows hissed and then thumped into the target wall. Running, climbing, over thirty hardened men were training in speed, attack, and defense.

That's right, Robin, we are not a horde of ruffians. We are your army. John stretched the muscles of his back. Yes, the lazy, lazy days were over. On three marked-out squares at the edge of the compound, the lieutenants instructed the divided troops. In middle of the field, Robin Hood supervised the archers. His orders spurred the men on, accelerating the pace of the firing sequence.

John shielded his eyes from the sunlight. Far away, on the other side of the field where the swordsmen were, he spotted a small brown hood. Marian!

"No, I'm not having that," he rumbled. With wide strides, the giant took off. He nodded at Gilbert Whitehand, who was practicing close combat with his men with fists and knives.

John paid no attention to Tom Toad, who was loudly counting as his companions, fully armed with bows, quivers, and swords, climbed up into the bare treetops, and then continued counting until they stood in front of him again, panting.

"Hey, giant! Here I am." Robin Hood ordered the archers to stop. But John paid no notice. He marched on toward Marian. The outlaw blocked his path. "Well? What happened with the spy?"

"He won't come back."

"So, talk!"

Menacingly, John pointed to Marian. "Who brought her here?"

"Our little condition?" Robin laughed. "You're worse than a brood sow with her shoats. Much fetched her. Let her have some fun!"

John trudged on without a word.

"At the next rotation, I'll send you five men," his leader shouted after him. "You start with training in staff fighting." Mockingly, he added: "And, by the Holy Virgin, leave the babysitting to the women!"

"Fine," mumbled John.

Marian glanced briefly at the bearded face and smiled. When John started to speak to her, she put her finger to her mouth and looked intently at Pete Smiling. Much and three of their companions were facing the experienced fighter, their swords drawn.

Pete threw his weapon into the snow. "Here I am. Come on, give it a go!"

One by one, he told them to bring their swords high above their heads with both hands and strike them down at him in the same movement. Only at the last moment did Pete step aside. The blows went nowhere. Before the broad, sharp blade reached the ground, the lieutenant jumped forward, bounced against his opponent's body, and knocked him off his legs. "That's how it's done. Now show me!"

Pete Smiling picked up his sword and waited impatiently until his companions' weapons were stuck side by side in the snow. "Remember! You must jump your opponent before he can strike again, or you are lost." His scar flared red up to his ears. "Don't be scared! Today I'll use the flat of my blade. But if you're not fast enough . . ." Smiling bared his teeth.

When it was Much's turn, Marian leaned forward. Much dodged, jumped. He was too late. The lieutenant turned only slightly, and the young man fell face down in the snow. Marian wrinkled her nose and laughed silently.

Still on the ground, Much saw her mocking him. He was back on his feet instantly. "Just you wait, little snipe!"

"Let it go, boy," growled John. His grim glare warned off the miller's son. Silently, Much lined up again behind the companions.

John put his hand on Marian's shoulder. "That's enough, little one. Go to the village. Go to Beth."

She pushed her hood back and shook her head.

"Listen to me!" the giant demanded. She shrugged at him.

Powerless, John dropped his hand. "All right. I'll take you back later." Marian smiled.

A short horn signal. The groups switched their teachers on the double. Robin Hood sent Vincent and the two newcomers to Little John together with two other men.

First, each had to choose a suitable, shoulder-high oak staff from the shed. The giant rammed his fighting staff into the snow. "You can handle using it for hiking, I think." He smiled. "The rest you'll learn from me." The heavy stick whirled around in his right hand.

Marian had followed Much and the others to Gilbert Whitehand. Knife fighting: the straight thrust, the thrust from bottom to top. Standing side by side, the men had to follow the fast movements of the lieutenant. Blades flashed, changing from right hand to left and back to right again.

Marian pressed her hand over her mouth.

"And now, lads, I'll show you why you have feet." Gilbert pointed to Much. "Go on. Attack me!"

Crouching, the two watched each other, circling around each other, evading sudden thrusts, tense eyes following the opponent's dagger tip. Marian gasped.

The lieutenant raised his knife much too high. An opening! Much saw his chance and stabbed toward the man's middle. Whitehand kicked up his right foot. The tip of his boot hit Much's wrist. The dagger sprang from his fingers. Gilbert had already grabbed the thrusting arm. He whirled Much around, pressed him against his chest, his left arm looped around the boy's neck him from behind. "That's it, Much."

Laughter.

Grinning, Gilbert raised his white right fist.

Marian's mouth dropped wide open. *He has a dagger! Must help. Must help!* The old terror flooded her head again. It filled her up. It broke forth. *Must help!* Marian screamed. She breathed in, screamed more, screamed herself into silence.

The two fighters and their fellows were frozen in place. Motionless, Gilbert still held the knife high in his white fist. He forgot to let go of Much. In startled, unbelieving amazement, all eyes were on the girl.

With giant strides, John stormed across the field. His roar cleared a path for him, the squads interrupting their exercises. His bellow drew all the freemen along behind him. John reached the fighting arena before any of them. He saw the knife, did not ask questions. Still running, he struck out with both hands. Gilbert and Much fell to the ground simultaneously. "Who did what to her?" He spun around, snorting. The three others immediately threw away their daggers and ducked.

Robin Hood and the others reached the arena. They helped the toppled men up.

Marian tugged at the giant's doublet. She cursed, silently. Her lips moving soundlessly, she repeated the scolding. A rattle came out of her throat. Some words made it into sound. "... Mean! ... Stupid! That's what you are!" She put her hands on her hips. Anger flashed in her blue eyes. "Why did you do that?"

"Because you ..." John trailed off. The big man's bearded chin trembled. He rubbed his forehead with the back of his hand. He drew his brows. "What?" He bent down toward the girl. "What? Little one?"

"They didn't do anything to me."

John gently touched her lips. "You—you're talking. You're back."

"You can hear me?" The blood drained from Marian's face. "Yes?"

He nodded.

"On your honor?"

"I'm not lying to you, little one."

She pulled his beard. "I shouted. But you didn't hear me. Nobody heard me. And then ..." she clutched at her throat "... then everything went quiet. I was always talking to you. But now you hear me." Marian looked over her shoulder at Robin Hood and the amazed men. "Do you hear me too?"

"Every word." The leader beckoned with his finger. "Try it again. What did you call him, a moment ago?"

"Stupid," Marian repeated.

"Plain and clear." Robin laughed. "I like your voice."

As grins spread across all their faces, Marian put her mouth to John's ear. "But that's not true," she whispered.

"It's all right, little one." John turned to the men he had knocked to the ground. "Gilbert. Much. I am sorry."

Whitehand gingerly touched his jaw and mimicked the giant's grumbly voice: "Fine, then."

"If . . . if it gets that . . . result, you can . . . you can beat me again." The miller's son beamed at Marian.

She threatened him with her fist. "Just you wait! *Snipe*, my foot. I could hear you the whole time, you know."

Tom Toad gleefully leaned over to Smiling. "It's best you never teach that little dragon how to use a sword."

Little John drew a breath into his mighty chest. He wanted to roar, release it all. He clenched his fists, opened them again, rubbed his hands together. "I don't know how to say how I feel. It's . . . good."

Marian pulled the hood over her curls. "Take me to the village! I want to tell Beth that I can talk again."

The brotherhood of outlaws watched John and the girl head off in silence. Although the giant tried to take small steps, Marian had to run beside him. She spoke, laughed, and talked. Her voice sounded bright and firm.

Robin Hood let his fingertips play over his chin. "Our little condition." He snapped his fingers. "A miracle for the New Year! King Arthur isn't the only one who gets one. Us, too. It's going to be a good year."

YORKSHIRE. DONCASTER.

Sir Roger held back his falconer. "I'll take him myself today! You bring the pigeons."

In the stone falconry, right next to the castle's farm buildings, his hunters sat and waited: six precious hunting birds, trained to obey only his command. Long leather fetters limited their freedom. Out of reach of their neighbor's claws, each of them sat enthroned on their own high wooden high bar, like a ruler in the middle of his empire.

"My flying bandit knights." The five mighty peregrine falcons alone were enough to make the gaunt baron the envy of his neighbors: steel-gray backs, the light, black-spotted chest. But it was the sight of the sixth hunter that had left even Prince John breathless last year.

Avoiding sudden movements, Sir Roger of Doncaster slowly approached the center, slightly higher perch. *"Mon roi de neige."* He beckoned the bird of prey. *"Mon roi de neige."* His pale green eyes glowed in the baron's hollow-cheeked face. This one was not dark like the others, but had snow-white plumage. What a feast for the eyes! A longer look revealed the needle-sharp claws, the sharp-edged beak, the big burning eyes that missed nothing. Woe to the wild goose, woe to the heron, whenever Sir Roger cast his Snow King into the air during a hunt.

The baron slipped a cuffed glove made of stiff black leather over his left hand, carefully gathered the fetters into short loops, and let the bird of prey cross from the perch to his left fist.

Noise. Voices from outside: "Not now!" "Shut up!" "You're not allowed past. No! Just wait."

Irritated, Sir Roger turned toward the commotion. His steward stomped into the birdhouse, pulling a ragged figure of a man behind him by a rope. The falconry master had tried in vain to stop the intruders.

"Diable," hissed the baron. With great effort at self-control, he calmly stroked the Snow King's plumage and put the gemstone-encrusted hood over the falcon's head and eyes. "*Par Tous les diables!* I forbade any interruption."

He headed out to the courtyard of the castle, where the steward helped him into his saddle. He trotted on his horse over the drawbridge, carrying his Snow King on his left fist. The ragged man, Charles, trotted beside the mare, closely followed by the steward and falconer.

He reported how he had been sent out to sneak into the outlaws' camp as a spy. He laced his report with embellishments, described Robin Hood as a wolf accompanied by a wild bear, breathlessly told of hard fights in which he was a bold hero. Sir Roger let him speak.

Not far from the castle, at the edge of an open field, the falconer set down the basket of doves. "Here is the most favorable place, sir! I am ready."

Questions were put to the spy: Where was the camp? How strong was the outlaw gang? Weapons? Plans? To none of these questions did Charles know the answer.

"So, you were superior to Robin Hood in combat?" The pale green eyes gleamed with scorn. "Why are you standing here in your undergarments?"

"Because . . ." The lad broke off, exhaled a breath. His shoulders sank. "Because . . ." He fell silent.

"I see." Sir Roger rubbed the falcon's chest. "You encountered this vagrant. I believe you did, Sergeant. But only because you look so plucked."

The steward spat in Charles's face. "And still you dare to steal our time." He swung the looped end of the rope back and forth with relish as if mimicking a noose. "Lord, may I . . .?"

"Silence! We are not murderers." Sir Roger pretended outrage. Charles wiped his brow. For a moment, the baron allowed him to feel relief, then he added calmly: "We leave the means of punishment to my friend, Thom de Fitz. We will tie up this great spy as he is and return him to the sheriff."

Charles fell to his knees. "Do not send me back! No one, *no one* could have found out anything. Believe me, this Robin Hood and his gang, they are devils!" Charles' eyes welled up. "They even eat ravens. It's the truth."

The steward scowled. The falconer shook his head in disgust. Sir Roger laughed and caressed the chest of his white falcon.

"Let me serve you!" Charles begged. "I would do anything for you. Just do not send me to Nottingham!"

"Enough! Send him to . . ." The baron paused. His bumpy nose flared. "Any service?" he asked. A new thought inspired him. "I am too indulgent, I know. Thom de Fitz will rightly reproach me. Nevertheless: I'll give you one chance. But if you fail again . . ."

"Never. Believe me! Give me a task, and I will fulfill it!"

Indignant, the steward shook his head. A stern glance from his master stopped him from saying anything further. Sir Roger smiled down at the ragged fellow. "Get up! I take you into my service as a man-at-arms. Once the snow has melted completely, you will have your chance. If you fulfill your task to my satisfaction, I will consider keeping you on. With the rank of sergeant."

Charles shuffled closer on his knees. "Thank you." He pressed his lips to the baron's boot. Sir Roger kicked him away. "Do not dare touch me again!" He waved his free right hand. "Now, leave! Wait for my steward at the castle gate! He will give you a new tunic. And you may choose a good sword from the blacksmith in the city."

"Thank you." Charles pulled himself together and stammered, "Th-thank you, sir." Thank you, I will be one of your finest, most loyal—"

"Get out of here before I change my mind!" Charles ran off in the direction of the castle. The baron looked after him with a sneer. "Idiot."

"But, sir!" The steward was displeased.

"It is time to hunt, sir," urged the falconer. "How long must the hunter wait for his meal?"

"You are right." Sir Roger's index finger stroked the breast of the white bird of prey as he apologized to the Snow King. "Pardon," he said nasally. "Pardon." Turning to the falconer, he said, "Wait until I give you the signal!"

A squeeze of his thighs, and the brown mare trotted off. Over his shoulder, he ordered the steward to follow along.

"Lord, why did you . . . ?"

"Not now." It was only when they were out of the falconer's earshot that Sir Roger replied, barely moving his narrow lips. "That fellow showed up just in time."

He stopped the horse the middle of a wide field and looked down at his breathless steward. "And you of all people should be pleased." He reminded him of what they had done two years ago. It was only because of that act, that a steward's high position in the castle had suddenly become available for the previously ordinary officer. He had, literally, stabbed his predecessor in the back in the woods below the town, near the mill.

"It was your wish, sir," the steward defended himself. "And the miller's son was to be accused as the murderer, as we had agreed."

"I don't recall that." The hollow-cheeked face froze into a mask. "There are two more witnesses to your crime. So beware! My hand lifts you, but it can also drop you."

The steward lowered his head.

"But I appreciate your loyalty. And I will help you. *Par la Vierge*, this fool was sent to us by heaven." The pale green eyes shone coldly. The plan was simple: Charles would go to the mill. His mission was to find out the whereabouts of the fugitive son. No mercy would be shown. Charles was allowed to go to extremes to break the silence of the boy's parents. "You alone will accompany him. And that fool will not return to Doncaster after his work is done." Sir Roger smiled. "No witnesses, no worries. You see how I care for your welfare?"

The steward sighed. He looked up at his master with gratitude.

"Mon Roi de Neige." The baron took the cap off the bird of prey. The falcon's head twitched back and forth—black, shining eyes. Quickly, the baron loosened the bird's foot strap with his right hand and with a mighty swing of his left arm, Sir Roger hurled the hunter into the air. The white falcon fluttered just for a moment, then it spread its wings, hovered, and then with powerful beats it rose, spiraling higher and higher. Only when it looked like it had reached the sun did it let itself be carried by the air currents, gliding in wide circles high above its master.

Sir Roger raised his hand, the signal. The falconer reached into the basket. A white dove whirled up, oriented itself, and shot away across the field. High above it, the hunter tipped over, accelerated its descent with short flaps of its wings. It pulled its wings in close to its body and plunged down, striking the unsuspecting dove, sharp talons reaching into its heart. Only a short distance above the ground, spread wings halted the rapid fall. The predator landed and crouched over its prey, and the sharp-hooked beak crushed the pigeon's neck.

"Mon roi de neige!" Sir Roger raised his gloved fist. He spurred the mare on and galloped across the snow-covered field. The bailiff rushed after him.

The falcon waited. Its master did not take the prey. "Eat!" Blood colored the white feathers of the victim. Blood colored the snow.

Sir Roger watched with satisfaction. Finally, he turned to the steward. "Just like this dove, Robin Hood will one day lie before me." He rubbed his bumpy nose. "A spy. The lord sheriff's idea was good. Almost good enough to have come from me." His lips stretched. "Only he should have trained a hawk, not a pigeon."

YORKSHIRE. BARNSDALE WINTER CAMP.

The snow melted by early March. Water thundered through the gorge. The stream swelled, washing away the mud and branches, its waves foaming and sloshing under the tree bridge. For days it had been flooding the bank at the main camp.

The air had become light. Thrushes greeted the morning, and the linden tree in the middle of the meadow showed bright budding tips. Among the tall beech trees rose the smell of rich black earth.

"In one week, we'll move to Sherwood," Robin Hood had ordered.

Old Herbghost and Gilbert Whitehand were to leave immediately. The most essential kitchen gear, and most importantly the unstrung bows, stocks of arrows, and a rough wooden reel wrapped in tightly twisted yet supple tendon cord for bow strings, as well as a sufficiently large selection of frocks, robes, and tradesmen's tunics—all this was carried by the band of men to the main road. There they pulled the cart out of its hiding place, loaded it, harnessed the strongest horse, and disguised as peddlers, Herbghost and Whitehand climbed onto the wagon seat. "See you in two weeks at the latest. We'll be waiting for you at the big oak tree!" Gilbert Whitehand took the reins and cracked the whip.

Beth worked ceaselessly. The outlaws exchanged their dark winter doublets for the green summer outfit. It was too much for her to do alone. Two neighbors gave the seamstress a hand.

"You must help too, princess!"

And so it started. Marian inspected the discarded black-brown hooded cloaks. What was damaged would be mended by Beth over the next months. Much carried the undamaged clothes to the cave and stowed them in the big oak chests under the supervision of Paul Storyteller. "No fleas. No moths," Storyteller assured him, as between the uniforms the old man sprinkled crushed roots of blessed knapweed.

John had been the first to come to Barnsdale Top for his measurements to be taken, and today he was the last to pick up his newly made uniform. Patiently he stood there, his head bent down so as not to bump into the ceiling.

"I've never used so much fabric for anyone before. Raise your arms." Beth stretched and pulled the seams. "By St. Catherine, you are truly a giant."

"I guess so." John grinned and patted his mighty stomach. "Need food for two. And a tunic that'll hold two other men." He laughed happily.

Beth was pleased with her work. "Nobody'll mistake you for a frog down there in Sherwood, more like a tree with legs." She joined in the laughter.

Marian had listened to them silently. Now she tugged impatiently at her brown doublet. "What about me? I can't . . ."

"Later, princess," Beth told her. "Once the fellows are gone day after tomorrow, we'll have time. Then I'll sew you a frock out of the best fabric, with a fancy collar, even. You'll look beautiful."

Marian gave a start of sudden realization. She gaped at the giant. "Gone? What about me?"

John turned serious. "Well, you see . . ." He took in an anxious breath. Over and over, he had postponed telling her, from one day to the next. Now they had to talk. He rubbed the scar in his beard. "You know, little one, you should stay here. It's better, believe me."

Marian shook her head. Her eyes grew big. Finally, she clenched her fists. "Liar," she stammered, "that's what you are. A mean scoundrel." With that, she rushed out of the hut.

Helplessly, John shrugged his shoulders. "She can't go down to Sherwood with us. She simply can't."

Beth turned the giant man around and pushed him to the door. "Go after her, you clumsy oaf. Explain it to her! Don't just *tell* her."

"Fine, then."

John found Marian behind the house. Knees drawn up, she was crouched on the piled firewood. She had her arms wrapped around her knees, staring at the clouds.

"Look here, little one . . ."

She ignored him.

"There are no proper houses down there, Robin says. We sleep in a cave or just under a bush. It is only comfortable when the weather is nice, Robin says. And we have to go from one hiding place to another. Always on the run because the sheriff's iron soldiers are after us. It is not pleasant. You see, there is no home for you down there."

"I don't care, no matter what Robin says. You promised: You'll never leave me."

"That's true. But I need you to be safe. And not live rough in the woods. I don't want that for you."

Marian wiped her eyes. "But I can do it. We have already lived in a cave, both of us, and slept on moss and in a ditch. And it was wonderful because you were with me. Please, John. Please take me with you."

"We were alone then. We had nothing. But everything's better now. You have to stay here, dearheart." He wanted to hug her.

She grabbed a stick of firewood. "Go. Go away! Since you don't need me anymore. Go to your dearheart Robin."

"I just . . . want to say," he muttered, "I do only have you and Robin. But Beth needs you, too. I will come visit often. With the loot. One of us lieutenants always has to come bring it here."

Marian lowered her head. The fair curls covered her face. "Go away!" Her shoulders trembled.

John wanted to comfort her, did not know how. "I do need you." At a loss, he walked away.

The days hurried on, and it was time to depart—the main camp was secured. On the high ground, the freemen had camouflaged all three pathways down with bushes. They had piled stones at the bottom of the ravine in front of the fourth entryway through the rock tunnel. For the first month, Pete Smiling was to remain at the base with three other outlaws. In case of danger to the main camp or Barnsdale Top, one of them would jump on horseback and alert the band in Sherwood. In April, Tom Toad and a few men would replace the current guards.

The departure was before sunrise. Little John looked around the camp furtively. Was Marian there? He wanted at least to say a farewell! "I need luck, little one," he muttered. But he hadn't seen the girl for two days. The giant sighed. He couldn't go back to the village to look for her there. There was no time for that now.

Robin Hood checked each man's weapons and equipment. No extra baggage permitted, only water, and provisions. Everything else was well hidden in the storage caves in Sherwood. "Our first meeting place is below Doncaster, off the trade road, by the creek near the little ford. But nobody goes to the mill, understand? It's too dangerous."

"But . . . but . . . You . . . you gave . . . gave me . . ." Much raised his hands, pleading.

"Patience, boy! I haven't forgotten you."

Simple caps and hats on their heads, green uniform, sword, and a knife hidden under shabby gray travel cloaks, the men set off in small groups. "Don't forget the signal!" The crack of a dry twig had to be answered with a double crack to confirm it was one of their own. "Avoid every village!" The final orders were short: no raids on the way. No hunting, no matter how tempting the prey. Above all, no fighting with any guards or royal forest rangers. "Avoid them! Hide or run away. Fight only when there is no way out. But if you have to fight, leave no one alive!" Gray eyes glittered in the sharply cut face. "We'll hole up secretly in Sherwood again." Only when his army had reached the summer encampment whole and safe did he want to strike. "Then, our game begins."

His army: twenty-eight fighters, strong, agile, deadly precise with the bow, and each wielding a dangerous blade. Loot was important. But their fight against the cruel attacks of the iron-encased men-at-arms on defenseless villagers was the most critical thing for Robin. "And I promise you, my friends: We will light a fire under the damned lord sheriff this summer and until he falls to his knees and prays God for mercy!"

With his fists on his hips, the outlaw leader surveyed his men. His brotherhood of outlaws trusted him to the full. "Go on, now!"

At short intervals, they left the base. Three or five of them scurried away at a time.

Soon, except for old Storyteller and the guards who were to stay behind, only John, Much, and Threefinger were left. Robin Hood pushed back his hood back and shook his auburn hair. "One of us is missing." He knelt down. "Without her, we cannot succeed. She must be with us." The men knelt beside him, as with a firm voice, Robin asked for the protection of the Blessed Virgin.

After his sincere prayer, he rose: "What harm could come to us now?" Laughing, he poked John in the side. "Wouldn't you say?"

John shrugged. "Fine, then." Again, the giant looked around. Marian had not come.

After another short salute to Smiling and his men, Robin strode out with broad steps. Much and Threefinger followed close behind him.

Only after a while longer did Little John finally leave the clearing. An apple struck the forest floor right in front of him. Two colorful feathers from a jay were stuck in it. John picked it up, and looked up. In the forking branches of a bare chestnut tree stood

Marian. She twisted a finger through her curls. "I can't go with you anyway. I have to help Beth."

"Fine, then, little one. I'll see you soon." John laughed and gave the staff a twirl around his hand.

Clay stuck to his boots. Despite the soft, sodden ground, they had made rapid progress. In no hurry, at an easy run that didn't tire them out, Robin Hood set the pace. Now and then, Much tried to overtake him, surging forward. He would see his parents again soon!

"You may be the fastest of us all, but stay behind me, boy," Robin commanded, smiling. "Otherwise, your legs will outrun your wits."

Around noon they crossed the main road below Doncaster and followed the cart track through the forest. Finally, Robin raised his hand. The men stopped and peered forward from the shelter of white-gray birch trunks. The deep cart tracks ended at the bank between chunky boulders. On the opposite side of the broad creek, they continued up the rising meadow hill.

They had reached the meeting point. There was no one to be seen, not at the banks of the ford nor nearby.

"Over to you, Bill," whispered Robin. "Do you see anything?"

Threefinger shaded his eyes and surveyed the scene for a long time. Finally, he shook his head.

"Just how I like it." Robin picked up a dry branch and snapped it. Two cracks answered: nearby, to the side, behind them. Little John spun around. Nothing. He only saw birch trunks. Farther away, there were bare, intertwining oak trees. Up in the wide forks of the branches, crouched some of the outlaw band!

Robin touched his lieutenant's arm. "Well, what do you think?"

John nodded appreciatively. "We have good men."

"The best, my friend. The best."

Robin stepped forward and sounded the hunting horn. Two short, low sounds. From behind the cliffs, from the thorny bushes, from the trees all around, the outlaws left their hiding places.

"No incidents," Tom Toad reported to the leader. He pointed to the creek. "But the ford water is high. We'll get wet up to our backsides. Better we backtrack to the big road and get over the bridge. If we hurry, we can just about make it to Worksop today."

Immediately Much was at his side. "Not back. Please!" Red flushed his face. "Our mill is a good place to spend the night. And there's a crossing below the mill."

Tom Toad raised his eyebrows. Cheerful mockery played in his voice. "Our downy-lipped pup wants to go home."

Much swallowed with difficulty. "I have ... because I ..." He rubbed the scanty fluff on his lips nervously.

"Leave him alone, Tom!" Robin interceded. "I promised. And there's time enough."

"I know you did." Toad put his hand on the youngest of their brotherhood. "Just kidding. I'm sure you have ale at home, too."

"You bet. Sometimes Father gets paid with a keg for grinding grain."

The troop was thrilled by the prospect. Now some of them wanted to leave immediately.

"Whoa!" Robin jumped onto a fallen birch trunk. "What are you? Oxen running for water?" The danger was too great. Roger of Doncaster was looking for the miller's son. "Don't think that fox has forgotten our little one!"

To avoid ambush, Robin Hood divided his army into three squads. Little John was to circle a wide arc with his men and approach the mill from the east, Tom Toad from the north. "Hide yourselves around the valley and wait! I, Threefinger, and the rest, we'll come up along the creek." Silently, the outlaws scurried away.

Robin waved Much over to him. "You stay with me. And no running off ahead! Understood?"

The sun hung like a silvery disc in the misty sky. Magpies bobbed on the riverbank willows. "Just after the bend," whispered the miller's son. "That's where our meadow begins."

With a snap of his finger, the leader sent a scout up a tree. From high above in the branches, Threefinger scanned the narrow valley beyond the bend in the brook. It took him a long time. Far too long. Much opened and closed his fists. "Stay silent, boy!" Robin cautioned him.

Now Threefinger relaxed, climbed from branch to branch, slid down the trunk, and jumped the last bit. His face was blank. "All is quiet. By the house, even by the barn." He looked past Much to Robin. "No chickens in the yard. No goose."

Much laughed softly. "Of course not. Mullers don't keep animals that eat grain."

Disregarding his friend, Threefinger added, "And the mill wheel."

A steep furrow grew on the leader's forehead. "Well, go on and say it, Bill!"

"It's turning slowly. Far too slowly."

"It's . . . just old." Much was growing impatient. "Are there any strangers about?"

Bill shook his head. "No danger to be seen. There's no one there. No one at all."

Much couldn't hold it any longer. "My parents must be in the house." He ran off, jumped over bushes, and charged onward. He was quickly gone around the turn.

"They're not in the house," muttered Threefinger. "Damn it all. They're not there."

Quick as lightning, Robin grabbed the horn. Two low, short tones, the signal for the others to come. In giant leaps, he and his men stormed after the boy. They rushed across the meadow.

Some of them drew their swords. Farther ahead, Much had already reached the small farm. "Ma! Ma? Where are you?" He disappeared through the open door of the house. "It's me! Hullo! It's me!" His cries echoed outside.

From the east, from the north, from far apart, the men ran toward the mill, closing in ever more tightly.

"Ma!" Much left the house and ran over to the barn. He called for his mother. Called for his father. "You don't have to hide! It's me. And my friends."

Outside in the yard, Threefinger pointed to the water wheel.

Robin groaned. "We're too late. Get out of here," he ordered his men. "But stay close by!"

One look at the mill wheel, and horrified, they obeyed. No one wanted to be witness to what would come next.

Only John and Tom Toad remained, waiting, with Robin. In silence. Just the groaning of the mill wheel's oak shaft, the scraping of the stones in the mill room.

Much returned from the barn. "They're not there." He gestured helplessly and came toward his friends. "But if they'd gone to Doncaster, they would at least have closed the door. And Father would have closed the mill chute. "He never goes . . ." Much trailed off. He looked from one man to the other. "What . . . what is it?" He followed their glances. He pressed both fists against his chest. His body convulsed: his mother's white face, her body tied to the mill wheel, the corpse plunging into the water as the wheel lumberingly turned . . . then his father's lifeless face, thin body. Much screamed.

He wanted to go to them, but Little John wrapped both arms around the boy.

"Don't look! Don't . . ."

Flailing desperately, Much kicked at the giant.

"Go ahead and beat me. Go on, boy! Yeah, go on."

As the lad's muscles slowly slackened, the screaming turned into broken sobs. John loosened his grip. "Hush, boy. Hush, boy."

"Make . . . make it stop! Please . . . make it stop."

Tom Toad and Robin ran, giving orders. The other outlaws hurried back. Above in the mill, the chute was closed. The wheel stopped.

John did not let go of the boy. "The others will take care of it."

They wrapped the dead in blankets and laid them side by side in front of the house. "Now go to your ma!" The giant gently pushed Much ahead in front of him.

Silently, the companions watched the boy. He knelt before his parents. His shoulders trembled.

Vincent quietly approached Robin. "Over by the river crossing. There's one more lying there."

The leader nodded at John, and they swiftly followed Vincent. Next to the small bridge's path, an armed man lay motionless, face down in the grass, arms outstretched over his head. In his right hand, he held a whip. The left was still clenched in a fist. His cape was dark blue. "That belongs to the Baron of Doncaster." Robin Hood sent Vincent back. "Tell Tom to dig a grave for the miller and his wife!" As the man left, Robin turned the dead man over on his back.

"By Dunstan," John gasped. "The spy. That's Charles, the louse from Nottingham." There was a black stab wound in his neck, just above his chain mail shirt. No distortion to his expression. He had died with a satisfied grin on his face.

How did this fellow get there? Why was he wearing the colors of the Lord of Doncaster? Who had killed him? Shaking his head, Robin brushed the hair from his forehead. "I don't understand *this* game." He examined the whip. They had seen welts on the bodies of Much's parents. "So, he tortured those poor wretches."

John bent down. From the dead man's left fist hung a string of small wooden beads. John pried the fingers open and found a silver cross attached. "That miserable bastard." John panted. A lump grew in his chest. *It was my fault. I let the spy go.* "My fault, Robin," he said aloud. "This is all my fault. Because I didn't want us to hang him." He stared at the cross. "What am I going to tell the boy?"

Robin took the giant by the arm. "Stop it, John!" His gray eyes flashed. "We don't kill defenseless men! That is our law. You reminded me of that, back when we uncovered this spy." He stepped up close to the giant. "And it was the right choice."

"And now these poor people are dead."

"It was right! And I don't want our men to doubt that. Do you understand me?" Robin gazed up at the bearded face. "By the Virgin, what more do you want? Even the saints do not know what will come to pass. We certainly do not." He pointed to the mill. "That is not your fault, my friend." He pointed to the dead man with a foot. "And this one? He was only one among the attackers. And then another of these henchmen stabbed a knife into his throat. That must have been how it happened. A mean game, indeed. But the real murderer is over in Doncaster, sitting there in his castle like a spider. And I'm sure no one will ever be able to prove him guilty."

Little John nodded. He saw that hollow-cheeked face before him, heard the nasal voice again—the baron in his black velvet robes. *One day, I'll break his neck.* With growing rage, it became easier for John to turn his focus. He was not to blame for the death of the miller. Robin was probably right. "Such a tragedy for the boy."

Silently, their caps and hats in their hands, the freemen stood by the open grave. The prayer was short.

"We move on," said Robin Hood. They had to force the miller's son not to stay behind. Only after three more hours of walking did they set up camp in a wooded area. Small campfires flickered, widely scattered. Tomorrow, they would be in Sherwood. The men spoke softly to each other. No one laughed.

Later, Much crawled close to the bush under which John had stretched out. "I . . . I can't . . . I can't find no place."

John beckoned to him. "It's all right, lad."

Much curled himself into his cloak beside the giant and hid his face.

Only when the whimpering faded away, when Much's breaths became calm and even, did John close his own eyes.

IX

YORKSHIRE. ON THE WAY SOUTH.

That first night under the open sky again, they lay with broken branches and moss as a bed. Nothing more.

Despite their cloaks, their new garments had become clammy. Before setting off, the freemen dried and warmed themselves by the fire. Everyone had a sympathetic touch, a sympathetic look for Much. With red eyes, the boy stood next to Threefinger. There could be no relief. Only a silent greeting, a hand on his shoulder: *You are not alone.*

The embers were doused, the ashes scattered. At intervals, the groups set off. By evening, they all had to have made their way to the great oak tree at Edwinstowe. Robin and his small troop were the last to leave the campsite.

From the corners of his eyes, Little John watched the miller's son. "Stay by my side!"

Much tried to smile, bravely shaking his head. "Don't worry! Where else can I go?" He walked with Threefinger and let Robin and his lieutenant go ahead.

They followed the trade road. The stone pavement, slightly arched from side to side, stretched straight in front of them. They could see well in advance who was coming toward them, and they could hear early enough when hoofbeats approached from behind. John ducked his head at each sound, and his hand slid down to the middle of his staff. *We should hide until any rider passes. Better safe than sorry.* But Robin Hood seemed unconcerned. Every now and then, they encountered a peasant cart, sometimes a wandering monk. No one was surprised at the men striding along.

"What if someone recognizes us?"

"No danger, John. We are in the border area between the counties. Sir Roger and the lord sheriff are far enough away." Robin spread his arms wide. "And spring is still young . . . so it's just the right time for us to head back to Sherwood."

Through the haze, they spotted the roofs of Worksop. "There's plenty of armed men over there," Robin informed them. "Like dogs chasing rabbits in the field, they could so easily hunt us down on the road. But those fellows are still hibernating." Only when the wealthy merchants were on the move, when the big wagon caravans started coming up from London and moved farther north via Nottingham, or rolled down from the ports via York to reach the market in Nottingham, only then did the soldiers step in to control every road, guard the tollgates in front of the cities, and collect duties. "If there is anything left for travelers to declare." Robin laughed. "Because before that, the moneybags have to go past us." Suddenly he became sober. He scrutinized the giant from the side. "You know every trail in Sherwood. Why haven't we met before?"

"Those were not my hunting grounds. All the way over to Edwinstowe and Blidworth—it was too dangerous. I stayed in the west by the monastery. Had to get the quarry to our village quickly." John closed his eyes. His village. The smell of hearth fires. The laughter of the children when he returned from a hunt. He saw the bodies. He saw Marian's mother. "And yet I was too late. One time, I was too late."

"Forgive me, my friend. I didn't mean to . . ." After a moment, Robin began again: "Soon everything will be green, soon it will be summer. Deep in Sherwood and along the road, we will have hiding places everywhere. And we have friends in every village now."

"Fine."

They entered Sherwood on a game trail. Around noon, a light smell of smoke rose into their noses. "That's Gabriel. I can smell his work a mile off." Robin Hood decided to pay a visit to his charcoal-burner friend. "Gabriel is a brave Saxon. He works for the Normans, but he does not cower. If it weren't for him, many old folk here would freeze to death in winter." The charcoal burner and his two farmhands made charcoal for the ironsmiths of Nottingham Fortress. He was not allowed to cut the wood for it himself. He specified the quantity, and the royal forest guards delivered the wagonloads to his three kilns. Later they picked up the baskets filled to the brim, and if there was not enough, he was in trouble. Gabriel understood his craft. He piled up kilns three-stories high. He also outsmarted the foresters, always ordering more logs than really necessary, always some left over. This way, he could provide wood to poor old people in the area. "Come along, let's have a drink at his place! Let him know that Robin Hood is back."

Two children were playing in front of the charcoal burner's secluded cottage. Full of curiosity, with big eyes, they looked at the stranger. John winked at them. He stuck out his tongue. They stuck out theirs. The giant made a grimace. The little ones tried to imitate him. A warmth spread through John's chest. How long had it been since he had unworriedly played games for children? He thought no further on that. Little John staggered back and forth in front of them, growling, turning like a bear. The little ones cheered and clapped.

"Hey, coalman," cried Robin. "Come out, Gabriel!"

Immediately a young woman appeared. As soon as she saw the strangers, her face turned to stone. She ran to her children, tore them away from John, and herded them into the house.

Robin Hood laughed. "Don't you recognize me? Where is your husband?"

Over her shoulder, she cried out, “Go away! You scoundrel. We have nothing.”

An old woman hobbled outside. She waited until the mother had taken her children to safety. Fearlessly, she approached the outlaw. “Robin Hood. I curse you.” She spat on the ground in front of him.

Robin stood paralyzed. “But why?”

The old woman held out two fingers to him. “You’re two-faced. You hypocrite. But Satan is within you. You’re lucky my son’s in the forest by the kiln. He would put a curse on you too. Miserable brigand. A plague on you and your murdering gang!”

Without a word, Robin turned around. John gave Much and Threefinger a sign. They quickly followed their leader.

John walked beside his friend in silence. Now and then, he looked down at him. Above the hard gray eyes was a deeply furrowed brow. His face was pale.

Finally, Robin shook his head. “Why?” he asked hoarsely. “With all I’ve done for these people?”

Never before had John heard his friend sound like that. “Not every curse brings bad luck.” He tried to placate him, but did not believe it himself. “She was just an old woman.”

“Don’t be an idiot!” Robin clenched his fists. At the giant’s reproachful expression, he relaxed his hands. “It’s not just the curse. John, I need people’s trust. Otherwise, we’ll never win this fight.” He quickened his pace. “And the worst part is, I don’t know what happened. The charcoal burner is an important ally. From him, we learn where the foresters are, what they are up to. Gabriel was on my side. And now his mother curses me.”

“I know,” mumbled John. “It is a bad start for us. First, the miller and his wife. Now a curse.”

“No, enough of this!” Robin turned waited for John to catch up. “We will fight if we have to, even without Gabriel. And, by the Virgin, it will be a good year.”

They took no rest. At dusk, they reached the meeting place. John was to stay behind, Robin decided, while he went on to the cave where Tom Toad and Herbghost were waiting for the army to arrive. Bill and Threefinger had to gather their friends in the thicket around the Great Oak and adjacent woods by the agreed signal.

The Great Oak. John looked up at it. *Even I am small beside it.* His gaze became entangled in the maze of branches. *This is not just a tree.* For a moment, it seemed to John as if some subterranean god had stretched out his mighty arm, spread his hand, and pushed the forest back.

Nonsense. The giant smiled at himself, rubbing the scar in his beard firmly. *But it is big. Five more like me with arms outstretched, we could perhaps encircle the trunk. And in summer, a good twenty men of my size could hide up there in the branches.*

By that evening, the band of men sat under the oak, caps and hats pulled low over their foreheads, their cloaks pulled closed around them. Robin Hood's army had safely reached the summer encampment.

There was no laughter. No one spoke. Nothing was like it had been the year before. Everyone stared into the fire, chewing on the leftovers of their travel provisions.

"There'll be soup tomorrow," Herbghost burst out, loud and angry. "Damn it! I didn't know you were coming today."

"Leave it, William. No one was complaining." Robin jumped up. With short, stiff steps, he circled the camp under the oak. The reports haunted him: One group had encountered two farmers in Sherwood. The men had addressed them amicably. Immediately the peasants had prostrated themselves before them and begged for mercy.

Worse still, Tom Toad told of an old woman: She had been gathering brushwood and could barely carry the load. He offered to bring the bundle home for her. The old woman had thrown her laboriously collected brushwood at his feet. "Here, take it! I have nothing more." And had shuffled off.

Gilbert Whitehand had tried to buy bread and fruit supplies in Edwinstowe three days before in exchange for good silver pennies. When he appeared, the villagers turned to hurry away, trembling.

"Wait a moment!" he had called.

Only a young swineherd had the nerve to raise his face to Gilbert. "Wait? For what? You've already killed three of our villagers."

"What?" Gilbert had demanded. "By Dubric, what are you talking about? Malcolm," he beseeched him, "you know me. I'm a friend of Robin Hood."

"I know you are. Everyone knows who you really are now." Bitterly, the young Malcolm continued, "Have mercy! You already raided here two weeks ago. Why come back to torture us more? Buy from us? Buy what? You've taken everything we have."

As Whitehand left Edwinstowe emptyhanded, he heard the tall swineherd curse the outlaws.

Again and again, Robin shook his head. The flickering glow of the fire fell on his pale face. John could see the grief in his friend's eyes. Determined, he stepped into Robin's circling path and grabbed his arm. "Rest! Tomorrow we will—"

"John, what happened? When we left last fall, people were slipping us apples and bread along our way. In every village, they offered us a farewell drink. My name alone meant hope. Because they trusted Robin Hood. Because I proved it: We Saxons can stand up to the sheriff, to the Normans."

"It'll be all right. I just think you should—"

"We can stand against injustice! We are not murderers. We will fight against injustice in this land until King Richard returns . . ."

"Enough!" John clasped the leader's wrist hard. Robin Hood stopped in stunned silence. John, too, marveled at himself. Before Robin could get angry, he smiled at him. "Stay calm! Perhaps I am wrong, but I just think somebody's playing a dirty trick on us. A dirty game."

Robin Hood broke free. "Don't you dare . . ." He faltered, and suddenly his face brightened. "Giant! By the Holy Virgin, you've learned quickly from me. A game—a dirty game! Yes, that's it!"

The outlaw leader strode close to the fire. He spoke briefly to his followers. The feeling of helplessness began to fall from the band of men. Courage and grim determination returned. The plan for the next weeks was clear.

Later, Robin crouched in the grass next to his friend. "Thank you, John. Since that curse at noon, my mind had simply stopped. I'm glad you're with me."

"Fine." John stared at the tips of his boots.

"I'd rip anyone else's head off for that arrogance. But you must always tell me if something seems wrong." The corners of his mouth twitched. "In the unlikely chance I ever make a mistake again." Robin laughed.

X

The latest dispatch from the Crusade: *In November of 1191, Richard leaves Jaffa with part of his army. In the destroyed town of Ramleh, he sets up camp. He celebrates Christmas even closer to Jerusalem. Despite sleet and storms, Lionheart lets the troops advance into Judea's hills during the last week of December. The Crusaders breathe a sigh of relief: The liberation of the Holy City is imminent. The Crusaders rejoice: Wealthy Jerusalem promises rich plunder. But Richard does not attack! He hesitates for five days, then he turns back. Through the thick mud, he leads the disappointed army back to Ramleh. "You gave away Jerusalem with your cowardice," grumble his allies. In January of 1192, many turn away from him. Some board their ships and return home.*

NOTTINGHAM.

The sky brightened, a light wind dispelled the morning fog, and pale sunlight reached for the fortress's battlements.

Horsemen had appeared, far to the north, between the hills. They had to pass through open terrain, first descending through the valley, then onward up to the defensive wall to reach the city.

The gate was still closed. Merchants, market women, ropemakers, knife sharpeners, poultry sellers, and fish traders had been waiting outside since dawn. They came from the surroundings of Nottingham and all knew one another. Some had dismounted from their high ox carts. Those who pulled hand carts had unhitched themselves. Chest and shoulder straps hung from the bars, thick stones behind the wheels prevented the carts from rolling backward. People rubbed their cold hands and chatted—no pushing and shoving. Everyone submitted to the unwritten law that whoever had reached the gate first was allowed to enter the city first. The best place on the market was reserved for the firstcomer, who was allowed to put their cart near the church, right in front of the lord sheriff's house. Next to it, the second, behind it the third, until the last one had to find a corner with his goods somewhere at the edge of the market.

Only here and there did some of the waiting people turn their heads at the sound of approaching hoofbeats. None of the conversation was disrupted by the troop of castle guards. Their chain mail and helmets shined dully. No one was surprised to see them. At the most, they shrugged their shoulders. It had been so almost every morning for weeks: Shortly after sunrise, armed men returned from a nocturnal ride.

A stone's throw from the gate were the traveling minstrels, jugglers, and beggars. They were evicted from the city at dusk and returned at dawn. During the night, Lord Sheriff Thom de Fitz did not tolerate any riffraff within the protecting walls. "Our citizens shall sleep soundly and safely."

The beggars, who came day in, day out, were restless. They cast hostile glances at six new ragged figures. The strangers had appeared a week ago for the first time: one-legged, slow-witted, limping. Or claiming to be—they knew every begging trick, and every morning they were back again.

"Where are you from?"

"London."

"Lincoln."

"York."

That's all that could be gotten out of them. The newcomers would limp through the alleys on crutches, crouch on corners, snatching the best spots. And how they could spin a patter! Hardly a townswoman passed by without putting at least half a silver penny into a stretched-out wooden bowl. The one with the white hand got the most money. As experienced as the beggars of Nottingham were, they did not know how he managed this trick. There was no paint on his skin; no, his fingers really were white. The man needed only to lie down in front of the sheriff's house and raise his right hand. That was enough. Nobody chased him away. On the contrary, every day at noon, the sheriff's wife had soup brought to him.

The horses snorted up the steep road, their breath steaming from their nostrils. "Make way!" At the head of the troop, the sergeant drew his sword. Hurriedly, the merchants obeyed, dragged draft animals and carts to the side, and cleared the way. But the strange beggars limped, hopped closer. One of them dared to approach the troop leader. Whining, he asked for alms.

"Get away with you!" The sergeant pulled at the horse's bridle. At the same time, he kicked in with his spurs, and his horse reared up. Its front hooves whirled dangerously. At the last moment, the ragged man threw himself to the side.

The armed men rode unhindered through the cleared lane. Ten riders. The nose guards of their helmets made their masked faces look alike. The last two iron men led two heavily laden horses behind them. Their load was hidden under linen blankets.

"Watch-Sergeant Baldwin returning with his troop," the officer shouted up to the narrow-slitted windows of the gate tower. A moment later, the iron grating rose, and the doors of the massive oak portal swung apart.

Following immediately after the troop, the market people moved into the city, and behind them, the travelers and beggars pushed through. Shouts, barking dogs, clucking and quacking, the creaking of cartwheels: The day in Nottingham had begun.

"*Par le ventre de saint Jacques!* You are worth your pay." The lord sheriff reached up and pulled his officer's face down to him and patted his cheek. "Keep this up, Baldwin, and I'll make you a rich man. But . . ." he stabbed his index finger against the man's chest. "Not a word to anyone. Or I will personally rip your heart out. You are responsible for your men. I pay you well, so keep their mouths shut."

Baldwin had not let his men dismount. The remainder of the troop was sent straight up to the castle. Baldwin hitched his horse in front of the sheriff's house, dragged the two pack animals into the courtyard, and locked the gate.

"Don't worry, Lord! My people know exactly what they can expect from me if they misstep." Baldwin put his hand on his sword. "They stay silent."

"Bien." Thom de Fitz walked around the heavily loaded horses. "Now show me what you brought me today."

Sacks of wool. Soft tanned sheepskins. Carved spoons and bowls. At the sight of the goods, the sheriff pulled a face. "*Diable.* The same as always. My cellar will soon be overflowing with this horrible junk. No embellishments, not the smallest carved ornamentation. These Saxons are nothing but unimaginative barbarians. Without culture, *sans finesse*. Regardless, down in the capital even the most primitive goods are in short supply. As soon as the large wagon caravan arrives from London, I will be rid of all this rubbish for good money."

The sergeant took the covering off the second packhorse. "That's all the supplies they had."

Thom de Fitz paid scant attention to the fruits preserved in honey. "You will divide this among your men?" He felt a bulging sack. "*Magnifique.* Grain seeds! Baldwin, the more you bring me before they plant their fields, the faster my plan will succeed. Grain is the most important thing they have. No seeds, no harvest. The villagers will never forgive their Robin Hood." He breathed on the gold rings of his right hand and polished them on his doublet sleeve. "And how many did you . . . ? Tell me!"

"Just one."

"And?"

"As you commanded. Don't worry, sir. No one in the village will forget it." Baldwin reported with an impassive face: First, the peasants themselves had to put their supplies and all the goods they had made over the winter on the pack animals. "Before we left, we chopped off the head of one of them."

"And nobody recognized you?"

"It was still mostly dark. We had green capes over our chain mail and the hoods over our helmets, like every time. And all the while, my people were calling to me. *Robin Hood!* or *Robin, come here!* No one knows it was us."

"*Bien. Très Bien.* Remember, kill no more than three at a time. And the others must watch it happen. We need witnesses to tell the tale." The lord sheriff raised his chin. "A few more villages, and the name Robin Hood will become a curse on Sherwood, and not just there. The whole shire will curse him. Soon no one will protect the outlaws. They won't be safe anywhere. You shall see, Baldwin—soon the first Saxons will come groveling before my judgment seat and tell me the bastard's hiding place." His eyes were shining. "My plan is succeeding! And I will show Prince John the gallows in the summer with the bones of Robin Hood, gnawed clean by ravens, hanging from it."

Abruptly Baldwin jumped forward, hurriedly threw a cloth over the loot on one animal, and reached for the second one. Too late. The sergeant snapped to attention, staring at the door. Thom de Fitz turned to look. His wife had entered the courtyard. Her hair was hidden under a cap, and she wore a simple high-necked robe. "Don't you have more than enough by now?" Her high forehead wrinkled as she frowned, full of reproach, at her husband.

"*Beatrice. Ma chère.*" Hurriedly, Thom de Fitz approached her and gave a gallant bow. Before he could complete the greeting by kissing her hand, she crossed her arms in front of her chest.

"Your manners do not impress me." She nodded over to the pack animals. "Why, Thom de Fitz? We have a fine livelihood and much more than we need. But you, in your greed, deprive poor people of everything they own. I am ashamed of you."

The blood burned in the Lord Sheriff's face, leaving the white spot of his false nose. "Please, Beatrice! Not here. Come inside! Not here, Beatrice." He reached for her arm. Over her shoulder, he called, "You wait for me here, Baldwin!"

Reluctantly, Beatrice let him lead her to the door. In the main hall, the Lord Sheriff moved his wife's carved armchair to the window. "Take a seat!"

"I prefer to stand." Only with difficulty did she maintain her composure, her voice trembling with irritation. "Day after day, you pass judgment on petty thieves, cruel judgments. While you squeeze the last belongings out of people. You are the true robber in Sherwood. No, let me speak! Did you think I don't know what you have been accumulating in the cellars? Ever since the snow melted? You shamelessly use your power. Crop seeds! Because of you, children will starve! And you smile as the peasant families plunge deeper into misery!" Bright tears stood in her eyes. "I couldn't help overhearing: You will not even stop at cold-blooded murder. Oh, Thom de Fitz, you bring shame and a curse on yourself and our house."

"*Diable.* Watch your tongue!" The lord sheriff bit his lower lip. He paused for a deep breath and began again, this time more restrained: "You're my wife, nothing more. What do you care about the serfs?"

"They're people."

"No, they're not. These Saxon vermin work for us. A Norman pays more for a decent horse than for two serfs."

In disgust, Beatrice turned away from him. She stared out the window. Thom de Fitz stepped up close behind her. "Why so angry? Appearances are deceptive. I would not let the villages be plundered merely for greed, *ma chère*. But it must be done. Unfortunately, I must—I will—destroy Robin Hood. This is all part of my plan. And it is succeeding. This time the outlaw will fall into my net. And Prince John will amply reward me." He pressed on, his voice flattering, "How do you like the sound of *Baron* Thom de Fitz?"

Beatrice's back stiffened. After a long moment, she coolly replied: "Even if you dress in the most expensive robes, wear rings on every finger, and cover the scar on your face with paint, even if you style yourself as baron or duke. You do not impress me. Underneath all those baubles, I always see the true Thom de Fitz."

The sheriff threw up his arms in exasperation. His wife turned around. Her bold stare made him back off, even as he threatened her with a raised fist. "Remember—just one word from me and you will spend the rest of your days in the deepest dungeon of the fortress. You would not be the first lady of noble lineage to perish there in the company of rats."

He could not withstand her unflinching gaze. Finally, he lowered his fist, and his shoulders sank. "I am the law," he proclaimed miserably. "I am the judge of Nottingham."

Beatrice nodded. "But there is a judge before whom you and all your friends must answer. He will mark this in the book of Heaven. Remember *that*, Thom de Fitz! Please, leave me alone now!"

Wordlessly, the Lord Sheriff turned around and stormed out.

Meanwhile, in the yard, Sergeant Baldwin had unloaded the plunder. No, the sheriff told him, he was not to take it into the cellar. The sheriff wanted to be rid of him quickly today.

"But the reward?" asked Baldwin. "I have to pay my men."

Thom de Fitz tossed him a heavy coin bag. "Here, take it! This time I'll give you a hundred twenty silver pennies. Pay each man five, put the rest in your pouch! I'm well satisfied with you."

In disbelief, Baldwin weighed the wealth in his hand. His master did not give him time to give thanks. He had already opened the courtyard gate himself. Together they led the unburdened horses out of the yard and through the narrow alley to the market, into the shouts and haggling, the flute playing intermingled with tambourine beats. The market bustle was in full swing. Nobody paid attention to the lord sheriff and his sergeant.

"Damn!" Baldwin let go of the pack animal, drew his sword, and stormed to his horse where it stood hitched. A beggar was unashamedly tampering with the saddlebag. His white hand was just pulling out a piece of green cloth. At a full run, Baldwin rammed into the beggar with his shoulder, who fell to the ground, still. "Damned thief!" The sergeant raised his arm for a thrust of his blade. In an instant, the sheriff was by his side, grabbing his sword arm.

"Let it go," he hissed. "I don't want any fuss."

"He found the cloak." Reluctantly, Baldwin sheathed his sword.

The lord sheriff nudged the toe of his boot into the beggar's side. The man lay motionless. "Don't be a fool," he reassured the sergeant. "He saw green cloth, nothing more." Thom de Fitz dabbed his forehead with a handkerchief. "I do hope he comes to. If you had stabbed him, it would be unimaginably awful: My wife would have never forgiven me for it. She's been fluttering around this foul creature for days." He tucked the kerchief back into his sleeve. "*Bien.* On to our plan. Which village is next?"

"Blidworth. First thing in the morning."

Neither the sheriff nor his watch officer paid any further attention to the beggar. He lay on the ground as if unconscious, but at the name *Blidworth* he had opened his eyelids a slit.

Thom de Fitz shook his head. "Not tomorrow." With a quick

glance at the windows of his house, he instructed: "Not so soon after the last. Wait two days."

"Yes, sir." Baldwin mounted his horse. "The day after tomorrow, then." He pulled the pack animals ambling behind him.

For a while, the lord sheriff stood and watched the fishmonger in front of his house. Fresh trout, eels. The dried fish hung on a rack. "That is how I want you, Robin Hood. You and your gang. Strung up. One by one."

No sooner had Thom de Fitz disappeared into the house than the beggar picked himself up, picked up his staff, and hobbled away.

XI

NOTTINGHAM SHIRE.
SHERWOOD FOREST.

A peaceful silence lay over Blidworth. The first twilight between night and day.

A dog barked. A second! A third one! The dogs tugged at their chains, lunged, were pulled back by their collars, lunged forward again. They growled, barked, turned in circles, barked on.

Torches blazed around Blidworth, and the noose tightened. The village was encircled.

Horsemen charged up the only road. Two each from both directions! They reined in their horses as they reached the first huts. With their sword pommels, they banged on every door: "Out! Come out!" The horsemen met in the middle of Blidworth. They looked around. No one. Nothing moved in front of the dozen or so huts. "Come out!" cried the horsemen's leader. "It's me, your *friend* Robin Hood. So show yourself!"

Only the dogs answered, barking more wildly.

"The people are scared," said one of the horsemen, excessively loudly.

"Oh, not at all," said another, just as loud. "They're still scrubbing their teeth and rinsing their mouths to greet us pleasantly."

All four laughed uproariously. In the weak morning light, the strangers could now be made out. They wore voluminous cloaks, the hoods pulled up, hiding their faces. The cloth was a deep green.

"By order of Robin Hood," cried the leader over the flat rooftops. "Shut those mutts' mouths!"

Immediately three men dismounted, stormed over to the dogs, and shoved blazing torches down their throats. The howls choked off into silence.

"For the last time: Come out!" The leader of the gang of horsemen waited no longer. "As you wish. Then we'll come and get you. We'll burn the huts over your heads."

"Have mercy. Have mercy!" A man stepped into the street, waving his arms frantically. "We're coming!" One by one, every door in Blidworth opened. In gray dresses, headscarves, and gray tunics, men and women stumbled outside. But only a few steps; each stayed close to their homes.

"Why didn't you just come out when we asked nicely?" Satisfied, the leader laughed. He blew a sharp whistle. Around Blidworth, his horsemen moved even closer to the huts. Escape was impossible. "Bring the packhorses!"

Everything seemed carefully practiced. Step by step, a cruel game. The leader ordered all the men in the village to come to him. Soon the peasants stood like lambs before their butcher, silent, head and shoulders deeply bowed. The man barely paid attention to them. He urged the others to hurry: The women were to bring the supplies, the seed, the sheepskins, ropes, simply everything they possessed. It was not much. There was no grain seed.

"You!" The leader chose one among them. "Come here!" The woman obeyed. "What are you hiding from us?" Humbly, face pointed firmly to the ground, she shook her head.

"Dismount!" he ordered his men. "Take a look! Search every hut!" The men spread out. "If they find anything else," he warned, "I'll cut off your ears. First you, then every woman here."

One of his men came running back. "Hey, Robin." He smirked and put a honeypot on the floor. "Look at what we have here."

The leader gave another sharp whistle. He waited until his men had closed their ranks around the gathered inhabitants of Blidworth. Now he threatened the men of the village. "If anyone tries to fight back, I'll smash his head in!" No one dared to move even a hand.

Slowly he got down from the horse, pulled the green hood even further over his forehead, and pulled out his knife. In a leisurely way, he approached the woman. She stood, her chin on her chest, hunched forward. "As for you, little pigeon. You have lied to Robin Hood. He doesn't like that." He yanked off her headscarf. She was almost bald, only a long braid dangling from the back of her head. The leader grinned broadly. "What an ugly witch you are!" He patted her shriveled scalp her grabbed her ear. With his other hand he set he set his blade against it.

The woman's fist suddenly flew up. A dagger blade sank deep into the man's right arm. He cried out in horror.

In the same moment, the villagers awoke. The men pulled out swords from under their long tunics. A horn sounded. More horns answered from the sheep pastures beyond. All the women raised their heads to reveal wild, bearded faces. Their skirts were slit up to the hips. They pulled the cloth aside, drew the swords from their belts. Steel flashed. The intruders understood too slowly. Much too late, they drew their weapons.

Despite the howling and cursing, despite the noise of battle around him, their leader simply stood where he was, staring at his bleeding wound in disbelief. Then he stared at the bald creature, stammering. "Spirits. Devils and witches!"

The creature set the dagger to the man's throat. "Devil? I don't like that at all," came a deep, husky voice. "Move, and you're dead!"

"A trap," gasped the leader.

"By Willick. You figured it out." Tom Toad grinned. He took a quick glance to the side. Some of the intruders lay dead nearby.

Men dressed as farmers drove the rest of the horde like rabbits before them. At both ends of the village, the runaways were being picked off by archers. The battle was over.

"Now as for you, my green pigeon . . ." Tom Toad imitated the voice of the leader. "There's no one left to help you." He flicked the man's hood back—to reveal a helmet. Tom Toad grabbed the green cloak and tore it from him with a single yank. "Well, well, well. An iron puppet of the sheriff."

Imperceptibly, the soldier's left hand slipped down to the pommel of his sword. He had already half pulled the weapon out of its sheath before Tom Toad noticed it. Tom's knee jerked up and caught the man between his thighs. Groaning, the man writhed, bent over. Tom's composure was gone. Hatred blazed in his face. He tore off the helmet from the gasping man, pulled off the chain mail hood, tugged his head up by his hair, and placed the tip of the dagger deep into one nostril. "What do you prefer? This one? The other? An ear?"

"I was only joking. Only joking. I just wanted to scare you."

"Shut up," cried Tom. His hand jerked, and the tip of the blade nicked the man's nostril. Blood poured from the cut. The man writhed more, in pain. Relentlessly, Tom held on to the shock of hair. "A joke? You shall have a fun little joke." He bent the man's head all the way to the side. An ear was exposed.

"Enough!" At the sharp command, Tom paused and looked over his shoulder. Robin Hood. The gray eyes looked coldly at him. Tom glanced around, at all his friends staring at him. Their faces were flushed from the fight. A few prisoners crouched on the ground.

"It's all right, Tom." Little John clasped his companion's knife hand tightly. "Let him go now."

Tom obeyed. He rubbed his eyes, stroking his shriveled scalp. "By St. William!" The smile returned. "That was close, friends. I almost soiled myself with this pig."

"I understand," growled John. "Not only you. I think there's such anger in all of us."

Robin Hood disarmed the leader of the mob. "Who are you?"

Blood ran from the man's nose wound, stained his mouth, soaked his beard. Blood ran from the right sleeve of his chain mail shirt, dripping from his fingertips. He remained silent.

"The game is over, you rat. Answer me, or I'll leave you to this one!" Robin pointed at Tom Toad.

His eyes widened in horror. "Sergeant Baldwin," he spat out. "Sergeant of Nottingham Castle Guard. We passed this way by chance."

No sooner had he spoken than Gilbert Whitehand jumped at him. "Coincidence? Robin Hood does not like to be lied to." His clawed right hand slowly approached the sergeant's face. "Remember this?"

"The beggar." Baldwin gasped. "You—you were digging in my saddlebag."

"*That's* what I call coincidence." Gilbert clenched his white fist. "So, out with the truth!"

Baldwin gave up … and, haltingly, he confessed, told them about the sheriff's plan. The robberies, the deaths.

Robin Hood listened with his lips pressed tight. Next to him, John stepped from one foot to the other, finally turning away. His breath almost died at the thought of Marian's mother. *Like then. Just like us.*

Every looted settlement, every village—Robin Hood made the man give a precise list.

"I only carried out the sheriff's order, nothing more," the sergeant concluded his terrible report. "My men and I, we are innocent. By the Holy Virgin."

Robin grabbed the collar of the chain mail and yanked the man toward him. "Don't sully the Virgin with your stinking mouth!

Innocent? That word should choke you, you and your gang of murderers." He pushed him away. The sergeant fell backward to the ground.

The sun had risen over the eastern pastures. "It's time." Robin nodded his chin toward it, gave orders. The prisoners were to remain seated back-to-back, hands on their heads. He had their four dead tied to the packhorses. He called Vincent over to him. "You're from here, aren't you? Is there a forge?" The freedman from Blidworth pointed to a solidly built hut.

"Nice. Little John, take two people. Stoke the embers! You, Vincent, run over to the thicket. Tell your sister and the others the danger is over! And tell them to fetch the sheep home."

The night before, all the village's inhabitants, along with their precious sheep, had been taken by the outlaws to a safe hiding place. Now they returned. The youths ran ahead of their fathers. Mothers carried babies in their arms. Shyly and incredulously, they looked at the prisoners, their damaged chain mail, their dented helmets. They saw the dead. *These* were the all-powerful men-at-arms? They crouched there beaten, moaning and groaning.

"This is what Robin Hood has done for us," Vincent told every man and woman. "He's our friend."

Silently, they picked out their belongings from the piles and carried them home.

"Leave the honeypot," Tom Toad asked. "Give me that."

John had just returned from the forge and had reached for the pot. He scratched the scar in his beard. "Find your own!"

"Just you wait, you runt!" Tom grinned broadly and continued to tend to the rounded-up horses of the soldiers.

"Wants a taste of honey, ha!" John stomped over to Robin. "The embers are going."

"Thank you, my friend. It'll be a spectacle." Robin rubbed his hands. "You'll see. There's never been a performance like this in Sherwood, I tell you, not in the whole shire."

One by one, the prisoners were taken to the forge. With their hands behind their backs, they were shackled on a long chain. Robin borrowed the only cattle cart in the village. As a pledge for its return, he gave the village elder a gold coin. "If I lose your cart, you'll have enough to buy two new ones."

He had Gilbert Whitehand tidy up the men-at-arms. "Turn around!" Under the laughter of his companions, Whitehand pulled the green cloak through the belt of each prisoner, plucking the cloth out over their rear ends like a tail.

The women from Blidworth knotted the helmets in a string to two ropes and tied the ends of the rope to the back of the cart.

Gilbert Whitehand stepped before his leader like a courtier, bowing and making a gallant flourish with his white hand. "Our jesters are ready."

"Wait! Wait!" Tom Toad brought the honeypot. He reached in and smeared one face after another with honey. He spent a particularly long time with Baldwin: "It's going to be nice and warm today, Sergeant. A glorious spring day. There'll be plenty of bees, mosquitoes, and blowflies."

The prisoners were herded onto the cart. While Much hitched the two horses loaded with the four dead to it, Robin Hood turned to the village elder. "Do you . . . have courage?"

The man shrugged. "We are in your debt."

"No. You do not owe me. I want a favor. Nothing more." Robin asked him to go with Vincent to take the transport down the road to Nottingham. He saw the frightened eyes. "I beg you. Be my witness. The people on the road will believe you. Don't be afraid. Vincent will be with you. He'll watch out for you. He'll drop you off safely, far away from the city. And besides: My men and I won't let you out of our sight for a moment. Even if you don't see us. We'll give you an escort. We will be in front, at your side, and behind you, always."

The village elder nodded calmly. "I have courage."

"Good." Robin laughed. His face became serious again. "You will tell everyone you meet what happened this morning in Blidworth. The prisoners are our proof. One more thing! And it's very important to me: Take the small detour via Edwinstowe. Stop in front of the church. Wait until the residents have gathered. Send for the priest as well. Let all hear the truth!"

Without a word, the village elder climbed onto the narrow wagon bench. Vincent hesitated. Behind him stood his brother and brother-in-law. He had brought them to Barnsdale Top in the winter, and since then, they had belonged to the brotherhood.

"Robin. I wanted to ask … the thing is, my sister said …" Vincent pointed briefly over his shoulder "… she needs them. And you paid them money for their services. Well, they don't want to come back with us." It was out. "But I'm still your man," he quickly assured him, and got on the cart.

For a moment, Robin Hood hesitated. He wiped his hand across his forehead into his reddish hair, wiping away the disappointment. "Agreed. But remember one thing!" He coolly examined the two farmers. "No one can leave our brotherhood. I demand fidelity and silence. You remain my freedmen." Both nodded hastily. Robin laughed. "So, it's agreed then—from this day forward, we'll have two guardians in Blidworth."

He mounted the sergeant's horse. Tom and Gilbert chose two good horses. Little John eyed the size of the others. "I'd better just run alongside," he decided. The remaining eight horses were divided among the men. All captured animals were to be hidden near the big road until evening. John shouldered his longbow. He winked at Much. "If you don't run too fast, the two of us can travel together later."

The boy beamed. "But one day, I'll show you how fast I really am."

The villagers waved and thanked the rescuers again. Robin put the horn to his lips.

The cart bounced out of the village. The prisoners' green cloth tails bobbed and dangled. Their helmets bumped and rattled loudly on the lines behind the cart.

Tom Toad rode his horse beside the giant. "And when the bees come out, this lot will sing for us. What a song it will be!"

John clenched his fists. "They have it coming. And more."

The village elder kept his word. Vincent backed him up. Outside the church at Edwinstowe, they outdid each other praising Robin Hood and the freemen's brotherhood. They were occasionally drowned out by the howls of the green-tailed soldiers when a new swarm of bees or mosquitoes attacked their faces. The pastor spoke on behalf of his congregation: "God bless Robin Hood!"

Children ran alongside the cart until it reached the main road again.

At the turnoff to Nottingham, Vincent had the village elder get off the cart. "Thank you. That was fun, wasn't it?" he said. "Better I do the rest of the work without you. And give my regards to my sister. I'll be back for Christmas."

Vincent cracked the whip, steered the team off the main road, and took the deeply rutted, gravel road toward town. No sooner was he alone than he pressed his lips together. The wheels creaked. Behind him, the prisoners whimpered and groaned. "How much farther?" he whispered. Again and again, he looked fretfully to the right and left. "Damn. Don't leave me alone out here."

At last, just before the cart left the hills north of Nottingham, Little John and Much stepped out onto the road. "Off you get!"

"About time." Relieved, Vincent jumped from the cart. Robin

Hood and his two captains, Tom and Gilbert, were suddenly there, too. The other men had been left behind long ago.

"Beyond the next bend, things are going to get dangerous," John stated.

Robin hurried over. He ordered Much to unhitch the packhorses and check the knots on the ropes tying down the corpses. "We will bring the horses down later."

Together they pushed the cart out between the hills to the edge of the open terrain in the midday silence. In the distance, Nottingham rose, and its mighty fortress towered over the city. Before them, the road descended steeply into the valley before rising again to the fortifications.

Robin positioned himself so all the captive soldiers could hear him. "You!" He pointed to the sergeant of the guard. Baldwin laboriously turned his head. Mosquitoes buzzed around him, sat thickly on his blood-encrusted face. He barely managed to open his swollen eyelids.

"Give the lord sheriff a greeting from Robin Hood. And tell him: The people of Sherwood are under my protection. Anyone who tortures or kills them will suffer my vengeance."

"I'll tell him nothing," the sergeant blurted out. "I'd rather die."

"Patience. Patience." A thin smile twitched at the corner of Robin's mouth. "The game is not yet over for you and your murderous brethren."

He calmly raised his hand. Tom and Gilbert led the packhorses aside. Little John sent Much aside with them and stepped alone behind the cart. At a tremendous push, the wheels crunched, the giant pushed a little more, ran, gave it more momentum; the cart rolled off and bumped driverless down the road, faster and faster. The green cloth tails fluttered. Loudly clattering, the two long helmet chains clanged and hopped behind the cart. The prisoners' howls of fear rang out all the way to the city.

John returned to the others. The outlaws stood, unmoving, next to each other. They stared after the cart. It was still rolling on in the deep wagon ruts of the road, bumping, tipping to and fro, racing onward. Suddenly the cart rose, took a huge leap, bounced back down again, and a wheel tore free and jumped away. The cart somersaulted, broke apart. Wooden fragments flew, green pieces of cloth. The chained prisoners flew with the wreckage.

Close to John, Much whispered, "Oh my God!" All blood had drained from his face. John put his hand on the boy's shoulder.

Robin Hood snapped his fingers. "Now, the packhorses."

Tom and Gilbert smacked the horses on the rump. Whinnying, the animals galloped into the open country, bucked, settled, then trotted down the road, side by side.

"There!" Gilbert pointed to the city. A horseman rushed out of the gate, bent low over the neck of the speeding animal, galloping into the valley. He circled the scene of the disaster and then rushed back. After a while, three more riders left Nottingham. Two armed men and a small man riding ahead of them, his light blue cloak billowing in the wind.

Robin shaded his eyes. Icily he said: "That's what I call luck. Here comes the man himself."

"Let's go," John warned. A stale taste on his tongue disgusted him. "It's enough. We've achieved everything we wanted."

Robin did not answer. His eyes followed the lord sheriff's every move as if they were glued to him.

Down below, Thom de Fitz dismounted. He shooed the packhorses off the road. With the toe of his boot, he pushed the bent and twisted bodies. A head moved. One of the injured shifted his foot. The sheriff gave orders. Immediately the guards jumped off their horses and drew their swords. Fragments of sentences reached the outlaws: "*Diable!* ... my order ... not executed!" And even more clearly: "Kill the traitors!"

When the armed men stabbed their cronies, Much hid his face. John clenched his fists. "Animals wouldn't even do this. Only humans. Not even animals would do that."

Unspoken rage shook Toad and Whitehand.

"He's eliminating the witnesses," Robin hissed through his teeth. "His plan failed. So he's murdering everyone involved." His right hand flew up, grasped an arrow; a shrug of his shoulder and the longbow was in his left hand; and in an instant, the feathered shaft was on the string.

He caught John's look. "No, my friend. I will not kill him." Robin Hood stepped out from cover into the open. He lifted the bow, stretching the string to his ear, and let the arrow fly. It struck the ground near the sheriff's boot.

Thom de Fitz swung around.

"Lord Sheriff? There's a witness here you can't kill. You murderer! Recognize me? Yes, this is Robin Hood!"

The sheriff raced to hide behind his horse. *"Maudit bâtard!"* he cried toward the hills. *"Enfer et damnation!"*

He made his men mount and serve as his shield. He led his animal on foot; only halfway to the city did he scramble into the saddle, pressing his head into the mane as he galloped up to the gate. "Alarm! Guard! Guard!"

Robin Hood laughed. Calmly he shouldered the longbow and returned to his friends.

On the way to the camp, Little John was silent. He tried to put his thoughts in order: *We had to help the people in Blidworth. There were deaths. It happens. That's just the way it is. And these iron men deserved what they got a hundred times over. And it's all for the good because now everybody knows we didn't rob from the villagers.* John rubbed his forehead. *That's the way it is.* But he could not swallow the stale taste.

For a long time, Robin Hood had only occasionally looked over at him from off to his side. Finally, he spoke. "Well, what do you say to all this?"

"I don't know," growled John. "About the cart. I don't know."

"Don't worry, my friend. Most of them were still alive when the sheriff arrived." Robin looked straight ahead. "This morning, the sergeant tried to convince us he was innocent. I tell you, John, nobody stays innocent in a war. Not even we do, even if our cause is just."

"I'll have to get used to that."

After a while, Robin laid a hand on his friend's arm. "You have a big heart. I know."

"It's . . ." Little John broke off.

Much later, he managed a smile. "We stick together. And that's good."

XII

YORKSHIRE. KIRKLEES MONASTERY.

"A shilling, sir!" The little one ran toward the horse, turned around, and ran back the other way to the squire. He held up his dirty hand. "A shilling, sir. For my mother."

The rider looked down at the child's feverish eyes. "For whom?" he asked in a tired voice. The boy pointed to the woman crouched by the wayside. Her face was encrusted with scabies, with festering cracks on her cheeks. "Sister Mathilda has an ointment. With it, my mother will get well again. I have collected two shillings already." He nodded proudly. "In just one week." His big eyes were fixed firmly on the convent gate a little farther ahead. "When I've got five, I can knock again, says the porter."

Without stopping his horse, the squire counted off a few pennies. "Only five. I can't give you more." Before he could throw the money to the boy, a coughing fit shook him. Dark mucus smeared his beard. "I am quite ill. I will need my money for Sister Mathilda."

The little boy nodded knowingly. "Her medicine is expensive." He held his open hand up. "She will only help if someone can pay. But I can, soon." They had almost reached the monastery. Ragged women, children, and men lay to the right and left of the path, marked by disease and misery. When the squire approached them, they begged, wailed. "Do not listen to them, Lord! I was here first," urged the boy. "Give it to me! Please!"

A faint smile glided across the rider's face. "You are clever." With that, he dropped the pennies into the little hand. The boy picked up four of them. The fifth coin slipped out of his hands. Immediately, two lame men pushed their crutches forward, pulling their bodies along with a swing. The little one was faster. Before they got close, he had the last penny safely in his fist. "Thank you, Lord!" A new coughing fit tormented the squire. Panting, he reached the monastery.

The sick by the wayside sank back again. The boy ran past them, proudly giving his mother the silver pieces. "Now, only two and a half shillings to go. Then you'll get well again."

He hooked both thumbs into the cord belt of his short tunic and waited.

The sun shone over the roof of Kirklees Abbey. The grass was fragrant. Bright, green-tinted light shimmered through the leaves of the hazel bushes—a warm May day.

The boy shaded his eyes. Riders approached—armed men in dark blue capes. Three of them side by side, behind them three more. Their shields were emblazoned with a red crest. The boy craned his head back and forth. At last, he caught a glimpse of the man riding in the middle of them, shielded by the two rows. His hat was adorned with a soft plume of feathers, and a dark travel cloak hung loosely from his shoulders. The boy had seen enough. Fearlessly, he ran straight for the escort. Before the guards realized, he had scurried between the horse's bodies and reached out his hand to the fine nobleman. "A shilling, sir. Please!"

"Begone, toad!" cried Sir Roger of Doncaster.

Undeterred, the little one asked, "A shilling for my mother. She is ill. She needs—"

A rough push with his heel hurled the boy to the side. Curled up, he lay where he fell. His mother whimpered. Only after a while did her son raise his head and crawl to her. Blood ran from the wide wound on his forehead. "I'll be fine, and I'll still get your coins," he said bravely.

The sick at the edge of the last stretch of the road had witnessed the cruel hardness of the lord. No one dared call out to him. Without an eye for the misery on either side of him, the baron rode by.

The escort's leader pulled at the bell. "Sir Roger of Doncaster," he reported to the white-dressed sister serving as porter. At once, the gate was opened wide for the monastery's great patron, and immediately closed again. The guards turned their steeds around and backed them up to the gate. As long as their master was within the walls, no one else was allowed to enter the monastery.

The baron got out of his saddle. He snapped at the nun. "Why are you dawdling?" Startled, the gatekeeper scurried away.

Sir Roger waited. Before him, the fruit trees were in full bloom. In long beds, carefully bordered with white pebbles, colorful spring flowers bloomed. The vegetable field was divided into small rectangles. Bent-over novices were weeding between the young bean and pea plants.

Nearby, a solid brick tower rose. It had been a gift from the baron. Behind its narrow windows, patients were treated and cared for. All the way up at the top, there was a single sickroom above the others. The convent's service buildings extended farther back. All was order and care. There was nothing to be seen of the decay, of the hunger outside the high walls. "And all this I get with my money." Sir Roger crossed his arms. "My salvation and health, both of which cost a lot."

He looked over to the whitewashed building just to the left of the church. The prioress emerged from the nuns' dormitory. As quickly as her old age allowed, she hurried along the raked paths, turning through the angles of the flower garden's layout. As she arrived in front of her guest, she greeted him breathlessly. "What a joy, Lord. Peace be with you!"

"And also with you, Mother Prioress, with you too."

"Did you have a good—"

"I am in a hurry. Bring me Sister Mathilda. I wish to speak to her."

Kindness and compassion radiated from the wrinkled face. Regretfully, the nun pointed to the infirmary tower. "She is treating a new patient. A dying squire. Wait until she has bled him. Come with me to the refectory. A cool welcome drink will—"

"Silence. Go, Reverend Mother, and send her to me!" The harsh tone made the prioress retreat.

"God bless you," she murmured as she hurried to the infirmary.

A little later, she returned with sister Mathilda—a tall figure, and under the starched veil, a narrow, smooth face, tightly framed by the white cloth of her wimple. She greeted the guest, holding her hands folded in front of her chest.

Sir Roger wanted to speak to her alone. "I will report to you later, Reverend Mother," Sister Mathilda assured her. No sooner had the prioress left than Sister Mathilda lost her humble look. With no hint of shyness, the dark eyes searched the baron's features. "You have complaints, Lord? A stone in your bladder tormenting you again? Is that it? I will give you . . ."

"Later. My health can wait." The baron barely opened his lips. "You know why I came here."

Looking at the busily working novices, Mathilda whispered: "Not here."

She hurried ahead, invited the guest into her herb garden, and locked the gate. "Curiosity sharpens the ear," she said. "It cures deafness even better than my drops of mother's milk and houseleek."

"To the point." Sir Roger tapped his fingertips together. "Have you thought about my plan? Will you give me your nephew?"

She didn't acknowledge the question. "Apart from this garden, there is no place in all the convent where my fellow sisters' curiosity does not extend."

"Par tous les diables!"

The look on her white-framed face became cooled even more. "Why so irritable? It only makes your bladder tense." Before Sir Roger lost his temper, she placated: "Yes, I've been thinking about it. However, I'm not satisfied with your terms yet."

"Don't overestimate yourself. My patronage has made all this possible for you so far. But the step from doctor to witch is a small one."

Mathilda lowered her head. Under the protection of her veil, she said in a falsely humble tone: "Forgive me. My family is dead except for my two nephews. The one is Robert Loxley, the son of my older brother. I do not care much for him, except that I make very good money from Robin Hood and his band of men. It's different with my nephew Gamwell. He's my favorite brother's child. I raised him. He's a part of me."

Sir Roger narrowed his eyes. "Then what is your concern? Out of sheer generosity, I shall take your Gamwell into my castle. There, he will live like my son. We already negotiated that in January. No—your hesitation does not stem from that sort of concern. I have known you too long not to know your greed. What do you want?"

Mathilda remained in her submissive posture. "First, the truth. I, too, have known you too long. I lie awake and wonder why the wealthy and powerful Sir Roger chose my nephew, of all people. Well, yes, he is handsome, knows how to behave—but, with respect, as your servant and doctor, I know about your physical ailments. You are certainly not looking for a . . . companion."

Sir Roger clenched his fists. "One more word, and you will see yourself burned at the stake!"

"We need each other, sir. And you know it." Fearlessly, Mathilda continued: "There are many poor squires from the old families, are there not? So why a boy who has no connections but an aunt?" The nun raised her head just enough to look the baron in the eyes. "What makes my Gamwell so precious to you?"

Sir Roger pressed his lips together and restlessly paced back and forth. The bad news from Nottingham had alarmed him, had driven him here. He alone knew how this Robin Hood could finally be brought down. But for his plan to succeed, he needed the nun's nephew, the cousin of that wretched bastard.

"To tell the truth. If I accept Gamwell, I expect a small service from him."

Sister Mathilda smiled soberly. "At last. What is it?"

Sir Roger smiled just as coolly. "A secret matter in the service of England. I am not allowed to say any more. Only this much: Gamwell must be thoroughly and properly briefed by me. This will take time. If he fulfills his task, our esteemed Prince John will personally elevate him to noble rank. I guarantee it."

"Good. I will help you." Sister Mathilda promised to send her nephew to Doncaster within the week. "However . . ." She hesitated. Finally, she continued: "When one hand gives, the other should be filled. This is how I see it. And not only with my patients. So, forgive me, I too ask a small favor."

Sir Roger did not want to jeopardize the plan when he was so close. "What is it?"

"Our abbey owes you much. but it could flourish even more."

"Your greed knows no limits."

"You have me wrong. I expect less, not more, from you. How easy it could be for more well-paying patients to be admitted here, and you would save the cost of our maintenance. Kirklees could almost sustain itself, if it weren't for the good Mother Prioress being so simple and humble. Day after day, she compels me to treat some among the sick outside the gate. For free, even! Oh, she is old and doesn't know how the world is now. But if I, if I could take her place, then . . ."

The baron fully understood her. "*D'accord.* Before the year is out. Only it would be easier to propose such a change to the abbot of your order if the Mother Prioress were bedridden with infirmity."

"Put your trust in the power of my herbs."

They looked eye to eye at each other for a long time. Neither lowered their gaze.

As a farewell gift, Sister Mathilda presented her guest with a large bottle in the presence of the prioress. "Take a few sips of this every morning. But warm the liquid beforehand. Iris root, crushed in wine, will soon dissolve your annoying stone."

Protected by his escort, Sir Roger left the convent of Kirklees. He smiled.

On the wayside, the boy stood next to his mother, his face still bloodied. "A shilling, sir!"

Sir Roger opened his bag and threw a handful of silver coins at him. "Take it, you greedy toad."

The little one didn't move. Only when the escort was far enough away did he pick up the silver pennies. He counted aloud, counted again. "Only half a shilling short. Don't worry, Mother. I can do it. I'll do it tomorrow for sure!"

XIII

YORKSHIRE. BARNSDALE TOP.

Marian had been waiting for Little John, and she was still waiting. He hadn't come to Barnsdale Top for months.

Much later than agreed, not until late April, Tom Toad and some men had taken over the second summer watch in the village and the two encampments. "He is well," they told her. "He sends his love."

After only a fortnight, Gilbert Whitehand had returned to the base above the main camp for a month. "Robin won't let the little man go," he reported back. "He needs him. But I'm sure he'll come up for a day or two when they next relieve the guard."

But even when June came, Pete Smiling could only bare his teeth. "Don't look at me so sad," he said cheerfully. "It's been raining day and night for weeks. It's bad enough for our people down there in Sherwood. Nevertheless, we've gotten good loot. Believe me, little one! Nobody's ever even touched a hair on your John's head. Well, a few bumps and bruises ... but everybody's got those now." The lieutenant had also brought two seriously injured people on stretchers into the camp. One with a deep flesh wound over his belly, the other with a splinted leg. "John's better off than those poor devils there. They'll have to go to Mathilda at Kirklees sometime during the night."

The girl clenched her fist. "He promised me."

"Well, you'll just have to wait some more."

Marian stayed on with Beth. Day after day, she helped at the sewing table, obediently but without enthusiasm. Now, in early July, the weather had improved. When the sun shone outside, Marian moaned, complaining of pain in her back. Sometimes she stabbed herself in the fingertip on purpose, then showed Beth the thick drop of blood. "I'd stain the good fabric."

Toad's wife played along. "That would be a pity, princess. So suck it clean and run along! But you be back before dark." In no time, Marian had taken off her light-colored, clean gown, put on the old, dirty one, stuck her dagger in her rope belt, and was out the door. She ran through the forest. In the kitchen at the hideout, Storyteller had old crusts of bread ready for her, just like every day. Behind the horse stable, the girl climbed onto the paddock fence and whistled on two fingers. Whinnying, one of the two white stallions answered, trotted up, snorted, ate the bread, and let Marian clamber up on his back. "My Lancelot! Run!" She rode him bareback.

In the evening, her hair hung tangled and disheveled around her head. "You're not a prince, princess." Beth sighed as she tackled the tangles with her wooden comb. "When you become a young woman, then—"

The blood flushed Marian's face. "Don't say that!"

"Well, just you wait. You'll be a woman whether you like it or not." Beth let the combed-out curls slip through her hand. "And then? Then I'll be alone again."

The next day, from early morning till about noon, Toad's wife seemed not to notice all the groaning and sighing. At last, she put the girl out of her misery. "Go on, run along!"

Not until the camp kitchen did Marian stop to catch her breath. The bowl with the leftover bread was empty. "Where is it?"

Paul Storyteller waved a hand, vigilantly stirring the ladle in the pot.

"Don't you have any crusts?"

The old man slurped the hot soup, his eyes gleaming. "Taste this, little one!"

"Where have you hidden them?"

"Try this first."

Marian sipped from the ladle. She frowned in surprise. "Tastes better than usual."

"I should think so." Storyteller tapped a step forward on his wooden leg. "There's no bread for your Lancelot today." He returned to the table, where he started chopping parsley. He glanced slyly at the girl and then returned his attention to the knife. Casually, he mentioned: "You see, Smiling took it all. He left last night."

Marian lowered the ladle. "They changed the guard?" She turned pale, bravely shook her head. "I knew that."

"Yes, our bald friend will be here through July."

"Paul!" Marian couldn't stand it any longer. "Please, Paul. Tell me!"

"Toad and his men stashed the loot in the caves. Now they've all gone to sleep." The old man continued to act all mysterious. "But, now, over there, from the shack next to the stables . . . I heard something, girl. Something terrible. Like a bear."

Marian had thrown the ladle aside and was already on her way out of the kitchen. She could hear the deep snoring from outside. Carefully, she entered the half-dark hut. Little John lay on his back. The mighty chest rose and fell.

Marian crept closer. She watched the giant. Soon her smile disappeared, her gaze turned angry. Marian grabbed the empty ale jug next to him and slammed it on the table. John jumped up from his sleep, knife in hand. He hit his head against the ceiling beams, knocked wide awake. "Little one."

"You remember who I am?"

"Little one," muttered John. He put the dagger down. *I'm home!* The thought warmed him. He bent down, wanted to squeeze her in a bear hug, reconsidered, and instead stroked her curls gently. "It took a while to get back. But I couldn't come any sooner."

"I'm doing just fine here. I'm helping Beth, and all." Marian took his big hand and held it with both or hers.

"Come outside with me! I want a good look at you."

"And I'll introduce you to my friend."

Marian ran ahead of him to the paddock. Little John grinned. *Her movements, her laughter! She's going to be like her mother someday.* When he heard her loud, sharp whistle on two fingers, he stopped in surprise. But when Marian threw herself off the fence and onto the stallion's back, and when she galloped off across the pasture, whooping, it almost took his breath away. Mixed in with the initial pride was fatherly concern. Finally, John frowned. "No lady rides like that. And whistles like an ox driver, too. Acts like a boy!" He scratched the scar in his beard. "No, I don't want any of that." John took it upon himself to have a serious word with Beth.

He made no comment to her about her horsemanship, not even his typical "It's all right." Marian didn't notice.

On the way back to the village, she was bubbling with happiness, showing him every tree she had climbed, boisterously recounting her shooting skills with her little bow.

I shouldn't have given you that, John thought. *I want something better for you than an outlaw's life.* So preoccupied was he with his thoughts that he had missed Marian's question. "What?"

"I said: When do you have to leave again, John?"

"Tomorrow, little one."

All joy died in her gaze. "So soon?"

"It has to be. July is the most important time, Robin says."

Marian swallowed hard. She didn't want to cry. She bravely lifted her chin. "Robin Hood? *He's* your friend."

"Yes."

Marian walked in silence beside the giant. Her hand slipped into his. “You’ll be back, won’t you?”

“You bet I will, little one!” John laughed. “But I’m still here now. And tonight, we’ll celebrate.”

Clouds had rolled in. Then in the late afternoon, the wind died down. The gray blanket of clouds hung heavy over the highlands and Barnsdale Top. The day’s heat did not cool.

Candles flickered on the table outside the cobbler’s tavern. Bowmakers and ropemakers, the blacksmith, the dyers, and the hemp weaver, whoever in the village felt like it, all had come for a drink. John and Tom kept the guests happy and full. For once, Marian was allowed to join in, much to the envy of the village’s other children and half-grown youths. She sat next to Beth and a pitcher of sweet cider made from apples. The girl pushed a cup over to her. “May I? Please?”

“But don’t be in such a hurry, princess,” Beth admonished with a smile, as she poured. She wore a new dress to celebrate her husband’s return, the loose, wide collar of her shift slipping down over her shoulders. It had been a long time since the girl had seen her so happy. Marian sipped the cider, enjoying the tingle on her tongue, and leaned her head against Beth’s shoulder.

The conversation roamed around the day, the weather, and the worry of whether there would be a good harvest. The ale tasted good in the muggy evening air. Each sip helped those present forget trouble and toil. They joked and laughed. Only one thing was missing. “Tell us a story!”

As usual, Storyteller waited before beginning. He wanted to be asked, and not just once. He wasn’t ready to entertain yet.

Marian brushed the curls from her forehead. Her eyes sparkled from the sweet apple cider. “Tell us about Sherwood!” Beth quickly tried to cover her mouth, but Marian pushed her hand away. “What did you do there? Tell me, John!”

The table fell silent. Little John put his ale mug down. "We . . . I . . ." He hesitated.

Tom Toad came to the rescue. "Well, we're having fun. All day. There are only fun times with Robin. Everyone here knows that."

What was he talking about? The giant peered at Tom, and his friend winked back at him. John caught on. "Right. That's exactly how it is, little one. We're having so much fun."

The merrymakers at the table breathed a sigh of relief. Nobody was allowed to ask the freemen such a question; nobody talked about what the outlaws truly did in the forest, nor did they want to know. In their hearts, Robin Hood was a hero, full of wit and cunning. He led the fight on their behalf. His gilded image was built from dreams and stories throughout the shire, even among the villagers in Barnsdale Top, and nothing was allowed to tarnish it.

Storyteller demanded their silence.

"I remember how, once, Robin met a deceitful beggar—"

No. They had heard that story too many times.

"All right. How about the cobbler from Wakefield? The churl demanded a toll from everyone who wished to pass armed through town. Whoever didn't pay, he thrashed. Then one day, Robin—"

The audience waved that one off. Storyteller glared at them angrily. "Then . . . the beautiful wedding. Who remembers that one: how Robin came across the poor vagabond Alan-a-Dale in the woods? Oh, how the ragged minstrel wept, because his lady love was promised to a rich old knight?"

Everyone except Marian and John knew what had happened. But the memory of it made his listeners smile. Paul took advantage of the silence and quickly carried on, embellishing the most important details. He showed them Robin Hood, disguised as a lute player, sneaking into St. James's Church near Papplewick. At the altar, the bishop was just about to bind the mismatched bride and groom together. Robin shouted, "This marriage must not take place. The bride's heart belongs to someone else." What a fight followed! And at the end of the day, the minstrel Alan-a-Dale won the hand of his beloved.

A distant rumble of thunder brought the audience back to Barnsdale Top. They filled their mugs with fresh ale.

Marian wanted more cider. "Did that really happen?" she asked.

"Don't even ask, princess!" Toad's wife studied the girl's eyes. "Best I only give you a little bit more."

Paul Storyteller had fortified himself. He wiped the ale foam from his beard with the sleeve of his tunic. "Oh—and that time Robin got the sack of flour thrown in his face. I was there to see it myself. There was a beggar—no, what am I saying, it was a miller. So: a miller lived with his wife in—"

Little John sat bolt upright. "Stop!" he snarled tightly. The mill at Doncaster appeared before him. He could see Much's dead parents tied to the water wheel. "I don't want to hear anything about a miller."

Toad put a warning hand on his arm. "Don't spoil the fun!"

But it was too late. Paul Storyteller was offended. He laboriously straightened his leg. "Then I won't, little man. Tell a story yourself, if you think you can do better! But something new."

"Please, John!" exclaimed Marian tipsily, clapping her hands. The villagers were also calling on the giant now. They demanded a new story, something funny.

Little John propped up his chin and rubbed his forehead. No, he didn't want to be a killjoy. *All right, something funny. Fine by me.* But try as he might, there was nothing funny in Sherwood to talk about.

Tom Toad nudged him under the table. "Follow my lead. But pay close attention!" he murmured. Loudly he called out, "Folks. John and I will tell this tale together. Many an adventure we've lived through. But the best is the story of the potter." Tom paused.

As the guests looked at him expectantly, he reached around to the back of his neck, brought the long braid of hair forward, and let it circle slowly around above his ale mug. "We're lying in the grass, as you do, full of food and comfortable. The sun is shining on our bellies. That's when Robin jumps up. 'Come on, you lazy bums!' he says. 'Let's see if we can't catch a golden goose on the trade road.' Only me, John, and Gilbert went along. The others didn't feel like it. That's how it went, wasn't it, John?"

"That's right." The giant grinned. What was he talking about?

"But no goose for miles. But then: Here comes a cart." Toad pointed ahead with the end of his braid. "We hear the clatter of pitchers and bowls. 'Hide,' says Robin. 'Want to bet the potter will pay me a toll?' We warn him, but he doesn't listen. Now you, John."

The giant rubbed the scar in his beard hard. *We don't rob poor people, do we? And definitely Robin doesn't! But this is just supposed to be a story. Just make something up,* he thought, *like in the old days when Marian wanted to hear about the hunt. I can do that easily.* He was ready.

John pounded his heavy fist on the table. "'Stop!' Robin jumps in front of the cart. Give me your money.' 'Who wants my money?' 'I, Robin Hood.'" For the potter, John lent his own deep voice, letting it rumble; for his leader, he let it resound as bright and clear as he could. "'I'll give you nothing willingly,' 'I'll take it, then.' 'You would rob an honest, poor man? I'll show *you*.' All at once the huge potter jumps off the cart. He lunges at Robin." John pounded his fists one then the other on the table. Startled, the audience rescued their tippling mugs. With a snort, John shouted, "The fight is on!" He drummed his fists ever faster and louder, raising them up and slamming them down on the wooden tabletop together. "There lies Robin flat on the forest floor. No sooner is he awake again than he's shaking his fist. 'I'll have your money in the end.' 'I'll beat you to death first.'" The giant raised his clenched hands again. The gathering at the table held its breath in anticipation.

"Stop! That's enough, John!" interrupted Tom Toad, laughing. "After all, *we* were also there." He let the braid circle again. Lightly, Tom went on with his story: Just in time, he, John, and Whitehand held back the angry potter. Robin apologized to the fearless man. After Robin looked a while at the clay pots on the cart, a new idea occurred to him. "'I feel like going to Nottingham. I want to pay a visit to the sheriff himself. I bet he won't recognize me.'" Tom held the braid tightly. The audience stared at the narrator in disbelief. John, too, frowned.

At that moment, there was a flash of lightning, bright as day, followed soon by thunder. Little John breathed a sigh of relief. *That's it,* he thought. A lightning storm means the end of storytelling time.

"It's not raining yet." Storyteller did not take his eyes off Tom Toad. "Go on. Go on with the story."

"So. The plan was simple." Robin bought the wagon and all the goods from the potter, as well as his tunic and cloak. Whistling a song, he set off for Nottingham market well disguised. "Now it's your turn." Tom turned to John.

John sighed in surrender. Brandishing his wares like a merchant, he hawked his tankard of ale, "'Cheap! Cheap! Come, folks, buy!' By noon, Robin is rid of almost all the pots. Five are left. He goes to the sheriff's house ..."

Lightning, an earsplitting crash. And rain. In a torrent, it pelted down on the table. John laughed and shouted, "By Dunstan! The story is over for today." No one was left to hear. The guests had jumped to their feet, and everyone fled home.

Tom Toad put his arm protectively around his wife's shoulder. "I'll take you home." After that, he still wanted to return to the camp with John. "But tomorrow night, I'll stay."

Marian was not tired. Elated from the sweet cider, she hopped through the puddles holding the giant's hand. "If it's really that much fun at Sherwood, I'll go with you next year."

"What?" John stopped. Despite the rain, he stopped and crouched down to her. Their faces were level. "They're only stories. Just stories, little one. They're what people like to hear about Robin Hood. I didn't know that, before, either. But down in Sherwood, things are really different than here."

Later, when Marian was dry and warm under the covers, John came to her bedside. "Tomorrow, when you wake up, I'll be gone."

"Come back soon!" Tearlessly, earnestly, she looked up at him. "And I'll pray for you with Beth, too. When we are alone, we talk a lot to the Blessed Virgin."

John nodded. "That's good."

John, Beth, and Tom Toad sat down together in the candlelight. There was one thing left on the giant's mind. Whispering, he asked the seamstress to pay more attention to Marian.

Beth could barely suppress a laugh. "You're worse than a wet nurse, giant."

"I'm just saying."

Abruptly, the mockery faded. "Leave the princess to me!" urged Beth. "As long as I live, she'll be fine."

John promised nothing. "Where else would she go?"

The storm did not pass until morning. Tom accompanied John to the base. There was no time for sleep. John had to get going on his way. "Or Robin will grab that overstuffed prize without me."

The freemen had known about it for a while. Bill Threefinger had been sent out first. For more than a month, he had waited outside the gates of London. Robin Hood did not rely on rumors. The scout was to return to Sherwood only when he had definite news. And he did. The goods caravan meant for Nottingham fortress was on its way! And the unusually heavy arms of the escort could only mean one thing: This time, the wagons were carrying more than just grain, wax, pitch, and salt.

"And too bad I'll be just sitting here. Someone's got to guard the camp." Tom Toad clenched his fists. "If it all works out, that'll be the biggest robbery Robin ever pulled off. Really too bad that I won't be there."

"What are you upset about?" With difficulty, John suppressed a grin. "You'll still get to tell the story later. And since you won't be in it, it'll be a pretty good story, too." With that, John strode off across the clearing. Without turning around, he called out, "See you soon. And don't get into any fights with old Storyteller!"

Tom Toad opened his mouth, said nothing at first, then laughed and waved a mock-threatening fist after his friend. "Get out of here, you runt! And . . . Take care of yourself, John!"

XIV

The latest dispatch from the Crusade: *During the winter of 1191 and 1192, Sultan Saladin does not attack the Crusaders. Lionheart has time to rebuild the city of Ascalon into the strongest fortress on the coast. Worries torment King Richard—quarrels among his army commanders, Christians fighting Christians. Also, month after month, alarming news from home: Prince John is trying to usurp the throne by any means. At the meeting of his army commanders in Ascalon on April 16, 1192, Lionheart demands that they establish orderly conditions in Palestine as quickly as possible. He announces his intent to return to England soon.*

NOTTINGHAM SHIRE.
ON THE WAY TO NOTTINGHAM.

Since daybreak, heavy rain had been pelting down on the high arched tarpaulins over the wagons. The teams of oxen trotted heavily in their harnesses. Water flowed in rivulets from the brims of the coachmen's hats. Four heavily burdened mules plodded between the first and second wagons; a fifth pulled the boxy feed cart. There was no need for anyone to walk in the rain and urge the patient mules on; a long rope, moored to the first wagon, connected one to the other. Their brown hides shone wetly.

The heavily armed riders of the escort pulled their cloaks tightly closed, with the soaked cloth of their hoods pulled low over their helmets and faces. Crossbows and shields hung from the pommels of their saddles.

Twelve mercenaries had been hired by a powerful merchant in London to protect his trade goods—rough, battle-hardened men. Four rode in front, two by two. They had relaxed their guard. The distance between them had grown to three horse lengths. Two mercenaries protected each flank of the caravan. The last wagon was followed by the rear guard. None of those four riders had kept to their positions. They had long since stopped riding in pairs. In this storm, it was much more practical to ride directly behind the horse of the man in front.

In the early morning hours, they passed Stamford. Although the cloudy gloom of the rain now blocked all view into the distance, Nottingham could not be far away. The mercenaries' thoughts hurried ahead. By afternoon, they would reach the campsite below the city, a fire in front of their tent, ale for their ever-thirsty throats, a game of dice with their mates.

Behind the last of the rear guard, three figures detached themselves from the roadside brush. As they stooped low, following the riders, Robin Hood leaped into the road as well. He cocked his short bow.

His arrow whizzed over the backs of his men, piercing a mercenary's neck. At once the three outlaws were upon him. They pulled the dead man silently and swiftly from the horse. Much caught onto the animal's halter and led it onward as the others unwrapped the mercenary from his rain cloak. Pete Smiling threw the cloak around his shoulders, put its hood over his green hood, and took a running leap over the haunches of the horse into the saddle. At Pete's signal, Little John burst from the bushes beside him. The blunt end of his staff struck the head of the next rider in line. Soundlessly, the mercenary toppled into the arms of the outlaws. They pulled him off the road. Soon an outlaw was draped in the man's cloak and was in his saddle. Little John moved swiftly to the next. His blows were hard and short: the third rider, the fourth. To a casual glance back, the view would not have changed, Just as before, four cloaked mercenaries rode behind the caravan, one after the other.

On both sides of the road, ten or so men left cover. They scurried to join Little John hidden by the last wagon. Not a word was spoken. Every sound was drowned out by the pattering rain.

The giant and Gilbert Whitehand communicated briefly, in silent signals. The men to the left and right of the wagon hurried forward. Gilbert swung himself onto the wagon's seat. The ox driver noticed nothing. His collar pulled up, his hat brim low on his forehead, he sat there holding the reins and staring at the swaying rumps of the four oxen. Gilbert stuck his clawed white hand in front of the man's eyes. "Holy Cedric ..." was all the ox driver got out. Whitehand slammed his left hand into the man's neck and pushed him off the seat. Little John caught the man, flung him off farther. In the ditch by the side of the road, two outlaws picked him up. While they gagged the man with a leather strap and tied his feet, John tossed his staff to Much. In a fluid movement, the longbow flew into his hand. Robin ran up alongside on the other side of the wagon caravan. The two men stopped simultaneously, took quick aim, and the next two mercenaries slumped forward. The horses carried them onward. The next arrows struck their targets, too. The path to the middle wagon was clear.

For days the freemen had been observing the caravan. The merchant rode in this wagon. Gilbert passed the reins of the rear ox team to another of the outlaws and dashed ahead. His white hand surprised and horrified the second cart driver just as it had the first.

The drumming of the rain lightened. They had to hurry! Vincent quickly hopped onto the driver's bench, his collar pulled up, the wide brim of his hat low over his eyes. Behind him, the curtain flaps of the travel wagon remained closed. The merchant had noticed nothing.

The small army continued to advance, past the mules, quickly replacing the driver of the first wagon. His place was taken by Whitehand.

The rain stopped completely, suddenly, as if an invisible hand had closed an ale-cask spigot above the road. The outlaws held their breath. In front of them, the first four mercenaries of the escort were still in their saddles. They still hadn't noticed a thing. At the slightest suspicious noise, these men would not turn back to investigate or fight, but would gallop off toward Nottingham and sound the alarm. All eyes turned to Robin. Everyone knew: the caravan could not be diverted to some hiding place; it was too big, too cumbersome for that. And if they stopped, reinforcements would be upon them before they could unload the goods.

Determined, Robin swung himself up to join Gilbert on the wagon. He whispered orders. Quickly he was back on the road, giving hand signals. Robin Hood, Little John, and a few other men overtook the ox team and hurried farther ahead. When they were almost alongside the mercenaries, they jumped right and left into the cover of the bushes.

Gilbert let out a shrill whistle and shouted at the guards. "Hey! Hullo!" He whistled again and shouted some more.

One of the armed men turned around in the saddle. Gilbert waved his wet hat. "Come here! Come!"

At last, the riders heard and turned their horses and trotted back. As they approached, one called out, "What's the matter?"

"You are to dismount. Orders from the master."

They reined in the horses. "Are you addled?"

Behind them and one either side of them, outlaws appeared. In an instant, they were surrounded. Arrows were aimed at their horrified faces. "Are you deaf?" hissed Robin Hood.

The horsemen stayed frozen in place.

"Well." Little John made short work of grabbing a mercenary's boot and heaving him out of the saddle. "If you won't follow orders." Before the remaining three had a chance to think about their choices in life, they too were whirling through the air. They sprawled motionless in the mud beside the road.

Gilbert pulled back on the reins of the first team.

"Don't stop!" Robin gestured ahead. "Keep going. Keep going!"

Pete Smiling came riding forward. He bared his teeth. "We did it!" He fought to suppress a cheer.

Robin's face stayed tense. "Quickly, Pete. You take the lead with three men! Everything must look the same as before. Quick!" Pete hastily obeyed.

"Much, Threefinger, go tell the others. Whoever is on foot, get off the road. See to the prisoners. Wait for my orders!"

Little John shook his head. "Why keep going?"

"I'll tell you later!"

The pack animals trotted by.

"Tell me now."

"I want to negotiate."

"What?" The giant forgot to close his mouth.

"Wait and see, little man!" Robin smiled. When the middle one of the covered carts reached them, he poked John in the side. "Come along! You stay outside next to Vincent. Only come inside when I call for you." He swung himself onto the cart's seat, and waited until John was seated too. Robin drew his hunting dagger and slipped inside the wagon through the loosely hanging canvas flaps.

Inside, crates were stacked on top of each other, secured with ropes. From the rear to the middle, the space between was filled with furs and bales of cloth. In front of it all, in a fur-padded armchair, sat the merchant, his fur-trimmed cloak spread over his knees. His head had sunk to his chest. He was asleep. Of his face, Robin could see only the half-open mouth, the flowing gray beard.

Nose, eyes, forehead were hidden by his wide square cap. A small oil lamp swung from an iron hook above a shallow bowl on the floor. The wick was trimmed low, but the dim light was enough for Robin. The color of the large hat he wore was yellow, marking him as a Jewish merchant. Jews were required to distinguish themselves from Christians by wearing such easily identified caps while traveling. Robin turned the flame higher. "When you sleep, you miss out on the best."

His voice woke the merchant. The man raised his head. After a briefly startled moment, his eyes scanned the stranger, the dagger, the green clothes. The merchant's beard quivered, but he strove for composure. "He who sleeps is cradled on Abraham's knees."

"Nice." Robin sheathed his dagger. Calmly, he sat down at the man's feet beside the lamp with his legs crossed. "It's easier to do business this way, eye to eye."

The merchant raised his brows. "I don't mean to be rude. But what are you doing here in my wagon?"

"I?" Robin shook his head, gravely. "Nothing. But you, alas, you have lost everything."

The lids half-lowered over the merchant's dark eyes. "Is that so?"

"John!"

Instantly both linen flaps were flung aside. The giant thrust his head in, his massive body filling the gap. "It's a Goliath," the merchant stammered, pressing back in his chair. "By the twelve fathers of Israel!"

"Thank you, dwarf." Robin winked at his friend. "That'll do for now."

"All right."

The giant disappeared. The merchant fretted with his beard, his breathing panicked. "And who are you? A Philistine?"

"No. I'm Robin Hood."

The man repeated the name silently. He sighed deeply. All at once, his features set, and calm and watchful dark eyes gazed at the robber. "My name is Solomon. I am a merchant and moneylender from London. Much have I heard about you. But wherever I went, I was never told that you rob from Jews."

"No poor Jews. That's right."

"Three years ago, my brothers in the faith and I were hunted down and slain all over England. I escaped the slaughter. And now that we are under the protection of King Richard, is the fate of my people finally to catch up with me?"

"I had nothing to do with that!" Robin clenched his fist. "We are outcasts ourselves. I know how it feels to—" He broke off. Sharply, he looked the merchant in the face. "You're smart, old man. You almost had me."

Solomon shrugged. "All right, then. Then put it plainly. As one businessman to another, I'm asking you: Do I have a chance, here?"

"If you're honest with me, yes."

"Lie? I have enough to do, exposing the lies of my contractors, much less create my own."

"How much is the entire cargo worth?"

Without hesitation, the merchant answered. "Three thousand and then another hundred pounds." He bent to the side and opened a leather casket. He took out some rolls of parchment. "Here. My letter of protection, the lists of goods, and the contract. See for yourself. Which I suppose has now become worthless to me." Solomon had already negotiated a price in London with Prince John's agent. A thousand pounds was quoted for the supplies for the Nottingham fortress. Then, in addition, silk, wine, furs, and spices, all manner of precious items, intended for the visit of the prince and his guests the next month. "That adds two thousand to the price."

"That adds up to only a sum of three thousand pounds. Guaranteed by seal. From where comes the rest?"

Despite his grief at his impending robbery, Solomon smiled disdainfully. "The lord sheriff is a vain little peacock. Though we Jews are hateful to him, he deigns to do business with us. For him, as every year, I have brought the latest fashions from France. He will pay the agreed three thousand from the fortress treasury, and his ostentation will be worth a hundred pounds to him out of his own coin purse."

Robin handed back the papers. "Answer me one more question: Do you carry any empty chests?"

"If not, I would be a poor businessman. In Nottingham, I was going to sell. In York, I was going to shop. The last wagon is loaded with empty casks, crates, and barrels."

"Nice." Robin's bright eyes reflected the light of the oil lamp. "Then you shall have your chance. Now, to our business."

The outlaw outlined his plan succinctly. Solomon listened, straightening in his chair. After Robin spoke his piece, Solomon excitedly slapped both hands on the armrests. "That's what I call the high art of cunning. Even if I have to shed some feathers. How lucky for me that you are not my enemy."

Robin rose and took the outstretched hand. "So, it's a deal. You'll lose a little, but not everything."

"And it's far better than looking hungrily at the sky and waiting for food to fall."

Robin laughed. He flipped the linen flaps apart. "John, stop the wagons!" Robin put the horn to his lips. Two short, low notes. His men emerged from the bushes. The men in disguise came galloping up to the travel wagon. Rich loot had been captured, with no casualties on their side. At last, the raid was over!

From the cart, Robin gave new, precise instructions. There were disappointed, perplexed faces all around. But the sharpness in his voice did not allow questions. "Hurry up! We mustn't keep the sheriff waiting."

The fortress towered mightily above the valley of the River Trent. When the afternoon sun found a gap between the clouds, the stones of the sheer walls glinted. The sentinels on the battlements spotted the caravan on the southern plain long before it reached Trent Bridge. When the last wagon had safely crossed the river, a detachment of the castle guard rode out to escort them to a campsite near the shore.

"Oh, by Father Abraham, by the twelve fathers of Israel. No no no!" The august merchant refused the lord sheriff's invitation. "I cannot come settle the sale at the city gate. I must keep watch over my guards." He pointed at to the ox drivers and mercenaries. They were a grim group, with cloaks wrapped tight, shadowed faces under their gray wide cloth hoods, their beards covered with dust and mud.

One looked much the same as the other. Only the whites of their eyes shone from the dark masks of dirt. "Left unsupervised, my expensive goods will quickly take wing."

The leader of the squad from the castle stared at the merchant uncomprehendingly. Solomon smiled. "Never mind, young man. What do you know about metaphors?" His voice became stern. "Offer your master my most humble greeting! Tell him: I await him here in the camp. All goods must be paid for and taken up to the fortress before nightfall. There are too much riffraff and brigands in the area. Now get a move on, young man!"

The squad leader nodded with relief. Following commands and obedience were the life of a soldier.

The sky had cleared of clouds. The sun was lowering toward the west. The air had been cleansed by the long rainstorm. An aromatic fragrance rose from the grass.

With five high-wheeled carts and a crowd of servants behind

him, the fortress steward came riding down to the camp on a donkey.

The three covered carts stood in a semicircle, the oxen not yet unharnessed. There was a bustle of activity. Tents were being pitched. Goods were unloaded. The merchant sat in a comfortable armchair in front of his wagon. The cargo lists lay before him on a folding travel table.

The steward saluted him with well-chosen words. Lord Sheriff Thom de Fitz sent his apologies. Obligations held him up for a while until the goods were loaded for departure. He would follow later to settle the business of payment.

Solomon smiled. "I thank you for the considerate overlay, my friend. You may as well have said: 'The lord sheriff is disgusted to be in the company of a Jew, so he sent me in his stead.'"

"I am only upholding the dignity of my office and . . . doing my job."

"That is so, my friend, that is so. The servant must bend down so that the master may eat from his back."

"Eat?" The steward hesitated in confusion, then shrugged. "As you say, Solomon. Let's start with the grain barrels." Every second lid was lifted. The grain was checked cursorily, and the lid closed again. Boxes, crates, bales of cloth, silks, furs—the steward tasted, felt, counted, compared the quantity with the list, and ordered goods to be loaded. Every now and then, he glanced worriedly at the two figures who always stayed one step behind the merchant.

Solomon noticed. "I bought this giant and his little brother from a Knight Templar. They're quite dark, under all that road dust."

"From a Templar? They are Moors? Two of them? They're rarely seen in England."

"They're certainly worth the cost. I keep them as bodyguards."

The steward shook himself. "With respect, I could never get used to having unholy foreigners around me."

Solomon took a breath. He lifted his hands. "They are quite capable. They guard me like the apple of their eye."

The goods checked, they were transferred into the steward's five carts.

"If you will acknowledge receipt?" Solomon held out a lead stylus.

With squiggling loops, the steward put his name under the lists. He drew two kerchiefs from his left tunic sleeve, stuffed back in the red one, and waved the white one over his head. Atop the battlements, the signal was answered with a white pennant.

A short while later, Lord Sheriff Thom de Fitz himself rode down the steep road. His light blue cloak billowed. A heavy cart followed at some distance. Two armed men of the town guard sat on the cart bench.

Thom de Fitz ignored the merchant's outstretched hand, saying only, "*Bonjour.*" He let his eyes wander disparagingly over the camp. "Your wagon drivers are lazy, Jew. They haven't unharnessed the oxen."

"There wasn't time yet, sir. After our little business is finished, I will have the animals fed and taken care of for the night."

"What about your mercenaries? The men look like pigs."

Solomon smiled. "A Jew does not surround himself with pigs, sir. Certainly, the men are dirty. They can't help it, out in the rain and mud. But first they work, then they may wash."

"Is this how you treat Christians?"

"They don't complain, because they are paid well."

"*Maudit chien!*"

The merchant kept a placid face. "My people have learned to endure slights, Lord Sheriff. You have known me long enough to know that your insults will not lower the price we agreed on. But to rid you of the sight of me as quickly as possible, I suggest we conclude our business at once."

On the lower, straight stretch of the road, the carriage bumped past the five heavily loaded carts and swung into the stockyard. As soon as the horses stopped, the steward hurried to the loading area and took hold of the large linen blankets.

"Halt!" Thom de Fitz was already out of his saddle. "Don't you dare!"

The steward looked at his master, puzzled. "I thought it was my duty . . ."

"Were the goods checked? The amount complete?"

"Yes, sir. Yes."

"Then what are you still standing here for?" Thom de Fitz yanked him away from the cart. "Go get on your donkey, man! Your place is out by the carts." Offended, the steward hurried away. Between the sheriff's two armed men sat the large money box, on the carriage bench. "Carry that over to the Jew!"

Meanwhile, Solomon had had his bodyguards prepare everything for the conclusion of the deal: a second armchair, a clothes chest right next to it with the lid flipped up.

Full of impatience, Thom de Fitz waited until his men-at-arms had set down the gold then barked, "Now get out of the camp! Stay over by the goods until I call you."

He lifted a gold-threaded brocaded tunic from the clothes chest and held it to his chest. *"Par tous les saints. Magnifique."* When he looked up, it was right into the dirt-covered faces of the bodyguards, who had moved closer. "Don't come near me, you bastards!" he hissed.

Solomon smiled. "They don't understand your language. But they know you haven't paid for the elegant pieces yet."

The sheriff gently put back the robe. Immediately the watchful bodyguards took their position behind the merchant again.

"Who *are* those fellows?"

"Oh, just Black Moors," Solomon said with a dismissive air. "So of course their names would be unpronounceable to you. That's why I call them Goliath and Samson." He tapped his chin thoughtfully. "I would be willing to let you have them for a good price."

The sheriff shook his head. "You cutthroat. I wouldn't want to meet those two in the daytime, let alone hovering near me at night."

"I can sympathize. To tell you the truth, they're hard to rein in. I shall breathe a sigh of relief when I am rid of them."

Thom de Fitz glanced up at the fortress. "It's about time to settle the payment."

As Solomon weighed bar after bar in his hand, and the sheriff's face turned red except for the stump of his white nose. "You don't trust me, greasy Jew?"

"Forgive me, I'm an old man. I trust in God. Otherwise, I trust only my wits."

Not a gold piece too much, not one too little. Only after confirming it was so did the merchant have the delivery lists signed and sign his own receipt. One copy was for the lord sheriff, and the other he tucked into his robe. Sighing, he gave a wave to the bodyguards. Goliath and Samson picked up the heavy money box and disappeared with it around the covered cart. After a while, only Samson returned.

The lord sheriff did not notice. He had been examining the robes from France, shimmering with their pearls and brocade. "How much?"

"A hundred pounds."

To the merchant's astonishment, Thom de Fitz immediately agreed to the price. "However, I offer you a countertrade. *Viens. Viens!*" Swiftly, he led Solomon over to the cart and tore the canvas tarps open. Carved spoons, ladles. Earthen jugs. Bulging woolen sacks. Spindles. Farming implements.

Solomon picked up a wooden spoon. "Excellent quality. The villagers here in the north are skilled craftsmen."

"*Bien. Très bien.* All this I offer you for the robes. And add fifty pounds on top."

"Too little!" Someone countered in a hard, clear voice.

"You usurer! Wretched Jew!" the sheriff snapped at the merchant.

"I said nothing," Solomon whispered close. "That was Samson. He's behind you."

"*Diable . . .*" The curse died on Thom de Fitz's tongue. He felt a dagger at the back of his neck.

"Don't turn around! There's a witness here you can't kill. Remember me?"

"R-r-obin Hood," Thom de Fitz stammered.

"Such a bright little noggin, even without a nose. Nice."

"Mercy. Spare me!" whimpered the sheriff. "Mercy! I'm defenseless. I'll give you what you want."

"You will, sure enough. And more than that," Robin promised icily. "Just once, I let you look me in the eye because I wanted to see you up close. The second time, I swear, it will be the death of you. But it's not that time yet." He gave a short whistle. Little John emerged from behind the covered cart. "Take the merchant!" ordered Robin. "We're on our way."

The giant replied with a low affirmative grunt. His left paw dropped on the merchant's yellow square cap and turned him around; his right grabbed the back of the merchant's coat, and he lifted the old man roughly off the ground. The old man kicked, wailing in utter anguish, "Goliath! Spare me. By all the fathers of Israel. Have mercy!"

"Shut up," warned John, "or I'll break your neck."

"I'll keep silent," the merchant promised. "I'll keep quiet."

John set him down. No sooner had Solomon regained his footing than he renewed his rant. John waited until he had fully lamented his misery to the sheriff: the raid on the caravan, he himself a prisoner of the robbers, and now, he said, all his beautiful gold lost.

"Shut up, I said!" The giant shook the scrawny merchant.

Thom de Fitz perked up hopefully. "Serves the Jew right. Take his money. And I swear I will not have you pursued."

"You sneaky thief!" Robin Hood increased the pressure of the dagger point. "Confess to what you've been doing to the villages, or . . ."

"Yes, it is true!" the sheriff admitted at the touch of the sharp edge. "I have robbed the villages. It's all here. Take it! And that makes us even."

Robin made no reply. Thom de Fitz pulled two pouches from his belt and passed them carefully over his shoulder. "Ten pounds in gold. That's all I'm carrying."

"Drop them, if you please!" hissed Robin. "My men will collect them anon." Again, he whistled. Immediately some of the outlaws disguised as coachmen and mercenaries left their work and sauntered over from the camp to the five heavily laden carts.

"No. You would not dare!" Thom de Fitz looked triumphantly up at the city walls. "As soon as you try to escape with the goods, the sentries will sound the alarm."

Robin jabbed his knee into the sheriff's rear. "Start marching, you rat! Don't run. Move with dignity like the great judge of Nottingham should! Or I'll cut you down in your tracks."

Solomon, too, walked in front of John at a measured pace.

Outside the camp, the harnessed horses waited patiently. The castle servants leaned against the cartwheels. At the head of the procession squatted the steward on his donkey. To the right and left of the long-eared animal stood the two town guards. From a distance, nothing seemed to have changed. But as they approached and the sheriff got a clearer view, he shook his head with a furious growl. Guards, steward, servants, and servants were tied up and gagged. Even the animals had leather slings loosely tied around their front hooves.

"Diable," Thom de Fitz cursed. Suddenly he gave a bleating laugh. "It's no good, Robin Hood. You fleeced the Jew. But not me." Without turning around, he warned, "You won't get far with the goods. So take the ten pounds and the tat made by those Saxon dolts. And get out of here!"

Robin had the three barrels unloaded. "Open them!" Thom de Fitz obeyed him. "What do you see?"

"Grain."

"Check it. Reach deeper!"

The sheriff burrowed in up to his forearms. Abruptly, he yanked his hands out. Sticking to his fingers were bran and bits of turnip. "Animal fodder. *Sang de Dieu!* Cattle fodder!" He lifted off the second lid, then the third. Under a thin layer of grain, he found nothing but bran and pieces of turnip.

"We needed space for our prisoners. So we took the liberty of transferring the contents of the feed cart into those barrels."

Robin had his men show the sheriff a bale of silk. Below the first layer were nothing but rags and blankets. "Want to see some more?"

All the blood had drained from Thom de Fitz's face. "Where are the goods? I paid for them. With money from the castle treasury." He faltered, horrified. "With my lord's money. Prince John."

"I am in possession of the entire shipment the merchant sold you. And you acknowledged receipt of the shipment." Robin pulled the parchment out of the sheriff's belt. He snapped his fingers. Little John snatched the matching document from the merchant as well and handed it to his leader. "These two lists are sharper than any sword. They will cut off your head, Thom de Fitz. That's the only reason I'm letting you live today. I will give them as a gift to your oh-so-indulgent Prince John when he sits in front of empty bowls next month as his ladies weep for the silk scarves and furs he promised."

"Mercy!" The sheriff sank to his knees in front of the barrels of useless fodder.

"Everyone knows what sort of judge you are. You're heartless and cruel." Robin's voice grew rough. "If only all the innocent condemned could see you like this now. You deserve death a thousand times over! Still, I'll give you one last chance."

The sheriff rose, trembling. "What do you want me to . . ." In a panic, he turned this way and that. Robin slapped the delivery receipts on his head. Thom de Fitz winced.

"Listen! You will buy the goods from me at the same price you paid the merchant. I know you have gathered far more money than that in your house. But I only want three thousand pounds. And I want it now. Besides, you will make it clear to your iron puppets up there that the wagon will leave the camp today with your express permission. Moreover, you will say that you will be celebrating the successful conclusion of the trade for a few hours with the honorable merchant over good wine."

"And . . . and . . ." Thom de Fitz swallowed hard. "How do I know you're not cheating me?"

"This is my game. I make the rules."

The sheriff complied. How else was he going to face Prince John? And avoid the ridicule of his citizens and peers? He feared that almost more than the deepest dungeon in the cavern under the fortress.

He mounted his horse, spurred it, and raced up the steep road. The outlaws watched him anxiously. When he disappeared from sight, they returned to the camp.

Sighing, the merchant took off his cap and wiped his sparse hair. "This kind of business would soon put me in my grave." He frowned and looked up at Little John. "Two goats are more than one."

"What?"

Thoughtfully, Solomon pointed at the outlaw leader. "Do the math, Goliath: pay the sheriff, and Robin Hood will have received three thousand pounds twice today."

The giant grinned. "Fear not! We're honest robbers. Robin gave his word, which means you'll get your money back. You go ahead and worry, pray on it if you need to! But we keep our word."

The sun had sunk. In the west, the sky was still glowing. Thom de Fitz returned alone. He drove his horse up to the merchant's covered cart. Plump bags of money lay crosswise in front of the saddle horn. Instantly, Robin and his lieutenants were behind him. "Dismount!"

Gilbert quickly counted the gold and poured it back into the leather sacks. He nodded to Robin.

"Tie up our guests! Back-to-back. But not their feet."

Pete Smiling pursed his lips. "This is going to be a feast for the sheriff. He never sat so close to a Jew before." He tied the two men together.

"Where are my goods?" gasped Thom de Fitz. No one gave him an answer.

The wagon bumped out of the camp. Solomon cried out. The sheriff banged the back of the merchant's head. "*Ferme ta gueule*, Jew!"

Silence all around. Without a sound, all the outlaws had dispersed. Thom de Fitz tugged at his shackles. "Where are the goods?"

Solomon moaned, "In the third wagon. The goods were there all the time. Except for the grain, the wretches merely reloaded everything. Why didn't you come back with a superior force? Then nothing would have been lost." He called again on Israel's twelve fathers, lamenting his fate, the loss of the gold, and several other things he happened to think of.

"*Enfer et damnation!*" Thom de Fitz cursed; he cursed Robin

Hood; he cursed Solomon. Solomon shouted louder and increasingly creatively. The mismatched pair stumbled around the campground back-to-back, their shouts filling the evening.

Late that night, the freemen reached Sherwood. They safely hid the wagon away.

"What a day!" Robin lay down under a bush near John. "You know, in a single day, we ..." He trailed off at the sound of loud snoring. His friend was already sound asleep.

A boulder thumped on John's chest. Again and again, the giant tried to roll it away, in vain. The troublesome stone bounced up and down.

"Hey, runt!"

John opened his eyelids. Beside him was Robin, squatting, making a large coin sack dance on his chest.

"What's the idea?"

"Don't you hear it?"

Not yet fully awake, John propped himself up on his elbows. He shook off the dream. It was dawn, cloudless between the treetops. "Gonna be a warm day," the giant growled.

"The *cuckoo*, little man. He never calls this early."

Now John heard it, too. "So what?"

An amused smile twitched around the corners of Robin's mouth. The saying went: *Whoever hears the cuckoo first, must shake his purse, and he'll have enough for the whole year.* Little John grimaced. "All I know is that the cuckoo shoves his egg into other birds' nests. We're more like the magpies."

"We're both, and yet much more." Robin Hood cradled the bulging pouch in his palms. "We caught more yesterday than we did all of last year."

"I wasn't with you then, of course," John mumbled. He scratched his beard.

Robin grabbed his friend's arm and held tight. "But I'm glad you're with me now." After a while, Robin grinned. "That cuckoo. Always calling out his name."

"Probably afraid no one will remember him."

"Well, we needn't worry about that." Robin jumped up, "Move it, little man! We've got to get going. We're the last ones out today."

Pete Smiling was long since on his way to the Great Oak with half the gold and a strong escort. Gilbert Whitehand was waiting below Blidworth with the remaining men, the wagon, and the remaining three thousand pounds.

Everything was carefully planned. As they made their way at a comfortable stride across the woods toward the rendezvous point, John learned the details. "Well, what do you say?" Robin asked. "A good plan?"

"It is. Just hope the plan works out as planned."

"You wait and see. And if it doesn't. I'll think of something new."

The giant nodded. *I can believe that. And yesterday! Selling the goods to the sheriff! I would never have thought of that. I would have taken the whole lot and disappeared.*

Around noon, the merchant's wagon train approached. The sun was burning down through the sky. Two armed men rode in front, two brought up the rear. Despite the heat, the oxen walked easily in their harness. The backs of the mules were empty. Solomon sat next to the driver of the second wagon. From the distance, the yellow of his cap showed brightly.

A shepherd drove his flock onto the road. Dogs circled them. The woolly animals shuffled toward each other, bleated, and finally stopped and milled about.

"Make way!" the merchant's guards yelled.

The bulky shepherd leaned on his stick and looked the other way.

"Damn!" The armed men had no choice. They turned and called

out a warning behind them. “Stop!” One by one, the reins were tightened. The wagon train halted.

Snorting with rage, one of the mercenary guards drove his horse through the herd. “Get your livestock off the road. Or—”

The shepherd wheeled around, his staff swinging. Just before connecting with the man’s head, Little John stopped the swing. The mercenary’s face contorted. “Not again!” He jumped away and tumbled out of the saddle. Startled, the sheep jumped too, bleated, and kicked up their hind legs. John set the blunt end of the weapon on the mercenary’s breastplate. “Hold it right there, lad, and I won’t dent you.”

He peered over at the wagons. The second armed man stepped stiffly and carefully out of his saddle.

“Don’t shoot. Don’t shoot!” the mercenary pleaded with a green-clad archer emerging from the trees. Farther back, the rear guard was already standing on the side of the road with their hands up.

Much easier than yesterday. John grinned and tapped his prisoner. “Stand up. Stand with your friend. And shut up!”

The merchant had climbed down from the coach. “Praise, and thanks. Shalom, Goliath!” He wore a loose, pleated robe today, his feet stuck in laced-up sandals. “I’m so very—”

“Leave it.” John took the old man’s arm. “You’ll have time for that later. I’m hot enough today as it is. Don’t feel like waiting for the sheriff’s soldiers.”

While the real shepherd appeared and drove his flock across the road to the nearby pasture, John quickly led the merchant through the low copse into a clearing. Solomon caught sight of the pouches in the open money box. He bowed slightly to Robin Hood. “You truly kept your word.”

“Come, sit with me in the shade for a moment!”

Robin offered Solomon a sip from the waterskin, then took a drink himself.

"You're not afraid to drink from the same vessel as a Jew?"

Robin laughed. "I should ask you that the other way around, Solomon. You certainly pay more attention to cleanliness than I do." Abruptly his face became serious. "I take it the sheriff does not suspect anything."

"Nobody has had to learn how to shield themselves more than a Jew." The merchant lightly tapped his robe. "And what's more, my letter of protection keeps me from molestation. Too many nobles need me for money: to wage a little war with their neighbor. To cover tax debt. Buy a nice horse. Even royalty are among my clientele. The only thing the parchment doesn't protect from is robbers."

"Good, good." Robin pointed to the money. "Do you want to count it?"

"What for? I trust my eyes and head. However, one thing does make me uncomfortable." He hesitated. "As you know, I'm an old merchant, through and through." He showed his empty palms, raised the right like one side of a scale, and lowered the left. "This is not a good deal. You're giving to me. And I?"

Robin pushed back his hood and shook his reddish mane. "No, you shouldn't get away this easily, in our game."

He offered the villagers' wares to the merchant to buy. Solomon narrowed his eyes. John poked the grass with his staff and hid a grin.

"What did you think?" Robin huffed indignantly. "Am I supposed to carry these bulky goods around to every village? No, distributing money is faster and more inconspicuous. All that grain is enough of a nuisance for us."

Relieved, Solomon agreed. "I'm happy to buy. My wagons are empty. I'll buy, but not for fifty—I'll pay the fair value." He opened a bag and counted out one hundred pounds in gold.

Robin waved Threefinger over. "Get some people, Bill. Take the wagon to the road and load up the merchant! Everything but the grain barrels. Hurry up!"

"You're in no danger today," Solomon assured him. "Thom de Fitz won't give away that he was tricked. To all outward appearances, the deal went as planned. But tomorrow, when enough time has passed, he *will* be looking all over for you."

"All right." Robin frowned. "Then there is time for one more trade." Every year, Solomon and his caravan made a stop at Blidworth on the way to York. "I'll make sure the Sherwood villagers get there in time to offer you their goods." In return, Robin promised to give the caravan safe passage in the future. "But you won't get a written contract. My hand must be enough for you."

"I trust . . ."

". . . my eyes and my head," Little John completed the sentence with a sigh. He wiped the sweat from his brow. *And what if the sheriff doesn't wait until tomorrow? By Dunstan, if I stand around here in the sun much longer, my eyes and head will boil.*

Solomon was enjoying the copse's supply of shade. He bared his head and smoothed down his sparse hair. "I had the dubious good fortune last night to be in close company with the sheriff for a very long time. I got to listen to his wrath. Aside from what you will face from him beginning tomorrow, he has prepared a great blow against you starting today." At daybreak, the sheriff had sent out two messengers. The first to London, asking Prince John to bring troops with him when he visits. The other to Doncaster: Baron Roger was also to have armed men ready. "Next month, he intends to have Sherwood combed from two directions. He wants to drive you out and defeat you in a battle."

Robin Hood laughed. "Sherwood is our fox's hole."

Alarmed, Little John lifted his fighting staff. "I don't like that kind of war. When I think of all the dead—"

"Thank you, Solomon!" Robin cut off his friend. He asked the merchant to bring news with him the next time he passed through. "Especially from King Richard."

"You ask for difficult news to report on, Christian!" Solomon stroked his gray beard. "Jerusalem—it is the city of my people."

"I have nothing to do with the Crusade," Robin replied. "I only want to know when our king will finally be back in England. England needs him. His throne is in danger."

"That's what I fear, too. All London is talking about a conspiracy of the nobility against him. Prince John grows more powerful by the month. As soon as Richard is back, I will send word to you." Solomon shook his head. "This Baron of Doncaster . . ."

Robin and John locked gazes. "What do you know about him?" demanded Robin sharply.

"He is one of the conspirators. Nearly tore my letter of protection in half last summer, this fine gentleman." Solomon had been on his way to York. An impoverished knight from the county had asked the merchant for credit. It was only four hundred pounds, but before Solomon could draw up the contract, Baron Roger had called on him personally. The old man sighed. "He forbade me. His reasoning was brief and impressive. He placed the letter of protection on my head and drew his sword. He threatened to split the parchment in half with one stroke." Solomon put his cap back on. "What could I do?"

"Tell me the name of the knight."

"Sir Richard at the Lea."

The companions glanced at each other. Little John grinned broadly. Robin consoled Solomon. "Don't fret. The man has found another moneylender."

Solomon understood immediately. "That's good." The wrinkles around his eyes deepened. He threatened with a mock-indignant finger, "But this is not to become the norm in our new partnership. Remember, moneylending is meant to be *my* business."

"Agreed." Robin laughed. John also chuckled in amusement. Together they led the old man to the road.

The wagon's load was stowed, the gold safely stored in the second covered cart. The mercenaries of the front and rear guard sat on their steeds again, relieved.

From the wagon seat, Solomon smiled at Robin. "Samson. By outward appearance, the name fits you and your wild mane, to be sure. But you are much more. Samson was only strong, but simple-minded. Still, watch out for your beautiful long hair!" He looked to Little John. "To you, I must apologize."

"For what?"

"I called you Goliath. That was wrong. You are not a Philistine. Shalom!"

The merchant gave the order to drive on. The oxen strained into the harness.

"Who are Philistines, anyway?" asked John uncertainly.

Robin shrugged. "You know, my friend, these traders get around. Who knows where Solomon met them."

Abruptly, Robin's tone became sharp. "Now to you. I don't want strangers to know our plans, remember that!"

John gulped. *What is he talking about? Never told anyone anything.* Fiercely, the giant thumped his staff on the ground.

Robin saw the offended expression. "Don't be silly, John! I didn't mean it that way. Earlier, I didn't want us to talk about fighting the troops in front of the merchant. If he doesn't know about our plans, nobody can beat anything out of him. It's better for the old man, and for us too."

John was silent. After a while he said, "That's sensible."

"Yes, and you are sensible too, my friend." Robin nodded. "No open battle. That's not our game." He clapped his hands together. "We're getting out of Sherwood for the year. We've got plenty of loot. We smacked the lord sheriff in the face. What more do we need?"

In an instant, John was ready. "And when we're gone, he can look for us until the worms crawl out of his nose." Despite the new rush, there was one thing the giant wanted to clarify: "I just got upset because I thought you were being . . . a bit unfair . . ."

"That's right," Robin grumbled to match his friend's tone, rolling his eyes. John laughed at the imitation. He would never be able to stay mad at Robin for long.

New orders were put forth. Vincent and Threefinger were to take the wagon with the grain, as fast as possible, down the side road to Blidworth. "Tell the elder I'll give him the wagon to replace his cattle cart. But the grain will be collected. It belongs to the villages the sheriff robbed."

Threefinger slapped the leather reins and Vincent cracked the whip.

"Don't get caught!" Robin shouted after them. "We'll meet tomorrow at the coal maker's."

Toward evening, fires flickered around the Great Oak. Herbghost was sweating and grumbling. "I never know anything ahead of time!" He rushed back and forth. He turned roasts on three skewers side by side.

"I'll tear your head off if the meat gets burnt!" John had threatened him.

While Robin Hood and Smiling discussed how to bring the captured money to Barnsdale without too much risk, the giant organized a quick retreat from the summer encampment. The seized weapons, chain mail, shields, and boots had already been rubbed with grease against moisture and safely stowed in the storage caves. The men had wrapped the precious unstrung bow wood and arrows in tunics, robes, and embroidered cloaks, piled them at the bottom of the cart's bed, and covered them with old, torn garments. Piled on top was a mountain of dented, greasy pots, jars, mugs, and ladles. As poor tinkers and scrap dealers, Herbghost and Smiling were to make the perilous journey up north first thing in the morning. "No man-at-arms is going to get his gloves dirty on that filthy lot."

John gave quick instructions. "The horse will still stay in the dugout overnight." He designated four men—"You push"—and put on the harness himself. With his might at the front, they rolled the heavily loaded wagon through the forest. Close to the main road, John had them camouflage the cart with bushes and branches until was he satisfied.

The wild boar back at camp tasted good, the brown crust crackling between his teeth. "Good job!" John winked at the cook as he wiped his beard.

"Please and thank you stuff your bellies and hurry and be done!" Herbghost gasped for air. Suddenly the skewers fell from his hands. "Damn it!"

John jumped up and took hold of the cook's shoulders. "Hey, William. What's wrong?"

The old man muttered, "They're looking for us, aren't they? And I'm meant to ride up to a road blockade disguised as a rag collector."

"It'll be all right, William. You'll have Smiling with you."

Herbghost shook off the big hands. "That one?" he scoffed, gathering up the skewers and continuing to rant, "I can't stand that perpetual grin!"

"That's the spirit!" John smirked. He walked over to the two men kneeling at the big fire. "How far along are you? Do you want me to start setting up the escort?"

"Hush hush, don't interrupt me!" Robin counted out the remaining coins to Pete, who placed the last stack next to the others on a spread-out cloak. All of the sheriff's money boxes had been emptied, the shimmering wealth divided precisely.

Smiling bared his teeth. "Three thousand pounds in five hundred beautiful gold pieces. That would be more than enough for my entire lifetime."

"Don't stumble now, Pete." Robin smiled softly. "So, one last time. Count along with me. You, too, John. There are thirty of us. There are twenty-five stacks here." On his fingers, he counted off. "We'll meet Vincent and Bill at the charcoal maker's first. Herbghost and Smiling mustn't be carrying any coins. And I'll send Much to the villages tomorrow. Good. We're ready to go, little man. Gather our people!"

A little later, all the band of men stood before Robin Hood. One by one, they took off their green garb, tied twenty gold pieces tightly wrapped in a linen cloth around their bare bellies, and slipped their garments back on. It was Much's turn. Robin waved the boy aside. "Not you."

"Why? I'm just as—"

"Leave it be, son!" John placated him. "Be glad you don't have so much hanging off your body."

Disappointed, Much squatted down on the grass. After Robin Hood and John had also donned the heavy bandages, the outlaw had his army line up under the Great Oak. Commendations were given for bravery, praise for courage, acknowledgments for obedience.

"Starting tomorrow, they will hunt us, like bloodhounds. But you are good men. The best! I have confidence in each of you. Touch those bundles at your belly, and you'll know I do. March out as soon as you're awake! But go in twos. One helps the other. No meeting place on the way. Each is responsible to me for the coins, and, by the Blessed Virgin, as I know you, you will bring me our gold bundles home whole."

Their eyes lit up. Yes, they were ready!

Only Much leaned listlessly against the trunk of the Great Oak. As Robin and John approached him, he turned away.

"Hey, lad!"

"You don't need me anymore."

"Oh, nice." Robin folded his arms. "Now that I can't get this done without him, he's grumbling like a child."

"I'm not a—"

"Then listen!" Robin interrupted him sharply. "You run tomorrow to the villages the sheriff raided in the spring. Go to the elders. Just tell them: Robin Hood has taken care of you! What you need to survive will be at Blidworth and with the charcoal burner Gabriel."

It was an important task! Much carefully memorized the names of the villages. Robin laid out the route, first in the south of Sherwood, then village by village farther to the north.

"I can't do that in one day."

"Pfft!" Robin allowed no excuses. "That's all the time you've got. We'll wait for you at the charcoal burner's. But only until tomorrow night." With that, he turned away, calling over his shoulder for Little John.

The giant murmured, "Don't get caught, boy! You can do it. Show him you really are the fastest of us all!"

Much smiled tightly. "I'll prove it to you all."

In long strides, John caught up with Robin. "Sending him alone? It's madness. And without a sword? He's only got his staff. I'd better go with the boy."

Robin was silent.

"What if he really can't make it in time?"

Robin gazed frankly at his lieutenant. "Well, then, we wait for him." John shook his head, uncomprehendingly.

"Oh, my friend." Robin looped his arm through John's. "I never ask for anything I wouldn't do myself, that's why the men follow me. But tomorrow, that will be different, for Much. He'll have to do something neither you nor I can manage. And so the poor villagers will have enough grain and money to last until next summer. That is more important than anything else to me. But—" Robin shrugged "—they should know who they have to thank for it. Through our messenger! Yes, I know, Much is risking his life. That's exactly why I goaded him, so that—you shall see—he'll run tomorrow like never before."

John scratched the scar in his beard. "The cuckoo."

"What's that?"

"The cuckoo sings out his own name." John stared intently into the fire. "We don't need that. Well. Much will do it for us."

Robin was silent. The corners of his mouth twitched. Finally, he tapped his fist against his friend's chest. "You certainly are a fast learner, little man."

A cart was settled in front of the charcoal burner's cottage, its bed loaded with baskets, filled to the brim with chunks of blue-black coal.

For well over an hour, John and Robin Hood had been watching the small clearing. They clenched their fists in impotent rage. Vincent and Threefinger kneeled not far from the oxcart. Two woodsmen stood over them, dealing blows, kicks, With unconcerned expressions, they carried out the ranger's orders.

"Who are you?" the ranger in the black leather jerkin barked. His head went back and forth. During the interrogation, he held the gaunt charcoal burner in check with a bow primed to shoot. Gabriel had no choice but to watch the beating. His soot-blackened face shone with sweat. He could not help, was not allowed even to move. His little sons were with him. Fearfully they hid behind their father's legs.

"Who are you?" The same question for an hour.

"Beggars. Just beggars," Vincent whimpered. Blood ran from his mouth, dripping onto his traveling cloak. Threefinger raised his hands protectively. His eyes were bruised and swollen. Again and again, the fist hit his temples, his cheekbones.

Gabriel shouted, “Stop it! Damn it. Stop it!”

“Shut up! Or you’ll get a taste of it, too.” And again: punches, kicks. “Who are you?”

In their hiding place, John hissed, “Those bastards.”

“Quiet. Stay calm,” Robin whispered.

John groaned. “Three arrows would do it.” But today, they carried no bows. To avoid attracting attention on the road, they had dispensed with the more obvious weapons. He began to rise up. “Come on! We’ll sneak up on them from behind.”

Robin yanked his friend back. “Don’t be an idiot!” He pressed his mouth to the giant’s ear to whisper. “We can’t risk the children! Besides, if that forester doesn’t get back to Worksop with the coal cart, Gabriel’s done for.”

“And our people?”

“Wait and see. They’ll tough it out.” Robin drew his hunting dagger, weighed the blade in his hand. “If I need to, I’ll take him down. But not unless it gets really bad.”

In the clearing, the ranger with the silver badge on his cap reveled in his power. “All right. Beggars you are. From what village?”

“No village,” Threefinger groaned. “From Nottingham . . .”

A nod to the woodsmen. Satisfied, the ranger watched Bill’s head snap back and forth at the blows. “You lie.”

Despite the danger, Gabriel took the chance—in two steps, he was on top of the ranger. He snatched the arrow from its string, gripped it like a dagger, and put the point hard against the man’s neck. Over his shoulder, he shouted to his children, “Run! Run!” Only when they had disappeared into the house did he relax the pressure of arrowhead against throat. “By Swithin! Leave them alone already! I *asked* them to come here.”

The ranger carefully pushed the shaft aside. Slowly, he took a step back.

Gabriel allowed it but held the arrow ready to thrust. "I wanted these people to do some work for me."

"Now, all of a sudden, you remember?"

Coldly, the charcoal burner looked him in the face. "Remember what? I put the word out everywhere that I need servants. It's no surprise strangers would show up."

"But those two?" The forester sneered. "They come sneaking in here. First, you don't know them. And now . . ."

"Think what you will," growled Gabriel. "Go ahead and beat them to death. But I swear to you, tomorrow I'll be in Worksop to report on it. And then you'll be rid of that nice silver badge on your cap. Our master has to deliver coal for the castle. How pleased do you think he'll be when I have to shut down one of the burn piles? Because you killed my servants?"

The forester gasped. "You wouldn't dare!"

With the arrow in his fist, Gabriel crossed his arms in front of his chest. "One thing is certain: Our lord needs me more than he needs you."

Seething with rage, the ranger shouldered his bow. "You false cur. I know that well enough. But you watch yourself! One day . . ." He turned away, called off his woodsmen, and went over to the coal cart. "I know there's something fishy here," he hissed. "And next time I pass, those scoundrels had better be working at the pile."

The gaunt charcoal burner shrugged. "Who knows? The work is hard. No farmhand lasts long with me."

The woodsmen reached for the bullock's muzzle strap. Without looking back, the forester followed the coal wagon.

Gabriel waited until the groaning of the wheels could no longer be heard. He turned around. The beaten men were huddled on the ground, breathing heavily.

"Thanks," Vincent muttered, spitting out blood.

Threefinger felt at his welts. "They would have killed us outright."

"You just wait—I can still make that happen!" growled the charcoal burner, grabbing them both by the collar and shaking them. "Bastards! You miserable bastards! Have you no eyes in your head? I'm standing here with this blackcap, and you lot saunter out of the forest, merry as can be? Why didn't you wait?"

"We didn't think," Vincent stammered.

"Stop!" pleaded Threefinger. "Yeah, it was stupid. Please stop!"

But Gabriel jerked them back and forth, pushing them against each other. "And my children? You didn't think about them either, did you. You don't care about my family, do you? I should give you—"

A harsh, clear voice rang out. "Stop it!"

Gabriel let go of his victims. He wheeled around. Robin Hood and Little John grinned at him.

"You, too," the charcoal burner snarled angrily. "Where did you come from?"

"From there." John pointed with his staff to the bushes at the edge of the clearing. "Nothing would have happened to your children."

Robin reassured the man: "You're right, Gabriel. But let it go!"

Indignant shouting came from the cottage. In the entrance, the two boys twisted out of their mother's grasp, tore themselves away, and rushed toward their father. Gabriel stroked their shocks of hair. Anger and worry dissolved. "Just ask me how you managed all that in Blidworth. Against the iron men." The charcoal burner pointed at Vincent and Threefinger. "With addle-pates like that, I wouldn't try to steal a sheep from a pasture."

Robin looked at him. "So, you know about that?"

"I know *all* about it. Everyone in Sherwood knows." He held out his hand to the outlaw. "I'm sorry. When the raids started in the spring, I thought . . ."

Laughing, Robin took the offered hand and held it. "The sheriff almost succeeded. But I had my addle-pates with me."

Gabriel sent the injured men into the house. "Let my mother take care of you. You'll be all right with a little spit weed."

Meanwhile, the two boys danced around the giant. They tugged at his cloak, made faces. John gave them a low growl. The children whooped and led their bear around in circles.

Concerned, Gabriel rubbed his chin. "You can't stay here, Robin. If the ranger comes back with armed men, it'll be bad."

"But we must. Our messenger is still missing." Quickly Robin explained why Much was on his way to the villages.

The charcoal burner listened in silence. When Robin Hood entrusted him with the coin purse containing a hundred pounds in gold coins, he said haltingly, "I've never seen anyone like you."

"But that's only because you don't have a mirror." Robin laughed.

The outlaws were allowed to stay. Not at the charcoal burner's house, but close by. Gabriel had cleared out the second charcoal kiln for them to tuck themselves around. "No one will look for you there. And the crumb coal is still warm." He promised to bring ale, bread, and ham later.

The charcoal burner's mother also came outside with Vincent and Threefinger. She stopped in front of Robin Hood. "Put your hood back," she demanded sternly. "Bend down."

Surprised, he obeyed. The old woman closed her eyes. "Mary's milk and Christ's blood . . ." Her voice sank into a murmur, rose again. ". . . And so no arrow shall hit you, no enemy shall hurt you." With the tip of her thumb, she stroked a cross on his forehead. "And so that nothing of the curse remains." She turned and limped back into the cottage.

Robin straightened up again. Only after a while did he come

back to himself and his smile disappear. "Come!" he snapped at the two companions. "Just wait until we get to the pile. I still have a few words to say to you."

Meanwhile, John had lifted both children onto his shoulders. They tugged at his hair. "Giddy-up!" they yelled. Their horse whinnied and ran.

Robin whistled. The giant waved and trotted toward the charcoal burner's house. At the entrance, he bent his knees to Gabriel's wife and let his little riders dismount. "Do you got any of your own?" she asked.

"What?"

"Do you got any little'uns?"

Little John rubbed the scar in his beard. "Yes. A girl," he said, drawing out his words, thinking.

"Oh, that's why." The charcoal burner's wife herded her sons into the house before her.

No, he wasn't going to the kiln. Not yet.

"You go ahead," he told Robin. "I'll wait over in the bushes. When Much comes, I'll show him the way."

Evening settled over the Sherwood. Gabriel had left the cottage with a pannier on his back and had walked away in the direction of the kiln. For a while longer, John heard the boys' laughter from his hiding place, then they fell silent.

John listened intently. When a twig cracked, leaves rustled, it was only the animals. He looked up at the full moon. *It won't be completely dark,* he thought. *That is good.*

A strange sound. It came closer. Footsteps. John heard a wheezing breath. Calmly he waited. A figure stepped out of the woods, lumbered into the front yard in the bright moonlight, stopped, swaying. Cautiously, Little John peeled himself out of the darkness. "Hey, lad," he murmured.

Immediately Much straightened, holding his staff defensively.

"Hey, son," John called softly. "Easy. It's me." He strode into the light.

"I . . . I showed you." The boy staggered toward the giant man. John caught him as he stumbled.

"Everybody . . . knows . . ." gasped Much, coughing.

"That's right, son. That's right." John lifted the boy and put him over his shoulder.

When he reached the kiln with his burden, Robin Hood was the first to jump up from the fire. "Thank the Blessed Virgin!" He reached out to help.

"Don't," Much gasped. "I . . . I want to stand."

Gently, John let the exhausted lad slide down from his back. He supported him until Much could hold himself up with his staff by himself.

"So?" Robin asked.

"Been to every village," Much reported. "Everyone knows . . ." He raised his voice: "Grain is in Blidworth. Money is with the charcoal burner. But be careful. You must . . ." His legs buckled.

Robin Hood caught the boy and laid him, unconscious, close to the fire, on his back.

"Damn it," the charcoal burner groaned as he got a good look. The others bent over Much as well. There were bloodied scabs on his face, neck, arms, and legs. Under his torn tunic, blackish crusted wounds covered his body.

Robin motioned to John, shoving the others aside. They examined Much all over. After a while, John sighed with relief. "Nothing bad. It's really just scrapes and scratches."

"What was it? A bear?"

"A bear would puncture deeper into the flesh. Looks like someone had at him with . . . needles."

It seemed the boy would be unconscious for the night. Gabriel promised to bring an herbal brew before they left the next day. One thing still worried John and Robin: Much's eyelids were thickly stuck together. Were his eyes damaged?

Vincent handed over his pitcher. "With the ale, you can—"

"Sit down, you addle-pate." Very carefully, Robin softened the crusted-over lids with spit and rubbed them clear. "Thank the Virgin!" Blood had only run down from a forehead wound.

Suddenly Much opened his eyes. "I stabbed him to death." He smiled.

"Who?" Robin demanded sharply. "Speak up!"

In a tired voice, the boy reported, "Between the lakes. I'd just finished at Carburton. My last village."

John nodded to Robin. "That's where the river narrows for a good two miles. That's the only place you can get across."

At the ford, armed riders from the lord sheriff had spotted the lad. When they called to him, he had not stopped. The patrol set one of their dogs after him. "At first, I thought I could make it. But the dog was faster than me." The memory lifted Much above the fatigue. "There was brush. All the way down the slope. Blackberries. I ran, jumped and pushed off with my staff, and landed in the middle of it. The dog jumped, too. He got stuck in the thorns right in front of my face. He kept barking, giving away where I was. I stuck the knife in his neck. That shut him up."

By the time Much heard the soldiers shouting and searching close by, he had already cut his way farther down the thorny slope. "That took time to get through. Else I would have been here sooner."

"You're a good man," Robin said gravely. "Nobody but you could have done it."

"Now I'm tired." He closed his eyes. The proud smile remained even after Much had fallen asleep.

"If it gets cold, he'll stiffen up and hardly be able to move tomorrow." While John wrapped the exhausted youth in his coat, Gabriel smoothed out a place on the warm charcoal bed. Together they covered Much up to the neck with the still-warm chunks of coal.

"This is going to be some journey back." Robin grinned. "Two bruised and battered, one scratched to bits."

"That's right," John agreed grimly. "Lucky us."

XV

The latest dispatch from the Crusade: *Jerusalem is not conquered! And yet, against the will of Richard the Lionheart, the army commanders have elected the ambitious Conrad of Montferrat as king of the Holy City. The news is brought to Conrad in Tyros. A few days later, on the evening of April 28, 1192, Conrad is stabbed to death by two hired assassins. Murder! Who gave the order? Was it Richard the Lionheart? Suspicion is stirred up by his opponents in Palestine and in Europe.*

YORKSHIRE. WINTER CAMP AT BARNSDALE.

What a summer! Grain. Peas and beans. Fruit! The farmers had reaped bountiful harvests. At the end of September, there were already more than enough winter provisions stored in the barns and cellars of Barnsdale Top.

What a summer! Without any losses, the band of outlaws had brought the lord sheriff's gold safely to their camp. Never had the raids in Sherwood been so profitable. In no previous year had the hoard buried under Robin's hut been so full.

There was enough money, to be used for the care of the severely wounded. For at Kirklees Abbey, Sister Matilda charged dearly for her treatments and her silence.

The early return from the Sherwood gave them extra time. Roofs were repaired down in the main camp, the bed sacks stuffed with fresh hay and straw. Robin had a new, spacious hut built right next to his own quarters. The men speculated, asked outright. He shrugged. "Whoever figures out what it's for shall have a gold piece." Smirking, he enjoyed the guessing games. Only Little John was given the secret: "For the monk. Remember? I want a priest just for us." He lifted his chin. "We have plenty of time to prepare this year. First, let's get his hut ready. And then we'll find one. Well, what do you say?"

John had barely been paying attention. Scowling, he grumbled, "That's all right."

"Hey?" Robin tapped his fist against John's broad chest. "Did you swallow a toad?"

"I'm fine," the giant assured him and stomped off. Shaking his head, Robin watched him go.

Everyone seemed happy—the peasants in the village, the men in camp. Only John was not. His wandering path led him over to Much's hut. Much was not there. "By Dunstan!" Though John had assigned him to the night watch, the boy would not rest. The scar in his braided beard flushed red. *That lout! All right, he can do what he wants on his rest time. But he should leave the girl alone!*

It had been going on for weeks. In the beginning, John had thought nothing of it. Much had come back from Sherwood so scratched up. Anyone would have wanted to take care of him. Why not Marian, too? But when the wounds had long since healed, and the two were still crouched together, a gnawing feeling stirred in John. He had watched them out of sheer concern. Very quickly, it had become clear to him why the young fellow had jostled for day duty up at the village, of all places. And every time the giant checked the guard posts, he found his Marian with Much.

Angrily, he had confronted Beth. "I don't want this."

"Leave the princess be!" the seamstress scolded. "She thinks it's nothing."

"But the boy—"

"Don't be a giant wet nurse! Our princess will soon be thirteen winters old. You can't tie her up forever."

Not a word had John said to Marian so far. But now his patience was at an end! For the third times this week Much had foregone sleep and disappeared from camp.

John sat down in the meadow under the big linden tree. It was a warm September afternoon. He leaned his back against the trunk, half closing his eyelids. Anyone passing by would have believed that he was having a comfortable nap. The giant was waiting.

Marian's bright voice! Chattering loudly and laughing, the boy and girl left the tunnel through the rocks. John rose to his feet. Exuberantly, Marian ran toward him. She showed him a large trout. "Look, I'm taking this to Beth," she exclaimed. "Much caught it—*by hand*."

"I learned that from my father," the boy said proudly.

John looked at Marian. Her frock was completely soaked, sticking to her body. Her small chest, her hips, and her bottom stood out clearly under the fabric.

John swallowed to calm himself. "Look at you."

"Well, I tried catch one too." Unconcerned, Marian laughed. "It's not that easy. I fell in the water, and the fish was gone."

"So, that's all what happened," John growled.

The two seemed oblivious to his irritation. Much tapped the girl on the shoulder. "There's still time before the watch. I'll take you up to the village."

"You stay where you are!" ordered John.

"But . . . but I . . ." Much began.

"Much Miller's-son! Let it be, or else . . ." the giant threatened. "Get out of here!"

Immediately the boy obeyed. Without a word, he ran over to his hut.

"Why did you do that?" Marian demanded indignantly. "What did he ever do to you?"

"Not here," John snarled. "Come along now, child! I'll take you to Beth."

Silently John climbed up the footpath behind the girl. On the way through the woods, he cleared his throat long and awkwardly, finally saying, "I don't want this, little one." Puzzled, Marian looked up at him.

"Well. The boy's fine." John searched for words. "You're still young, though. I mean, too young for this."

"I don't understand." Marian brushed back her half-dried curls.

"What I mean is, there are only men around, in the camp, and . . ."

"What's that got to do with me?"

"Much is a man, too, that's what I meant to say."

Marian stopped and stood in his way. Her blue eyes darkened, full of anger. "I don't want anything from Much! I feel sorry for him. About his parents. Because I know how he feels."

"Then why, by Dunstan, are you going with him into the water, with your dress all . . . wet?"

She held the trout up to his face. "Because we were catching fish. What do you think of me?"

"It's all right, little girl. It's all right," John relented. "Believe me, I only want what's best for you."

Marian wasn't listening anymore. She shoved the fish into his hands, "Maybe I don't want the same things anymore!" She ran away from him. But just as suddenly, she stopped and came back. "Don't be angry! Please. I was just angry. Because I don't like men at all. Except for you. Because you're the best. Even Beth agrees."

John smiled. They walked side by side in silence. After a while, he mused aloud, "I'll manage something. I'd like you to wear fine clothes someday. And live in a nice house. You know, my lamb, much nicer than our huts here."

"I hope that doesn't happen," Marian blurted out. Quickly she crossed her fingers behind her back. "Yes, that would be nice." She winked at him. "And later, I'll find myself a husband. But only if I feel like it."

The leaves of the linden tree turned yellow. The outlaws had long since exchanged their green summer garb for the brown-black winter garments again. On the last Monday in October, Robin summoned his lieutenants and the two cooks to his hut. "The day after tomorrow, midweek, the knight's year ends. And by his guarantor, the Blessed Virgin, Richard at the Lea will keep his word."

They were to move up to the other camp that same day. "Maybe he'll come sooner, maybe a little later," Robin allowed. Herbghost and Storyteller were instructed to prepare a delicious meal for each evening of that week.

Little John patted his stomach. "If he doesn't come until Saturday, that would be fine with me."

No stranger found his way to the hideout on his own—it was too well camouflaged. And neither could Richard at the Lea. So, one of the men was put on the lookout for him along the main road. "You take turns," Robin ordered. "John, it's your turn today. Take Much and Threefinger with you. Wait above the bridge in the same spot as last year. But please, do kindly welcome the knight. Don't ambush him."

"It's fine," John replied. "He'll be glad to see his squire again."

Smiling offered to get the green and yellow-striped cloak for John. "So he won't mistake you for someone else."

"Don't even move!" the giant threatened, struggling to stay serious. "Or there'll be no more grinning."

That evening they returned without the knight. "Such a shame," John said with mock regret. "We'll just have to eat alone, then."

Gilbert Whitehand also waited in vain above the River Went.

No one was angry with the knight. On the contrary. "Such a shame," remarked John.

Late Wednesday afternoon, the guard post's horn sounded: Long. Short. Short. Each note in the signal stayed at the same pitch. No danger, but: Strangers had arrived!

"Toad will bring him." Robin laughed. "Nice. Our debtor is punctual to the day."

But when the men reached camp, Robin's expression darkened. Yes, Tom was bringing a guest. But the guest was sitting on a mule, wearing a plain black robe. His eyes were blindfolded.

"Our knight seems to have joined a monastery." Smiling bared his teeth.

Whitehand grinned, "And ate all the other monks."

John didn't join in the laughter. He stared at the monk. Where had he seen him before? *I know that holy man from somewhere.*

Robin confronted Tom. "Hey, toad head, are you missing more up there besides hair?" He pointed a thumb at the prisoner. "That's not him."

"I know. But I just couldn't resist. All day we were staring south and waiting. Nothing. Then I turn around, and this one's coming up the road. I would have let him ride on, only he had two guards with him. So, I thought . . ." Tom snapped his fist shut ". . . where there are guards, there's bound to be something to guard. We tied the two iron men together and left them right by the road."

John took another look at the bulging neck, the large, round head "By Dunstan!" He pulled Robin aside. "I know that bastard," he murmured. "He's the cellar master at St. Mary's Abbey in York. He was there last year when our knight paid back the money. I could gladly still wring his neck today."

"Don't say anything for now!" Robin rubbed his hands together. "Can't wait to see what kind of game this is going to be." He stood, stance wide, hands on hips, beside his lieutenants. "Help our guest off the mule, and take off his blindfold!"

When the cellar master was freed, Robin smiled obligingly. "Forgive the unkindness, father. My men can be a bit rough. It was supposed to be an invitation."

"Invitation?"

"Is that not what they told you? How unfortunate. Very well. Let me introduce myself: You are the guests of Robin Hood."

"Murderer," groaned the monk. "You bandit. Vile thief . . ." As he continued to sputter and curse, his eyes wandered back and forth, searching for an escape route. "You spawn of hell. You and your henchmen, you should be—"

"Enough flattery," Robin interrupted him coolly. "As I'm sure you've concluded, there is no escape. But don't worry, it won't cost you your life today. And so, the truth, if you please: Who are you?"

"I am . . ." The cellar master covered his eyes. When he lowered his hand, his expression had changed: so pitiful! From one breath to another, the voice became plaintive. "I am an unworthy servant of the Church. A sinner. With a stain of shame. I come from Fountains Abbey, far up north. They call me Friar Tuck . . ." he swallowed, and whispered in shame ". . . the drunkard."

Whitehand marveled, "We've heard of him." He poked Robin in the side. "Back when we were transporting wine . . ."

"Hush!" Robin hissed. Frowning, he asked their guest, "A drunk? Why is a drunk traveling through our beautiful countryside with two armed men?"

"Because . . . because . . ." The cellar master pursed his lips, sorrowfully lowering his gaze. "First, Father Abbot banished me from the dormitory of my brethren. To the remotest corner of the monastery grounds! There I had to live alone in a hut. But despite all my prayers, wine and ale rule me like Furies." He uttered a long sigh. "The two guards were escorting me to London. There I must answer for my wicked vice before the superiors of my order. A harsh errand." He wrung his hands. "Therefore, I ask: Let me move on!"

John was speechless. *That plumped up, deceitful priest. If I didn't know better, I'd believe him.* Warningly, he gave Robin a sign. Robin winked quickly and turned back to the cellar master.

"Poor Friar Tuck. We don't want to keep you from your penitential pilgrimage. But be my guest and dine with me. Enjoy some peace of mind. Who knows what torment awaits you ahead."

They took their seats on wooden benches in front of the horse stable. Robin clapped his hands. When Storyteller appeared at the door of the kitchen shed, he ordered, "Serve us two fried chicken legs!"

John sighed with relief. The good food would have been wasted on this liar.

The cellar master hastily refused a sip of Malvasia.

"A brave decision," Robin said with a serious face. "Nice."

"I am . . ." The monk searched for an explanation. "I am striving to conquer the devil within me."

Robin pointed to the man's half-gnawed chicken bone. "After this excellent roast, I ask you, venerable father: Pay me for the hospitality shown. Then you may move on."

"How?" The monk was aghast. "I-I don't carry anything with me. But Heaven . . ."

"Enough!" Robin barked at him. "I hate being lied to. You want to be Friar Tuck? From Fountains Abbey? Well, we'll see." He signaled John.

The giant stomped toward the cellar master and wordlessly plucked the chicken bone from the friar's fingers. "Put your hand on the middle of that beautiful silver plate!"

Reluctantly, the monk obeyed.

"Don't you remember me anymore?"

The monk shook his head.

"Just as well." John drew his dagger and scraped the blade across the back of the cellar master's hand. "But I know who you are. Like to play with knives, eh? A year ago, you were torturing that little prior at your monastery. You know, the one with the hump."

The monk's jaw dropped. "You were with . . . you're the squire."

Sneering, John nodded. "Thought you wouldn't remember me, since I'm not wearing my nice colorful cloak today." And very casually, he pressed the sharp edge into the man's skin.

"By all the saints! Wait!" Beads of sweat sprang to the monk's forehead. "I am not Friar Tuck. I'm the cellar master from St. Mary's Monastery in York. Yes, I lied out of fear. Everyone here can understand that, can't they? Can't you?" He glanced around the group. "Right?" None of the men so much as blinked.

"Then at least tell us the truth now." Robin's voice was dangerously soft. "How much money do you have on you?"

"Not much to speak of. Twenty marks in silver. That's all."

"Not worth mentioning? A farmhand toils all year in your monastery's fields for far less. And all so you can stuff your belly." Robin signaled again. Smiling and Whitehand walked over to the mule.

"Not there," the cellar master blurted out. "Not in the baskets." He drew a pouch of money from his robes. "I carry all my coins—" Before he had finished speaking, the bulging leather sack was already in the giant's hand.

Again Robin signaled.

"Don't . . ." the monk pleaded.

"Shut up," John growled.

To the right and left of the mule hung tightly woven travel baskets. Smiling and Toad dug their hands into them. Provisions. Laced sandals, a crucifix. Suddenly Smiling bared his teeth. Whitehand laughed. They each lifted a gold bar from the depths of the basket and held them up. "And there are many more," Smiling announced.

"Again, you lied to me," Robin said coldly. "Now that chicken bone will cost you everything you carry."

The cellar master blanched. "Not the gold. That's my monastery's annual tax debt. Eight hundred pounds. I must take it to London."

Only when he stood naked, save for his much too short under-tunic, before the outlaws, did any color return to his round face. Red with anger, the cellar master shouted, "Satan shall take you. And, Robin Hood, when you are finally in chains, I will be there. I will cut out your tongue, your nethers, cut off your hands . . ."

John grabbed at the monk's face, squeezing his lips between his fingers, twisting them. "One more word, and I'll rip them off!" He held him like that until Toad put the blindfold back on the man.

After a little over an hour, Tom was back. He had sent the cellar master away toward the main road with a rough blow on the mule's hindquarters.

In good spirits, Robin and his men sat down at the now richly laid table. Fragrant mushroom soup. Roast wild boar. Sweetbreads.

"A toast, friends!" Robin raised his silver goblet. "No woman is kinder than our Blessed Virgin." At the inquisitive faces of his companions, he patiently explained to his disciples, "A year ago today, she stood surety for my four hundred pounds. So? The debtor didn't return. But in exchange, she sent us the cellar master of her monastery and made him pay me back double." Laughter rose. Enthusiastically, the men drank to the health of the generous Blessed Virgin.

John set down his goblet. "At that interest, our friend Solomon would even agree to do business with her."

Later, Robin leaned, maudlin, toward the giant. "One more thing, friend, but keep it to yourself!" John nodded. Quietly, Robin continued, "That cellarer, he lied, but that was a good thing. No, not not telling about the gold. He gave me an idea."

Uncomprehending, John shook his head.

"Friar Tuck. I hadn't thought about it. But he could be our priest. Well, what do you say?"

John struggled to hold in his thoughts. *What do we need a friar for? But if Robin wants something, then . . . ah, never mind. Just the one can't hurt.* "I suppose." But, seriously concerned, he added, "Only before we can—before that, we need to get some barrels of drink here. Otherwise, there's no point to even ask Friar Tuck." He turned his empty goblet upside down. "Otherwise, there won't be enough wine. You understand?"

Around about noon the next day, Pete Smiling led the knight's steed across the clearing to the base. Sir Richard at the Lea sat upright in the saddle. His gray hair curled over the fur collar of his coat.

"We'll be right there, sir!" called Smiling to him. "Please. You may remove your blindfold now."

The knight untied the cloth. In front of the huts, Robin Hood and his men stood ready to receive him. Sir Richard turned to look behind him. The white stallion had followed the black horse without saddle or bridle. Behind that, the two outlaws pulled three heavily laden packhorses. Sir Richard looked ahead again.

He did not return Robin's smile. Still in the saddle, he pounded his fist accusingly against his own chest. "He who is late has robbed the waiting man of a piece of his liberty, no matter what good reasons he gives. But if a debtor is late, there is no excuse. Nevertheless, I first had to settle a dispute in one of my villages. Therefore, I beg your indulgence."

Before Robin Hood could answer, John patted his stomach. "Don't mention it."

The men laughed, and Robin joined in. "Yes, enough of the formalities. Sir Richard. I greet you as a friend. The one-day delay has gained us all much. In more than one way." He graciously helped his guest out of the saddle.

Herbghost came storming out of the kitchen. "That's rudeness for you," he grumbled, planting his hands on his hips in front of Sir Richard. "Too early! You are far too early. Do you think we started cooking at sunrise? Storyteller and I, we're not your personal chefs after all." He stuck his index finger right under his guest's nose. "Dinner won't be until tonight." With that, he turned and disappeared back into the kitchen.

The knight stroked his elegantly trimmed beard. "A strict regimen."

"Let's leave those old men to it." Robin shrugged. "It'll taste all the better for the wait."

Half sighing, half smiling, Sir Richard said, "Apparently conditions here are similar to mine at Fenwick Castle. Good cooks are rare. Therefore, my family and I live by the principle, never bite the hand that holds the wooden spoon."

"Nice. Although a little bite now and then wouldn't hurt either of us." They shared relaxed laughter. Little John kept on laughing until Robin poked him in the side. "Quiet, now! Or our guest will think you have nothing else but food on your mind."

There was plenty of time until evening. Robin called for drinks. "Wait," the knight asked, pointing to the white stallion. The white horse pranced back and forth in front of the paddock gate. "First, I want to give you back the most precious item."

Robin's eyes glittered. "He knows he's back home." He stepped up to the stallion, greeted him with gentle strokes over his nostrils, and let him out to pasture.

The wine jug was passed around. Sir Richard reported a good year, a rich harvest. Above all, he had news from Palestine. "Lionheart wants to be back in England as early as next year. And with him, I hope my Edward will return."

Together they drank to the much-longed-for return of their king.

The knight touched John's arm. "Be once more my faithful squire! Please, bring me the two saddle chests!"

"Don't you dare give orders to my men!" Robin interjected.

Startled, Sir Richard turned to him. The rest of the men frowned uncomprehendingly. For a moment, Robin held everyone's gaze, then the corners of his mouth twitched. "Don't bother with it, Sir Richard."

"I just want to pay back the four hundred pounds."

"Done. The debt has been repaid."

"But you can't refuse..."

"Forgive me, Sir Richard. But this is my game. Remember? I make the rules." Sternly, Robin now looked at Little John, dropping his voice low. "Bring me four hundred pounds." With his eyes, he indicated the hut next to the stable.

This time John immediately saw through his friend's plan. He obeyed and returned to set one gold pouch next to the other in front of the knight.

Sir Richard pressed his lips together. He stared at the wealth, stared at Robin, at the others, and again at the gold. Finally, he stiffened his back. "I came too late. Good, I deserve this humiliation. But I will, by—"

"Enough!" Robin swiped a hand through the air. "Enough, Sir Richard. I forgot how hard you find playing games." He sat down opposite the gaunt man. Robin told his guest of the Virgin's generosity, took Richard's hands in his. "It is straightforward: I have my four hundred pounds. You brought me four hundred, and I don't want it because I already have *my* four hundred. Follow me?" Seeing the knight's raised brows, he didn't even wait for the answer. "There are these four hundred pounds here now, and I have too much. I don't want these either, because I . . . oh, I said that already. So, Sir Richard. You keep your four hundred, and I beg you to take these four hundred pounds off my hands. This is the interest that our Blessed Maiden in her kindness has given me. And I mean that you should distribute the interest to all who reaped the harvest for you this year."

Little John rubbed the scar in his beard. "Even I could have explained that more simply."

"Stay out of this!" threatened Robin.

By now, Sir Richard had composed himself. "You always give me new riddles. But one thing I know: You are a true friend. And I say it freely: Were you not what you are, I would openly stand by your side."

Robin grew serious. "It is better if we fight in different camps for the same goal."

Moved, the knight asked Robin and the others to follow him to the packhorses. "Not knowing how richly I would be gifted again, I wanted to express my gratitude with these." He flipped back the linen blankets. There were short and long bows of the best quality. A hundred bows of Spanish yew. And quivers! A hundred quivers loaded with arrows, with perfectly feathered shafts.

"By Dunstan," John whistled through pursed lips.

Robin lifted his chin. "This will hold us until King Richard returns."

Marian and Beth had also come to the camp for the feast. They took seats to the right and left of the guest at the head of the table.

"You've grown even more beautiful." Sir Richard smiled at Marian. "Do you like to study? My Patricia hates her lessons. She prefers to play the lute."

The blush rushed to Marian's cheeks. Beth came to her aid: "She's good at handwork. The girl is very industrious."

"And riding. And shooting," the girl blurted out. "And—"

"Enough." Beth squeezed the girl's hand and smiled at Sir Richard. "She's interested in all sorts of things. Yes, my princess is a quick and easy learner."

"I'm sure she is." Sir Richard nodded at her approvingly.

Silently, John had listened to the conversation. An idea was growing in his mind. But then the cooks served up. Every thought now belonged to the delicacies.

The aroma of the game pie was surpassed only by its flavor. "Today—" John licked his lips "—today I'd beat up anyone who tried to bite our Herbghost or Paul Storyteller's hand."

No sooner had the giant awakened the next morning than, despite his heavy head, his new thought returned.

"Let me escort Sir Richard to the road," he asked Robin. "Got something to talk to him about."

"But the yellow-striped cloak stays here." Robin shook a fist in mock warning. "No walking away from me to squire with him."

"I know where I belong."

Robin took a good look at his friend's solemn face. "All right, John."

Sir Richard made his farewells. "The gate of my castle is open to you and your brethren always." He made his departure. "With the help of the gracious Virgin, we shall win the battle."

"God save our king in the Holy Land!" Robin replied.

For a long time, John paced in silence beside the knight's horse. Finally, he said, "That would be nice."

"What do you mean?" asked Sir Richard.

"You said earlier that we could go to the castle. And if it's true, it would be nice."

"Are you doubting my word?"

John shook his head hastily and sighed. A few words and he had offended the man. *This isn't getting me anywhere.* "Lord. I have my Marian, is all."

"Any father would envy you."

"That's just it. I want something better for the child. A solid home. Can't she come to your castle? I mean, and learn. To write and to read. She should become a lady. Music and all that. I have enough—I'll pay whatever it costs. No matter what." Uneasily, John wiped sweat from his black hair.

Sir Richard at the Lea reined in the horse. "It costs nothing."

"What?"

"I don't want your coin. On the contrary, because of the hostility shown to me by my neighbors, my daughter is often alone. She lacks companions of the same age. You would give me, my wife, and certainly my Patricia the greatest pleasure."

"You mean my Marian may come?"

"She will be received with open arms. Shall we go back? I'm so delighted, I would be happy to take her right away."

The joy drained from John's face. "First, I have to talk to Beth. Then I have to tell the girl. By Dunstan." Now he felt a gnawing feeling in his gut. "It won't happen so fast."

The Knight looked down at him searchingly. "I understand. This is your plan, and not Marian's wish?"

"Not yet," John grumbled.

From the saddle, Sir Richard held out his hand. "You have my word. When Marian comes, she will live with us as my own daughter. Just tell me, when may we expect the child, so we can prepare?"

John thought it through. "For the Christmas feast. No, when the snow is gone. I'll make it so by then."

"And don't be shy, Little John! I saw how familiar that girl is with Tom Toad's wife. Tears between them are unnecessary—there would be no problem if Mistress Beth comes to the castle, too. As her nursemaid."

"Yes, yes, that would be very fine. And . . ." No, he didn't want to think about the conversation he would have to have with Marian and Beth now. "Thank you. It will be what's best for the child."

YORKSHIRE. ON THE TRADE ROAD TO THE NORTH.

They rode as simple Cistercians on the road northward. Two monks leading a packhorse. That was all.

Usually, we lie in wait for them, now we're ones ourselves. John scowled, tugging his too-small hood over his forehead. Although Beth had sewn two of the light gray tunics together for him, the fabric was stretched taut across his chest. Moreover, sitting in the saddle as he was, the hem had ridden up almost to his knees.

"Suppose Friar Tuck doesn't want to come along?" grumbled John.

"That's enough of that!" said Robin. "You wait and see, Brother Runt."

They rode side by side in silence. Hooves clacked on the stones. It was a cold, dry December day. Slowly they approached the edge of the plateau. Before the road dropped down toward the River Went, John's brow furrowed. *There to the right and left in the thicket, that's where we usually wait for prey.* He quickly checked the leather scabbard on his rope belt. If only he at least had a shield and sword! The other weapons—staff, quiver, and bow—lay rolled up in blankets behind them. Not ready to hand. Well hidden under their provisions.

"Suppose someone attacks us?"

"Who?"

"Well, the likes of us."

"Don't be an idiot, Little John!" Robin gave him an irritated look. "What's wrong with you?"

"I don't know."

"What do you think will happen? Armed men? So what? Nobody would recognize us. We're two brothers of the Cistercian order, on our way from the monastery in Canterbury to Fountains Abbey.

We just want to visit our brothers in the wilderness over Christmastide."

John sighed. No, it had nothing to do with the priest. It was something else. Danger was looming. Ever since they'd left the camp this morning, he'd felt every hair on the back of his neck.

"I have such a bad feeling."

Robin snapped his fingers. "It's obvious. Nobody's comfortable putting on a monk's robe." He laughed.

"That's right." Now John was smirking, too. "That'll be it. I only know how to take them off other people."

XVI

They followed the wide sweeping bends of the road down into the valley. Robin pointed to the other side of the river. "We'll have a drink at the inn. That's what everyone who comes through here does."

They had almost crossed the high arched stone bridge when John reined in his horse. "Up ahead on that log," he hissed. "Right next to the alehouse, by the stable."

Red—scarlet—from the cap to the doublet to the hose and even the boots. Only the cloak was woad blue. The man was sitting on the fallen trunk, his sword stuck into the ground in front of him, his hands relaxed on the cross guard, his chin resting on the pommel.

"Some pompous squire," Robin murmured. "We don't care."

They let the horses go on at a leisurely pace. They dismounted in front of the inn. Out of the corner of his eye, John looked over at the log again. The scarlet was gone! Before Robin could hold him back, the giant was already around the corner of the inn. Nothing. There was no sign of the man anywhere. "I don't understand it," he muttered.

"Dammit. That's no way for a monk to behave." Robin warned his friend, "Keep it up, and we won't get far."

"Who was this man?"

"Never mind, John. Don't worry about it. We mustn't attract attention now. Who knows who's watching us from inside? Rangers. Men-at-arms from York. Maybe even some from Doncaster. They love to lurk around in the bridge taverns."

But the inn was empty. The innkeeper greeted the pious brothers with a silent nod and brought two jugs. No questions about *where from* and *where to*. The innkeeper bit down on the silver penny before pocketing it. He nodded a farewell.

The ale tasted good. Satisfied, John climbed back into the saddle. He wasn't that uncomfortable anymore. "He really thought we're holy brothers," he said.

"They all will. If you don't open your mouth."

Just beyond the inn, the road rose steeply from the Went valley to the ridge. Breath steamed from the horses' nostrils. The lead line of their trailing beast of burden tugged at John's saddle horn. He glanced briefly over his shoulder—nothing out of the ordinary. The horse plodded along behind them, letting himself be pulled. But then, John twisted his head around again. "By Dunstan. There he is again." Back down the road: Scarlet red, in the middle of the road he stood, shadowing his eyes, staring after the monks.

"I'd better get him."

"Ride on!" Robin command sharply. More kindly, he added, "We've got better things to do today."

After a while, John looked back again. "He's gone."

"By the Holy Virgin. Forget about that little red bird already!" Robin smirked. "Are you afraid of him? The way he's dressed, we could spot that one from miles away, even if he flies from tree to tree."

"That's all right." John pressed his thumb against each nostril, blew each side, and wiped with his sleeve. *Yes, Robin is right. Besides, I need to have a talk with him today. And that's more important than Red Cap, really.*

On the hill, the two companions allowed the horses to amble along slowly for a while, then they lightly slapped their flanks and continued at a trot. They wanted to reach Fountains Abbey before sunset. Only after they had left Pontefract behind did John casually lead the conversation to Richard at the Lea.

"If only there were more knights like him." Robin sighed. "England would be saved."

"Yes, he's a good man," John muttered to himself. "And it's best for Marian."

Puzzled, Robin looked at his friend. "What do you mean? What has our little condition to do with Sir Richard?"

"Don't you dare laugh," the giant threatened. "And I'm not a giant wet nurse. Let's be clear about that from the start."

Full of curiosity, Robin raised his hand to promise not to laugh.

"All right, then." John explained his plan hastily and asked, emulating Robin's typical tone, "Well, what do you say?"

"Our Marian, a little lady." Robin clapped his hands. His horse sprang forward. Laughing, he reined it in again. When John caught up with him, he said enthusiastically, "Nice!" His expression turned serious. He looked up at the clear winter sky. "Ah, poor friend. Before this comes to pass, I see dark clouds for thee. You have two people to persuade—Marian and Beth."

"I know. Pretty sure that's going to be a grim task."

In the late afternoon, they reached the turnoff to Fountains Abbey. Leaving the main road, they followed the cart path into a narrow valley. The deep ruts were frozen. For a while longer, they rode one behind the other. Above them, the bare branches of the trees clawed at each other. The sky shimmered pale. Then it became too dangerous for the horses to be ridden. Leading them by the halter, John and Robin guided their animals deeper into the valley.

"I wouldn't think there's a monastery here in the wilderness," John said.

"Wait and see!"

The plan was simple. As soon as the buildings appeared before them, they would take off their robes. No stray travelers would be turned away at any monastery gate. Especially not if they were paying for the night's lodging. "We'll quickly find out where Friar Tuck is. We need only keep our ears open." Robin was quite sure. "Either he's still lodging with his brothers after all, or they really have banished him from the house. It doesn't matter. Somehow we'll be able to talk to him alone tomorrow."

The forest grew lighter, and echoed with distant singing. The two travelers stayed under cover. Below them, the valley widened into fields, meadows, and scattered woods. To the west, rooftops peeked out from behind monastery walls, overlooked by the mighty abbey church.

"I like this." Robin stroked his chin. "As hidden as our main camp."

"They've got guards, too." John pointed. "Singing guards." Just ahead of them, the path dropped and ended at a wide stream. On the opposite side stood a cottage fashioned of stout logs. White smoke rose from the opening of the moss roof. "Look at that good-for-nothing."

From the opposite bank, a rotund monk worked his way step by step through the frozen stream. His robe was gathered up to his waist, his legs were in high, water-soaked boots. In a steady rhythm, he swung a massive club and let it crash onto the ice, then pushed the broken floes aside. As he did so, he sang the Gloria at the top of his lungs.

"You wait here." Robin's eyes glittered. "But promise me, you won't come until I call you."

"Are you going down there like that? In a monk's robes?"

"That big little man is wearing it, too, isn't he?"

"But he belongs in it."

"How do you know?"

"Well, since he sings like that. Weren't we going to be travelers?"

"Later. When we go to the monastery. Give me a little time!"

Robin slung the shield over his shoulder, winked at John, and, humming along with the song of praise, strode down the path to the stream, his hood low on his face. As a precaution, John pulled the short bow and two arrows from his pack. "Better safe than," he grumbled.

The monk had already cut his channel past the middle of the stream. He did not notice the stranger. Too fiercely did he slam the club on the ice. Too vigorously did he chant the Gloria. He stretched out the *O*, letting it rise and fall in long loops.

Only when the monk had waded to the shore on the other side did he see the strange brother. His song broke off. He braced the club on the ground in front of him.

Robin bowed his head. *"Pax tecum."*

"Et cum spiritu tuo." A firm, round face, freshly flushed from exertion, watched him from wide-set, dark eyes. Surprised, he eyed the stranger. "I did not hear you approach." He rubbed the shaved tonsure on the back of his head with the flat of his hand.

"Nor could you have. The way you praised the Lord."

"My abbot has given me the unfortunate duty of keeping this ford in repair. In summer, I watch for loose pebbles at the bottom. In frost, I see to it that it remains ice-free. A cold task. Only singing warms me." He didn't take his eyes off the stranger for a moment. "I see we wear the dress of the same order. Where are you from, brother?"

"From Canterbury. I have to deliver a message from my prior to your father abbot."

"From so far? And on foot?"

Robin sighed. "Yes. Humility often demands arduous undertakings from us."

The monk pursed his lips. "If it is from the heart, then I gladly agree with you."

Sighing deeper, Robin showed off his soft leather boots, pointing to the far shore. "You, dear brother, are already wet. I beseech you, for the sake of St. Christopher, carry me across!"

The monk closed his eyes. When he opened them again, his expression was cold. But his voice remained gracious. More than that, his tone had become submissive. "Gladly. I am used to serving." He tucked the club under his arm. "Give me your sword while you ride! It will be easier for you to mount that way."

"I don't . . ." Robin quickly checked himself. "You are prudent, dear brother." With that, he handed over belt and weapon.

The monk bent over, and Robin Hood sat astride the broad back.

From up high, Little John watched as Robin allowed himself to be carried through the barely knee-deep ford. "Another one of those games. Sitting there like a gray frog on a toad." He lowered his bow.

The monk reached the other bank with his load. Abruptly he stretched, shook himself, and let out a wild cry. Robin flew through the air, landing hard on the ground. The monk stood over him, club in his left hand, the drawn sword in his right, the tip aimed at Robin's heart. "*Pax tecum*, you scoundrel!" All submissiveness was gone. "You are anything but a man of the church."

"But you are, father." Robin laughed miserably. "Spare me! I am defenseless."

Up in the cover of the trees, John had drawn back the arrow on its the string again. He grimaced. "Told him so."

The monk kicked the fake brother in the side. "No, I'm not going to kill you, even though, sincerely, I'd enjoy confessing that. Come on, get up. Now you play Christophorus. Carry me over, and then get on your way! As punishment, I'll let you freeze your toes off." He lowered his club and crouched on Robin's back, holding the sword blade at Robin's side, driving him through the water.

"Serves him right," John grumbled in amusement. He was still grinning when the rider dismounted. But then his breath caught.

As if of its own accord, a dagger leaped from Robin's sleeve into his hand. Quick as a cat, the outlaw was behind the monk, choking him with his left arm. The dagger's point sat against the man's stocky neck. "So swiftly heaven and hell change place, venerable father. Away with the sword!" The monk obeyed. "Before you do me the kindness to take me across again, tell me: What did I get wrong?"

The monk showed no fear, not even anger. "Everything, you charlatan. I have not yet met a brother who wears such good boots and then speaks of humility. Besides, you claim to have come here on foot? Show me a single brother in England from our rich order who still walks. And even more: There is no Cistercian monastery in Canterbury. I have visited the tomb of the pious Thomas Becket. He was an Augustinian, and the monastery—"

"Enough," Robin interrupted him. "My game was poorly prepared."

"A game?! May Hell devour thee!"

"That's enough. Carry me over, you fat knave! I haven't got all day."

Halfway across, the monk stood straight up then dropped to his side. Both of them, Robin on the bottom and the monk above him, broke through the ice. The monk got to his feet faster. He grabbed the fake brother, dunked him under, yanked him up, dunked him again. Robin gasped, yelled, "John!" His head disappeared again.

"Ask for mercy! Ask for mercy!" the monk roared. "For mercy!"

Little John was swiftly approaching in great leaps, stomping through the water. He seized the monk from behind, lifted him, and tossed him aside. The ice cracked. The monk sat in the floes.

"By Dunstan, now, that's really enough!" John helped his friend up. The monk seized the moment. As he scrambled to his feet, he put a small silver flute to his lips and whistled twice.

Bellowing rang out from behind the cottage. Barks! A pack of dogs raced into the water—five long-legged, shaggy gray dogs.

"O Sancta Catherina!" the monk called out to them. The pack split. Two rushed at Robin. Three rushed toward John. Water splashed. Crouching, the giant braced himself for them. He grabbed the first by the scruff of the neck, yanked it up, and shook the animal. The next two were already circling, barking, baring their teeth. The other two dogs jumped and snarled at Robin, too, cornering him like a deer.

"Call them off!" shouted John. The greyhound in his fist struggled, its tongue hanging out of its mouth. "Or I'll crush his neck."

"O Sancta Dorothea!" Immediately, the beasts backed away a little. They lay in wait. Slowly, John put the dog down in the water. It staggered off to join the rest.

Robin glared at the pack, glared at the monk. "By the Blessed Virgin. I've never met such a priest."

"Silence!" the monk ordered him. "Just one command and they'll tear you apart." He warned John, "Even if you kill one, before you can grab the second . . ."

"Fair enough." John folded his arms in front of his chest. Reproachfully, he looked over at Robin. "I'm tired of this."

Robin shivered with cold. "But this game was a good one. We're not searching any further. We found a better one. What do you say?"

It took a moment to understand him, then John nodded. "Fine."

Robin managed a stiff bow. "I beg mercy, reverend father, please deliver us from this damned ice water! And I pray, warm your heart. Let us talk together by the fire." He held out his hand. *"Pax tecum."*

Suspiciously, the monk looked from one to the other.

"He means it, this time," John assured him.

"All right, peace." The monk rubbed the tonsure at the back of his head. "But only because I'm cold too." He commanded his pack, "O Sancta Martha!" Immediately the dogs ran across the stream to the house.

"Follow me!" The monk waded ahead.

Warmth! Not from the hearth fire alone. The monk lived his pious life with his dogs and four sheep under one roof. There was storage for hay and wood, and a wide gate showed that the rear part of the house was intended as a stable. The rest of the living space was open. Except for the circle around the cooking place, the tamped-down floor was covered with straw. The sheep camped close together, right next to the monk's sleeping mat, exhaling warm, comforting breaths.

"This is what I call an inn." Robin Hood crouched close to the hearth embers. "So, father, I will give you—"

"Silence!" Panting, the monk freed himself from his high boots. "Take off your robes, both of you. Only when I see you without these disguises will I know who you are. But you had better be careful. Just one false move, and I won't call off my dogs this time."

John had stopped near the entrance. "There's plenty of room in here."

"What are you standing there for?" the monk snapped at him.

John pointed to the sheep, to the dogs. "We've got three more, too."

"Off with your robe!"

"I'm trying to say, we've got three horses. Up in the bushes."

The monk looked up at the giant. "Good. Bring them here!" he ordered. "Where there' s shelter for two scoundrels, there's indeed room enough for God's innocent creatures."

As John led the packhorse in through the stable gate, the dogs growled.

"O Sancta Clara!" They fell silent.

A little later, the horses were standing close together in the rear of the hut. "With you three, my ark is filled to capacity," their host told them as he fed them hay and water.

John grinned. The monk had taken off his habit and wrapped in a blanket, a hemp rope holding it up on his belly. In only his undertunic, Robin sat by the hearth fire, silent, his eyelids half closed. Water dripped from two light gray robes hanging from the ceiling beams. "Hang yours next to them!" the monk ordered. "Well, get on with it!"

Strictly guarding the giant's every move, he had him hand over his dagger, pommel first. He accompanied him to the packhorse. "Don't touch the weapons!"

"It's all right. It's all right." Deliberately slow, John pulled the blankets he had brought with him out of the pack.

John squatted beside Robin as the monk stood by the fire. "Now then," began the monk. "Who are you? What do you want in Fountains Abbey?"

Robin looked up. "I'm Robert Loxley. This is Little John." Cautiously, he added, "Perhaps you know me better by the name Robin Hood."

The monk took a step back. "Not another word." He clenched his fists. "Never! You churls will not rob Fountains Abbey." He was reached for the silver whistle.

"Wait!" begged Robin. "Pray, wait."

Hesitantly, the monk returned to the fire. "What are you planning to do here?"

"Not a raid," John grumbled. "Though it looked like we might, earlier."

"Prove it."

Robin showed his open hands. "Simple: There are only two of us. I would have come with an army. Enough of that! We came to find one of your brothers, Friar Tuck. But now . . ."

"I . . ." The monk broke off. Almost imperceptibly, the corners of his mouth twitched. He moved a stool to the fire. "All right, then. I am Brother Jerome. What do you want from Friar Tuck?"

"Nothing, anymore, from that drunkard," John grinned broadly. "Just—"

"Drunkard!"

"Well, that's why they chased him out of the monastery, isn't it. Now he's got to live out here somewhere."

"Convenient lies." The monk glanced quickly from one to the other. "Rumors are always easier than the truth. Yes, Brother Tuck is shunned by his monastery. Because he admonishes, because he criticizes. And if he indulges in wine, it is not for drunkenness, but merely a desire to forget his lot for a while."

Robin frowned. "Forgive me, father. You are defending Friar Tuck? So, he has a friend. There are two of you."

The monk laughed boomingly, slapping his thighs. He laughed until tears ran down his cheeks.

Stunned, the companions stared at each other. All at once, the monk stopped. "Now I do believe that you and this giant have come here with peaceful intentions." He folded his hands over his belly. "The solution is simple: There are not two of me. My name may be Jerome—Father Jerome—but everyone calls me Friar Tuck."

He gave his guests no time to let that settle in. "So here I am. What do you want?"

John rubbed the scar in his beard. *He knows a game or two himself. That's all right. A priest like that could be really good for us.*

Robin quickly composed himself. "By the Blessed Virgin." He pressed the heels of his hands against each other, lightly tapped his fingertips, and started telling Friar Tuck about the life of the outlaws in Barnsdale, about the struggle against injustice and humiliation, about the raids. He left nothing out. "We, too, are a brotherhood. But we wear only the green or brown battle garb, and use the sword and bow. We lack someone who wears God's tunics."

Sitting up straight, staring into the flames, the monk remained silent.

After clearing his throat a bit, John added, "There's a hut. There's plenty of food. And we plan to build a chapel in the village. Someday."

Silence. Friar Tuck rose. He took a jug from the niche in the wall, drank, and handed the wine to John. "The most beautiful rule of my order is *ora et labora*. Pray and work. The first Cistercians cultivated this valley with their own hands. Farming and sheep breeding. But what about today? Like Norman barons, we too have servants tilling the field, shearing the sheep." He passed the wine to Robin. "I want to go back to the *ora et labora*."

Robin set down the jug. "Does that mean . . . ?"

"Yes. I'm ready." He grinned. "You offer me life in a wild field with unshorn sheep carrying bows and arrows."

"Thank the Blessed Virgin!" Robin jumped up.

John slapped Friar Tuck's shoulder in exuberance. The monk flinched in pain. Then laughed. "Well, just wait until you feel *my* punch."

From a storage pit, he took out three wineskins. They drank and planned their departure.

When? First thing in the morning. Farewell? No, no goodbyes for the holy brethren. "I will drive my sheep to the monastery flock. That way, they'll know I've gone. The abbot will breathe a sigh of relief."

They camped down around the hearth fire. Friar Tuck wanted to take his dogs with him. John propped his head up, "How does that work, with the saints?"

"The abbot wanted to charge me with poaching. In the royal forester's presence, he even brought a hare and released it in front of the pack. Whatever he ordered them to do, the dogs didn't budge."

The monk folded his hands. "But every now and then, when I wander through the forest and speak to them in the name of the saints, some venison is miraculously brought to me."

"Nice," Robin murmured, half asleep.

"All right." John lay back. "Only a monk would think of such a thing, and only our new Friar Tuck."

They rode south on the trade route as simple Cistercians, their light gray hoods pulled up to shield their faces. It was cold. A squad of armed men approached them. The red crest of the Baron of Doncaster shone on their shields and mantles. A silent salute was exchanged. Nothing more. None of the men-at-arms wondered at the strangely bulky baggage the pious gentlemen had strapped behind their saddles; none noticed the dogs that silently accompanied the monks in the undergrowth.

The road dropped steeply down to the River Went. They could already make out the roof of the bridge tavern. John straightened his back. "There. By Dunstan!" Below them, in the middle of the road: scarlet red. "There's that fellow again."

"A fox on hind legs." Friar Tuck grinned. "You don't see that often."

"*We* do," John growled. He reached behind him.

"Leave the bow!" commanded Robin. "Take it easy. You're a monk. So act like it!"

"Quite so." But the bad feeling was back: Danger was imminent. John felt it all the way down his neck.

What was the man up to? As the riders approached, the scarlet man sprang aside with a light leap and was gone among the trees.

John opened and closed his fist. *Robe or no robe. If I see him again, I'll grab him.*

Before they reached the inn, the monks dismounted. Friar Tuck stood at the side of the road. He gathered his robes under his ample belly and crouched. His companions waited indifferently. After a low whistle on the silver flute and an "O Sancta Clara," Friar Tuck dropped the robes back into place again and quietly said, "All right. My darlings will wait patiently until you're ready to move on."

John poked Robin lightly in the side. "He gets it, eh?"

"Yeah. We got lucky." Robin laughed. "And we got a priest."

After their rest stop, the monks made their horses prance awkwardly in front of the stone bridge. Clearly, they were clumsy riders. An amusement for anyone who watched them. While they struggled to keep the horses in check, five gray dogs scurried across the bridge ahead of them.

"Courage, my brothers!" shouted Friar Tuck emphatically loudly. "Hold on to the reins. And with faith in God, go on."

Soon the horses were snorting. They had almost reached the high ground. The men rode toward the last long sweeping bend. Above them, the scarlet man stood again in the middle of the road. He seemed to be waiting, arms folded, his blue cloak tucked behind the hilt of his sword.

"Stop!" hissed Robin. "You're right, John. Now I want to know what he's up to, too."

"At last." The giant pulled the bow from its blanket sheath.

"Wait! We won't learn anything that way."

"But if we get closer, he'll disappear again."

"Fox or deer." Friar Tuck reached for little flute hanging around his neck. "My hounds know how the prey is driven."

Robin agreed. John, too, nodded. They held themselves ready to ride off at a moment's notice. Friar Tuck steered his horse to the side of the road. At his whistle, the pack loped out of the bushes. The monk pointed to the scarlet man. "O Sancta Catherina!"

The greyhounds raced off barking. The stranger stood motionless. A stone's throw from their quarry, the pack scattered. The scarlet man did not move. The dogs surrounded him, their barking intensifying. From all sides, they rushed at him. Then the stranger crouched low and sprang jumping over one of the beasts, drawing his sword as he leapt. The dog threw itself around, snatching at the blue cloak. Even as it sank its teeth into the fabric, a mighty blow severed its neck. Howling, the other four jumped on the man. He lost his sword. They pulled him to the ground.

Now the horsemen were at the scene of the battle. Brother Tuck issued the command, and the greyhounds released their victim. The scarlet man lay on his back. Groaning, Brother Tuck sank to his knees. "What have you done?" he wailed. He loosened dog's the fangs from the stranger's cloak.

Slowly the stranger sat up. His clothes hung in tatters, but he himself seemed intact. He looked directly into the monk's face. "I had to fight back." He looked up at the other two. "You are witnesses, aren't you? Aren't you?"

They gave no answer. Friar Tuck tenderly carried dog's head to the side of the road. As he lifted the blood-streaming torso from the stones, the other greyhounds whimpered. "Yes, mourn, my darlings. Mourn Secundus!" He crouched down among the pack.

The stranger reached for his red cap and slapped the dust from it on his knees, indignation in his gray eyes. "Don't stare at me like that. I'm not to blame for the mutt's death. You monks set the pack on me."

Reluctantly, John nodded. Robin frowned. "Where have I seen . . . ?" He shook off the thought, set his fists on his hips. "Get up!"

With a skillful roll, the stranger twisted to the side and grabbed the hilt of his sword. John was quicker, his boot on the blade. "Don't even try it, lad!"

"Enough!" Robin commanded.

The stranger jumped to his feet. Fearless, he relaxed his shoulders. "What monastery are you from? Where are pious brothers allowed to hunt with dogs?"

"Shut up!" growled John.

Unimpressed, the stranger pointed at his red tatters. "And who's going to pay for my expensive clothes?"

Like a snake's head, Robin's right hand flew to his rope belt, and he had his sword in his fist. With the tip, he lifted the man's chin. "I'm asking the questions," he said, dangerously softly. "And if you don't answer nicely, you won't have need for any clothes."

The stranger's smooth face turned pale. Cautiously, he nodded.

"That's the way I like you." Robin asked quick and curt questions.

The man had been waiting for weeks now. He had watched every traveler. Whether they came on foot or on horseback down to the River Went. He only wore the red clothes so everyone would actually look at him.

"Who are you waiting for?"

"When he comes, he'll recognize me."

Robin lifted the sword's tip a little more. "Who?"

"A relative."

"And his name?"

"If you kill me. I can't tell you."

"You do have guts." Again, Robin frowned.

Meanwhile, Friar Tuck had returned. He stood beside John, muttering, "The misfortune is done. And we bear the blame. Why magnify it yet more?"

"You're right." John expelled a breath. "We should keep going."

"No, wait!" commanded Robin. Unblinking, he stared at the stranger. "Who are you?"

"Gamwell. Gamwell from Maxfield."

Robin lowered his weapon. "Do you have an aunt?" he asked gruffly.

Cautiously, the scarlet man fingered his neck. "Yes. She's a nun. The prioress of Kirklees Abbey."

"Prioress!"

"Yes, so she has been for the past month."

"What's her name?"

"Sister Mathilda. She knows all about the healing arts."

Robin sheathed his sword. He winked at his companions. "So, Gamwell. I know who you're looking for." He smiled. "Me."

"And you are . . . ?"

"Hush. No names." Robin put a finger to his lips, then laughed. He held out both hands. "Well met, cousin!"

Lithely, Gamwell stepped close, and he let himself be embraced. He laughed, too.

Robin called to the others over his cousin's shoulder. "Well, what do you think of that? Is this a remarkable day? The last time I saw this little fellow, he was a toddling babe. And I was just thinking, 'That face! Why do I know those eyes?'"

Little John fiercely rubbed the scar in his beard. He had never seen Robin like this before.

Gamwell extricated himself. "I've been waiting . . . because I don't know where to go anymore. Because I need your help."

"First of all, I'll bring you with me. Family blood belongs together. Later . . . we'll see." Robin led him before the others. "This is my friend, Little John. You were lucky, Gamwell. He was a hair away from shooting you."

John took the outstretched hand. *He has strength, yes.* Openly, warmly, Gamwell returned his scrutinizing look. And yet . . . John wasn't sure about him. He still felt the tug at the back of his neck.

"I'm glad to meet you," Gamwell said in a melodious voice.

In reply, the giant growled.

"And this is the only true Cistercian of us. Brother Tuck."

Silently, the monk clasped his hands in front of his stomach. Gamwell grew serious. "Forgive me, father. What was I supposed to do?"

Brother Tuck nodded. "You proved to me on the very first day how thorny my new path will be. My son." He pointed to the pack. "These are Primus, Tertius, Quartus, and Quintus. Obedient, and incorruptible. And while they are in mourning, beware them."

"We'll be friends," Gamwell said, his gray eyes cold.

Robin handed John the packs from his horse and let his cousin mount behind him.

The two rode ahead, searching for shared memories. There were few of them. Gamwell had not seen his older cousin since the raid on Loxley after Robin's father's death.

"I had to fight, constantly." Robin held up his fist. "First for food. But now—for much more." He laughed.

Friar Tuck and Little John followed them. The giant held the reins loosely in his hand. Beside him, the monk hunched silently in the saddle. How fast thing were going! John sighed. *Yesterday we were traveling alone together, wanting only to find a priest. And today, we have a priest, a cousin, and four dogs.*

"How was it with you?"

Robin's question to Gamwell snapped John out of his thoughts. Tensely, he listened.

"The plague came to Maxfield. Both of my parents died. On the same day. That's when Aunt Mathilda took me in."

"That nun! Not a word did she tell me about this."

"She hid me from you. So I wouldn't turn out like you."

After a pause, Robin asked, "And what happened then, Gamwell?"

"She provided everything for me. I learned from her. Now I can read, write and . . ."

". . . handle a sword," Robin added dryly. "Our Mathilda is very capable. She is prioress now, after all. And she even knows something about the art of combat."

Gamwell laughed. "No, I didn't learn that from her. I learned that at Doncaster."

John held his breath.

"Where?" Robin shot a look back at his cousin.

"At Sir Roger's, the Baron of Doncaster."

The giant sped up his horse until he drew even with Robin's. "Say that again!"

Chagrined, Gamwell looked from one to the other, then lowered his eyes. "I had to obey. Aunt Mathilda wanted me to be a squire." At the castle, he had learned to fight, hunt with a falcon, shoot crossbow, make polite conversation, and had learned proper table manners. Everything had been taught to him. And he even enjoyed it. "You'll be a real Norman yet," Sir Roger had told him, pleased with him.

Robin looked ahead again. From the side, John saw his friend's frozen face.

"A Norman, are you!" Little John took over the interrogation. "So why did you suddenly appear here?"

Gamwell seemed oblivious to the looming tension. Without faltering, he answered, "Because I killed the steward. Because I couldn't stand the injustice any longer." He paused. "Outwardly, Sir Roger pretends to be charitable and plays the pious patron. But I quickly saw through him. Power is what he wants. To enforce his evil plans, he orders torture, even murder. And this steward was his henchman." Gamwell wiped his eyes with his sleeve. "With the baron, I lacked courage, but I finally confronted his bailiff. He took up his sword. I was better."

John's jaw dropped. Robin had turned halfway around in the saddle. "You dared to do that?"

"I had to, for the sake of those innocent victims. I hid the body behind some barrels. But it was discovered. Before anyone could suspect me of it, I mounted my horse and rode away."

"That's fine, boy." For the first time, John looked kindly at Robin's cousin. "Glad I didn't shoot you. And you'll have to tell our Much that story, too."

Robin's eyes smiled. "Good thing you waited for us."

Before they rode off the main road and into the wilderness, John ordered his cousin and Father Tuck to dismount.

"Don't get carried away with it!" Robin advised John.

"It's your rule!" John grinned. "It applies to all strangers. To reverends and also to relatives." He tore two long strips from Gamwell's red jacket. "Blindfold yourselves until we get there."

Gamwell obeyed, and with a mighty swing, John put him back on the horse behind Robin Hood.

"Hold on, son!" Friar Tuck called to the dogs. "O Sancta Ursula," he instructed them.

"Now it's Ursula?"

"No matter where you take me," the monk said. "With Sancta Ursula, they will stay by my side."

The first sentry sounded the horn on their arrival. The second relayed the signal onward. When they entered the main camp, all the men gathered in front of the kitchen shed. While Robin Hood introduced the priest and his cousin outside, the two cooks inside poured some more water into the steaming soup to extend it, complaining and cursing.

John did not get a word in edgewise, nor would he have wanted to. After the meal, Robin reported in detail and cheerfully about the two last days' adventure. "We made provision for Friar Tuck," he concluded, "but until Gamwell's hut is ready, he'll stay with me."

Ale was dispensed, and even wine! Tom Toad circled his braid around his tankard, eyeing Robin's cousin. "Gamwell? Don't like it. We'll have to change that."

"You're right." Robin stroked his chin thoughtfully. "Gamwell. Gam. Well." He tried the name. Smiling faces all around.

John slammed his paw on the table. "It's simple: Will! And because he was standing there in the road looking so pretty and red: Scarlet!"

Robin whistled appreciatively. He drew his dagger, placed his splayed hand on the tabletop. Three times the "No!" rang out. The blade tip pointed between his last two fingers. "Will Scarlet?"

"Yes!" the chorus answered.

After Robin's cousin was baptized with ale, Smiling bared his teeth. "And our frocked newcomer?"

Friar Tuck set down his jug. "Wait. Debate no further, you ruffians." Flushed with wine, he rose, paced back and forth in front of his congregation. "My name was Jerome. But because I . . ." he gathered his robe up to his belt ". . . always waded through the stream like this, they call me Friar Tuck." He dropped the hems again.

Enthusiastically, the companions drummed on the tabletop. "Friar Tuck! Yes! That's the way it stays: Friar Tuck!"

The jugs were refilled, again and again, until the singing and the last laughter were drowned in gurgling snores.

Soon he would go talk to Marian and Beth—John was determined. *Before Christmas. Right after the men have gone to their homes.*

By torchlight, Brother Tuck celebrated mass outside under the big linden tree on an icy Christmas Eve. Nothing dimmed the perfusing joy. Marian and Beth sang and prayed together with the freemen who had remained in the main camp.

By Epiphany at the latest, John told himself. *There's plenty of time.*

Marian helped in the horse stables. Day after day, John watched her exuberantly ride the white stallion across the snow-covered paddock.

"No, not today. But definitely tomorrow."

One by one, the men returned to camp from their villages. And John had said nothing, neither to Beth nor Marian.

On the Feast of the Epiphany, Brother Tuck swapped places with the priest at Wrangbrook. *"In Nomine Patris, et Filii, et Spiri-*

tus Sancti." He read three masses in a row. At the church entrance, Marian held out the offering plate, beaming. Three times the villagers were allowed to clear the mountain of pennies.

"I need time and rest to do this," John said to himself. "And now the men's training must come first."

Every day John found new excuses. Sometimes it was training in archery, in fighting with staff; then he postponed because they were celebrating the new hut for Will Scarlet. Then it was a critical meeting with Robin Hood.

The leader looked from one lieutenant to another. "Is there anything to be brought against my cousin?"

Toad and Whitehand shook their heads. Smiling bared his teeth, "If Scarlet also handles his sword like he does in practice when the fighting is real, then he can manage four iron puppets at once."

"And what do you think, John?"

"Got used to him." He nodded thoughtfully. *Scarlet does everything well. With a crossbow, he's better than any of us. And he can talk. Sometimes I think ...* John wiped the thought away. *Scarlet is Robin's cousin! And that's that.* "It's all right. I'm all for it."

"Nice." Robin clapped briefly. "It gives the Brotherhood of Freemen a fifth lieutenant, Will Scarlet."

By the end of January, the snow was melting. John couldn't delay any longer. First, he sat down secretly with Robin.

"All right, my friend," Robin replied. "Agreed. Our little condition, I'll gladly give him. But as for Beth ..." Robin shook his head. "It would be bad if we had to walk around all raggedy in the future."

"I'll find a way to handle that," John assured him.

Then he talked to Toad and asked him to go with him to Barnsdale Top. He didn't reveal the reason. And while Marian tended Lancelot at the base, he trudged silently beside his companion to the village.

“Tell me now,” Tom urged.

“Wait just a moment more!” After a few long strides, John added, “This is not easy.”

Beth sat at the table after John spoke, her eyes wide. “You want to take her away from me?” she whispered. The seamstress felt for her husband’s hand, clasping it. “Tom, he can’t do that, can he? He can’t, can he? Tell him, Tom. He mustn’t.”

Toad found no answer. Unblinking, John stared at the tabletop in front of him.

Beth jerked her hand back. “So that’ s the way it is. Tom, you knew!” Her lips quivered. “You two, you’ve been working this out for a long time! Get out of here ...”

“I knew nothing until just now, believe me, Beth!” Tom gently took her shoulder.

“Don’t touch me!” The seamstress shook him off and bent forward over the table, in tears. “My little princess. She’s the only thing I have left, she is. She’s my child. Mine!”

Tom Toad ran his hand over his gray scalp and tugged his braid. “Damn it, John. There—you see the mess you’re making.”

The giant put his hands flat beside each other. “My word’s my bond. To the knight. Because I want the best for Marian.”

“Because you ...?” Beth sobbed. “And me? What am I to do?” She struggled for breath. “By the merciful Virgin, I beg you, John: Don’t take our little princess away from me!” She shook his arm. “Look at me!” When he raised his eyes, she asked, “If Marian is gone. What’s to become of me?”

“It’ll be ... all right.” John cleared his throat awkwardly. “Well, Beth, I’d know what you ...” He began again, “Why don’t you go along with her? There’s plenty of room there.”

The seamstress opened her lips silently. Tom Toad let go of his braid. After a while, he growled, “You have it all planned out, don’t you.”

Beth didn't believe the hope. "Please, John, I can't stand being mocked!"

Quietly, John told them of the knight's offer. "And I'd prefer that, too. Richard at the Lea says you could be the girls' nursemaid. You'll just watch over them both."

Through her tears, Beth laughed. "As always. Doesn't leave me much choice." She dried her cheeks. "And you mean for us to leave soon?"

"It's time." John expanded his chest in relief. "By spring at the latest, I promised."

"I'll need a few more days," Beth began. "First, I have to get us dressed up properly." She glanced at the bales of fabric stacked against the wall. "Oh! For Marian, I already know what—"

"Stop, damn it!" Tom slammed his fist on the table. "This is no good, no good at all."

"Shut up, Tom Toad! You have your gang," Beth rebuked him, but took it back immediately. "I don't mean to be harsh. But in the summer, you're traveling. And in the winter, well . . ." She waved a finger at him. "I'm sure I'll have a chamber to myself at the castle."

"That simple?" Ruefully, Tom grumbled, "When you become a lady, I bet you'll have me strumming something and singing some balled before you'll even let me in."

Beth paused with a sudden thought. What about her work? Could the village women even manage on their own?

John confessed, "Already talked it over with Robin." It wasn't far from Fenwick Castle to Barnsdale Top. "If you need to, you can come back here. Before we leave to go to Sherwood. And after the summer, when we get back." He grinned. "Besides, don't you think I'd want to see how the girl is doing?"

Beth pulled her hair over the scar on her left side. "My princess is going to be a princess."

Tom Toad watched his wife. After a while, he nodded to John. "All right, then."

The door slammed open and Marian rushed in, hair disheveled. Her cheeks glowed. "Beth. I was with Lancelot today . . ."

She noticed the men at the table and furrowed her brow. "What's the matter, Beth? You've been crying." The girl glowered at Tom and John. "What have you done to Beth?"

"It's all right, princess." The seamstress rose quickly. "But look at the state you're in! One of these days, I won't be able to comb that at all anymore."

"Then cut it shorter!"

"Don't say that. A woman only cuts off her hair if . . ."

Marian groaned. ". . . she's being taken to be executed." She let her fingers snip like scissors. "I know, I know."

"So, Princess, keep your hair long." Beth scooped milk from the jug. With the cup in hand, she led Marian to the table. "Sit down. John has something to tell you."

"Why me?" John pouted. "Can't *you*, Beth?"

She shook her head sternly, pulling her stool close beside the girl. "Do it now," she commanded.

By Dunstan! But he was no help now, either. "You see, little one, you know Sir Richard at the Lea," John began.

Marian nodded, unconcerned.

"You know . . ." Many more *you know*s and *I mean*s followed. When John finally finished, Marian was silent.

The giant could not bear the silence. "Don't be sad, little one!"

Marian stayed silent.

The gift! John wiped his brow. He almost forgot about the present. "And also, little one: Robin will let you have Lancelot. The white horse is yours."

Marian's eyes glinted. "Mine alone?" He nodded.

"And Beth comes, too?"

The seamstress nodded.

"And you're not sending me away just because you want to be rid of me?"

John shook his head.

"Swear!"

He raised his hand.

Marian drank the milk. She set the empty cup down hard.

"Agreed."

"Yes?" John felt a twinge in his chest. Almost indignantly, he braced both fists on the table. "You're not mad, at all?"

"No." Marian blew a curl off her forehead and said, "It's all right." She set her voice in as low a growl as she could muster.

Beth laughed and hugged the girl. "We'll have a fine time. We'll ride up to the castle like two ladies. You wait until you see what I'm sewing for both of us."

"Just like that," John grumbled. "Like I'm nothing. Just says 'agreed,' and that's that." Only after a while did he remember that, in fact, he wanted it that way, and that he had now achieved what was best for Marian. "I really hope it is. All right."

Beth and her princess planned their departure for the next week. "If it doesn't snow again," John advised. He was overruled. "That's fine. But I'll take you to the castle."

"Both of us will," Tom decided. "After all, I need to know where to find my wife."

Beth pushed the men rudely toward the door. There was still much to prepare.

On the way back to the camp, the men strode side by side in silence for a while. At last, Tom poked the giant in the side. "You're a clever one." He looked up at him, mockingly. "I had no idea. Always thought you were all strength."

"That's right. But you're better at telling stories. And I'm looking forward to hearing you sing soon."

XVII

The latest dispatch from the Crusade: *August 1192: Another battle for Jaffa breaks out. The Crusaders wade to victory through the blood of Muslims. Nevertheless, Richard abandons the conquest of Jerusalem. He negotiates with Sultan Saladin.*

September 2: The enemies sign a three-year truce. The Crusaders retain the coastal cities. Only Ascalon must be destroyed. Peaceful pilgrims are allowed to go to Jerusalem and pray unhindered at the Holy Sepulcher. The Crusade is over.

After all the misery, after all the killing, what a price! Guilt stains the white mantle of the Crusaders.

October 9: King Richard leaves the Holy Land. Autumn storms separate his ship from the fleet. Between Venice and Aquila, Lionheart makes landfall. He knows that enemies and rivals lie in wait for him. Disguised as a merchant, he tries to make his way north.

December 22, 1192: Near Vienna, Richard the Lionheart is caught in the net of his enemy Duke Leopold of Austria. On the same day, he is taken to the strongly fortified castle of Dürnstein.

Hard negotiations ensue for the precious prize. The duke delivers Lionheart to Emperor Henry VI.

King Richard a prisoner! The news shocks his followers in England.

King Richard a prisoner! The news delights his brother Prince John.

Ransom! The emperor demands 100,000 Cologne silver marks for the prisoner's release.

NOTTINGHAM SHIRE.
SHERWOOD FOREST.

Gold bars, silver coins, even a box filled to the brim with precious stones—by the end of June, the Brotherhood had successfully pulled off three raids. Without any casualties, almost without any fights, the outlaws had been able to capture goods on the great trade road. The loot was safely stored in the main camp under Robin's hut.

"I like this summer better every week." The outlaw shouldered his bow and girded his sword.

"It's been good so far." John poked thoughtfully at the bark of the Great Oak with his staff. "Almost too good." He pressed his lips together.

"Yes, my friend. The people of Sherwood are firmly on our side. And since my cousin has been with us, we have a lucky star."

Will Scarlet spied for the freemen. Sometimes decked out like a squire, sometimes dressed as a wealthy merchant, he rode to Nottingham. He always lodged at the inn below the fortress. Sometimes he stayed away for ten days or more. But when he returned to his fellows in Sherwood, he always brought good news. Success boosted his standing. He soon became Robin's closest confidant after John.

The information he had brought with him to the summer encampment the day before once again promised fat, easy pickings. "The Bishop of Hereford's emissary is on his way to York! It wasn't easy to get anything on that. But after the third jug of wine, I had the servant ready to spill: During the journey, his pious master sits in his litter on a box brimming with pearls and jewels." Anticipation glittered in his gray eyes. "We should pull the eggs out from under that hen." Best time to gather eggs: the next day around noon. Most convenient place: at the crossroads three miles north of Edwinstowe. Escort: four mercenaries who'd rather drink than fight. "You, Little John, and I will lift the bishop from the nest. It'll be quick and easy."

"Thanks, Will! I couldn't have planned it any better." Proud, Robin had nudged the giant. "Well, what do you say?"

"Right." That was all John had answered.

The sun had not yet risen. The sky shimmered reddish through the foliage of the Great Oak. Spread across the circular clearing, the men lay rolled up tightly in their blankets. Friar Tuck was snoring. Even the dogs were still asleep. Only their leader and his chief lieutenant had risen at first light, had put on their weapons, and now they waited.

At last. A low whistle. The two immediately left the campsite through the surrounding brush.

"Look at you!" Robin walked around his cousin. Coat, doublet, and all were the most expensive in the clothing cave's stock. Scarlet had turned himself into a landed Norman lord. Three pheasant feathers bobbed from his hat. But his right sleeve and stocking were torn, his knee above his boot bound with a blood-soaked rag.

"Looks like I fell off my horse. Am I right?" Scarlet enjoyed the amazement of his companions. "As soon as the troop with the litter arrives, I'll limp around in the middle of the crossroads and wave. If the bishop's emissary sees me like this, he will stop. I'll distract everyone with my wailing until you get there."

John grinned. "Better you than me." *I wouldn't have thought of such a thing*, he admitted to himself, without envy.

The morning was crisp, the sky cloudless, the sun slowly rising above the treetops. Robin winked at John. "Gonna be a good day. Maybe you'll like something from the jewelry box. A pearl necklace or a nice brooch made of gold."

"Why?"

"As a gift for Marian. Now that our little condition is becoming a lady."

"That *would* be something." The thought of bejeweling Marian like a lady pleased the giant.

Will Scarlet snapped off an elder branch, played with it for a while, then tossed it away. Barely a hundred paces farther on, he snapped a beech branch, was dissatisfied, and broke a second. He put it between his teeth. A little later, he spat the branch on the ground.

"Are you hungry?" growled John.

"Ah, never mind." Will laughed boisterously. "I'm fine." After a while, they reached a narrow valley. A stream gurgled its way through the tall grass. "There's one thing I've always wanted to know." Scarlet stopped the others. "Who out of the three of us shoots best? We've got plenty of time. What do you say?"

Robin clapped his hands. John shrugged indifferently. "*I* know," he said. "But if you need to know, too, fine by me."

Scarlet pulled one of the pheasant feathers from his hat and pointed to a thick beech tree beyond the dale. "Wait. Be right back" He ran into the meadow, leaped light-footed across the stream, fastened the feather in a knothole, and sped back.

"What's the wager?" he asked.

"Enough to make this worth it." Robin grinned. Ten shillings for the winner was agreed upon. Payable as soon as they returned to camp that evening. Their bows were to be identical. For the raid, John and Robin each carried a short bow. Robin lent his to his cousin. Scarlet fired. The arrow whizzed across the valley and struck the feather's gleaming white edge. Robin fired. His arrow also nailed the pheasant feather to the trunk.

"That's all right." Calmly, John raised his bow and drew. With a *crack*, the top of the wood snapped back with the string, whirling past John's head. The bow had broken.

The cousins laughed. Robin grinned. "Don't know your own strength."

"Now what?" John frowned.

Robin handed him his bow. "Here. But be careful with it."

By a finger's breadth, John missed the target.

"Our runt has lost!" Robin raised two fingers. "That's ten shillings for each of us."

Scarlet grew serious. "One bow is not enough for me. If I'm standing there in the road, I'd like to have two archers at my back."

He was right. John tucked the broken bow into his belt. "Keep moving along. I'll run back and get another one. Won't be long."

"We'll wait," Robin decided. He stretched out on the grass. His bow lay beside him. "There's time. Hurry up, though. I don't feel like having to run to catch up with those gems."

John turned back toward the camp. Not a twig snapped as he silently dove back into the forest.

No sooner had the giant disappeared than Scarlet crouched anxiously beside Robin. "I don't know. What if our mark left Nottingham early? Don't you think I should hurry to the crossroads, just in case?" His hand was on the hilt of his sword. "Be a shame if that hen with her golden eggs got away from us."

Robin sat up. "That's what I like about you, cousin. You're thinking ahead. Glad you're with me. Agreed. Go ahead. But no heroics! Wait till John and I get there."

Scarlet sprang to his feet and strode along the edge of the meadow. Before he left the valley, he whistled and waved a hand at Robin one last time. Then he ran off in the direction of the road.

The brook murmured. Birds were chirping.

Suddenly, a foot planted itself on the bow in the grass. At the same time, a sword blade slapped against Robin's neck. "Sit still!" ordered a hoarse, hollow voice. The outlaw froze. Out of the corner of his eye, he saw a leg beside him. Not a boot. Fur—brown, smooth fur to the tip of its foot. "What are you?" Robin breathed carefully, trying to buy time. "Are you human?"

The blade turned, the sharp edge cutting into his skin as his assailant gave a muffled, satisfied laugh. Then the voice rasped: "Your giant can't help you. Nothing will help you."

Suddenly, Robin threw himself to the left, rolled over, leaped to his feet, and had his sword in his hand ready to thrust. He stared in disbelief. A beast stood there. Motionless. Its head was a horse's head, a mane hanging long over its neck, its eyes far too deep in their sockets. From neck to feet, a brown coat covered its entire body. Robin sneered. "What carnival have you sprung from?" The horse-man carried his bow shouldered, his quiver high—the sword was in his furred right hand, a shield on his left arm. Two long daggers hung down from his belt, and a spiked metal ball dangled from a chain and short staff beside them.

Slowly Robin walked backward toward the edge of the meadow. The horse-man did not move.

"Well, what is it you want?" the leader teased. "C'mon! Though I have no bread scraps for you to nibble." He taunted with his sword. "But you'll like this."

"Don't take another step, you coward," commanded the voice from the horse head.

"Of course." Robin stayed in place, the sword held in front of him. "May I know who is scaring me so?"

"Before I smash you to pieces, I am Guy of Gisborne. The man who hunted down Robin Hood." With that, he leaped, a tremendous muscular force rushing forward with wild, sweeping strokes of his sword. Robin barely managed to ward off the first blow, but he had no shield and had to dive away from the second blow. The horse-man forced Robin backward. The blades of the swords struck against each other. A terrible duel raged in the narrow dale.

Little John ran without too much haste, deftly following the well-marked path back. He saw the bent beech branch. He spotted the discarded elder branch. *This cousin. Otherwise, he's serviceable, but in the woods? Makes tracks like an ox.* He resolved to talk to Robin about it. After a while, he grinned. *But what about me? Not much better. Snapping a bow as if I had never shot one before, even if it was a small one.* As he ran, he felt the two pieces of wood. John stopped abruptly. He stared at the fractured ends. His fingertip brushed over the edges. First, he could feel a tiny smooth cut, then the roughness where the wood had splintered under force. "I don't understand," he muttered as he walked, slowly now. *Who gave me this bow? Someone brought the bows from the weapons cave for Robin and me last night.* Ahead was the well-camouflaged entrance through the thicket. John bent down to pass through.

Nets fell from the trees, with thick ropes. They dropped heavily on the giant. He reared up with a cry of rage, pulled at the ropes, and pushed with his legs. He giant tugged, twisted, fell to the ground, squirmed, tangled himself more, lay shaking. "Ambush!" he roared. "Ambush!"

Loud laughter was the response. Four of the sheriff's men-at-arms approached their prey—four spears aimed at the giant's chest.

"Ambush!" shouted John again.

"Shut up!" One of the iron men kicked him in the face. "It's long past too late for your friends."

Three miles away, the peaceful valley had become a battlefield. The fight raged between Robin and the horse-man. The grass was trampled down all around them. They leered at each other, panting, leaping at each other again and again. Robin bled from a shoulder wound. Twice in a row, his blow broke through the other man's guard. Twice the broad blade rebounded harmlessly off the horsehide. Robin backed out of reach, shouting, "What do you want from me?"

"Your head," roared the voice from the horse-head helm. "Alive, you are worth eighty pounds in gold to the sheriff. But I'll make do with less." The horse-man charged forward, swinging his sword over his flowing mane.

Robin ducked, breathlessness and exhaustion taking away his voice. With a last burst of strength, he ducked under the blow. His head crashed against the man's stomach. His opponent tumbled over Robin. He lost his shield as he fell. But his back barely touched the grass before he sprang again to his feet with wild laughter. "He'll pay forty for your head, and that's enough for me." The man pulled the flail with the spiked iron ball from his belt. In his left hand, he swung the ball. In his right he held the sword, ready to strike. Prancing back and forth, he approached Robin.

Robin's eyes flicked from one weapon to another, looking for an opening to attack. "In the name of the Holy Virgin!" roared Robin, swinging the sword, striking blade against blade. He swung the sword again, and the flail's chain wrapped around the blade with a tremendous jolt. But Robin held his weapon tightly. He was jerked forward, and crashed to the ground.

A hoarse howl of victory rose up. The horse-man dropped the flail, threw the sword aside. With both hands, he plucked the long daggers from his belt. Robin rolled onto his back. The horse-man threw himself onto his opponent with a mighty leap. Desperately, Robin threw up his sword—

His enemy fell onto the blade, pierced through the neck on the point of the sword. His arms whipped about wildly as, gasping, he tried to stab at Robin with the daggers. Robin heaved him aside. The horse-man toppled to his knees in the grass. A dagger slashed Robin's sleeve. Robin also scrambled to get to his knees. And still, the mortally wounded man tried to thrust at him. Robin grabbed the sword with both hands, and swung the weapon back over his right shoulder, and brought it crashing down. The tremendous blow separated the horse's head from its torso. Robin's arms went limp. He let himself fall forward, dropping face down into the grass.

A horn called out. Robin raised his head. Another. One long note, two quick blasts, another long, drawn-out note. One of his brothers was calling for help! Again and again to signal sounded. Robin groaned. "Holy Virgin, don't abandon us!" He dragged his horn to his lips. Only on the third try did he succeed in answering the call. When his breathing was calmer, Robin struggled to stand up. There beside him lay the bleeding torso, beside that the horse's head. "Guy of Gisborne. You—"

"Robin!"

He turned. Much came rushing out of the forest, hurrying across the meadow. "Raid! The ... the camp. Come! The ... the sheriff has ... has ..."

Barely able to calm the boy, Robin shook Much by the shoulders. "Damn it. Get it out." The boy had been sleeping with Tom Toad and some of the others. Suddenly they heard noises, cries of battle from the Great Oak. "Tom sent me running. I ran. Then I saw the sheriff's men. They were climbing the trees at the edge of the thicket. And inside, at the camp, our people were yelling, louder and louder. I hid. And then ..." Much faltered, weeping.

"Then what?"

"Then, John came." He sobbed. "Nets. They used nets to catch John."

"John!" Robin clenched his fists.

"They dragged him to the oak tree to the lord sheriff. And ... and I went back to the caves. Tom told me to find you and Scarlet. So ... he's waiting. Because there are too many of them."

Robin Hood wiped his sweat-stained face. His expression hardened into stone. "All right, boy. Run back to Tom. Tell him to sneak up as close as he can with his men. Tell him to keep watch, not to attack." Coldness glittered in his eyes. "I have to try this alone. It's the only chance John, Friar Tuck and the others have—if they're still alive. But if it doesn't work, then Tom must strike at once!"

Much nodded, turning.

"Hold it!" Robin gave another command. "After that, run to the road. Stop Scarlet! He's alone. Bring him back!" The boy rushed off.

Determined, Robin bent down to the horse-man's torso, turned him on his side, and loosened the straps that closed the horsehide coat.

Little John was tied naked to the Great Oak. His hands were bound. Thick ropes pressed his neck, chest, and legs to the mighty trunk. In front of him, the lord sheriff, in a shining breastplate, strutted up and down like a fighting cock, poking him repeatedly in the stomach with a club. "*Sacre Dieu.* Who are you?" He thumped John on the head. "I've seen you before. Where? Open your mouth!"

The giant didn't answer. *Just strike me dead,* John thought. Out of swollen eyes, he looked across the clearing. His friends lay tied together on the ground.

They had not even had time to get out of their blankets. Next to Whitehand, Brother Tuck sat tied under a net. His four dogs lay dead around him, slashed open like hunted boars. John turned his head with an effort, looking over at the pile of corpses: seven brave men, and Pete Smiling was one of them. One of the armed men, guffawing, had reopened the dead man's scar with a knife. "He's really laughing now." The sheriff's men had had their fun.

The sheriff had accomplished his raid with only twelve of his iron puppets. Only twelve! *Ah, Robin, my friend, I tried to be a good right hand to you. And let myself be caught like a fool.*

"Guy of Gisborne!" an armed man announced. Thom de Fitz

lowered the cudgel. *"Maudit bustarin!"* he threatened the giant. "I am far from finished with you." He turned, staring expectantly at the edge of the small clearing.

A horse-man stepped out of the thicket. The men-at-arms fell silent, fearfully stepping aside. Slowly the sinister man strode to the oak tree. He had one bow on his shoulder, another in his fist. A head was impaled on the curved end of the bow, so crisscrossed with slashes and wounds its face was no longer recognizable. Proudly, the horse-man stood before the sheriff.

"Mon ami." Excited, Thom de Fitz dabbed his handkerchief around the stump of his nose, "Is it . . .?"

"Robin Hood," replied a hoarse, hollow voice. The frightful figure held up Robin's horn, and shook the bow and severed head. "You'll find his green remains in the valley, scarcely three miles from here."

"Magnifique. Quel jour. Magnifique!" Then, mock regret poured from his voice. as Thom de Fitz lifted his hands theatrically. "*Quel dommage, mon ami.* I would have liked to put the noose around that bastard's neck myself. But if there is no neck . . ." He broke off to laugh at his joke. Taking a deep breath, the sheriff said, "This day is my day. I, Thom de Fitz, Lord Sheriff of Nottingham, have brought down the band of outlaws with a single blow. What a triumph! And Prince John will sweeten this for me with honor and gold." He called to his men: "Your work is done. I will reward your bravery with ale and gold tonight in Nottingham. But now rest yourselves for a while!"

Enthusiastically, the men laid aside their heavy crossbows, swords, and shields; chattering, they squatted down on the grass beside their prisoners.

"Now that we will be undisturbed, *mon ami* . . ." Smiling, the sheriff took a step toward the horse-man. "To our business. Forty pounds in gold you have earned for the head. But I offer you eighty for a small favor more."

Just a nod in reply.

The sheriff took another step closer. He lowered his voice. "Eighty pounds for your silence. Let me have the glory."

No reply at all.

"*Sacre Dieu.* Your business is hunting people. Mine is politics. Prince John will soon be king of England." He pointed to the head's bloody grimace. "With this head, I will stand high in his favor. But there are still many enemies to eliminate. Without a fuss. I will not forget you and your talents, *mon ami.* Therefore, take the gold and stay silent!"

"A good deal," came the hollow voice from the horse's head. "But I don't want your gold."

The sheriff's face turned red. Before he could utter a curse, the horse-man added, "I'll let you have the head and the glory. In return, want that fellow there." The hairy hand pointed to the trunk of the Great Oak. "That's all. I killed the master. Now I want his servant too."

"You know this one?"

"Ever since you gave me the task, I've been watching this band of men. This is the right hand of Robin Hood." The man's hollow croak grew louder. "As a reward, I demand the runt!"

John perked up. Robin! New courage rose in him.

"Runt? That giant?" Surprise and greed alternated on the sheriff's face. He rubbed his hands together. "*Bien. Bien.* If you're satisfied with just him." He yanked the bloody head from the bow by the hair and cradled it in his hands. "*Voilà!* In return, this *maudit bustarin* is yours."

The horse head nodded. "But you will not interfere with what I do to him. Your people will stay where they are. No pity! No matter how I choose to deal with him. No matter how loud the shouting gets."

"On the contrary, *mon ami.* I will watch from here. Hang him, slaughter him like a pig, whatever you want. *Par tous les diables.* I'd love to watch you work." He ordered his men to remain where they were. He could not, though, stop the pleading and entreaties of Brother Tuck and the other prisoners.

Wordlessly, the horse-man approached the oak. John groaned, "Mercy. Mercy."

"Come up with something else!" whispered Robin. "Scream a little!"

John screamed. With languid slowness, the horse-man leaned the second bow and quiver against the trunk. In a flash, he drew both long daggers from his belt. He let the blades whirl in his hands, prancing back and forth in front of his naked victim, leaping forward, making quick cuts, prancing back, darting forward again, more quick cuts. "Louder, damn it!"

John roared like a stuck boar. The huddled prisoners screamed in sympathy and cursed.

At his safe distance, Thom de Fitz laughed, enjoying the spectacle.

The monster struck the bound man again. This time he slashed his blades crisscross across the broad chest. The howls of pain were awful.

"All the ropes are cut." The blades made a show of slicing up and down over the giant's legs. "Bow and quiver just to your left. By the Blessed Virgin, here we go."

John roared on.

The horse-man stepped back. The daggers were back in their scabbards. His right hand sprang up, grasped an arrow. A shrug of his shoulder and the bow was in his left hand. He pulled back the arrow on the string.

"Bravo!" exclaimed Thom de Fitz. "You are a true artist."

The arrow strained on the string, aimed at the naked prisoner. "Only the Blessed Virgin can still help you."

The ropes burst. The giant reached for the bow. An arrow hissed from John's string and hit the sheriff's face, piercing his head all the way to the feathered shaft. Robin's arrow pierced the breast-plate. Thom de Fitz hit the ground backward, the head of Guy of Gisborne rolling away.

The surprise and horror gave them a moment more. John flung the quiver over his shoulder. With his bow cocked, he threatened the iron soldiers. "One move, and you're over!"

Robin pulled the horse mask from his head. He sounded the horn. At once there was a response from outside the clearing. All around the in the brush and trees, horn calls rang out.

Abruptly one of the soldiers reached for his crossbow. John's arrow pierced him through the heart. "Don't any of you dare!" the giant shouted. But all the men-at-arms sprang to their feet. One found his sword, another his lance, a third had nothing, but all of them fled.

Robin caught hold of his friend's bow arm. "Let them run!"

The men rushed from the clearing and plunged into the thicket, out of range.

"By Dunstan!" cursed John. "Why did you stop me?"

Robin stayed silent until death cries rang out and then cut off.

"Tom Toad and the others were waiting." His grim face was smeared with dirt and sweat. "It's over."

He tore the horse's hide from his body. Thick black blood caked his shoulder wound, as black as on the scars on his back. He sat down and propped his forehead in his hands. "But what about Scarlet?"

"Much is missing, too," John muttered. His blazing rage had faded. The iron puppets had not stood a chance. *Good, our people didn't have a chance this morning either.* In vain, he tried to choke down the stale bile rising in his mouth. All at once, he felt the pain. Every kick, every blow. Face, chest, stomach. Exhausted, he sank into the grass beside his friend. "A disaster. A damn disaster," he muttered.

They left the freeing of the prisoners to Tom and the others.

Herbghost had made dressings for the wounds. At dusk, the men trudged together deeper into Sherwood. Two pits had been dug at the edge of a swamp. *"Requiescant in pace,"* Friar Tuck chanted and prayed for their seven dead. He stood silently by the grave of his dogs.

Thom de Fitz and the guards, they tossed in the swamp. The prayer was short.

Later, the first fires flickered under the Great Oak. In grief and perplexed anger, again and again, one asked the other: Why had no sentry heard attackers' approach? How did the sheriff know the way to the camp? And then again, they wept for their lost friends. Tom Toad, Whitehand, and Brother Tuck sat together, the truth of it heavy between them: Pete was dead. Each held on silently to his thoughts.

Away from the men, Robin and John stared into the flames. At last, Robin said, "If your bow had not broken . . ."

Abruptly John straightened.

Robin waved it off. "I don't mean it that way."

A memory was back. The bow! Someone had nicked the wood above the handle. "I've got to tell you—" John began.

"No, leave it." Robin sighed.

John rubbed his swollen lips. Where were the two pieces? *Where they netted me. They must still be there. I'll get them first thing tomorrow. Then let Robin see for himself.*

The sentry signaled. Low and long. High and short. Almost simultaneously, John and Robin sighed and said, "Here they come."

Much rushed into the clearing first. "Where's Bill Threefinger?"

"Here I am."

Much hugged his friend fiercely. "The guard told . . . told us everything. But . . . but the fool didn't know if you were alive."

With a serious face, Scarlet set an ornate box down in front of his leader and John. "Here. A little comfort." He crouched down with them. Quietly, he said, "First, I stopped the priest and his squadron with my poor injured leg. Then Much came along. The stupid boy just came running down the middle of the road." He patted his sword. "What else could I do? I took care of it on my own. Short and quick."

Robin opened the lid. Over the dull shimmering pearls, brooches, and jewels, he quietly looked into his cousin's eyes.

John felt that tug at the back of his neck, fiercely. He shook his head. "Four mercenaries. The priest. You alone?"

"They fought back. But I was better."

A smile creased Robin's face. "I know you are. Thank you, cousin. I am very glad we have you." Robin touched the giant's arm. "There's never been worse than today. But you'll see, my friend: We'll go on." He raised his chin. "Even if our hearts are bleeding. You and I must be the first to lift our heads again, John. The men expect courage from us now. Therefore, that's the end of it. This day is over. Tomorrow we break camp. We'll retreat slowly to the north. Well, what do you say?"

"Probably for the best. Pretty soon soldiers will be looking all over for the sheriff."

"And never find him." Angrily, Robin laughed. "We'll wait for the Jewish trader beyond Worksop. We can sell him these glittery baubles. And then that's done for this year. Then we're going home to winter camp."

"What Jew?" Scarlet wanted to know.

"Tomorrow, my cousin." Robin lay back and pulled his cloak up under his chin. "I'll tell you about Solomon tomorrow."

Will Scarlet also stretched out beside the fire.

John rose with difficulty. Every bone in his body ached. "Still thirsty," he grumbled. Carrying a mug, he shuffled past the mighty trunk of the oak tree. At the edge of the clearing, he sat down under a bush. He had half emptied the mug when Much joined him.

"May I?"

"Go ahead and lie down, boy."

For a time, they were silent.

Then Much whispered, "At first, I thought Scarlet knew the priest."

"What's that, now?" John let himself sink back. "Scoot closer, son. What happened?"

"I didn't run into the road right away," Much whispered. "Because Scarlet was drinking wine with the monk and the mercenaries. But I had to let him know, didn't I? And . . . so I . . ."

"Just say it!"

"And no sooner did Scarlet see me than he had his sword in his hand. First, he did in the priest, then the mercenaries. It happened very quickly." Much stammered, "No one . . . no one had a chance to fight back. And, and he was laughing. Laughing terribly."

John propped himself up heavily, leaning over the boy. "Don't tell anyone about this! And if you see anything else, you tell only me. Do you understand me?"

"But if . . ."

"Hush, boy. Scarlet is Robin's cousin. And—" he hesitated a long moment "—and a good man."

For three days, it rained. For three days, they waited near Worksop for the merchant's caravan. Just John, Robin, Scarlet, Much, and Threefinger.

A week earlier, the Brotherhood had retreated from Sherwood. When Robin Hood had seen how grief and horror still held the men captive, he'd made up his mind. "We'll split up." He sent most of his army ahead to Barnsdale, led by Whitehand and Tom Toad. "Rest up. The Blessed Virgin be your witness, you have earned it. We will follow."

Since then, group of five had camped in the abandoned barn near the main road. There was laughter, talk of the ordinary. No difficult questions. No one talked about the terrible day. Anxiously, John made sure that Much always stayed close to him. The boy must not betray himself in any way. Neither with a glance nor with a thoughtless word.

Until now, John had kept silent in front of Robin. He was always looking for a better chance to talk to his friend alone. But at noon that day, Threefinger had come to the barn with news: "The caravan is already past Edwinstowe. Tomorrow Solomon will pass this way."

John was determined.

The two friends trudged across the pastures in the rain, between wet grain fields. "What is it?" Robin was getting impatient.

"You once told me to tell you when something seems wrong. Lest you make a mistake."

Robin grinned uneasily. "So, come on then, tell me!"

Wordlessly, John handed him the halves of the broken bow wood. Robin looked at them. Abruptly his face changed. "Notched. With a knife."

"Do you remember who brought us the weapons that night?" Robin struck the pieces of wood against each other; he was silent.

John watched him out of the corner of his eye. *So, you do know.* He prepared each of his next sentences carefully, wanting to go lightly on his friend. "I just want to tell you how it was."

Robin grabbed him by the arm. "Do you? Why should my cousin, of all people ... Oh, come now, that's no evidence. *You've* had something against Scarlet ever since we met him."

John didn't answer.

Robin took a deep breath. Struggling to control himself, he asked, "And what was his plan? What if I hadn't sent him ahead that day myself? What then? Do you think my cousin would have stood by calmly while that monster stabbed me? No, never. He would have fought! By my side!"

"Then it was a coincidence," John said. "All of it coincidence. Even that Guy of Gisborne knew full well we'd split up in the valley."

"Because he'd been following us."

"You know this forest, and so do I. Were we asleep all the way through, then? Why didn't we spot him?"

To this, Robin had nothing to say.

"And what about the net? The iron soldiers were waiting right where I would come back. Only there. Not on the other paths."

Robin stopped, pulled back his hood, held his bare face up to the rain.

Quickly, John counted off: Who had told the sheriff where the camp was? Who had fed Friar Tuck's dogs the night before? They had not barked a warning, because they had been still soundly slumbering when the iron soldiers speared them through. Who had been drinking wine with the pious gentleman and the mercenaries by the road? There was only one answer: Will Scarlet!

"Never!" cried Robin. "He's my flesh and blood. Can't you get that through your skull! A family stands together, faithfully."

John wanted to wrap his arm around his friend. But he didn't. He simply said, "It's all right, Robin. It's all right. Even in a family, sometimes wicked deeds are done. Such things do happen."

Robin hurled the bow into the field. He laughed bitterly, breaking off abruptly. Somberly, he looked up at the giant. "If that's the way of it, Little John, and I'm so wrong, then I'm not worthy of any of this." He held out his hand to him. "You are the leader of our brotherhood from now on. Go on! Take my hand on it! You know everything, better than I! You're a smart giant after all!"

John turned away.

Behind him, Robin hissed, "Well, well, going off with his tail between his legs? What's the matter? Don't have the nerve to take on my job? Is your courage deserting you?" Robin laughed. "Nice. Ah, Little John: you'll never learn to play the game. All right, then: I stay what I am, and you stay you, just another one of my men."

"Why are you talking like that?" John's shoulders shook. "I-I thought you were . . . my friend."

Harshly, Robin replied, "You know, to a man in my position, *friendship* means something different."

"What are you saying?" John clenched both fists over his chest. "We're not friends?"

Robin's face fell, and he ran at once to him. "No—I don't mean . . . I'm your friend, and I have none better in you. But—but I also must be a leader to them all, that's what I mean." He laid his hands over John's large fists, and looked up at him.

The warmth between them returned. "It's just as well," John sighed. "If I had to take over, it'd be bad for everyone."

As they walked back, they decided: not a word to Will Scarlet for now. But they would remain vigilant. Robin wanted one more clear proof of it. "Then I'll see. Maybe we'll just send him away. To London, maybe. Somewhere he can't hurt us."

John nodded. "Fine." *If Scarlet knows all about us, then he can do harm no matter where he goes. But I won't say that until the time comes.*

Poor petty traders in gray cloaks, their heads covered with squared-off yellow caps, Robin Hood and Little John strode toward the merchant's caravan. They used their staffs as walking sticks. The giant carried a sack over his shoulder.

"Out of the way!" warned the riders at the front. "Come on, get a move on!"

The two men stopped in the middle of the road. Politely, Robin offered a greeting, "Shalom, gentlemen. Me and him here, we ask to wish the grand merchant a good day."

"Who's asking?" snorted one of the four mercenaries.

"Samson and Goliath from Worksop."

"Does our lord know you?"

Robin put his hand to his chest, indignantly. "We're his nephews! His brother's sister has another sister, and she married my mother's sister's father. I'm Uncle Solomon's little nephew. This is his big nephew. Uncle Solomon's sister's brother married the sister of—"

"Stop it. Just shut up!" The mercenary waved him off. The first covered cart had almost reached them. He quickly consulted with his comrades. "What do you think? It'll be fine. These Jews have such huge tangled families." The others nodded indifferently. "All right, then," the mercenary told Robin. "But make way first. Our oxen must not stop."

John and Robin obeyed.

"What were your names?"

"Samson and Goliath."

They were told to wait. The mercenary rode back, informed the guards on the flank, and spoke to the driver of the second team of oxen.

The canvas flaps were folded aside. As soon as the old merchant saw the two men at the roadside, his face beamed. "What a surprise!" Hastily, he sent the rider forward again. Like a beneficent uncle, he spread his arms. "Shalom, my nephews. Come up—what a joy!"

Solomon leaned back in his chair, his goods piled up behind him. Robin and John sat on the floor in front of him. Sweet wine was shared in greeting. But the joy of reunion quickly gave way. Gravely,

Solomon plucked at his gray beard. "In these months, England is coming apart at the seams."

Robin straightened his back. "But the sheriff is no more . . ."

"Hush. I don't want to know the details." The dark eyes looked soberly from one to the other. "Yes, vain Thom de Fitz disappeared with a whole troop of men. Nobody knew what he was up to that morning. They've been looking for him all over Sherwood. To no avail. It seems as if the earth swallowed him up. But who benefits?"

"All of us, I say." John frowned. "I mean, all the poor people in the shire. With that scoundrel gone, it stands to reason—"

"Don't be a fool, my good Goliath. Within a month at the most, Prince John will appoint a new lord sheriff. Nothing will get better. Nothing will change but the name."

The giant stared blankly. "Then, it will never end, this fight?"

"Enough of this." Robin clapped loudly. "Since when are you so gloomy? Last time we met, you said your people never give up hope. That it was the secret of your strength. That's how we live in the Brotherhood, too. We hope. That's why we fight." He took the small wooden box out of his sack and opened the lid. "This is what we want to sell you. And when our king returns from the Holy Land—"

"Richard the Lionheart was captured."

Robin's face stiffened. John set his cup down. The merchant continued grimly. "Until the ransom is paid, Richard the Lionheart remains a prisoner of the Emperor. A hundred thousand pounds in silver! Who knows whether the Queen Mother will ever be able to raise the ransom?"

No word had yet reached the Brotherhood of this misfortune. They listened silently to Solomon. New taxes, levies. Courtiers and noblemen, artisans and bishops, Norman, Saxon, Christian and Jew, everyone in the country had to give up some of his property.

"But then the sum should soon be raised," Robin interrupted excitedly.

"You forget the king's brother." The old man lowered his voice. "I have it on good authority that Prince John is playing an insidious game. He is collecting the levies in his shire's monasteries and castles with the king's forged seal. The levies never reach London. John robs and hoards jewelry and coins with his allies. One of these scoundrels is Sir Roger of Doncaster. Heavens lament. How could it be otherwise? No, my friends. I fear it will be a long time before Queen Eleanor can buy Richard back from the Emperor."

Robin ran his finger over the rim of his cup. All at once, his countenance brightened. "At last, I can do something for my king." He grabbed John's arm. "Well, what do you say?"

"What, now? Without our people? We can't just go to Doncaster . . ."

"We'll talk about the details later," Robin cut him off. He laughed and pointed at the twinkling and glittering contents of the small box. "I mean this." He set the wealth before the merchant's velvet boots.

"I see." John had caught on. "I like it."

"I don't mean to be rude." Solomon raised his hands slightly. "But I'm too tired to solve riddles. If it's a business matter, let me know."

"We're not selling." The leader looked frankly into the old man's eyes. "Take the box into your possession. As soon as you return to London, could you take it to the queen? Say this is the share Robin Hood and his Brotherhood will contribute to the ransom." He paused, corrected himself. "No. Not my name. Just say King Richard's most loyal followers gave it."

Solomon breathed heavily. The wrinkles around his eyes deepened. "You trust such a fortune to an old moneylender, a Jew, no less? Without surety?"

Quietly, Robin said, "When I see a man's eyes, I know him. And

I am never—" Sensing John's gaze, he hesitated and then added, "I am seldom mistaken."

Solomon poured a parting drink. "I usually only trust my head." He smiled. "From you, in my old age, I may yet to learn to trust the heart as well. Shalom, my friends!"

Scarlet was immediately enthusiastic. "Yes, we will gut Sir Roger like a goose. I've waited a long time for this. And I know how we can get into the castle secretly, too. I know of two underground passages. They are unguarded. And if you want—" he jumped up, squared his shoulders, and clapped his hands like Robin "—we'll not only take that bastard's money. No, we'll rob him of his greatest treasure." With relish, he stretched out the pause. "We'll free the *roi de neige*!"

John, Much, and Threefinger stared at Robin's cousin in silence.

"Slowly. Slowly." Robin tamped down the young man's enthusiasm, giving a sober assessment of the situation. "There are but five of us. Sir Roger has well-trained men. More than enough to nail us to a beam three times over."

"What else do you have me for?" Scarlet squatted down close to Robin. "Send me out first thing in the morning. And tomorrow night, I'll bring you the plan: Where they hid the ransom. When the guards will change."

John grumbled, "I thought you weren't allowed to show your face in the castle anymore?"

"Don't need to, giant," Scarlet scoffed. "I know a fellow in Doncaster. He always has free entry to the castle."

"And who is that?"

"The blacksmith. He supplies all the weapons. Sir Roger trusts him, but in reality, the blacksmith is his enemy." He looked frankly at Robin. "I'll bring you the plan, and then we'll strike."

John propped his forehead on his fist. *The blacksmith? That scoundrel. I asked him for work that day. He didn't want Marian there. "Sell her to a beggar!"* John could still hear the greasy voice. No, that blacksmith was loyal to the Baron.

"Nice, cousin." Robin seemed to agree with Will. Lightly, he nudged his foot against John's boot. "Hey, are you asleep?"

"What?" The giant looked up. "No. Just tired."

"Well, what do you say?"

"It's all right. If it works, it's good."

For a long time, John stood outside the barn. The weather had cleared. Misty vapors rose from the wet meadows. Silently, Robin stepped up to his friend's side. When he noticed him, John murmured, "Think I'll go hunting with Much tomorrow—heading north. Pheasant or duck. Got an appetite for it."

"Is that the only reason?"

"No."

Robin was silent. Then he said, "Good."

They stood together in silence. Above them, little by little, the stars rose.

"Here." Robin swung a small string of pearls between his fingers. "For our little condition." He smiled. "I'm sure King Richard would approve."

Mushrooms and grains, boiled with water, early in the morning. Robin Hood sat alone with a bowl and his cousin by the fire. They spooned their porridge in silence. Their companions still lay quietly in the back of the barn, their cloaks pulled over their faces.

John was not asleep. He had spent half the night brooding, then finally dozed off, but Scarlet's first movement had awakened him again. Since then, he'd been lying there, watching the two cousins through half-closed eyelids. Scarlet munched unconcernedly, eating his fill. Robin took little, poked about in the pot with his spoon. *Oh, my friend. I wish I had been wrong!*

Scarlet jumped up, bouncing on his feet. He squared his shoulders and threw on his blue cloak with a flourish. "I'll be back tonight."

"Think it over, Will!" It was an offer, almost a plea. "You're riding right into Satan's lair. If it's too dangerous, just say so! No one will hold it against you."

"Oh, come, cousin. I can handle this easily." Scarlet waved off the plea. "And in any case, I'm sure I won't even need to go into Doncaster myself. I'll send some boy to the blacksmith with a message: Gamwell is waiting at the mill."

"Mill?" asked Robin harshly. "Where our Much comes from? Do you mean that one?"

"Yes, the one in the south. It's the best meeting place. It's been standing idle since the miller and his people died." Will embraced his cousin, not noticing that Robin did not hug him back. "Don't worry. I know exactly what I'm doing. I'll learn everything I need to know from the blacksmith." He mounted his horse. "A fat haul it will be." He clicked the horse into a short trot, then spurred it to a gallop.

John stepped out of the barn. "Fat haul?" he growled. "The only question is for whom."

Both of them looked after the rider.

"He's lying." Robin rubbed his knuckles against his teeth.

"That's right."

At the far side of the meadow, the blue cloak disappeared into the brush.

"No, John. Not about what you told me yesterday. I still want proof of that. But now, just now." Anger flashed in his gray eyes. "He brazenly lied to me. Who does he think I am? The mill! He gave himself away with that. It belongs to the baron. He needs it for flour. Why would it stand idle?"

Little John said quietly, "It's time for the hunt."

Staff. Daggers. A short bow. Arrows full in the quiver. When Much and the giant had laced their light sandal straps, Robin once again called his friend aside. "Just remember, Will is my cousin. Maybe he is telling the truth after all."

"We'll know tonight," John replied, nothing more.

They ran cross-country, jumping streams, avoiding any homesteads. A good five miles lay behind them. "Hey, Much!" Only now did John enlighten the boy. There was to be no hunting for pheasants that day. The hunting ground was the mill. The prey was Scarlet.

"And what . . . what if we see . . . ?"

"Then nothing, lad. What we see, we report to Robin."

They ran northward at a brisker speed, and Much was always a good three paces ahead. Sometimes he would smirk over his shoulder. "Should I slow down?"

"Save your breath, lad!" Sweat shone on John's forehead. John still felt the sheriff's hard blows. On his ribs, in his stomach.

By late morning they reached the creek above the mill valley, waded through the ford, and rested among the birch trees. "No matter what we see, you stay by my side," John cautioned the boy. "That's not your home anymore over there."

Much swallowed. "I . . . But my mother and father are lying . . ."

"No, boy!" The giant continued sternly: "Another miller is living in the house now. And the grave is probably no more. Do you understand me?"

The boy's chin quivered; only after a long while did Much nod.

"It's all right, son." John firmly planted his hand on the young man's shoulder. "Now go on ahead. You know your way around this place better than anyone."

They took advantage of the shelter of the riverbank willows. Along the edge of the narrow depression, they made their way upward, close to the buildings. There they stayed in the bushes.

The water rushed through the millrace. The wheel turned evenly. The sound of heavy stones scraping came from the millhouse.

"Robin was right." John nodded grimly. Though Scarlet was nowhere to be seen, his horse stood in the shadow of the house. They waited. Now and then a farmhand shuffled to the barn, returned with a sack over his shoulder, and hauled it into the millhouse. The sun was rising. It was getting hot.

Hoofbeats approached from the direction of Doncaster. John carefully parted the hazel branches. Two riders. Their faces could not yet be made out. Yet he recognized one by his leather apron, the other by his plume of feathers, his dark velvet tunic, and his billowing dark cloak.

"Thought so," he growled. "The devil comes himself. And his blacksmith brings him here."

The riders had barely reached the courtyard when Scarlet, followed by the miller, emerged from the house. It was impossible to make out any words. Much and John only saw Will bow politely.

With a wave of his hand, Sir Roger dismissed the blacksmith. At once, the fellow turned his horse and trotted back. The baron tossed the miller a purse. The man bowed low and continued to bow until he had disappeared backward into the house.

Only now did Sir Roger dismount. A smile twisted his thin lips. Like an obedient pupil, Scarlet bowed again. With two fingers, Sir Roger lifted Will's chin. He patted his cheek.

In the bushes, Much groaned. "But, I thought Will killed his steward. And that's why . . ."

"Remember everything you see!" murmured John. He rubbed the scar in his beard. *Poor Robin. Today, I'll bring you proof.*

Scarlet eagerly ran to the baron's stallion, grabbed the halter, and led the animal behind him. Together with Sir Roger, he left the yard. They walked, leisurely, along the bank of the brook.

"Where does that path lead?" murmured John.

"To the jetty. And a bit farther down, there's a lake. Not big, but deep. Father and I used to go there in the boat . . ."

"Not now, boy. Come!"

Soundlessly, they left their hiding place. They followed Sir Roger and the cousin at a safe distance. John wanted to get closer but couldn't. There was too little cover from the trees.

Then the baron and his pupil left the wide path and followed a branching-off between reeds and bushes to the lake. Sir Roger stopped close to the rugged edge of the shore. Patting his horse's neck, he listened intently as Scarlet spoke, explaining with his hands, laughing, letting his whole body play it out, snapping his fingers.

Gently, the outlaws moved. No stem broke, no leaf bent. John and Much silently crept closer through the reeds. Bits of sentences drifted over.

". . . But not in the castle . . . In the church . . . All the money is under the stone behind the altar. Tell him that!"

Scarlet asked, "When?"

Closer still. They heard each word plainly and clearly:

"Starting tomorrow: every evening for a week. Tell your cousin that right after the last mass is the most convenient. And I promise you, my people will be there. With swords, axes, and lances."

Sir Roger steered the horse around by the halter. "There's one more thing." With a finger, he beckoned Scarlet closer. Only hesitantly did Robin's cousin obey.

"Fear nothing, my son! I do not blame you for the *affaire fatale* at Sherwood." A little smile. "On the contrary, you have learned from me. Your plan could have been devised by me. That sheriff! Thom de Fitz was always nothing but a greedy, vain, brainless wretch. You presented him with victory on a platter, and he failed."

Scarlet bowed artfully before his master. "*À votre service.* I do my best. Soon I will deliver you Robin Hood and his gang. And I hope you will not forget me."

In hiding, Much groaned. Firmly John pressed his hand over the lad's mouth.

Sir Roger pinched his pupil's cheek and patted it. "I'll see to your future," he said, nasally. "Deliver the bastard to me, and as I promised, my new bailiff shall be Gamwell of Maxfield. And that will be only the beginning. For soon, Prince John will ascend the throne of England. Yes, my son, I still have great plans for you." Suddenly troubled, the baron frowned. "There's one more little problem."

"Tell me," Scarlet urged, "just say the word!"

"You're a good boy." Sir Roger barely opened his lips. "You know nothing must jeopardize my plans—especially no superfluous witnesses. That vexed affair with the miller troubles me still. All I need to settle it once and for all is his son. Take care of him."

In hiding, Much squirmed under the grip of the giant. Only when John threatened him with his fist did the boy settled down quietly on the boggy ground.

Scarlet laughed, clapping once. "Done. While the trap for Robin Hood snaps shut in Doncaster church, I'll be skinning that mouse with relish." He helped Sir Roger into the saddle.

"You wait here. As yet, we are not to be seen together, if possible." The baron's pale green eyes looked sternly down at his apprentice. "Make me proud of you, Gamwell!" With that, the baron trotted through the reeds and shrubbery over to the wide path.

"I will never fail you!" exclaimed Scarlet to his master. "Never. Neither you nor my aunt."

Sir Roger did not look back.

In hiding, John let go of the boy. It was hard for Much, so hard. *And, oh, Robin. My poor friend!*

On the shore, Scarlet bounced on his knees, stood again, flexed his shoulders.

Much could hold back no longer. Before John could grab him, the boy leaped up, burst through the reeds, raced screaming toward Will. Scarlet stood stunned, mouth agape. "Bastard!" The boy rammed headfirst into the traitor, throwing Scarlet back. Much kept moving, pushing both himself and Scarlet over the rocky edge of the bank. Both tumbled into the water.

John was on the spot at once. Two heads resurfaced not far from him. Both sputtered, gasped for air, went under again. Neither of them could swim. They surfaced, splashing wildly. Scarlet spotted the giant. "Help me!" He managed to grab the boy's hair; he pushed Much underwater, keeping himself above the surface for a moment. "Help! John! Help me!" Gurgling, he sank.

John couldn't swim either. He threw himself half over the edge of the bank, holding the staff at the ready. Much rose up, gasping, spitting water, screaming. John held out the end of the stick to him. "Grab hold of it, boy. Hold on!"

Much's arms flailed desperately. At last, the boy reached for the wood. Scarlet sprang upward from the bottom. He threw himself over Much, gasping, trying to push him away, to reach for the staff himself. Smoothly, as quickly as he could, John guided the boy with his staff out of the traitor's reach. "Hold on! Just hold on, lad!"

Slowly, he drew Much closer to the shore, pulled him half out of the water, and heaved the boy up to him.

In the lake, Scarlet still struggled. "John!" He splashed about wildly. Sank, surfaced. "Help me!"

John lifted Much to his knees and bent him over. As he spat water, gasped for air, convulsed, the giant held his head. He pressed both hands tightly over Much's ears.

Only John saw Will's death throes and heard the cries for help, saw his head break the surface one last time, heard the desperate gurgling. The water sloshed in waves, smoothed. The lake lay flat and calm.

John released the boy's head. Gradually he caught his breath. Much looked up at him. "What . . . what . . . happened to . . . ?"

"Was too late," John muttered. "Had to pull you out first."

The boy turned warily. The still water frightened him. He slumped forward. "Thank you." Just a whisper.

"You heard everything you needed to." The giant stroked the boy's head. "Now get some rest, son. It's a long way back." John fell silent. And then what? He thought of Robin.

Deep in the night, they finally reached the dilapidated barn near Worksop. The boy had needed frequent rests. Progress had been slow.

Robin and Threefinger were waiting by the fire. Robin saw John's face and was silent. Only after the two had eaten did he ask, "How was the hunt?"

Much beat John to it. "Scarlet has ... has betrayed us all. He ... he's ..."

"That's all right, boy. I'll tell it."

Robin Hood listened with a fixed gaze. John reported only as far as the Baron's departure, then broke off.

Robin snapped. "Go on. Something is missing. Where's my cousin?"

Much folded his hands over his chest. "It was me. I ... I just had to. Because ... I ran at ... Will. Then ... then we both fell into the water." He looked to John. "He saved me first. And Scarlet ..."

Robin abruptly jumped up and stormed away, then returned to the fire. "Threefinger! Much! Go sleep. At once! Did you hear me?"

Startled, the two retreated into the barn.

Robin Hood stepped into the embers. Sparks flew. "Why, John? You had clear orders. Proof! You were to bring me proof! Nothing more!"

The giant straightened his back and stood up in front of his friend, breathing heavily. "I got the boy out. Then it was too late."

"Too late?" Robin clenched his fists. "Why, John? Why didn't you try to save Scarlet first?"

John shook his head. "No, you don't mean that? No, you don't mean . . ." Wildly, he shook his friend by the shoulders.

"Don't you dare!" Robin shouted at him, his hand going down to clutch the hilt of his dagger.

John released him, calmly taking a step back. "It's all right," he placated. "I didn't choose which one first. Much was at the staff first. That's why."

The anger in Robin's eyes died out as abruptly as it had flared. Tears stood in his bright eyes. "Even if he did betray us. He was my cousin, after all," he whispered. "Do you understand?" Looking tired, he huddled back down by the fire. "Stay with me. Please."

John nodded.

After a while, Robin raised his chin. "So. We're not going to Doncaster."

"Better not."

"Not yet. But someday, sometime, when this devil isn't lying in wait for us."

Out of the corner of his eye, John watched his friend. "You know, back in York, when I was Sir Richard's valet, the baron wanted to see my face. I promised him, you won't see it until I break your neck." John waited. The corners of Robin's mouth twitched. He added, "And if I meet him, then I'll keep my promise, I promise you that."

There was a grim smile in response.

John exhaled. *Done. By Dunstan, it's really over now.*

XVIII

YORKSHIRE. BARNSDALE WINTER CAMP.

John missed the laughter. Since returning to the main camp, Robin had driven the men hard. "He who works, forgets!"

He had a stockade built around the base at the top of the ridge: trenches with needle-pointed logs planted in them, camouflaged by loose tangles of branches and leaves. And the leader himself pitched in. From morning till night, he showed no fatigue.

At the end of September, Robin called his lieutenants to him. "You have worked well," he told them. Except for two heavily guarded access roads, deadly pits now surrounded the hidden compound. "But it's not enough." In addition, a stockade fence was to be erected around the huts, stable, and paddock. No rest. "Tomorrow we'll continue," he ordered. "We have to be finished by winter." More to himself, he added, "And no sheriff, no Sir Roger will surprise us here in our sleep."

For another week, Little John watched his friend. Robin's countenance remained sober, grave. Not even a mocking smile at the corners of his mouth. The giant threw up his hands. "Well, if you've got something to say, go ahead and say it."

Robin's eyes were cold. "What do you expect? Do you want me to clap my hands with glee?" He clenched his jaw. "Our losses at Sherwood were high. Only hard work will distract these men. Their courage and fighting spirit are gone. And that's what worries me. And that is all."

"Just as well." John fell silent. *He who works, forgets?* He shook his head slowly. *It's true for our people. They already carry their memories easier than you.*

In mid-October, the leaves of the big linden tree in the camp turned yellow again. It was once more time to trade their summer clothes for the warmer winter ones.

Tom Toad and John sighed with relief and looked at each other; they had been waiting for this moment for weeks. In Robin's hut, the giant did the talking. "These garments need to be patched up. Better get Beth." Anticipation lifted his voice. "And Marian can help. We'll leave in the morning and be back by evening."

"No." Terse and sharp.

"What?" Little John did not understand. Tom Toad stroked his scalp, pulled on his braid, and said, dangerously low, "By Willick. For what reason . . . ?"

"Don't you dare question—"

"That's all right." John pushed Toad aside and joined Robin at the table. Their eyes were level. "Why shouldn't we fetch them?"

"Stop! My friend." Robin put his hands together, fighting for self-control. "A few months ago, I had five trusted lieutenants. Now there are only three. I'm sorry. Until the palisades and gate are finished, I can't do without any of you." He gave Tom a frosty look. "Let the village girls mend our clothes this time. Beth won't mind."

He turned to John. "Marian is in good hands with Sir Richard. I think she can wait a little longer." With that, he tried to dismiss his men.

Tom did not stir. John remained seated, motionless.

"All right." Robin drummed his fingers on the tabletop. "Our men have fought long, and they always had the goal clear in their minds: King Richard will soon return. By our Blessed Virgin, I promised you and you, I promised everyone. But now?" He fell silent, then continued: "So our fight will take much longer. And we must prepare for that."

John murmured, "We'll make it through this together. For certain."

Outside, he wiped his brow. "Damn. If it hadn't been for Scarlet—"

"Don't worry about it. He just needs time." Toad groaned exaggeratedly, slamming his fist into his hand. "But what about me? We last visited the castle in May. Oh, it's going to be too long a wait."

"Just as well." John grinned mockingly. "This'll give you more time. To compose your song."

The work at the base was finished in time for Christmas. Robin seemed pleased. The stiffness had gone from his visage. He was talking, even laughing now and then. But those who knew him well sensed that his cheerfulness was only labored pretense, only a veil. "Take care of yourselves!" he called to the few who had family and were allowed to wander home. "Don't get lost!" No one laughed at the joke.

"What about us?" Ready to depart, Toad and the giant stood before him.

The corners of his mouth twitched slightly. "All right, get out of here. But be back tomorrow! Friar Tuck won't start Christmas Mass without you." He grabbed Tom's arm with a worried look. "Do you have your lute?"

"Not you, too," Toad groaned. He put on a haughty face. "Thank you, friends. Thank you. I packed everything I need."

Neither John nor Robin had another joke to make.

Toad grinned.

The fire was crackling in the castle hall. After the midday meal, hosts and guests waited for the girls' performance.

At first, Marian had vehemently refused. "Don't feel like it." At a toss of her head, her carefully combed curls tumbled over her forehead.

Angered, the priest lowered his brows. "Why this unruly

disobedience? Don't you want to show everyone what you have learned?"

Marian persisted. "Don't feel like it."

Patricia, Sir Richard's daughter, dared a brief admiring glance at her friend, then she bent her head low over her trencher. She tried hard not to snort.

Beth begged the baroness for indulgence. Her voice became stern: "Princess. Don't forget our agreement!"

This helped. Marian pouted. But then she smiled at John. "Only because you're visiting."

Relieved, the tutor-priest rose from the table. "Come, my children! One more rehearsal." He quickly left the hall with his pupils.

John shifted cautiously. As soon as he moved his weight on the chair, the seat and wooden legs creaked precariously. He had sat very stiffly during the dinner of stuffed bread and three crispy chickens. *Sir Richard's cooks understand,* he mused. *I'm happier when I'm full. If only everything here wasn't so uncomfortable.* He didn't know yet if the dainty armrests would hold his arms. And the wine goblet? Was it smaller than the ones in the camp? Just as well. He drank more slowly, more deliberately.

Out of the corner of his eye, he watched Tom. The man sat, unconcerned, next to Beth. How his eyes shone as soon when he looked at his wife. Nothing bothered the man. And Beth? To see her now. She was like a fine lady. But she still gazed at her Tom the same way she did in Barnsdale.

The girls returned. Each carried a lute on a velvet shoulder strap. The priest placed two stools in front of the table. Gracefully, Patricia and Marian took their seats.

The lord of the castle's daughter turned her brown eyes on her friend. A wink. Almost in unison, they plucked the strings.

John took in a deep breath. *Oh, my little one. Sitting there like a highborn damsel.*

Two bright, high voices sang: *"Natus est Jesus, natus est Deus, natus est Salvator noster . . ."*

John swelled with pride. His thoughts went to Marian's mother. *I promised you. You see? I'm taking care of the child.*

The song ended and the audience clapped. John thumped his heavy hands together and had to restrain himself from drumming his fists on the table.

The girls curtsied. As the priest bowed to Sir Richard and his wife, Marian nudged her friend in the side. Both of them struck their lutes again. Full-throated, they sang out: "In the rose garden, there I spied a bold young knight waiting by and by. It was merry May, the air was warm and fair . . ."

Horrified, the priest took a step back. He tried to end the song with hand signals, in vain.

"There rose from the well a damsel, bare . . ."

Sir Richard soothingly placing his hand on his consort's. But a smile remained on his lips even as the lyrics turned more and more raucous. Beth covered her eyes. Tom liked the song. He twirled his braid along with the tune. John didn't even hear the words. Marian sang like a lady! The two outlaws alone applauded the singers this time. Before their tutor could recover from the embarrassment, Patricia and Marian were already running out of the hall giggling.

"I beg your forgiveness, sir." The priest folded his hands in front of his black robe. "The burden of my office grows heavier every day. When it was only your daughter . . ."

"I pray you!" Sir Richard pointed to the door. "We each do our duty. And yours seems to me among the easiest."

With bowed head, the teacher left the dinner party.

Tom Toad tried to give Beth a hint. Seemingly indifferent, Beth ignored his glances. At last, Sir Richard rose from the table.

The nursemaid turned to lady at the Lea. "Do you still need me, mistress?" A shake of the head. "Thank you." Beth strode out.

The baroness stood beside her husband, waiting. She looked over at Little John. He was the only one still seated at the table. After a few patient moments, she decided to overlook his ignorance. "Squire John." Her voice sounded warm and serious at the same time. "I wish to offer you my gratitude, for Marian. The child means a lot to us. Patricia has found not only a playmate but, above all, a friend. However . . ."

John waved his hand, wanting to interrupt, but he came to his senses in time and closed his mouth.

"However," the lady at the Lea continued with a smile, "we are also glad that Beth is at our side. Otherwise, the girl's temper would be hard to control." With that, she took her leave until evening and left the hall through a side door.

As soon as he and Sir Richard were alone, John squeezed his body out of the narrow chair. The armrests did not break. "Why did she thank me?" He stood before the knight. "It's the other way around. I am in your debt, my lord. Because you've given the child everything, and she can already sing, just like our brother Tuck at mass. And pluck the lute. Oh, that was beautiful." He thumped his hand against his chest. "Tonight at the meal, I will thank your wife."

Sir Richard stroked his trimmed beard. He mulled something over, then reached a decision. "What do you think, my dear Little John, the girls are doing right now?"

The giant lightly shrugged his shoulders. "Well, at their learning. Surely they're reading something with the monk." His eyes lit up. "Or writing. Yes, surely . . ."

"My dear Little John." The knight took his arm and slowly paced the length of the hall with him. "So that you see how everything has two sides, I want to show you something."

The corridors were cold and damp. They followed a wide curved staircase up through other corridors, descended a narrow staircase.

Before Sir Richard opened the door, he asked, "Do you remember how Mistress Beth persuaded Marian to obey? No? She asked the girl to remember the bargain she had made."

He pushed open the portal and led John a few steps along the battlements.

Orders were yelled. Clipped shouts. More orders. Marian's voice, Patricia's voice echoed up from a small courtyard.

John leaned over the ledge. His breath caught. Below him, the two girls stood facing each other, wooden swords in their hands. Attack and defense. Marian was showing her friend just what thrust to use to break through an opponent's guard.

John rubbed the scar in his beard. He saw bales of straw and target cloth on the courtyard wall, and he saw bows and arrows. "By Dunstan. Just like ours at the camp. I thought—"

"There was no other way to negotiate with Marian." Sir Richard frowned. "And she's keeping her end of the bargain. She studies, is diligent, wears in public the clothes Mistress Beth puts her in. In return, she gets to frolic down there as she pleases. And, if I'm honest . . ." Sir Richard lowered his voice ". . . why shouldn't a woman be able to handle a weapon? In moderation, of course. I don't forbid my daughter to do so. And since the baroness has seen for herself Patricia's enthusiasm, she has no objections either."

John leaned over the parapet again. Marian spotted him. Cockily, she whirled the wooden sword around her head. He tried to calm her with his hand. Concerned, he turned back to Sir Richard. "But, she's learning as well? I mean, writing too, reading too? Because, after all, she is to become a lady."

"Don't worry!" Sir Richard tried to ease his concerns. "Get used to this! Marian possesses all the good qualities a father would wish for his daughter. And a few more besides. Why shouldn't those talents be nurtured as well?"

"If that's the way it is." He was not entirely convinced. But if even a distinguished gentleman like Sir Richard did not object? "All right, then." *Then I'll just get used to it.*

Back in the castle hall, Sir Richard sat down by the fire with his guest. They talked for a long time. About England. The shires, which the lords called counties.

John memorized the name of the new lord sheriff. Walter de Monte. An ally of the prince. Cruel and greedy like his predecessor. Nothing had changed. "I'll tell Robin. At least we know the name of the villain we're fighting."

"But perhaps, my friend, everything will change for the better soon, after all. No—I'm sure of it."

"If only." John thought about Robin. "But we'll fight, no matter how long it takes."

The baron abruptly set down his goblet. "You don't know?"

"What?"

Sir Richard jumped up, slapping his forehead. "What a fool I am. How could you have known?" Excitedly, he grasped the giant's shoulders. His face lit up. "My friend, my brave squire. The ransom, a hundred thousand pounds in silver marks! England has raised the sum. I understand from a trusted source in London that Queen Eleanor is already on her way to see the Emperor." John's incredulous expression only increased Richard's excitement. "Yes, the old Queen Mother herself is accompanying the transporting of the ransom. If God is merciful to us, King Richard will soon be in England."

John emptied his cup in silence. It was not enough. He picked up the wine jug and drank directly from it. At last, he wiped his beard and mouth with his sleeve. "If Robin hears this . . ." He hesitated, wanted to inquire more, desisted. He grinned broadly. "That's all right, sir. If Robin . . ." He struggled to choose the right words. "I mean: when Robin Hood hears this news . . . Oh, nonsense! It's not simply news. It's a marvel!"

"And not only for England. For my family, too," the baron added quietly. "So many young men have already returned from the Holy Land. And still, we wait for our son. But I know him. Surely Edward has stayed by his king's side. Even in captivity. When Richard the Lionheart returns, my son will come home, too."

Beth and Tom stayed away from the night meal. John did not care. Everyone should enjoy themselves that day! He looked at the richly laid table—fragrant minced-meat of veal, accompanied by a cream sauce with red and black currants.

And the giant ate! After all else had finished, accompanied by astonished looks, he continued to eat on alone. Nothing remained of the tasty dishes.

John made a request. Marian and Patricia were happy to sing him the Latin song once again. They curtsied gallantly, then rushed off to their shared bedchamber.

With jug after jug, the good news mingled in John's head with the good malmsey from the castle's wine cellar. Only with difficulty did he find his bed for the night. He snored away until a servant pounded on his door in the morning.

First, a farewell from Sir Richard, his wife, and Patricia. The hosts remained behind at the gate. At the end of the drawbridge, Tom promised to his Beth to return soon.

"Wait, little one!" Circumspectly, John searched in the provisions bag. With two fingers, he pulled out the small string of pearls. "Here. I thought . . . well, it's sure to fit around your neck."

Marian took the necklace. "That's all right," she said quietly. Then she laughed happily. Suddenly, her blue eyes grew serious. "I like it here, John. But only because you're not far away."

The men left briskly. Beth and Marian waved after them, standing close together on the drawbridge for a long time.

“He is coming?” Robin slowly turned his back on his friend and leaned his forehead against a post in his hut.

No sooner had the giant and Tom returned that afternoon than John had given him the good news.

“He’s coming.” Hope grew in Robin’s voice. He pounded his fist against the wood. “An end at last. I promised you. Not someday, my friend, but soon. Soon we’ll reach our goal!”

Robin abruptly turned around. The mask he had worn for the last months had fallen off. A new fire glowed in his gray eyes. “Oh, John. So long have we fought against injustice and oppression.” He paced back and forth in front of him. “Perhaps to the sheriff, to all the Norman plunderers, we are nothing but outlaws. Robbers. But, by the Blessed Virgin, Richard the Lionheart will see us. With a gaze from which nothing can be hidden.”

“He will.” John puffed up his chest, proudly. He didn’t care what Robin was saying. He only saw his radiance, heard the clear, powerful voice again. Finally.

Robin laughed. “Our king is coming! That’s the most wonderful news. Especially coming today.” He took his friend’s arm. “For tomorrow we celebrate Christmas. And not just tomorrow. We shall feast into the new year. Roasts. Ale and beer. Well, what do you say?”

“That’s all right.”

Robin hugged the giant of a man fiercely. “That’s all right. That’s all right. Is that all you have to say? Oh, my friend.”

Without a by-your-leave, the giant lifted Robin up and sat him down hard on the table. At Robin’s stunned face, John had to laugh.

At midnight, torches blazed around the big linden tree. Joy was reflected in the eyes of all the freemen. Friar Tuck celebrated the Christmas Mass, proclaimed into the frosty night: *“Ecce, rex venit sanctus et salvator mundi. Gloria! Gloria!”* And the brotherhood sang, *“Gloria in excelsis Deo.”*

Day after day, Herbghost and Storyteller stoked the fire in the long kitchen shed. Water boiled. The smell of soups rose from stewpots, and the smell of roasts drifted through the main camp down by the river. Night after night, the men gathered together. Robin wanted to hear stories—stories of King Arthur.

Storyteller transformed the kitchen shed into Camelot Castle. The outlaws sat next to the noble knights of the Round Table.

"How the Lady of the Lake saved good King Arthur from a cursed cloak that would have burned him."

"How King Arthur knighted brave Perceval."

"How the Red Knight dueled with—"

That evening, John slammed the flat of his hand down on the table. "No. Not that story. I still don't know what happened to the Green Knight. Only that he put his head back on and left."

Gilbert Whitehand remembered. "No, no. First, the fellow told Sir Gawain that he would be waiting for him at the Green Chapel a year from then. Then he rode off on the green horse."

"Yes, tell the tale!"

As usual, Storyteller wanted to be begged, drinking his ale with relish. He awkwardly adjusted his stiff leg. "But the story will turn out different than you think. Very different."

"Get on with it!" Robin pointed warningly toward the door. "Or else . . ."

"Don't interrupt me!" hissed Storyteller. His hands reached for invisible reins. "On All Saints' Day, Sir Gawain rides out through the gates of Camelot Castle. At once, the drawbridge is closed back up behind him. He sets off alone in search of the Green Chapel. It's cold . . ." Storyteller showed a measurement with his fingers. "That's how thick the ice was on his helmet, on his shield. Sir Gawain rides deeper and deeper into a wild forest. On Christmas Eve, he suddenly comes upon a castle. The knight is cordially welcomed therein. He sits by the fire with the lord of the castle. Then the door opens . . ."

Storyteller pushed his tankard toward John. "I am in want of ale."

The giant hurried to return. Hurriedly, he poured more from the jug.

"By Willick," Tom Toad growled. "You are meant to be telling! You can drink later."

The old man set down the cup and wiped the foam from his chin with his sleeve. "That's when the door opens, and the beautiful lady of the castle comes in. So beautiful. Such a woman as our knight has never seen. Such beautiful eyes he has never seen. And she makes beautiful eyes at him." Storyteller scratched his head at length. "It wasn't much farther to the Green Chapel. It stands only two miles away, in a deep ravine. So, Sir Gawain has some time to spare for the castle's lovely mistress."

Tom Toad slapped his thighs. "Good on him. But what did the lord of the castle say to that?"

Indignantly, John rubbed the scar in his beard. "If that was my wife. I would have pushed him headfirst through the ice into the moat."

"And I would have—" Gilbert spoke up. So did Much. Each man present announced what he would do to a rival.

"Enough!" Robin smiled expectantly. "I want to know what happens next."

Every morning, the lord of the castle and his guest set out separately to hunt. They give their word to share the spoils in the evening.

So, Sir Gawain receives half a deer, a hare. He, however, returns to the lady of the castle first thing every morning. First, he kisses the lady's hands ... And as an honest knight, he must keep his word. And so, he also shares this with the lord of the castle.

Tom Toad opened and forgot to close his mouth. Amused, Storyteller grinned at the crowd. "First he kisses the lord's hands ..." He did not elaborate further. The laughter all around showed him that everyone understood well enough.

Robin demanded silence. "You made that part up. You louse. If you don't know the rest of the story, you know what happens to you." He pointed sternly toward the door.

"It's true, though," Storyteller grumbled. He hastily continued. On the last day of the year, it is time for Sir Gawain to leave. The lady of the castle gives him a green belt. "Wear it!" she says, "It will protect you."

Sir Gawain rides two miles into the deep gorge. At the Green Chapel, the Green Knight awaits him. His ax is even bigger than last year. Sir Gawain just stands there quietly. The Green Knight takes a wide swing. The blade whistles through the air. But just short of the knight's neck, it stops and slides away. The Green Knight tries again. Again the ax slips. Only on the third blow does the edge touch Sir Gawain's neck, but only lightly scratching the skin.

"'Now it's my turn!'" Storyteller boomed in Sir Gawain's threatening voice. "He thrusts his lance. But the Green Knight just calmly swings his ax in his hand. 'It is well, my friend,' says he. 'All this was but a test.' He strips off the green mask. Standing before Sir Gawain is the lord of the castle. 'You kept your word. You came at the appointed time. You shared honestly with me all that you had won, even my wife's kisses. Only the belt you kept from me, so I had to wound you.' Before Sir Gawain can reply, the lord of the castle turns and vanishes."

One by one, the freemen returned to their food. Unsatisfied, John shook his head. "Where did he go?"

"How the hell should I know?" Storyteller scoffed indignantly. "That's it for today." He reached for the mug himself and poured himself a cup. "Make up something for yourself if you don't like it."

On the penultimate day of Christmastide, the day before Epiphany, water was again being heated over the fireplace. The freemen stood outside in the snow. One by one, they undressed, then smeared themselves with grease, salt, sand, and ashes.

"Our pure Virgin and the saints have refined noses!" Robin laughed at his men. "Our King Richard, too." Thus he declared the Great Bath Day begun, and was the first to scrub himself, until his skin glowed. John had bucket after bucket brought to him. What a steaming treat. Last of all, Friar Tuck pulled up his robe, and this time not just up to his belt. He started scrubbing at his feet and didn't stop until he reached the carefully shaved circle on the back of his head.

After each service in the little church at Wrangbrook, Much held the penny plate in Marian's place. The adults took gratefully, the children pecked twice, and the congregation's reverend father emptied the lavish remainder into his lifted gray robe.

The Brotherhood of Freemen trudged through the snow back to Barnsdale. Robin let the others lead the way. He took John's arm. "My plan is set." While the snow was still melting, he wanted to leave for the summer encampment. "We have to be in Sherwood early."

John shook his head. "We have time."

"No. I want to know as soon as possible what the new sheriff is up to. We'll ask the charcoal burner, we'll ask around Blidworth, we'll ask all our friends. I want to know exactly what the new situation is. We're sure to pick up a fat morsel or two along the way on the trade route. Besides, we must secure our terrain around the Great Oak. Get supplies and fine clothes into the caves. And do you know why?"

He didn't wait for an answer. With a flourish, he yanked his cap off his head and spun it upward. His reddish-blond hair shone. "Oh, John!" He snatched the cap out of the air. "And in June, we'll wait below Nottingham for Uncle Solomon."

"You mustn't," growled John. "We promised. No raiding his trade wagons."

"Don't be a . . . ah, never mind, I'll keep my word. I just want to ask him where Richard the Lionheart is. By then, I'm sure the king will be back in England. And then . . ." He paused. "Then you and I will dress up like fine nobles. That's how we'll go to London, to our king."

"What? You mean to do what?"

Robin resolutely looked up at the giant, hardness in his eyes. "Yes, dear friend. We will appear before King Richard. First, I will tell him all about us—the plain truth. Then I will tell him of the sheriff, about every one of his barons, of every abbot, and how they bleed and torture the people. I want him to know everything. And then . . ." Robin spread his hands as if it were drawn before them. "We kneel. And await his judgment."

John's breath caught. "What if he's a completely different man? I mean, we may never be done with this game."

"None of that!" Robin laughed. After a while, he shrugged slightly. "And what if we aren't? Only you and I would be headed to the hangman. Our men won't. Think of our great goal. For that, the stakes are worth it, even if I don't know all the rules this time."

Little John bent down and gathered some snow. While shaping it into a ball with his big hands, he said, "I'll always stay by your side." He smiled. "The first time we were together here in Wrangbrook . . . that time you threw the snowball over the church for the children. Do you remember what they shouted?" He handed the snowball to his friend. "Here. Try it again. Hit the sun for us!"

XIX

NOTTINGHAM SHIRE.
SHERWOOD FOREST.

The Brotherhood of Freemen safely reached their summer encampment in Sherwood in the middle of March. As every year, they had set out separately, in twos, in threes. Along the way, all of them were on high alert: if possible, escape; if necessary, fight to the death . . . of their pursuer. But no one had paid any mind to the wandering men. "If we had marched in the middle of the trade road," Tom Toad reported as he rubbed his shriveled scalp, "the iron puppets wouldn't have cared."

Whitehand and Friar Tuck reported royal troops and tents around Tickhill, in southern Yorkshire. "We dared not go near the castle," said Gilbert.

Reproach sharpened the monk's voice. "It would have been easy for me to mingle with the mercenaries. No one would have refused information to a humble Cistercian."

"You . . ." Gilbert swallowed whatever curse was coming with some effort, threatening Friar Tuck instead with his white fist. "And if it had gone wrong?" Seeking support, he turned to Robin. "No risk. That's what you ordered, tell the holy man. Tell him!"

"Stop." Robin was leaning against the trunk of the Great Oak. At a new thought, he snapped his fingers. "Nice." He nodded to John. "So, our charcoal burner was right. The castle is under siege. And if that is true for Tickhill—" his voice grew rough "—then, friend, it is also true for Nottingham."

"Good thing, too." Grinning broadly, John added, "Before the eagle comes, the magpies are driven from their nests."

The news had been astounding! Robin had asked twice. Gabriel had stuck to his story: The newly installed Chancellor of England, Hubert Walter, Archbishop of Canterbury, was preparing for the return of his king with an iron fist!

The chancellor was alarming Prince John's supporters throughout the country: "Richard the Lionheart is coming!" It was both a warning and a threat. "Remember your oath of loyalty!" The cowardly renegade nobles blanched. To them, politics were only a means to personal gain. So, the news was enough—"Richard the Lionheart is coming!"—and one stronghold after another raised the royal standards again, the leopards and the lion of England fluttering side by side on the battlements. All the intrigues, all Prince John's treacherous plans forged during his brother's absence, blew away in the wind.

Nottingham and Tickhill alone defied the chancellor's messengers, chasing them out to the gate. "Lies!" they declared. "Richard will never return. We stand under the banner of the future King John."

Both fortresses had been besieged for more than three weeks. The charcoal burner had gotten the news from Tickhill: Besiegers and defenders were engaged in fierce battles. Losses on both sides, but no victory.

What was the situation outside Nottingham? Robin lined up his men under the Great Oak. "This time, there are no armed men from the sheriff looking for us. But there will be troops from those earls and bishops loyal to the king everywhere. By summer, we may have reached our goal. But I warn you: The game is not yet won." Whitehand and Toad were to lie in wait with the main body of the brotherhood above Edwinstowe. "You will capture spoils. Keep a keen eye out for me for monks heading north! I imagine the priors, in particular, will be trying to quickly transport some more money bags under their robes to Doncaster, or some such place, before it's too late—before our king reinstates law and order in the monasteries of that shire as well." Robin would travel from village to village with John, Friar Tuck, Much, and Threefinger. "And if we don't glean enough information, we'll sneak up to the tents camped outside the city. I want an accurate view."

It took the brotherhood a few days to settle back into Sherwood. They retrieved weapons from the caves, checked bow wood and sinews, resharpened arrowheads. Finally, after a week, Gilbert and Tom moved the men to the main road.

Friar Tuck knotted his rope belt over his sword belt. John and Robin shouldered their bows. Only Much and Threefinger were still squatting listlessly under the great oak.

The giant let his staff hover dangerously close to their feet. "Getting up soon?" he growled. "Or shall I help you along?"

Obediently, Threefinger tried to get up, but Much held him back. He looked up boldly at the giant. "Why can't we go to the road with the others?"

"By Dunstan!" John thrust the stick into the soft moss between them, grumbling. He pushed up the sleeves of his green tunic. "I think . . ." he opened and closed his huge paws ". . . I think I need to have a good talk with you two."

In two quick steps, Robin was beside him. "Hey. What are you up to?"

John hefted his staff. "Wanna teach these two a lesson." John grinned tightly.

Much and Threefinger crawled backward away from him before scrambling up. "He wanted to beat the crap out of us," Much grumbled.

"Ah, no, lad." John twirled the staff. "It was just a game."

The corners of the leader's mouth gave a telltale twitch. "It looked pretty serious." He murmured appreciatively, "Game? By the gracious Virgin, you certainly are a good student."

Friar Tuck rubbed his tonsured head. "Better if we leave these two in Herbghost's care. As kitchen servants."

"By all the saints, anything but that!" Threefinger blurted out. "If . . . if I . . ."

Robin didn't wait for Much to get the sentence free. "Hush! So. While we're in a village talking to the elder, you two will be watching the trade road. When troops pass by, you'll make note of their crests, each flag. I'll want to know precisely what they were. But as soon as something worthwhile turns up, then let me know at once. I don't want to miss a chance at something. Is that clear?" Robin held up a finger on each hand and brought them together. "For that, I need my best scout and my best runner. All good?"

There was no questioning him. With great haste, Much and Threefinger made ready to depart.

"Lord Sheriff Walter de Monte sentenced three cutpurses to death. Put the rope around their necks and pushed them out of the windows of his own house. That's how he hanged them." Robin paused. "They were just children."

He went on: "Because a farmer could not pay the interest on a loan, the sheriff's soldiers took away the man's only milk cow."

He went on: "In the presence of Walter de Monte, the forest rangers chopped off both hands of a poacher. Because he had caught two partridges with one net."

The trail of terror left by the new lord sheriff in his short tenure so far stretched from village to village.

But what was happening outside Nottingham, around its walls? None of the villagers had been able to answer that question.

On the twenty-fifth day of March, John, Friar Tuck, and Robin Hood sat in the cottage of the village elder of Blidworth. At last they received the information they needed: "The fortress is under siege. Yet, by day the troops can move no closer. The archers and crossbowmen have a clear line of fire down from the battlements of the walls. And at night?" The elder shrugged. "The weather has been too bad. If only the moon would shine."

"So they're making no progress?" Robin furrowed his brows. "You'd have to take that fortress by surprise."

"It's not so easy," came the reply. "The new lord sheriff is different from Thom de Fitz. He knows a bit about warfare. He thinks himself as something of a field commander."

"They'll have to be starved out," John grumbled.

The village elder sighed. "It's more likely the king's troops who are doing the starving in the tents outside the city."

Much rushed in breathlessly. "Quick! Someone's coming. From the direction of Nottingham. Maybe two miles away."

Robin jumped to his feet. "Easy, boy! Who?"

"Four parsons. Black robes."

"Any escorts?"

The boy shook his head.

"You're certain?"

"Bill only saw the four of them. On horses. Riding slow. Bill says fine frocks. Sword scabbards gleaming. And spears. That's all he could make out so far. I headed back right away."

Robin clapped his hands. "Four in one fell swoop. Nice."

John was already at the door. Friar Tuck had no intention of staying behind. "When it comes to my fellow brothers, I want to give succor. No matter to whom."

Robin quickly said goodbye to the village elder. "Thank you! But duty calls." He laughed.

Much ran in front, through the forest. They would receive their victims to the north of the turnoff to Blidworth.

They reached the main road without a hitch. There was still no sign of the reverend lords. At the apex of the long sweeping curve of road, Robin stopped. Here was the most favorable spot for watching for travelers.

"We have plenty of time." He ordered, "Much, fall back, half a mile. Wait until they pass and then join Threefinger. Both of you follow the parsons. But don't let them see you!"

The boy rushed off.

Robin handed Friar Tuck his leather waterskin. "Stow that away!" He pointed to the bare bushes on the other side. "You hide yourselves there. And, by the Virgin, please keep quiet! Until I call for my cupbearer."

A smile flitted across the monk's plump face. "My outrage alone shall shut my mouth." Friar Tuck crossed the trade road.

"Shall we go forth together?" asked John.

"I'll go alone. You always say it's better to be cautious. Who knows how brave these gentlemen are? You cover me."

The giant took the bow from his shoulder, looked for a good shooting position among the trees. *No matter what, my friend, I will let nothing happen to you.* From where he stood, he could see Robin leaning against a tree trunk on the slightly elevated embankment, and past him, John could easily see the ribbon of the road up to the knoll. With a turn of his head, he could see anyone approaching the bend from the north.

Now came the waiting. The clouds hung heavy; it seemed they almost touched the bare crowns of the trees. But there was no rain.

Far to the south across the hill, four dark dots appeared, slowly growing larger. Four riders, dressed in black. Three brown horses, one white. Four robed priests, their wide hoods pulled low over their foreheads, riding leisurely into the hollow, getting closer.

Robin whistled. From beyond the road and behind his back, soft whistles answered.

Voices could be heard. The four travelers were conversing in the Norman tongue.

Calmly, Little John put a feathered shaft on the string. He pinched his brows. The tall one on the white horse, the one with fur on his cowl collar, that man was leading the conversation. *If I have to, I'll take him down first.*

Robin detached himself from the trunk and stretched his back.

The dark monks rode along the bend, almost reaching the top.

Robin flew off the embankment with one leap, barely touched the ground, took a second springing jump. He landed standing in the middle of the road.

The horses spooked and pranced. *"Merde!"* Eventually, the priests had their steeds back in check. All reached for their lances and had them half out of their saddle straps.

A shrug of his shoulder and the bow was in his left hand; his right hand whipped behind his head; and the arrow was on the string. Robin drew it back. "Now, now!" His tone was sharp: "Don't even dare!"

The monks froze in midmotion, staring dumbfounded at the green-clad man.

"Mon ami . . ." Deliberately slow, the tall one on the white horse slid his lance back into the saddle quiver. A nod of his head and his companions followed suit. He showed his open empty palms. "I am not angry with you, my son." He spoke the words carefully, unpracticed, as if searching for the correct words in the Saxon tongue. "Surely it has escaped your notice who we are. See—we are Dominicans from . . ." he hesitated ". . . from Keyworth. *Bien.* And I am the Father Abbot of the monastery." The timbre of his voice was full and strong. "We are hunting for a strong stag that has been spotted farther north in Sherwood near Edwinstowe. So, clear the way!"

"In due time, your reverence. In due time." Robin smiled. "Just rest for a little bit. Then, I will relieve each of your heavy burdens, then you may continue on your hunting trip."

The squat monk next to the abbot threatened with his fist. "You, bastard, dare—"

"*Taisez-vous!*" Sharply, his master reproached him. From the shadow of the black, fur-trimmed hood, the whites of his eyes shone, his beard gleamed red. Calmly he turned to the robber. "You are very brave. But alone. Despite our dress, we are skilled in the use of our weapons."

"Enough of this!" Robin commanded gruffly. "Get off your horses! All four of you. Get a move on! And keep your hands where I can see them."

In his hiding place, John drew the arrow shaft up to his right ear. The point was aimed at the abbot's neck. *One wrong move, and you're done.*

The men reluctantly climbed down from their saddles.

"Now, two steps forward." Robin grinned. "Nice." A short whistle. Behind the monks, Much and Threefinger crept out of the bushes. "Get the horses off the road," Robin called to them.

The expressions of the four men darkened. None dared to turn their heads.

After they carried out the order, Threefinger returned alone. Unnoticed by the monks, he made warning signs, pointed south, and mouthed words over and over. Finally, Robin understood. "Armed men." Now John, too, spotted the troop. Riders were charging up to the road at full gallop. *By Dunstan!*

"Reverend fathers. Forgive the inconvenience!" Bow still taut, Robin pointed with the arrow up the embankment. "It's better to talk there in the woods."

Wordlessly they obeyed. The abbot led the way, climbing effortlessly, his fellows following him closely as if to protect his rear. Robin drove the gentlemen deeper into the forest. None of them noticed the giant, Threefinger, or Friar Tuck, who crept behind them at a short distance.

"Take a seat!" Robin invited them. His guests squatted on the wet moss. He told them, and his voice brooked no argument, "Keep quiet!"

Hooves clattered over on the trade road. They came closer, grew loud, then quickly receded.

"Merde!" cursed one of the Dominicans between his teeth. With a perplexed expression, he looked at the others. The abbot, too, seemed changed all of a sudden.

Controlling himself with obvious difficulty, he forced his face into a thin smile. "*Alors, mon ami.* We are in a hurry. What can I do for you?"

"No." Robin cut him off, aiming at the black-robed chest. "I make the rules here. You are my guests."

"Guests?" the abbot sneered, not taking his eyes off the arrow. "Strangely uncouth manners seem to be practiced here in Sherwood. May I at least know the name of my host?"

Robin replied in the same tone, "Our customs are in accord with the visitors we receive." He lowered his bow. "Before you stands Robin Hood."

The three monks sat agape, sliding back a little on the wet moss. Only the abbot strained for poise despite his uncomfortable position. "Robin Hood?" He stroked his red beard and looked right and left at the others. "Then, *messieurs*, I suppose our hunting trip is over for the day."

"Now, now," Robin assured them. "Do not fear for your lives. You are my guests, and later I will allow you to hunt the treasures of my sprawling summer woods."

"Do you presume to—?!" The abbot was indignant. "This forest is not your property. It belongs to the king!"

"Quite so. But until Richard the Lionheart is back, I am his steward."

"Appointed by whom? Say it, you dishonorable rogue!"

Abruptly Robin's countenance changed. "Guard your mouth, priest! My people and I know more about honor and loyalty to the king than most of the barons and abbots in this county. And I warn you, the bogs in Sherwood are deep. No one will ever find you and your monks." He smiled again. "Enough of this. A welcoming drink will do you good." Robin whistled, and called, "Cupbearer!"

Immediately Friar Tuck stepped out from behind a tree.

"Feed our guests!"

The squat Cistercian's round face was flushed. "Gladly, sir." His voice sounded menacingly soft. "I'll take care of these fine Dominicans." He pulled off the leather stopper and approached the monks with the waterskin. "Open your mouths!" Holding the horned mouthpiece a handspan from their lips, he squirted a stream into the guests' mouths one by one. One choked and coughed. Friar Tuck did not care. "For you thirsted, and I gave you to drink."

Lastly, he stepped before the abbot. "And you, redbeard, lean your head back. For you, I have two sips."

When the priest refused, Robin threatened him with the arrow. That was enough.

Friar Tuck splashed the closed lips with water. "For King Richard!" he demanded. No answer. "To our king's happy homecoming!" The lips parted, but the abbot said nothing. Friar Tuck emptied half the contents of the skin over his mouth and red beard. "To Richard Plantagenet. King of England." The priest spat and shook himself.

"And that was the refreshments." Carelessly, Friar Tuck dropped the waterskin. He breathed deeply and looked down at the abbot. "And now for some more edifying conversation, as is customary among Cistercians and also Dominicans." He raised his voice to a loud chant, *"Beati, qui habitant in domo tua, Domine . . ."* He paused, waiting. Nothing. The abbot just stared at him.

"Go on. Complete the verse!"

When there was still no answer, Friar Tuck swung his arm back and gave redbeard a resounding slap. He hit him again with a second slap, striking right and left, continuing the chant "*in saecula saeculorum laudabunt te*" and marking the beat of the words with his hard blows. "Amen." Enraged, he folded his arms. "Liar. There is no monastery in Keyworth. You and this brood of yours! Oh, how I detest it when one dishonors the dress of the church."

The stricken man lowered his hand to the pommel of his sword. Friar Tuck did not see. He was far too agitated. He blocked Robin's aim.

Abruptly the abbot threw himself forward to his knees, and the weapon hissed out of the scabbard. Too late did Friar Tuck realize the danger. The tip of the blade pressed against his belly. "In the name of—"

"Drop it!" commanded Little John. The abbot jerked his head around. The giant stepped out of the bushes behind him, his arrow aimed at redbeard's face. "Drop it!" he growled, taking two steps to the side so that he had all the monks lined up in front of him. "At this range, my shot will go right through your skull—" John drew the feathered shaft up to his right ear "—and through those three empty skulls beside you, too."

The sword dropped into the moss. Robin dared to move again. "It's all right." John cautioned him back. He was not yet satisfied. "You others, too! Set your swords down in front of you!" They obeyed mutely. The giant relaxed his bow and grinned at Friar Tuck. "You know a few things about the mass, brother. But other than that . . . well, it's all fine now. Gather up the weapons and rest yourself a bit!"

Now Threefinger also left cover. Smiling, he took the swords from Friar Tuck.

Robin shouldered his bow and drew his dagger. "And now for

you scoundrels. You are Normans—that I can tell by your language. And you are up to something—that I can tell by your disguise. No matter what you have planned, you will not succeed against my king."

In impotent rage, the stout monk clenched his fists, snarling, *"Maudit bâtard."*

Redbeard ordered him to be silent.

Robin spun the knife around in his hand. "We've wasted enough time. From liars, and especially from lying monks, we take everything." He bowed gallantly to the false abbot. "Such is our custom in Sherwood. Mind you, everything: horses, clothes, coin. But I will spare your naked lives." Robin winked at John. "It'll be days before these fellows stumble out of the woods naked and barefoot. Well, what do you say? If the wolves spare them. For the cause of our king—"

"Par tous les saints!" Despite the danger around him, the false abbot jumped to his feet. With both hands, he tore the robe off his chest, "I am your king!"

A dazzle of chain mail gleamed, the three leopards on his tabard shone. He threw back the black hood, and the chain-mail hood beneath it, too. Red hair flowed down to his shoulders. "I am your king!" he roared at Robin, holding him with his dark gray gaze.

Silence fell.

Friar Tuck's shoulders slumped. *"Kyrie Eleison."* He made the sign of the cross and fell to his knees, muttering, "What have I done?"

The gathered swords clanged to the ground. Threefinger knelt hunched beside the monk, hiding his face.

John felt the blood pounding in his neck. In his chest. All they had done—all in vain. There would be no mercy. He threw his bow into the moss. He dropped heavily to his knees.

Only Robin Hood still stood before his king. His eyelids twitched. He did not lower his gaze. It seemed as if he was absorbing every feature of the face before him.

"Will you not greet me?" demanded Richard the Lionheart.

"My lord," Robin said in a raspy voice. He pushed the green hood down around his neck. His reddish-blond hair fell in straggly curls to his collar. He bent his knee. Unblinking, his light gray eyes locked with the king's storm gray ones. "My lord."

The king's three attendants sprang to their feet, rushed to their weapons, and the stout sergeant returned his sword to Lionheart. Murder was in his voice. "Shall we—"

"Silence," the king commanded gruffly. "Just silence, *sieur.*" A flick of his finger commanded the man and the others to move a few steps away.

With his sword, the king knocked the dagger out of Robin's hand. "None of my subjects kneel before me with weapons ready to stab."

"Pardon me!"

"You are forgiven." Richard Lionheart smirked. "You have already demonstrated more than clearly to me and my captains just how uncouth the manners are in Sherwood."

The sound of horses trotting, from the north—they were approaching fast. "*Vite!* Stop the troops!" the king ordered one of his attendants. "Tell them to wait!" Seeing Robin's questioning look, he declared with a slight sneer, "Even had you sent me away without my clothes, my escort would not have ridden past their naked king. And the laughter that would cause tonight in the tents outside Nottingham? I would myself have ordered my scribes to record it for posterity."

For the first time, Robin bowed his head.

"Look at me!"

The outlaw obeyed.

Richard turned serious again. "Time is of the essence. I rode out here to find you. Yes, you are the stag I wanted to hunt for, farther up Edwinstowe. I did not expect that you would find me first."

"Why, my lord . . . ?"

"Don't interrupt me! I have things to say to you, you self-appointed steward of *my* Sherwood. Or should I say, you king of the outlaws?"

The corners of Robin's mouth twitched.

"Bien." Richard returned the smile. "Rise, then. One ruler to another."

Tickhill had surrendered the day before. Early in the morning, Richard the Lionheart had joined the besiegers outside Nottingham with an army. Despite the royal banners, despite the fanfares, the fortress had not surrendered. He had even approached the walls himself, protected by shield bearers, to within shouting distance. He had been showered with jeers and taunts from the battlements. Lord Sheriff Walter de Monte believed it was a ruse. Faithful men had fallen dead to the ground on the king's right and left in a hail of crossbow bolts. "I must force Nottingham to surrender," he vowed. "I will take it! Now, and quickly. And I need your help to do it."

Robin spread his arms. "Anything, my lord. I give you—"

"Don't interrupt me!" At once his tone became calm and steady again. "A week after Easter, at the request of the Queen Mother, I will be crowned for the second time. At Winchester. By then, I must have settled all the affairs here in the north. Therefore, Nottingham must open its gates to me within the next few days." He looked at Robin. "How many archers can you give me?"

"All my men, except for Friar Tuck. Twenty archers. Longbow and short bow."

Disappointment darkened the king's face. "I was told there were more."

Robin lifted his chin. "Each of us is worth ten. So, in truth, I offer you two hundred bows."

Richard smoothed his red beard. "That might be enough. When?"

"This very evening."

The king laughed. "Tomorrow morning. Before first light."

"We'll be there. But . . ." Robin hesitated.

Coolly, Richard looked at him. "I understand. *Bien.* Only those who negotiate a price do not cheat." He ordered his companions closer. "You, *sieurs*, will bear witness to my words." Richard Lionheart hesitated. He asked, "What is your real name?"

"I'm from Loxley. Robert Loxley."

"*Bien.*" The king raised his hand. "We, Richard Plantagenet, King of England, hereby assure you, Robert of Loxley, called Robin Hood, and each of your companions of our mercy. We promise: After assistance is rendered, you will all be granted a general pardon. No one shall dare to persecute nor punish you for past deeds. . . . Is that enough?"

A dull, slapping sound made Robin spin around. Little John was kneeling, but now he thumped his fist into the flat of his other hand, his bearded face beaming.

Robin bowed to Richard. "Thank you." He raised his head. "But, forgive me, My Lord . . ."

"*Bien, d'accord.* I know what you would ask." The king gave a sober look to his companions. "Moreover, it is decreed: Every one of your men shall be raised to the rank of a freedman. To no baron, to no monastery shall you be beholden, but to your king alone."

There was a stifled cry. Little John pressed his hand over Threefinger's mouth. Only Friar Tuck still stayed with bowed back.

"You are generous. Thank you!" Deeply moved, Robin placed his right hand on his heart. "But, forgive me, My Lord, who . . ."

"*Par les saints!*" Richard frowned. Measured respect resonated in his voice. “You are the equal of the Sultan’s negotiators. You know how to use your advantage. *Bien, d’accord.*” Anew, Richard drew in his companions. “Furthermore, it is decreed: Barnsdale, in the county of York, the whole region to the left of the trade road, with forest, valley, and village, is given to you as a royal fief.”

“Nice,” Robin blurted out. Immediately he lowered his voice. “Thank you! But forgive me . . .”

“Don’t overplay this game!” the king snapped at him.

“I’m not playing . . .” Robin paused. “By the Holy Maiden, this day, it is not a game,” he amended. Resolutely he began again, speaking quickly. “Pardon me, My Lord, but who taught you so accurately about us? That is all I was trying to ask. From whom do you know of Robin Hood?”

Richard the Lionheart laughed.

With a bow, one of the attendants stepped in: “Forgive me, Sire. The time. You must reach Nottingham before . . .”

The king waved him off. *“Un moment.”* He slid his sword back into its silver-studded scabbard, looking at Robin, his eyes flashing, “You mean to say that you would have rushed to my aid even without asking anything in return?”

“I and every one of my men,” Robin replied simply.

Richard Lionheart beckoned him closer. “Now I know you even better.” Moved, he added, “Who is willing to give himself so freely to his king? I know none among my noble lords. And, my friend, a king knows how to give thanks.” His voice grew louder. “How did I know about you? The great merchant Solomon, who delivered your treasure chest, your share of the ransom. The Queen Mother invited him to an audience. And nothing remains hidden from her for long. You have chosen a wise advocate in him.”

Richard offered his hand to Robin. Robin reached to take it. “No, my friend.” Lionheart smiled. “This time, you must submit to courtly custom, as practice for the next few days. Simply bend over the ring and kiss it! Yes, like so, that is enough. And again, on behalf of your companions."

Robin obeyed.

"Allons, sieurs!" With long strides, Richard followed his captains. When he reached Friar Tuck, he paused. "Stand up!"

The monk rose guiltily. "By St. Cedric, I am your servant, sire."

A mighty blow snapped his head to the side. At a second blow, Friar Tuck crashed to the ground. "I hope so, holy father," the king said. "For both our sakes." With that, he continued on his way.

Little John helped the monk up. "No harm done," he grumbled. "Luck is with us today."

Tuck carefully fingered his chin. "An eye for an eye, a tooth for a tooth." He gave a pained smile. "It seems our king knows the Scriptures."

Only at Robin's own command was Much willing to bring the captured horses back to the road. "Why?" he asked.

"Hush!" muttered John. "Not now."

Lionheart settled into the saddle of the white stallion. He glanced briefly down at Robin Hood. "Tomorrow. Before daybreak! The camp guards will be informed."

"We'll be there." Robin raised his hand, looked around at his companions, looked openly at the king. "I swear it by the Holy Virgin."

Richard the Lionheart put his spurs to the horse. At a sharp gallop, his companions and escort strove to catch up with the king.

Much was displeased. "Why did you give away those good horses? I had them safely hidden."

No one answered.

Much complained some more. "First you make me wait and wait. Then the iron men stop right under my nose, too. And then . . ." He saw that no one was listening to him, and that the others were only gazing after the riders. "Who … who is that fellow on the white horse?"

"Our king," John muttered, wiping his eyes with the back of his hand. "Our king has come."

XX

NOTTINGHAM SHIRE. NOTTINGHAM.

Dawn lay on the horizon. Ponderous clouds pushed eastward over the fortress and ramparts. From the northern hills down to the valley stood tent upon tent with leopards billowing on royal banners. It was cold. In front of his spacious pavilion, Richard the Lionheart knelt with his captains. The Archbishop of Canterbury was celebrating mass for his king.

At the edge of the camp, makeshift canvas tarps were stretched over poles. Robin and John also knelt, and behind them Whitehand and Tom Toad, and behind them the rest of the band of men. *"Deus, qui conteris bella . . ."* Friar Tuck implored God's assistance on their behalf. *"Alleluia!"*

Fanfares sounded.

"Bonjour, mes amis!" the king greeted the king of outlaws and his lieutenant. With a grim face, Richard surveyed their bandit army. Three-times-six green-clad men, their hoods pulled over their heads, each bearing a longbow and a short bow. Each carried two quivers, stocked with arrows.

The stocky sergeant next to Lionheart pursed his lips, then blurted out, "Forgive me, sire." Doubtingly, he pointed to the small gaggle of men. "This is supposed to be the miraculous weapon? These men are meant to turn the course of the siege? They've no helmets, no chain mail. Sire, no battle can be won with rabble like this."

John roared, leaping forward. "Hush yourself!" He grabbed the scoffer by the iron shirt, lifted him over his head, shook him.

"Enough!" ordered Robin sharply. "Don't break that doll! He may be needed."

The giant put his victim down hard. "That's all right." He stepped back. "Just keep your mouth shut."

All color had drained from the captain's face. Smiling, the king admonished him. "The customs are rough in Sherwood. You had better guard your tongue, *sieur*!"

He turned to Robin, pointing to the fortress. "*Alors.* This is my castle. Built so that no enemy should ever conquer it. Little did I know that I would have to try it myself one day." He pointed down to the valley. "From the battlements, the archers control the whole terrain." Time and again, the besiegers had managed to work their way up to the knoll under their shields. But fifty paces from the garrison walls, if they chanced a sally, it would be halted by the unerring crossbowmen and bowmen. Under the deadly rain of arrows, the attackers would have to retreat again. "If I manage to advance ten catapults over there to the halfway point, only then will we have a chance at least to cause confusion in the fortress, with stones and incendiary bolts."

The command to Robin Hood was clear: "I expect you and your men to stop those archers from firing on my men until the catapults are in position."

Robin shaded his eyes and scanned the terrain. John rubbed the scar in his braided beard. There was no cover, not a single tree, no brush. *We're good in the woods. But by Dunstan, they'll shoot us down like rabbits, here.*

Robin conferred with his lieutenants. At last, they nodded.

"Yes." Robin looked candidly at the king. "This game can be won—my lord, forgive me, but only by my rules."

"*Merde!*" Again the captain objected. "How dare you speak to—"

"*Taisez-vous!*" Lionheart commanded him. He calmly demanded of Robin Hood, "*Bien.* Your plan?"

Robin listed his conditions. Without hesitation, King Richard agreed.

Additional quivers of arrows were to be kept ready in baskets. A broad, man-size shield and a shield bearer were assigned to each outlaw. Robin ordered slits to be pierced into each shield, to look through.

He laughed. "For our beloved England!" Louder, he shouted, "For King Richard!"

"For King Richard!"

And so, the little army moved down into the valley. John glanced behind him anxiously, looking for Much. As he had been ordered, the boy marched in the rearmost line. The first enemy bolts and arrows whizzed from the walls, slamming into the ground a few paces ahead of them. Robin paused, estimating the distance. Over his shoulder, he called to Threefinger. "Bill, you and your shield bearer stay between myself and them! But don't you dare show those scoundrels up there so much as an ear. If you do and they don't hit it, I'll cut it off myself tonight. You're our eyes. Understand me?"

Threefinger hissed through his teeth. "I understand." His chin trembled.

"Tom and Gilbert! Watch the ranks. Wait for my command!"

Robin winked at his dearest friend. "Well, what do you say?"

"Ready to go," John grumbled. He instructed his shield bearer to raise the shield enough to cover the giant's head. "We'll just have to watch out for our feet." He grinned.

"Two more steps forward!" ordered Robin.

Up above, crossbowmen and archers stood, relaxed and open, among the battlements. They thought they were safe. Their arrows thudded into the ground close to the outlaws.

"You take the one to the right of the city gate!" decided Robin.

Both had their longbows in hand. The feathered shafts were set to the bowstring. Together, Robin and John stepped out of cover. The bowstrings sang as they loosed their arrows.

Two arrows flew to the wall. Two castle guards threw up their arms and fell howling backward from the battlements. In response, a rain of arrows pelted down, not quite reaching John and Robin. The two men fired steadily. Their movements were fast, each shot deadly. Four, then six, then eight archers fell. Only then did the archers on top of the wall duck behind the stone parapets. Now and then one emerged, ventured a wild shot, and immediately took cover again.

"Forward!" shouted Robin to his troop. Together with their shield bearers, the outlaws charged thirty more paces up the hill. The archers on the wall immediately seized the opportunity. Bolts pierced the shields—a terrible scream cried out. One of the outlaws staggered, a crossbow bolt lodged in his neck. A second bolt pierced his chest. The man must have been dead before he hit the ground, but the men to his right and left tried to help him. "Leave him!" Robin's command was absolute. "Back in line! Shoot! Aim at anything moving up there!"

And shot after shot flew at the walls. "Well, what do you say?" Robin called over to John.

"We go on!" replied John, thinking just one of them was already too much for the archers above. He let loose one more arrow. Soon no helmet could be seen on the battlements. The besieged men fired blindly from behind cover, missing their targets.

Orders rose from the camp, horn calls. Creaking and groaning, the catapults began to move. Their long arms loomed menacingly high. They reached the valley. There were cheering shouts. The horns set the rhythm. Mercenaries pulled and pushed the ponderous machines up the hill one by one. They had almost reached the line of outlaws.

The city gates opened. A good twenty armed men charged the

attackers on horseback, lances ready in their fists. And the outlaws left their cover. Standing in the open, they shot the iron men from their saddles. But some city soldiers made it to throwing range. A lance struck Whitehand. The tip stuck out from his back. He fell without a sound.

John roared, dropped his bow, tore the shield from his bearer, and charged toward the horsemen. He knocked one lance aside, fended off the next, lunged among the horses. John howled and knocked a man out of the saddle with the edge of his shield, then hit a second. The shield crashed against the iron armor of the third man-at-arms. The struck soldiers rolled in pain on the ground. John raged on. The iron men screamed in horror, turning their horses around. Only five of them reached the city. The gate slammed shut.

New archers popped up between the battlements, firing arrows and bolts. At the catapults, three mercenaries slumped forward. The noise of battle grew.

"Shoot! Shoot!" The outlaw army ceaselessly sent death up to the battlements.

"Where is Gilbert?" roared John, not taking his eyes off the city wall.

"He's dead. Leave him!" Robin stepped from behind the shield, fired, stepped back. "We'll get Gilbert later."

John breathed heavily. Impotent rage burned in his eyes.

The barrage from the wall eased. The archers ducked behind the stone parapets again.

"Forward!" Thirty, forty paces closer toward Nottingham. "In a line!"

Behind the outlaws, the catapults groaned and crunched. "Position reached!" reported a sergeant. "Pull down the beams. Bring the stone balls!"

More arrows from above, scattered but well-aimed shots. Mercenaries on the winches screamed, died.

"By Dunstan!" cursed John. There was not an archer to be seen on the battlements.

"Bill!" Robin roared. "Where are they coming from? Where are those archers?"

"There are three embrasures! In each gate tower!"

John peered through the viewing slit in his shield. For a moment, iron arrowheads flashed in the dark embrasures before the arrows themselves whizzed out. "There you have it," he growled, calling to Robin. "I'll try to get the one on the right."

"We're the best, my friend!" Robin laughed. "Good luck!"

They peered around the edges of the shields, a flash marked the target, they took a step to the side. Their arrows flew, slamming through the narrow openings in the wall. Simultaneously, arrows flew out of the other embrasures, missing John and Robin by a full foot's breadth.

"Not bad!" Robin sneered. "But not good enough for us."

Another flash.

At the same time, the two men stepped out of cover. Both hit their target.

More arrows came in return.

One whizzed past the giant's head. Robin groaned and dove behind cover.

"What is it?" John shouted. "What's happened? Say something! Talk to me!"

"It's fine," came the strained reply. "A scratch."

Bill Threefinger was closer. "Robin!" he exclaimed. He called to John. "The arrow! It's in his leg!"

"Shut up!" Robin ordered, his voice firm again. "No one is to know. Shut up!"

The giant's throat tightened. "I'm coming over there!" he shouted.

"Stop! There are two more rats in those holes. Show me your best, my friend!"

Again, arrow tips flashed. John stepped to the side. Robin hopped out of cover on his left leg. Both fired. John reached for the next arrow, aiming into the embrasure of the left gate tower. No one returned his shot.

"Nice!" Robin gasped from behind his shield.

Muffled thuds resounded. Stone catapult balls howled their way away from the ten throwing arms, over the ramparts, crashing down inside the fortress. Shouts rose from Nottingham.

The jeering howls of the royal soldiers answered them, and a second volley. The shouting beyond the walls grew louder.

The king's trumpeters blew, ordering the retreat. Soldiers rushed down the slope, each with his shield on his back. They dragged with them the three wounded men John had knocked from their horses.

"Walk backward!" Robin ordered his men. "Slowly. Don't let that wall out of your sight. Bring our dead with you!"

Tom Toad found Gilbert. He broke off the spear shaft and put the lifeless body over his shoulders. The others brought the second fallen man.

John called out to Much.

"I . . . I . . ." Much tried.

"It's all right, lad," he soothed. The giant pushed himself and his shield-bearer closer to Robin. He saw a feathered shaft still sticking from Robin's right thigh. The arrow had pierced through the leg, the bloodstained, triangular tip protruding from the other side. Robin dragged himself backward, limping, barely daring to put weight on his right foot.

John wanted to help. But the twitching at the corners of his friend's mouth held him back. Robin watched him from a pale face. "By the kind Holy Maiden. You learned archery quite well from me. You and I could keep Nottingham at bay all on our own. Well, what do you say?"

"Almost," growled the giant, "only almost." He pointed to the leg. "As soon as we get out of range, I'll—"

"Not another word!" Robin set his jaw. "When it's all over, you'll take me to Kirklees. Aunt Mathilda will be pleased to see me."

"You can't wait that long."

"Quiet now!"

Down in the valley, Robin was at last willing to unstring his longbow and use it as a walking stick.

"Nos compliments, mon ami!" There was undisguised admiration in King Richard's gray eyes. *"Tu es vraiment le seigneur des arcs."*

Robin looked questioningly at his king. "We are in England, my lord. Forgive me if I do not understand the Norman language."

The sergeant next to Lionheart gritted his teeth but dared not speak up.

Richard stroked his red beard. "*Bien.* I think we understood you. And you are right. If We rule the land, then We should also make an effort to speak our subjects' language. *Alors*: We appreciate you and your men. We express our gratitude to you." Only then did he notice the arrow. "You are wounded."

"Not even worth mentioning, My Lord."

"He needs help." Courageously, John stared down at the king.

Richard smirked. Without raising his head, he wagged his fingers at John. "Step back a bit so We can see your face!" John obeyed.

Serious again, the king made a decision. "*Bien.* Take Robin Hood to his quarters! We will send him our *medicus*."

"My lord," Robin cried out. "What of Nottingham?"

"Don't worry, *mon ami*! You and your men have given the lord sheriff much to think about. One more little demonstration, and by evening, the fortress will be delivered to me."

Richard nodded to John. "Take care of your friend! Later, We will call on you again."

The doctor cut off the arrowhead, shoved a piece of wood between Robin's teeth, and pulled the shaft out of his thigh. Blood welled, but it didn't gush and splatter. "You're lucky." The doctor dribbled a pungent-smelling oil on the wound. "No veins seem damaged," he said, pressing ribwort and shepherd's purse over it. He wrapped on a bandage.

"Will I be able to walk?" Beads of sweat stood on Robin's forehead.

John wiped them off. "If you can't, I'll carry you."

The *medicus* looked from one to the other and shrugged. "With enough rest, even such a wound as this will heal quickly in men as vital as yourselves. I've been watching you out there." Pensively, he said, "During the Crusade, I was constantly at our king's side. I saw Christian knights and Muslim soldiers fighting. But men like you? No, I've never met such fighters."

"Thank you! That's what all the fresh forest air will do for you." Robin laughed. John joined in. Shaking his head, the doctor took his leave.

Ten catapults stood menacingly in front of Nottingham. Their throwing arms rose rigidly to the sky. Down in the valley, three gallows had been erected. Loud blasts of horns called to the sentries on the battlements. They were to be witnesses.

Robin could no longer stand stay in his tent. "Help me go see!" John carried his friend out to the cleared field, to Tom Toad, Friar Tuck and the others.

There was no trial. One by one, the sergeant pushed the three injured castle guards off the gallows. They kicked, twitched, hung still.

The soldiers waited. The cloud cover over the fortress had broken. Now and then, a ray of sunlight grazed the dead on the gallows.

The city gate opened. Two horsemen with white flags galloped past the catapults, down into the valley, and reached the encampment. A little later, they hurried their horses back.

"I would love to know what that was about," Robin pleaded impatiently, "Please, John. Go over and find out. I need to know!"

The giant grinned. "I'm not letting you out of my sight today."

"That's an order!"

John growled, "Have patience!" As Much pushed his way through the others, John added, "We have people for these errands."

Before the boy had even reached him, Robin called out, "So?"

"They . . . they just came and looked at the king. Wanted to know if it was really . . . really him."

"Calmly, Much! What did Richard say?"

The boy tried to imitate the voice: "Well? What do you see? Am I Lionheart?" He swallowed. "They fell to their knees. And mounted their horses and went right back again."

Robin straightened himself as best he could. He tried to imitate the voice as well: "Well, what do you see? Am I Lionheart?" He clapped. "Oh, John! That's our king."

The flag with the three leopards was raised above the fortress tower. White flags fluttered on the battlements. Both halves of the city gate swung back. The lord sheriff rode out in a flowing cloak. And behind him, in orderly rows, men-at-arms and castle guards exited the gate. Not a sword, not a lance point flashed. The garrison marched helmetless down to the gallows.

A fanfare sounded through the camp. King Richard trotted forth slowly on his white stallion. Accompanying him on a black horse was the Chancellor of England, Hubert Walter, Archbishop of Canterbury. At a suitable distance followed the sergeant and his captains.

"Ah, I'd like to be there." Robin sighed.

"It's all right." John rubbed the scar in his beard. All at once, he felt empty. The fight was over. Now what? He breathed in deeply. He didn't want to think about it. Later, maybe. Not now.

Tom Toad grabbed the giant's arm. "We dug a hole up in the

hills." Sadness was in his eyes. "Friar Tuck thinks now is the best time."

While down in the valley Richard the Lionheart had the lord sheriff kneel and surrender the fortress, Friar Tuck prayed at the graves of two of the brotherhood. *"Requiem aeternam dona eis, Domine."*

Heralds raced off in all directions. They had royal orders to summon all barons and abbots, all dignitaries and officials of the counties of Nottingham, Derby, and York to the fortress by noon the following day. Richard the Lionheart was in a hurry. No one was allowed to be absent, unless they were confined to their bed by illness.

Pack animals brought the king's robes, weapons, and luggage from the camp up to the city.

Early in the evening, King Richard and his chancellor strode through the rows of tents. Before they entered Robin Hood's makeshift quarters, Lionheart addressed the brotherhood in the small clearing. "It has pleased Us, how you have fought. From this hour, all the shackles of the past are taken from you. You are free men. Freedmen!"

The companions looked at each other sheepishly. As Tom Toad and Friar Tuck bent their knee, the others followed their example.

"Freedmen?" whispered Threefinger. "We already were, weren't we?"

"But now we really are, I think," murmured Much. "Well, let's wait and see!"

With a curt gesture, Lionheart yielded the space to his chancellor. The broad-shouldered Archbishop of Canterbury smiled. "You have done England a great service. For that, my thanks! Tomorrow you are to stand ready. My clerk will enter your names and give each of you your charter."

"A letter, too?" Threefinger sighed. "I can't read."

"Don't be so silly!" hissed Much. "All we have to do is show anyone this ... parchment, then ... then everybody knows what it means."

Sternly, the chancellor pointed to Friar Tuck. "Now, as for you!"

The monk lowered his head.

"Your shameful offense, your assault on His Majesty the King, must be atoned for. The law demands death by hanging."

Friar Tuck staggered on his knees. Beside him, Tom Toad clutched the hilt of his sword, "By Willick! I won't let you touch him! I'd rather—"

"Silence!" Hubert Walter took a step forward. Unmoved, he continued, "But, given yesterday's circumstances, the following sentence is passed on the Cistercian, Father Jerome: banishment from the monastic community. This will still be submitted to the superior of his order. Furthermore, Father Jerome must serve the inhabitants of the remote region of Barnsdale as a priest for the rest of his life."

First disbelief, then beaming smiles. Friar Tuck folded his hands in front of his robe. "With humility, I—"

"Don't thank me, my son. Thank the benevolence of your king!"

Impatiently, Hubert Walter ordered the men of the brotherhood to retreat to the edge of the clearing. The king wanted to speak to Robin Hood and his best captain alone.

"Remain seated, *mon ami*!" Richard settled himself on a log. "And you, giant, relax!"

John grinned sheepishly, standing at attention beside the chancellor of England.

"*Bien. Alors.*" The king's gray eyes coolly regarded the leader's pale, pain-stricken face. "Without further delay, all the promises I made to you yesterday are confirmed." He gave a questioning look to the chancellor. Hubert Walter nodded in agreement. "*Bien.* But that's not all. I expect you to present yourself at the fortress tomorrow to receive another favor from me. In the presence of the noble assembly, I will elevate you." He paused for a moment. "Tomorrow, you will leave the hall as Sir Robert of Loxley."

John took in a startled breath. *Ah, my friend.* He expelled the breath. *You will be a lord now.*

Robin bowed his head. "My lord." His voice barely obeyed him.

"No, look at me!" the king commanded. "It was not gratitude alone that drove the Archbishop of Canterbury and me to this decision." Quietly he smiled. "*Mon ami.* You gave me a taste of your manners. *Alors,* now learn from me: Yesterday I promised you land that you had already appropriated anyway. A war against you would only cost money and is hardly likely to be won. So, I give it to you in fief."

"My lord—"

"Do not interrupt me! *Alors*: Tomorrow you will be made my liege. I know you have always been loyal to your king. But as Sir Robert of Loxley, you also have duties to the crown. In the future, you can only buy your way out of sword duty with gold. My officials will be counting on your annual tax payments in the future." He paused, stroking his red beard. "So not only gratitude, *mon ami,* but as a ruler, I have to consider the benefits my gratitude brings to the kingdom."

"Forgive me, My Lord." The bright gray eyes sought the king's gaze. "You're giving me more than you know." Robin pointed to John. "You give us freedom. We fought against injustice and oppression, and now I firmly believe—"

"Pardon, sire!" Hubert Walter took a step forward. "We are expected in Nottingham." Immediately the king rose.

"Please, my lord!" cried Robin quickly. "Do not go yet! I must warn you—"

"Warn?" Lionheart arched his brows, signaled the chancellor to wait. "I'm listening. But be brief!"

"You have enemies up here in the north. Allies of your brother. Dangerous traitors." Robin spoke quickly, drawing a terrifying portrait of the lord sheriff, reporting on Sir Roger of Doncaster. "All the threads of the conspiracy tie together at this scoundrel!" Out of breath, Robin fell silent. Little John pressed his lips together. *Baron of Doncaster. At last, you bastard, you're losing your head.*

"Merci, mon ami." A flick of the finger to the chancellor. "Are we acquainted with these gentlemen?"

"We knew of Lord Sheriff Walter de Monte. Also, of his predecessor. *Mais pardon*, sire, that Sir Roger of Doncaster is also among the conspirators was unknown to us. We will consider this allegation."

"Consider it?" Robin blurted out. "I beg your pardon, my lord—consider it? That man deserves to die a hundred times over. The lord sheriff, too."

Richard looked down at Robin in wonder. "Why so agitated? Death? If I acted like this against all my secret adversaries, a third of England's castles would be depopulated. No, *mon ami*. Your information was very valuable to Us. But enough."

Robin pounded his fist against his forehead. "But, my lord, what good is it if I know the wolf that tears apart my sheep, but I don't kill him?"

The chancellor pressed the king to move along. But Richard took his time. "That may be the right course from your point of view. And in my heart, I feel the same. But I am the king. This is a matter of politics. I will not even have the lord sheriff beheaded. I'll even let him out of jail! For that he will pay a ransom, so much that he will not dare to rise against me again any time soon. And Sir Roger of Doncaster? Most assuredly, he will remain my enemy."

Richard smiled coldly. "But he will soon know that I know. And he will support my next war in France with much gold."

Robin fingered the bandage on his leg. "Then our fight was pointless after all." His voice became rough. "Forgive me, my lord, but then nothing changes for the poor."

"Yes, it does, my son. All the wolves in my enclosures have their fangs blunted. Only when that fails to bring them to their senses will their heads fall."

"Sire, you must not delay any longer!" Hubert Walter finally decided to end the conversation. "Equal law and justice for Normans and Saxons. I will enforce that with an iron fist throughout England." He looked down at Robin. "Is that promise enough for you?"

Beside him, John nodded. *Fine. I'll believe it. We still have to be careful. Better safe than sorry.*

Robin Hood nodded to his king. "Thank you, my lord. Then I have achieved my goal, after all."

"Par tous les saints." Richard laughed, threatening him with a raised fist. "Tomorrow, in the castle hall, I expect a Robert of Loxley without a sword in his scabbard, and above all, a silent Loxley, who gratefully receives the honor and silently departs. Otherwise, my lands and castles in France will be lost before I even reach the mainland after my coronation."

Robin returned the laughter. "I promise, my lord. Tomorrow I will submit to the custom of the court."

The friends gazed after King Richard and his chancellor. Only after they had left the clearing did John grumble, "They just let those villains walk free. Instead, it's nothing but talk. What kind of game is this?"

Half closing his eyelids, Robin propped his chin in his hand. After a while, he said, "Not a game, John. I don't understand the rules, but they call it politics."

Fanfare: Bells rang in the city. The citizens of Nottingham crowded the road to the fort. Their faces were drawn by deprivation. Children's eyes sat deep in their sockets. There was no rejoicing. The siege had lasted too long. After the winter, the town's supplies had been nearly depleted. Only the bellies of the armed men were kept filled. No one in the city had been able to get enough for weeks from what was left. There was not a cheer, not a waving hand.

Hastily and as solemnly as possible, the barons, abbots, and royal officials strode through the impassive crowd.

Fanfares: In the castle hall, the noble lords were silent. *"Messieurs!"* The chancellor opened the meeting in a harsh voice. King Richard himself announced new laws, harsher taxes, point by point. None of the nobles dared murmur an objection. Each feared for his post, for his coffers.

Outside in a corner, right next to the wide-open portal, John and Robin waited. The giant had rolled over an empty barrel for Robin to sit. Concerned, he looked into his friend's pale face.

"Don't be a wet nurse!" sneered Robin. "I'm not Marian." The pain in his leg had grown overnight. And because Herbghost had stayed behind in Sherwood, John himself had tended to the blackening wounds torn by the triangular arrowhead. *I know how bad it is, even if you try not to show it.* The wait was taking too long for him. "By Dunstan. Best we just get out of here."

"Patience, John!"

Out of the corner of his eye, the giant watched the hustle and bustle of the castle courtyard. Like a genteel chicken coop! Women and men stood together in groups. Others paced up and down. Whispering, quiet conversations. All were festively dressed. John grinned. *Ah, my friend. We wanted to go to the king in the finest robes, too. And how do we look? Barely washed the dirt from our faces. Our green robes are torn from battle. If Beth saw us like this. She would be ashamed.*

The bailiff stepped out of the hall into the open air, setting his staff gracefully in front of him. “Lady Beatrice!”

All heads turned in one direction. Accompanied by a maid, the emaciated, slightly bent woman slowly moved forward step by step. Whispers buzzed all around.

“Poor thing.”

“Five months down in the caves.”

“That bastard Thom de Fitz!”

“He threw his own wife into the dungeon.”

Without a glance for the onlookers, Lady Beatrice allowed herself to be led into the hall.

Robin tapped John’s arm. The giant leaned down to him. “I’m glad the swamp in Sherwood is so deep,” Robin murmured. “Not just for our sake. For the poor woman, too.”

“Even so.”

A knight appeared, his chain mail gleaming. His gray hair fell to his fur-trimmed coat collar. From the threshold, he looked searchingly over the crowds.

“Sir Richard!” Robin called softly.

The baron turned. “Thank the Virgin, you are on time!” He walked quickly over to the two men. “After Lady Beatrice, it’s your turn, Robin.” He gave them no joyful greeting, just a smile. “I, as your nearest neighbor, am to present you before the king.”

“How is Marian?” John could hardly wait to see her again.

Sir Richard’s eyes in his long, angular face showed nothing, dull. As if he had to think about it, he hesitated. “Yes, the girls are fine.”

“Excuse me, Sir Richard.” Robin touched his arm. “But you are so changed.”

“My son is . . .” His voice faltered. “The king is back from captivity. But my son. He was not in his company.” Richard at the Lea straightened his back. “According to a sergeant, he was last seen in the Holy Land during the storming of Jaffa. And that was almost two years ago now."

John wanted to hug the gaunt man in sympathy, reconsidered it, and said only, "That damned crusade."

"Quiet!" The baron looked around. "Don't say that! Not here."

Lady Beatrice was carefully led out of the hall by her maid. Her face was wet with tears, but her eyes were smiling.

They were followed by the bailiff. "Robert of Loxley!"

"That's us," John grumbled. He lifted his friend to his feet, carefully straightened his garments. He tried to give him his staff for support.

Determined, Robin refused. "Just make sure I get in there! I can manage the rest on my own."

The bailiff strode forward. John and Sir Richard flanked Robin, staying close by his side. Robin dragged his right leg, only lightly planting his foot on the floor. John braced him as he limped ahead. Torches lined the walls. In the semidarkness of the hall, the light twitched across the faces of the noble assembly. "When I say so, you let me go on my own!" whispered Robin.

The central aisle ended at the stairs to the dais. Light fell through the high windows, spreading like a radiant ornament over the dais and reflected in the gold of king's crown. Richard the Lionheart was enthroned among precious tapestries. Near him, at the broad oak table, sat the chancellor. In front of him, he had carefully arranged rolls of parchment and writing tablets.

Three times the bailiff pounded his staff on the stamped earth. "Robert of Loxley!" he announced in a resounding voice.

The murmur in the hall died away. All eyes were fixed on the baron. The men so incongruously dressed in his company were regarded with frowns.

At the halfway point, Robin halted the others. "You can let go now!" he murmured.

"If anything happens, I'll catch you in a flash," John grumbled. He remained standing where he was, like a shepherd leaning on his staff.

"Shall I?" Sir Richard offered his hand.

"No." Robin clenched his jaw. He put the wounded leg forward. Only the first step was uncertain. After that, he stepped forward firmly. With a sure stride, he reached the raised platform beside his guide.

"Sire." The baron bowed. "Richard at the Lea brings you the freedman Robert of Loxley." Backing away, he did not straighten from his bow until he was beside Little John. Robin just stood where he was. Tense silence built in the hall.

King Richard arched his brows slightly. "You must come up to me!" he said half aloud. "It is the custom, *mon ami.*"

Robin nodded. With his sound foot first, he climbed the high step.

Richard rose from his throne. "Kneel!"

John suffered for his friend, watching him bend his left knee and angle his right leg outward. The gray bandage was soaked with blood. But warmth flooded the giant's powerful chest to see Robin honored before the king.

Richard Lionheart touched both of Robin's shoulders with the blade of his sword. "Rise!" In a powerful voice, he announced, "Sir Robert of Loxley!" He continued, "We, your lord and king, expect from now on and for all time to come that you will be loyal to England, honor all women, and protect all places of worship, widows, and orphans." The gray eyes smiled.

"Stand back!" commanded the chancellor.

Robin obeyed, and a without stumble he stepped off the dais, finding secure footing again on the hall's stamped clay floor.

"Sir Robert of Loxley, receive the sword from the hand of your king."

The bailiff brought the weapon on a cushion. Robin took the sword and slid it into the leather scabbard at his belt.

Restrained, polite murmurs arose in the hall.

"Messieurs!" With a lifted finger, Lionheart silenced the noble lords. "I gather from your meager applause that this man is unknown to you, and yet he has been a terror to many of you. We, King Richard, give him the territory of Barnsdale in fief. From this day forward, he may call himself Sir Robert of Loxley. But, *Messieurs* ..." Lionheart relished the suspense "... before Us and you stands Robin Hood!"

There was breathless silence. Here and there, one of the gentlemen groaned. Suddenly a single voice shouted: "*Magnifique!* Bravo!" A gaunt figure pushed his way out of the ranks, hurrying forward. The dark blue coat swung. "Our hero of Nottingham!" With arms outstretched, Sir Roger of Doncaster strode toward Robin. "I will be the first to greet you thus."

Little John slid his fist down to the center of his staff. "By Dunstan," he rumbled, putting a foot forward.

At the last moment, Richard at the Lea yanked him back by the collar. "If you do this now, we are all lost," he warned hastily, "Robin, you, and me too."

The giant's chest rose and fell. "Even so." He subsided.

In front of the dais, Robin clenched his fists. But Baron Roger did not stop. Tapping the once-outlaw's shoulders with the fingertips of both hands, he shouted enthusiastically, "To neighborly friendship!" He hissed between his teeth, *"Maudit bâtard!"* And then loudly again, "*Visitez-moi!* My castle is open to you!" Softly, without losing the smooth smile, he said nasally, "Today, you have won. *Mais, sacre Dieu,* I will never forget!"

Robin's hand clasped the hilt of his sword. He struggled to keep silent.

Gallantly, Sir Roger of Doncaster took a step back, thumped his velvet-encased chest, and bowed to the king. "Sire. It will be my honor to assist the young lord of Barnsdale in all ways as he reclaims the wilderness you have given him as a fief." With that, he hurried back to his seat. Robin stared after him in anger. He did not notice the bailiff beside him.

"Sir! You must move along now," the dignified voice admonished.

Robin came back to himself. "Even so." Straightening, he strode to Little John and Richard at the Lea.

"Mon ami!" As Robin turned back to his king, Richard called out, "Remember, the wolves' teeth are blunted! Even in the wild. Now go! We have other things to worry about."

"Yes, my lord," Robin whispered. To the giant he murmured, "Take me away. Quickly! Before I split that wretched baron's skull."

"First I'll break his back," growled John.

"Silence!" admonished Sir Richard. He escorted his friends to the entryway. Despite his grief, he seemed visibly relieved. "You are always welcome in my castle." Their farewell was short. Sir Richard returned to the assembly.

Robin now willingly took hold of the giant's staff. He dragged his bloodied leg.

"Herbghost will make you a fresh bandage."

They had tied their horses in front of the sheriff's house. John helped his friend up. "Are you all right?"

The corners of his mouth twitched. "With a nurse like you? How could I not be?"

They left Nottingham. At the grave beyond the valley, they took silent leave of Gilbert and their other fallen companion once more. Then they let the horses trot, heading north among the hills. "I told the others to meet us at the Great Oak," said Robin.

In the early afternoon, they neared Edwinstowe. For a long time, Robin had been silent, hunched over the saddle horn. *Shall we rest?*

John kept asking. Each time, his friend just shook his head. *No, no rest.*

The roadside shrubbery ahead at the turnoff moved. The giant raised his staff, ready to shout a warning. Too late. In front of them, behind them, and from the sides, figures jumped out onto the trade road. The horsemen were already surrounded. John lowered the staff. "By Dunstan!" These highwaymen wore green hoods pulled down low over their foreheads. "Enough!" he threatened them with a fist. "Bring Herbghost here!"

No one obeyed.

Grimacing, Tom Toad planted himself in front of Robin's horse. "Sir Robert of Loxley. How much money do you carry?" He warned, "If you lie, you will lose everything you own!"

With tired eyes, Robin looked down at his lieutenant. "I share with you and with all."

Horrified, Toad noticed the state of his leg. The hose was soaked with blood all the way down to his boots. "Damn! Didn't know it was that bad!" He yelled to Herbghost.

The old man tended the wound with fresh herbs right there at the roadside and wrapped it with a new bandage. "You must lie still! Otherwise, the wound will tear again and again."

Robin resisted. "First, I want to go to Barnsdale. Then I'll have time enough for rest." He brooked no argument. Quietly he asked John, "Put me on the horse!" Robin Hood braced himself in the saddle. "Come closer, all!"

His small army gathered in front of him. Their expressions were tense.

"I have a lot to say to each of you. But . . ." he pointed to his leg ". . . when it heals. But there's one thing I want you to know right now." He set his chin, his voice clear and strong. "There's a piece of land for each of you in Barnsdale." He laughed. "Even if the next few summers don't bring in a crop, there's money enough in the treasury. Those who have families shall come to us with their wives and children. Friends! We have fought injustice side by side. Now we will live together in freedom."

There were exhalations of relief. Hands were squeezed. Joy shone in the bearded faces.

Friar Tuck pushed his way forward. "Behold my habit. It is the robe of the Cistercians. I know how to turn a wilderness into fertile . . ."

"Enough!" It wasn't said as a command, but the monk fell indignantly silent.

"We will do this work together. You, too, will have your hands full." Robin took a few deep breaths. "A chapel. I want to build my chapel, finally."

"By all the saints . . ." Friar Tuck began.

"Later." Robin's voice grew fainter. "Tom, you take charge! You break up the summer encampment. Seal the caves and hide them well, even if we don't need them anymore. Get some carts. Bring everything to Barnsdale!"

Tiredly, Robin turned to John. "Well, what do you say?"

"Nice." The giant grinned.

"That's right, nurse."

John leaned over from his saddle, taking up his friend's reins. "Better safe than sorry." He clicked his tongue. The horses trotted off.

XXI

ENGLAND. WINCHESTER.

No time to spare!

Prince John had managed to escape his brother's grasp at the last moment. His ally, King Philip of France, had invaded Normandy. It was war!

Richard had no time to spare. Right after Easter of 1194, on April seventeenth, Lionheart had England's crown placed on his head for the second time. He hardly noticed the jubilation, the congratulations of the Queen Mother. In the weeks that followed, he stared impatiently at the sky. At last, the storm subsided. On the twelfth of May, Richard Plantagenet set sail with his fleet. A hundred sails billowed. The port of Portsmouth quickly receded into the fog.

And on the island kingdom, his chancellor tightened the reins with a firm hand. To the horror of the Norman barons and ecclesiastical princes, and the delight of the Saxons so long subjugated and exploited, he restored law and order. Serfs, villagers, and freemen breathed a sigh of relief. Hubert Walter, Chancellor of England and Archbishop of Canterbury, kept the promise he had made to Robin Hood the night after the siege of Nottingham.

YORKSHIRE. FENWICK CASTLE.

In the autumn of the second year, a ragged man reached the moat of Fenwick Castle. He dragged himself across the drawbridge. Lowering his lance, the sentry barred his entry.

"Tell your lordship . . ." Spent, the man slid down to his knees by his crutch. His body sank forward. His face bent low over the planks of the bridge. He stammered, "It's me . . ." He fell silent.

In the castle hall, the guard hurried to his lord. "Forgive me, sir! A stranger is waiting outside."

A stranger? Sir Richard put his hand on his consort's arm. "I'll go alone."

The lady at the Lea shook her head.

Together they hurried to the gate, then cautiously approached the cowering figure.

At the sound of footsteps, the man slowly raised his head. "Mother." His eyes searched for his father. "I beg your pardon. I . . . I am late."

And happiness returned to Fenwick. Two days of sleep and care. On the evening of the third day, Marian and Patricia stood before the festive table. They plucked the lute, and first sang artfully, and then, to the horror of their tutor and the delight of young Edward, performed an earthy minstrel's song.

YORKSHIRE. BARNSDALE.

The Brotherhood of Freemen had put aside their bows and swords. With ax and plow, the men worked their land—grew grain, turnips, and fruit. In the third year, they brought a rich harvest to the common barns, and filled the storage cellars to the brim.

The bright ringing of bells resounded above the cottages at the former outlaw base.

"Deus, cujus misericordiae non est numerus et bonitatis infinitus est thesaurus . . ." For the first time, Friar Tuck celebrated mass in the completed chapel.

And there were guests! From under half-closed lids, John let his gaze wander along the front row. *Marian! What a beautiful lady you are now. Her light hair curled around her fine collar.* Beside her knelt her friend, Patricia. Tom Toad furtively held his Beth's hand. Sir Richard, his lady, and their son seemed absorbed in prayer. Robin sat on a low stool at the end of the row, his right leg outstretched, his gaze fixed on the small carved Holy Virgin, a gift from Sir Richard.

John sighed softly. *Oh, my friend, eventually, that wound will heal properly. Just you wait and see.* Sometimes Robin was free of the pain, moving as swiftly and smoothly as ever. But from one week to another, his thigh swelled, the flesh became hard, the wounds burst open. "Aunt Mathilda will be pleased," Robin would remark, as John took the sick man to Kirklees. Only bloodletting gave him relief. They willingly paid the enterprising prioress for new ointments and herbs.

"Per Dominum nostrum!" Friar Tuck ended the service.

YORKSHIRE. BARNSDALE.

The base had become a fortified estate. In spring of the fourth year, John accompanied his friend down to the main camp. Flowers bloomed around the big linden tree. They checked the huts, noted any damage to the roofs. "Got something to tell you," the giant growled, hesitant.

"Come on, talk!" The corners of Robin's mouth twitched. "Is it about our little condition?" He leaned against the trunk of the linden tree expectantly. "Is there finally someone she wants?"

"What?" John winced. "No, she's headstrong. Nothing's wrong with Marian." He rubbed the scar in the tangle of his beard. "You know, I've already talked to Tom and the others. We want to leave this place."

Robin was silent, slowly brushing back his hair. "So. that's the way it is."

Irritated, John fought back. "No, not like that. Just to earn some money. That's all." And he explained: with Toad, Much and Threefinger, they were going to offer themselves as escorts for wagons. "Offer our services to Solomon. He'll be glad to have us, I'm sure. Given our experience with ambushes." The giant didn't dare look at his friend. "It would be only one trip in the summer."

"Nice." Robin's voice remained even. "What about me?"

"I know." John shrugged. "If you think we should stay here, we'll stay."

After a while, Robin said quietly, "That's all right, my friend," and he added, "Tomorrow we start training."

"We?"

"Sir Robert of Loxley does not ride as the escort of a wagon train. That would not be proper. But I'm still the best at archery." Robin clapped his hands. "And each of you can still learn a little something from me." He laughed.

FRANCE. CHALUS FORTRESS.

For months Count Adomar refused to obey his king. More than that, a suspicion became a certainty: The rebellious count was in negotiation with Philip of France.

"We will bring him to reason." Coldness set in the king's gray eyes. "We will take away his fortress at Chalus."

In the fifth year after his second coronation, in March 1199, Richard's troops closed in on the castle. An unceasing hail of arrows pushed the defenders from the battlements. "Dig a tunnel. Undercut the walls!"

Late in the afternoon of March twenty-sixth, Lionheart, accompanied by his sergeant, inspected the progress of the tunnel work. High up among the battlements, a bowman stepped out from cover. He raised his crossbow. The bolt struck the king's neck, penetrating deep into his shoulder.

Richard staggered a few steps, then told the horrified sergeant calmly, "No fuss, *monsieur*. Lead me back!"

In his pavilion, the king tried to yank the bolt out with a single hard jerk. The shaft broke off. The iron point remained deep in his flesh. His personal physician cut open the shoulder, dug with a knife, finally succeeded in removing the bolt from the cartilage of the spine. After only two days, the wound became gangrenous. Richard was feverish. He knew death was near. He sent for his mother. On the early morning of April 6, the old woman kept vigil at the king's camp. Before the chaplain, he confessed his sins and received the last rites. Toward evening, Queen Eleanor closed the eyes of her beloved son.

"The king is dead!"

ENGLAND. LONDON.

"Long live the king!"

Barons, earls, bishops, the noblest of the land led the coronation procession. There were no cheers. The citizens silently craned their necks. Fear marked their faces. "Line the road between St. Paul's Cathedral and Westminster!" they had been commanded. Only under threat of punishment had many of them heeded the call. "Greet your king!"

In the crowd, the tinker scratched his beard. "Now what?" he grumbled. Ever since King Richard's coronation, he had kept postponing his return to Nottingham. Life was good here in the big city of London, and there was plenty of work. But he had never given up his desire to return home.

King John strode under a silk canopy. The purple coronation mantle hung from his angular shoulders. He held his small head high. His eyes twitched to the right and left. Whoever was met by that cold gaze turned away in fright.

"Long live the king!" John's followers mingled with the people, pushing and kicking the citizens. "Open your mouths!"

"Long live the king!"

The tinker also obeyed. "Long live the king!" But it sounded like a curse.

After the solemn coronation, John received his barons and lord sheriffs, his closest confidants. "Despite my brother's rule, you have remained loyal to me all these years. Now you may raise your heads again. Now, *mes amis*, I will reward you. For the throne is mine. I own England!"

Ale and roast were shared with the people! Gradually the mood in the streets of London improved. Late in the evening, the tinker returned to his dwelling. "I suppose I will stay on," he mused as he curled up drunkenly on his bed. "It isn't be as bad here as at home."

XXII

NOTTINGHAM SHIRE.
SHERWOOD FOREST.

He pushed through the thicket. He quickly estimated the position of the sun among the green treetops. Roderick nodded with satisfaction. He carried his quiver tied high, diagonally across his right shoulder, the arrows ready to hand beside his thick blond hair. He reached for his belt. The dagger was secure yet loose enough in its leather sheath. Roderick straightened the bow at his left shoulder with a practiced grip, then slid his thumb under the string and let it snap against his chest. He laughed. "No question about it. I'll win."

Light-footed, he continued on his way. He wanted to be in Edwinstowe by noon and at the gates of Nottingham by evening. And tomorrow! Tomorrow was the day. The lord sheriff had organized an archery contest. Even King John and his court would be present. Prizes beckoned. Money. Lots of money. "If I win, I'll buy us a cow," Roderick had promised the village elder.

Laughter—loud roaring! And not far ahead of him. Roderick deftly used the cover of the broad beeches and reached the edge of the clearing. Leather tunics! The silver badge flashed on the black cap of one of the men. "Ten," Roderick counted hastily. "Ten rangers and a forester." They squatted in a semicircle in front of a tree in the middle of the meadow, drinking and toasting to the sky. Above them, a naked man trembled, tottered, in supreme agony balancing himself with his left foot on the end of a thin staff, his right leg rowing in the air. A noose was looped around his neck, the rope lashed to the branch above his head.

The rangers were waiting. When the desperate man seemed to regain his balance, they slapped his thighs.

"Those damn dogs." Without another though, Roderick stepped out into the clearing. Jaw tight, he strode directly toward the howling horde.

"Who's that coming?" The royal forester grabbed his bow and jumped up. "Who are you?"

Undaunted, Roderick walked on.

The woodsmen stood beside their master, ready to fight—eleven arrows aimed at the stranger's chest.

"Stand still!"

Roderick obeyed. Behind the woodsmen, the eyes of the tortured man stared pleadingly at him. Roderick stretched his empty hands out. "What do you want from me?"

"Shut up!" roared the forester. "I ask the questions here!" He ordered his men, "Don't let this smooth-faced boy out of your sight!" He lowered his bow and eyed the young man. "So, you're out hunting."

"Why, no, sir. I'm on my way to Nottingham." Roderick smiled thinly. "I plan to win the competition."

"Are you that good?"

"The best."

There was a glint in the forester's eye. "Milksop, you're in luck. We have a competition for you right now." He pulled a rabbit from his hunting bag, held it up. "Here is your target. We took this off the poacher up there. If you hit it, it's yours." He grinned slyly. "And if you don't, we'll even give you a second chance." He gestured to the branch. "And if you still miss . . . there's plenty of room next to that swineheard from Edwinstowe."

Roderick pressed his lips together.

"The little boy is scared." One of the rangers stepped closer and spat in his face. The others grinned broadly.

Roderick wiped away the spittle with his sleeve. "I'm ready." He pointed to the rabbit. "But he's already dead, isn't he?"

"You only think it is, my boy." The forester shook the prey. "Don't you see how he's still wriggling?" Laughing, he tossed the rabbit to one of his men. "Go on!" He pointed to a beech trunk at the edge of the clearing. "Pin it with your bow."

The target was a good seventy paces away.

"One false move," the ranger warned, "and my men will spit you like a roast. Because you are the best, you will now show us how you nail this rabbit's right ear to the trunk."

Roderick positioned himself sideways to the target, slightly spreading his legs. A flick of his shoulder, the bow jumped into his hand, he reached for the quiver, and the arrow was on the string.

Such speed! Amazed, one leather-clad man after the other lowered his weapon.

With great calm, the archer tilted the bow, drew, lowered the arrow toward the target. The arrow whirred away, pierced the hare's right ear, and stuck in the trunk.

The men stared over at the beech tree.

"I want another prize," Roderick said into the silence. He still held his bow outstretched in his left hand. "I want the naked man up there." He tensed his arm.

"You'll get nothing at all," the ranger behind him sneered. "You just hunted royal game. You stole a hare from our king. The penalty for that is death."

His hand whipped to the quiver. The arrow sped away, severing the rope just below the branch. The swineherd crashed to the ground. Roderick ducked, his knife flashing in his right fist. He jumped at the first ranger. A slash, and blood shot from the man's neck. Roderick whirled around, stabbing the second man in the chest. His blade tore into the throat of the next. Around him, three men sank to the ground. But they still pressed close. Danger loomed from all sides. Dagger ready to thrust, Roderick pranced in a circle. "Who else? Come on!"

The men backed away. "Robin Hood," one whispered, dropping his bow. "I-I knew it." He waved his arms wildly. "Only Robin Hood fights like that!" He ran from one to the other. "Run! Before it's too late." He tugged them by their leather tunics. "His men will be here any moment!" Screaming, he fled. The name was a signal. A second man, then a third stammered, "Robin Hood!"

Roderick took advantage of the confusion. In mighty leaps, he put distance between himself and them. The next arrow was on the string. "Get out of here! All of you!"

"Shoot him!" the forester commanded, looking around at his men. "You cowards! This fellow is alone! Go ahead and shoot!" They threw down their weapons. In a blind panic, they rushed across the clearing.

"Cowards! You bastards!" Hatred blazed in the eyes beneath the black leather cap. "Then I'll show you how." He yanked up his bow.

Roderick's arrow nailed the silver badge to the man's forehead. The ranger dropped backward into the grass.

Cries of "Robin Hood!" rang out from the edge of the clearing.

"He's killed our master!" And again, now farther away, "Robin Hood is back!"

Roderick did not pursue them. He ran to the tree and knelt beside the motionless swineherd. "Hey? You still alive?"

The eyes in the dirtied face blinked. "Are they gone?" A deep voice.

"No question."

"And my rabbit?"

Roderick held his bare shoulders. "What?"

"Tell me!"

"By the Virgin! It's hanging from the tree by its ear."

The swineherd sat up swiftly. "All good, then." A grin. "Thanks! That was close." He loosened the noose and slipped it off over his head. He regarded the cut end thoughtfully. "Damn good shot. The only other man I know who could—"

"Hold on!" Roderick frowned. "That's it for both of us! Do you understand? No competition. No more pig herding!" His dark blue eyes glared at the naked man. "Damn it. Don't just sit there. Come on, move it! We've got to go." He hurried over to the dead bodies.

Abruptly, the swineherd understood. "They're going to hunt us down." He jumped up. He found his tunic under the tree trunk, slipped it on, grabbed his walking stick. "What's your name?"

"Roderick of Crossway. Come here!" Roderick had gathered as many arrows as he could and stuffed the bundles into three quivers; two he handed to the swineherd, the third he slung over his own shoulder. "And what is your name?"

"Malcolm. Up from—"

"Edwinstowe. I know." Roderick checked the ranger's bow. "Here. That's the best one."

Where to now? They glanced at each other. Deeper into Sherwood? To Crossway? Malcolm rejected that idea. "They'll come with weapons and dogs. If they follow our tracks to your village, they'll kill everyone. No, we have to get out. Out of the shire." The swineherd clenched his fists. "North." Grimly, he added, "And I know where to go, too. To Barnsdale!"

Roderick shrugged. "Fine by me. Let's go, then!"

After just a few steps. Malcolm halted. "Wait!" He ran to the beech, returned with the rabbit. "For the road. We have far to go."

They ran cross-country through Sherwood. Soon they had reached the old path and made faster progress. After a while, Roderick asked, "You know anyone up there in Barnsdale?"

Malcolm laughed. He called over his shoulder, "Sure do. A real sir, even, and his name is Robert of Loxley. But before that, he was . . ."

Impatiently, Roderick urged, "Well, tell me!"

"Why, Robin Hood, you milksop. Who else?"

XXIII

YORKSHIRE. KIRKLEES ABBEY.

The lad awaited the carriage far below the abbey. Two servants led the horse by the halter. Quietly the young man inquired, "A sir or a lady?"

"We are taking our mistress to Mother Matilda."

He walked beside the carriage. "Lady!" And again. "Lady!"

The curtain was pushed aside a crack. "What do you want?"

"To make you well, lady." With practiced skill, the lad opened the sack at his side; he pulled out three linen pouches one by one. "Bitter clover for fever? St. John's wort for a cough? Bloodroot for the sick stomach? Whatever you need, lady. Each medicine costs but a tuppence." He had a narrow face, a deep scar across his forehead. He urged, "Don't pass it by, my lady. Up there in the abbey, herbs will cost you three times as much."

"You can't help me." Slowly the curtain closed.

"Too bad." As the cart rolled on, the lad stayed behind. "But next time for sure."

Horsemen! Armed men in dark blue cloaks. A red coat of arms was emblazoned on their shields. They rode three abreast, and behind them another three. The lad knew only too well the noble lord who was being protected by these men-at-arms. A soft plume of feathers adorned the man's hat, and he wore a dark traveling cloak. Before the escort approached, the young man jumped away, hiding among the flowering bushes. Only after the abbey gate had closed behind the Baron of Doncaster did the boy return to the wayside.

Full of impatience, Sir Roger stared across the heavily laden fruit trees to the whitewashed building just to the left of the church. *"Par tous les diables!"* He stretched his thin lips into a smile. "No matter how long it takes. No quarry escapes my nets."

Mother Mathilda left the nuns' residence. With a firm step, the tall figure followed the raked path between the flower beds.

Sir Roger straightened. Regret, even slight compassion now dominated his countenance.

"Peace be with you, sir!"

He gave a nod. "I must speak with you, Reverend Mother."

Boldly, her dark eyes searched the Baron's features. "You seem free of complaint to me today." She raised her brows. "And yet you seem changed."

"Not speak with the healer, not with the prioress. Today I want to speak with my dear friend Mathilda."

The nun understood. "Then follow me, sir!"

In silence, she led her visitor past the infirmary tower into the herb garden and locked the gate. She smiled. "What can I do for you, sir?"

Sir Roger folded his arms. "You are a strong woman, Reverend Mother. Under your leadership, the abbey has continued to flourish. Indeed, its success exceeds my boldest hopes."

"Your praise shames me." She lowered her head. From cover of her veil, she surveyed the baron. Her tone remained humble. "Is that the only reason for this secretive conversation? I would have gladly received such praise in the refectory before all ears."

Sir Roger clasped his hands in front of his dark velvet tunic. "You may wish to sit down for this, Holy Mother!"

"I am always prepared."

"Your nephew." Carefully, the baron loosed the first sting. "He failed. Gamwell did not live up to my high expectations."

Mathilda gave no reaction. Calmly, she said, "I am astonished at that. True, you have never spoken of his secret mission. But in all these years, even on your last visit, you've been full of praise."

"Only to spare you, dear friend. You had enough to do with the expansion of the abbey. Besides, we all suffered under King Richard's rule." Sir Roger made of show of having to wrestle the words from his mouth. "I took Gamwell to my heart as a son. I prepared him for a great task. But, dear friend, I will conceal it no longer. Your nephew was chosen to hunt down Robin Hood. For the good of England! In return, I promised to raise him to the rank of a squire. More than that, with my influence, he would be a valued man in King John's court today." Chagrined, the baron continued. "Moreover, I promised Gamwell a thousand pounds in gold for the head of this filth."

"So much?" The prioress' eyes gleamed. "I beseech you, sir, give my nephew another chance!"

"*Attendez*, dear friend. You do not know everything yet." Sir Roger struck the final sting. "Gamwell is dead."

The blood drained from her white-framed face. Mathilda took two steps away, to escape the baron's gaze. "Dead?" she whispered. "How I loved him."

"Yes, dead. Disgracefully murdered. More than six years ago."

Behind her back, Sir Roger flicked some dust off his sleeve. He raised his voice, lamenting, "My miller found his body on the shore of the lake. He sent word to me—what a gruesome sight. Too many wounds in his back to count. But that is not all . . ." He trailed off.

"Go on, sir," Mathilda pleaded. Her strength returned. "I want to know everything."

"The body was mutilated. His hands and feet were missing."

The prioress turned. "Who? Who did this?"

"Gamwell was living with the outlaws as my spy at the time. And he was found out." The baron raised his hands. "Robin Hood. He slaughtered your nephew. Forgive me, dear friend, there is no kinder word, he slaughtered Gamwell." Sir Roger pressed his fingertips together. "And today, he lives safely as Sir Robert of Loxley on his estates."

Chillingly, Mathilda replied, "He is ill. You know this, sir. His leg will not heal. He comes to Kirklees monthly."

Sir Roger did not take his eyes off her. "And you will continue to treat him?"

"With all diligence." Like scales, she held out her open hands. "When one gives, the other shall be filled. That is how I see it, sir."

Sir Roger smiled. "*D'accord,* dear friend. A thousand pounds."

For a long time, the two gazed at each other. Neither lowered their eyes.

XXIV

YORKSHIRE. BARNSDALE.

Marian and Beth had come two days earlier. They would not reveal the reason.

"It's to be a surprise," Beth told Tom late the first night. "So don't ask any more questions!"

"I don't care." Toad leaned over his wife. "Things aren't as fine here at the estates as they are at your castle at Fenwick." He smiled at her. "You're there. And that's best of all."

The next morning, Marian set her hands on her hips. "I told you yesterday, John. It's *all right*!" She wore her hair down. Curls cascaded over her shoulders.

Full of pride, the giant looked at the slender young woman in her dress of soft dark leather. "You are beautiful, little one," he began, "Isn't it about time—"

"No! Please, John." Her blue eyes flashed. "I'll find a husband on my own. That's what we agreed."

The giant sighed. He stroked the scar in his graying beard. "Still, I'd like to know why you and Beth—"

"Wait and see. It's going to be a surprise for Robin. And until it's ready, we'll stay here. Will that do?"

"Very much."

Marian looked anxiously toward the estate's large manor house. "How is he today?"

"He's gotten worse. He's dragging his leg again."

"Can't Herbghost help?"

"The old man's trying. He's been trying for years, when the pain comes." But what good were michelwort and fleawort? The wound was festering deep inside his thigh. And only at the very beginning had William's herbs provided some relief for the sick man. No longer.

"Why don't you take him to Mathilda at Kirklees?"

"It's not my decision." John shrugged. "Robin is like you. 'Wait and see,' he says. 'I'll tell you when it's time.' So, I have to wait."

"Oh, John." Marian nestled against his arm. "You're the best man I know."

"Indeed, little one." He didn't give up: "But surely there are others."

She winked up at him. "Don't start that again!"

The second day, right after morning porridge together in the hall of the spacious manor house, Friar Tuck rose. "If our ladies are ready?" He clasped his hands. "I am at your disposal."

"You sound like my tutor," Marian scoffed.

"Hush, Princess!"

Only Robin, John, and the three closest friends—Friar Tuck and the two old cooks—lived together the old base's main building. Those who had families lived with their wives and children in Barnsdale Top, or on their land around the heavily fortified manor. Marian smiled from one to the other, demurely asking: "Forgive me, Brother Tuck." Mockery rippled through her voice. "I understand. We are the only ladies in this men's household." She pushed her stool back hard. "Come on, Beth. To work!"

Toad's wife sighed in dismay at her charge. She took the narrow wooden box. "Holy father, you lead the way!"

After they left the room, Robin leaned toward John. "I don't like this." His pale face perked up; feigning outrage, he continued, "Why go to the chapel? What are the ladies up to with our poor brother Tuck?"

"Don't ask me!" groaned John. Much and Threefinger grinned. Tom grinned across the table. "Let it go, Robin. All of us have tried. None of us got anything out of the women."

At the chapel, Tuck bolted the narrow door carefully from the inside.

"Clear everything off the altar, princess!" Only now did Beth flip open the lid of the box. With pinched fingers, she removed a white cloth of the finest silk. She spread it across the altar.

"By all the saints!" Friar Tuck approached full of awe, not daring to touch the cloth. A wide, embroidered border lined the edges. Roses and crosses wrought of gold and silver threads. "Truly, this is a surprise."

Beth smiled. Marian shook her head. "We're not done yet." Quickly, she stooped to the box, laid glittering strands of thread over the edge. She lifted a sharpened charcoal pencil. "I still want words on it, reverend. Beth and I thought it over. But we couldn't agree. You know best what words are right for Robin—I mean Sir Robert … never mind. What holy words are appropriate for Robin? After all, you are the priest here and also the confessor."

Friar Tuck glanced at the carved Madonna above the altar. "I don't have to think long about that." *"Ave Maria gratia plena,"* he said.

"So it will be!" Marian was triumphant. "I was right, I told you, Beth!"

"Hush, princess!" Toad's wife pushed the silk cloth back a bit, smoothed it over the side of the altar stone. "Here. We'll embroider it above these roses."

Obligingly, Friar Tuck asked for the charcoal pencil. "Good, I'll write out the text."

Marian huffed. "I can write fine myself, if you please. You just make sure I don't forget a letter!"

Ave Maria gratia plena.

They sent the priest away. He was not to come knocking until dinnertime.

Was that a horn call? Long, short, short. Strangers, the sentry from the tower above the palisades reported.

Much rushed ahead of the strangers into the hall. "Robin! John!" Frantic, he pointed to the door.

The two young men behind him halted after a few steps. Their faces were filthy, their hair greasy, their tunics torn in many places. Each had a bow and two quivers at his back.

Sir Robert of Loxley frowned, looking from one to the other. Finally, his gray eyes returned to the tall, dark fellow. "I know you."

Before he could answer, Much blurted out, "That . . . That's Malcolm! Remember? The swineherd from Edwinstowe!"

"Shut up, boy!" growled John.

As quickly as his pain would allow, Robin lifted his ailing leg from the stool and put his foot down. "Welcome to Barnsdale, Malcolm."

"Sir Robert." The swineherd gulped. "It was like this—Roderick and me—we had to get away from Sherwood. There was the ranger, and the farmhands—"

"I killed them!" Roderick spoke out clearly, firmly. "I had to kill them."

The way he spoke . . . John took in a breath. *I know that tone.* But he pushed the thought aside.

"You had to?" asked Robin.

"Yes." The young man pressed his lips together.

"Because I was hanging from a tree," Malcolm explained hastily. "I caught a rabbit in a snare. But they were on me. And when I balancing was on the stick—"

"Enough!" Robin slammed his fist down on the table. With a

glance at John, he demanded, "One thing at a time, Malcolm. The whole story, but from the beginning."

And the swineherd told them: about Edwinstowe, about the raid by the lord sheriff's soldiers. Even though the villagers paid all their taxes on time, soldiers had stolen the crops. As *just a warning*! The iron men had laughed. Nothing had been left for the villagers. Hunger reigned in Edwinstowe. "That's the only reason I went hunting."

John listened with clenched fists. Just like it had been in days long before. He saw the hungry eyes of the children in his village again. *Oh, Robin, it's starting all over again.* As the swineherd recounted Roderick's fight, the two friends sat at attention. From the corners of their eyes, they eyed the young man's powerful figure.

"And that's what happened. And if he hadn't come along . . ." Malcolm wiped his hands on his torn tunic.

"Why?" Robin's expression was stony. "Roderick, what did you care about some naked poacher hanging from on a tree?"

"Did you expect me to just move on?" Indignation sparked in his dark blue eyes. "I hate injustice! That's why, Sir Robert."

"And for that, you have given up the competition?" the Lord of Loxley probed further.

John tried to calm him. He lightly touched his friend's arm.

"No." Robin shook him off. He continued, teasing, "And the beautiful milk cow? You wanted to buy it for your people, didn't you? Such a fine cow is worth more than five Malcolms. You're an idiot, Roderick. What do you care about injustice if it doesn't affect you?"

"Enough!" the young man yelled. His bow leaped into his fist.

Already John was on his feet, yanking up the stool. "Dare me!" he roared. Beside him, Much held his knife, ready to throw.

Roderick faltered in midmotion. "I don't want to break the rules of hospitality. But tell him to shut up!"

"Enough!" Sharp and cutting. Robin spread his arms. "Easy, friends, easy! Much, put away the dagger! Sit down, John!"

A smile twitched at the corners of his mouth. "And you, Roderick," he said softly, "set down your bow and tell me where you're from."

"Crossway." After a while he added, "Sir Robert."

"I like you, Roderick from Crossway. Welcome to Barnsdale." He looked at his wound dressing, soberly summarizing. "You killed a forester and his servants. Through necessity, you took a stand. True, you were in the right. But no one will believe you, my boy. And you, Malcolm, you hunted royal game. Who cares about hunger in Edwinstowe? I'm sure Lord Sheriff Walter de Monte has long since passed sentence on you both." Robin raised his head. "He will hunt you, and not only him. You are outlaws."

"That's why, Sir Robert . . ." Malcolm took a step forward. "That's why we came here. Because we need help."

"I can provide protection." Robin added harshly, "But only you can help yourselves. You'll have to fight."

"No question." Roderick brushed the tangled strands from his forehead.

"He always says that, Sir Robert." The swineherd extended his open hands helplessly. "Fight? That's what the people at Blidworth tried to do. And now . . ."

"What happened in Blidworth?" John snapped at him. "I was there only a month ago with Solomon. We bought wool, pots. Everything was fine." He raised his fist. "Tell me! What happened at Blidworth?"

Shortly after the trader's wagons train had moved on, the sheriff's men-at-arms had closed in on the village. They had demanded all the proceeds. Desperate, the residents tried to fight back. The elder's head was cut from his shoulders by the soldiers, then another villager. "Nobody's alive there anymore," Malcolm whispered. "And we're supposed to fight that?"

"I'm not afraid," Roderick said cockily. "Not of the sheriff or his iron puppets. Nor of the foresters."

"Do you even understand what you're saying?" growled John.

"You have to fight!" cried Roderick passionately. "By the Virgin, these fellows will eat us up if we don't."

"That's right, lad."

Coolly, Robin smiled. "To truly win a fight like this, it takes a lot more than hate. You seem to have that." He snapped his fingers. "Much, give them both a bedchamber! And make sure they wash up! After all, we have ladies visiting."

Closing his eyes, Robin leaned back in his armchair. John waited. After a while, John murmured, "By Dunstan. We divided up the money for each village. The elder from Blidworth was a good man."

"You heard their story. 'Robin Hood,' the woodsmen shouted. The sheriff will get that name stuck in his craw." Robin lifted his eyelids. His pale face became animated. "And by now, everyone in Sherwood knows it, too: Robin Hood is back! You see, John? That alone gives hope to the people!"

"What?" John stared at his friend in disbelief. "What do you expect to do? You with your leg? And me with my gray hair. Look at the pair of us!"

"This is the game. Wait and see!" Robin laughed.

Candles flickered on the long oak table. For the ladies, the two old cooks had outdone themselves: crispy fish, roast in bread dough, fragrant pheasant pie. And malmsey to go with it.

Beth watched her princess. Her food stood untouched before the young woman. "What's wrong with you?" she whispered.

"Nothing." And as if caught in a lie, Marian hastily explained, "I'm not hungry. Nothing else."

The ladies had been the last to enter the hall.

"These are Malcolm and Roderick," Robin had announced. "Visitors from Sherwood."

The young man had smiled. For a moment, Marian faltered, as if startled by his open, bright face.

A stern look from Beth was enough to bring her back to herself. A polite nod of greeting and the women had settled into the seats of honor.

Ever since the beginning of the feast, Marian had just sat there, upright, her fingers stroking the rim of her wine cup.

Roderick and Malcolm enjoyed themselves. Starved, they gobbled up the delicacies—no time for conversation. Sir Robert, the other men, and Friar Tuck also ate with great appetite. Such a feast came only ever so often. And yet, there was an oppressive silence in the hall. Everyone already knew what news the visitors had brought from Sherwood.

John poked at the pie on his plate with his knife. His throat was tight. *Is it going to start again? By Dunstan—sleeping every night under a different bush?*

And all that running? Oh, my friend, even if you don't want to admit it, we're too old for all that.

Sir Robert of Loxley raised his silver goblet. "Not only our ladies have something for us—I also have a surprise!" Everyone, even Marian, turned eagerly to the head of the table. "But first, drink with me!"

Robin waited until everyone had put down their goblets. Then he set his hands on the table and braced himself. He looked at Roderick and Malcolm. "Six years ago, it was, when King Richard gave my men and me a general pardon. Our fight was over. Not only for us in Barnsdale, no—law and order were also extended to the villagers in Sherwood. But those six good years are over. John sits on the throne of England! And all his noble rats are coming out of their holes again. Oppression. Cruel despotism. You two have reported it to us: They bleed the villagers in Sherwood without mercy, more terribly than ever."

Beth reached for Marian's hand, squeezed it. All around in the faces of the old band of outlaws, the memories were revived. Heavily, Malcolm propped his head in both hands. Roderick tensed. He listened with a blank expression.

Robin's voice grew hard. "Fight back! Only our resistance can keep these rats from the people's houses and cottages."

Don't. John crushed the rim of his cup. *Don't say it, Robin!*

"But for me and my loyal friends, the fight in the forest is over. We cannot go back to it. Many of us have families. Protecting their lives has to be my task now."

Easing, John let out a sigh of relief.

Robin's gaze fixed on Roderick. "I've made a decision. If you consent, I can give you more than just protection in a safe place."

"What?" The young man waited.

"In that time, I called myself Robin Hood. That was the name my men followed. The innocent rallied around Robin Hood, not Robert of Loxley. The name alone terrified my enemies and gave the villagers of our shires new courage to resist. And today? All over Sherwood, the word is out again: Robin Hood has returned. But it wasn't I who killed the rangers. It was you."

Roderick placed his clenched fists on the oak slab in front of him. His face flushed.

Robin took note. "I see you're catching on quickly." After a pause, he turned to the others, and spoke clearly and forcefully, "My friends, beginning today, Robin Hood is no longer a name. It is an honor. As long as there is injustice in England, there will be a Robin Hood!" Sir Robert offered both hands to the young man. "Take this title from me, Roderick! You can win this fight. Take it, be a new Robin Hood for the desperate! Let hope return." Sir Robert of Loxley fell silent.

Breathless silence.

“Yes.” There was a glint of light in the dark blue eyes. “I’ll take on that honor. No question about it. I’ll fight, even if I have to do it alone.”

“There are two of us already.” Determined, Malcolm brushed back his black hair.

“I . . .” Marian hesitated, then said, “You will win this! I know it.” Her hand bumped against her cup. The wine spilled across the table. Marian laughed. And it was like a spark. The old brotherhood slapped each other’s shoulders, joined in the laughter; they drummed their fists on the table.

“All right, now, enough!” The noise broke off. Coolly, Sir Robert took the measure of the brawny young man. “One more thing, young Robin Hood. You claim to have shot Malcolm off the rope as you turned? Are you really that good?”

“The best.”

“Even with the longbow?”

“Of course.” A confident smile.

“Don’t stuff your mouth too full, boy!” John huffed; he’d caught on to Robin’s game. “Tomorrow at the archery range, you’ll go up against us oldsters.” He grinned broadly. “Bring pennies to lose.”

“And get them from where?” For just a moment, Roderick hesitated, then he lifted his chin. “I won’t need any money.”

They rose early, while the others still asleep. John brought a saddled horse. But his ailing friend refused. “No, John. By the good Virgin, not today. I can walk that short distance on my own feet.” He clasped his hands. “I’ll manage. We should set out right away. We’ll be the first ones there.”

Immediately after the morning meal, the other old former outlaws set out with the young new outlaws. Roderick carried a longbow. His gait was light. He had tamed his golden mane with a headband.

Marian gazed after him.

"Why are you dawdling about?" Beth saw Marian's expression, which made her admonish the girl all the more sternly. "Come along, princess! Otherwise, we'll never finish the altar cloth."

Friar Tuck unlocked the narrow door into the chapel. Marian could contain herself no longer. "I have to . . . oh, please, Beth." Her eyes pleaded. "Can't you go on working alone today?" Hastily she tried to explain, "I have to be there when they shoot, don't I?"

"You have to?"

Marian nodded.

After a moment the nursemaid smiled. "You have it that bad?" The blood rushed to Marian's cheeks. "Oh, princess." Beth squeezed her hand. "Run along, then. You won't be late."

Marian ran, stopped, returned. Breathless, she asked for some coins. "Only a loan! But at least a shilling. Please!"

Friar Tuck was able to help out.

"Thank you, father!"

"Why do you want it, princess?"

"Because he doesn't have any!" Already she was on her way out again. She called back over her shoulder, "But we won't need it. I know that."

Just in time, Marian reached the wide training area from the secret path outside the palisades.

The archers had taken their positions. A good hundred paces from them, Much pinned a target cloth to the straw-padded wall.

"What are you doing here, little girl?" John's voice sounded gruff. The tension was plain in him, as well as the other men.

"I've come to see who's the best." Marian shrugged. "Why else?"

With a stick, Toad parted a straight furrow through the grass. He was in charge of the morning's shooting contest. He collected five pennies each from John and Sir Robert then insistently he held out his hand to young Robin Hood. “The stake must be paid first.” He stretched out his little joke. “Or else, wee lad, you lose.”

“I can’t,” the blond man hissed. “You know I can’t.” He glared angrily at his opponents. “And so do all of you.”

“I’m covering the bet!” Marian announced, brightly and decisively.

Heads wheeled around. “For me?” asked Roderick, dumbfounded, face softening for a moment, smiling. “Just like that?”

“No.” Their eyes, Marian approached him. “Just because I want to. Just because.” Before she could hand Roderick her the silver pennies, John was at her elbow.

“It’s all right, boy,” John assured him. “You can pay the stakes later.” Gently but firmly, he steered the young woman away. “Little one, get back there with Malcolm and Threefinger.”

“Don’t tell me what to—” Marian caught herself. “Oh, right! Yes!”

She waved at Roderick and obeyed. “Thank you!” exclaimed Roderick after her.

Sir Robert had watched the scene intently. The corners of his mouth twitched.

“What?” the giant growled.

“Wait and see, my friend. Wait and see!”

Tom Toad ordered the archers to take their positions. They stretched their arm and back muscles, slipped a leather guard over their right hands. Then they stepped up to the line Tom had marked, standing sideways to the target, legs slightly spread.

Speed and marksmanship were required for the first pass. Each of the five white target circles had to be hit. Toad divided the target cloth: Sir Robert was to work his way down from the top, outer ring to inner, John was to shoot in a line on the right side, Roderick the left. “No mistakes. Whoever does it first gets the whole stake.”

“No contest.” Roderick pressed his lips together.

Silence. Focused only on the target, they waited for Toad's signal. Tom snapped the stick with a loud *crack*.

Three arrows flew from the bowstrings. Three arrows struck the outer ring. The archers were swift. Hands whipped to the quiver, drew, fired. Second arrow, third. A show of power in matched rhythm! The fourth. Roderick drew the bowstring a fifth time. His arrow whizzed away. A heartbeat later, the more arrows flew through the air, hitting the fifth ring—a heartbeat too late.

The archers waited.

Marian pressed her hand over her mouth. Next to her, the swineherd clutched at his hair.

"How looks it, Bill?" asked Toad solemnly.

Threefinger shaded his eyes. "Good. All the arrows are right on target."

Much ran to the target cloth. He pointed to the left side, raised his fist.

"Roderick!" blurted out Marian, exultant. "Yes! I knew it!"

Malcolm danced from foot to foot. "We were faster!"

But full of respect, the young Robin Hood turned to his opponents. "Just got lucky. By our Maiden, that was close."

"You're good," said Sir Robert, in simple praise, with no mockery. He winked at the gray-bearded giant. "Remarkable! Nobody's ever managed that but you and me."

"At least his shooting matches his bragging." Grinning broadly, John added, "Now he can prove how good he *really* is."

The bet was ten pennies this time. Tom asked only John and Sir Robert to put in for the second round. He stopped briefly when he reached Roderick and stroked his shriveled scalp and tugged on his braid. "Anything I said was in jest. No one here seriously mocks each other. That's just how it is with us."

Roderick stretched. "So I see. I'm learning that fast."

"All right, then." Tom turned to his old companions. "As is proper, this time, the wee lad paid his bet beforehand." He ordered the archers to the second target.

Before Roderick got into position, he waved at Marian. "Thank you again! For the bet."

"That's enough, wee lad," John grumbled angrily into his beard. "One thank you will suffice."

Sir Robert quietly teased, "I think our little condition has already hit her own target. Now, make an effort this time, so we can do the same."

The giant frowned. Target? What did he mean? *Don't worry, Robin, we'll show the lad a thing or two.*

Dead center on the target was the aim this time. "One shot each," Tom Toad announced. "One after the other. Winner takes all. John, you go first. Then Robin—" He corrected himself with a grin, "Then Sir Robert, and last, young Robin Hood."

John stepped up to the line. He reached for the quiver. One gesture flowed into the next. The arrow buzzed through the air and a hundred paces away, it struck the black dot just above center.

No one made a sound.

Sir Robert shifted his bad leg back a little with his hands. He was ready. Clear gray eyes locked on the target. The string sang. A feathered shaft appeared in the dead center of the target.

Roderick's brows knit. He lowered his bow. "Where do you expect me to shoot?"

"Whatever do you mean?" Toad pointed sternly toward the straw-padded wall. "In the middle. Where else?"

"There's no room there."

"Oh, I see." Tom folded his arms. "So, you're giving up? Then Sir Robert—"

"No! He's not giving up!" Marian urged him on. "Go ahead, Roderick. Shoot!"

The young Robin Hood glanced over at her, looked at Tom. "Only jesting," he apologized.

"Get on with it, boy!" urged John.

"No trouble at all." His face turned serious. Roderick tightened and loosened his grip on the bow. He took an arrow from the quiver, weighed it, chose another. Satisfied, he moistened the notched end with his tongue and carefully set the arrow on the string. Eyes cold, a brief moment of calm, then he pulled back and released the arrow. The glinting point bored into the bright feathered shaft, splitting Sir Robert's arrow and lodging in the middle of the target's eye.

The Lord of Loxley was the first to break the silence. "Nice." He laid his hand heavily on the young man's shoulder. "Yesterday you showed me your head and your heart. And today . . ." His voice became hoarse. "Yes, you are the one. Find the right companions, and you will win the battle."

The two locked eyes in silence. Little John stepped up to them. "You can handle a bow, boy." He grinned. "But if you want to be Robin Hood, there's more we old ruffians can teach you. You only have to . . ."

". . . ask," Roderick finished, grinning at himself. He looked candidly at the men. "I never want to be without your advice."

Sir Robert poked his friend lightly in the side. "Lest you ever make a mistake." The two laughed, and Roderick joined in.

The laughter attracted the others over.

"But who, who won?" Malcolm wanted to know.

"Robin Hood always wins, of course!" Marian brushed back the curls from her forehead. "The victory is yours."

"The stakes, too?" Roderick asked tentatively.

The tall young woman nodded. "Yes. Yours, too."

"Then I have . . ." he counted on his fingers ". . . thirty pennies!" He could hardly believe it.

With a slapping of shoulders, the congratulations, and coins, were given to the winner.

Sir Robert eyed the young men. "You may not stay here in the manor. But don't worry. We have a safe place for you. No sheriff or iron soldier will find you there." He motioned to Tom Toad. "Take Much and Threefinger, and show them our main camp down in the gorge!" He turned to Roderick. "From this day on, it's yours."

"I'll take him." Marian stood beside Roderick, hands on hips. She looked at John, daring him to object. "I want to show him, myself." Her voice caught slightly, but the tone brooked no argument. "We'll take the path through the rocks. It's shorter. The others can go down the supply trail with Malcolm."

Before the giant could compose himself, she called out, "Come on, Robin!" and led the way. Roderick quickly caught up with her, staying close to her side.

John froze in place. *There she goes, just like that, with that young fellow!*

At his back, Sir Robert signaled to the rest to move along. Quickly Toad headed off with Malcolm and the others. "Well, my friend?" With no hint of mockery, he said, "I like them."

"Who?" John huffed.

"Well, those two. Our little condition and our young Robin."

John swallowed, resistant, but the idea grew, pushed its way into his head. At last, the giant understood. He saw her angry eyes again, back on the road to Barnsdale Top. *I'll find a husband on my own.* John wiped his forehead with his sleeve. First, she didn't want one. Now she does? So quickly? "She knows her own mind," he said at last.

"And I'm grateful for that." Robin pressed a hand against the bandage on his right thigh. "You'd better take me to Kirklees. First thing in the morning. Before this swells up any bigger." He clenched his jaw. “When Friar Tuck rings the bell for them, my friend, I’ll be the first to dance with the bride at the feast.” He poked his friend lightly in the side. “Well, what do you say?” Smirking, he demanded, “Just say it!”

“That’s all right,” John grumbled.

XXV

YORKSHIRE. KIRKLEES ABBEY.

The lad awaited the two horsemen far below the abbey. Swiftly they came nearer. Good customers. He knew the slender gentleman on the white stallion, the giant on the strong bay. Both carried bows. They had been coming here for years, and never rode by without buying something from him, too.

"Sir Robert!" The lad walked along beside the white horse. "I can make you well, sir." With practiced ease, he pulled out his linen pouches one by one. "Bitter clover for fever? St. John's wort for the cough? Bloodroot for the sick stomach? Each medicine costs only three pennies."

"Three?" Little John scratched the scar in the gray tangle of his beard, looking stern, "Last time you only charged two pennies for your herbs."

Robin played along. "Move on. We're not buying from grifters."

The two friends trotted along lightly. But the efficient peddler kept pace. "Don't say that, Sir Robert! But everything has gotten more expensive." He held out the bags to him. "Don't pass it by. Up there in the abbey, herbs cost four times as much now."

Robin reined in the stallion and counted out nine pennies. "Here, little one. You can't help my leg. But once you know more about the healing arts, I'll come only to you. Then we'll ruin the prioress's business."

"Thank you, sir!" The lad clutched the silver pieces tightly in his fist, pressing them against the scar on his forehead. "And may the saints protect you!" He watched the men go until the monastery gate closed behind them.

"All is prepared." Prioress Matilda stepped out of the gate of the infirmary tower, in her bright, pure robe and starched veil. "Come, Robert!" Only her mouth smiled in the white-framed face, not the eyes that looked coldly on her nephew.

"Oh, aunt!" Painfully, Robin dragged his leg. "How fortunate that you exist!"

John tried to support him. But his friend shook his head.

At once, the prioress asked for the fee. "I must ask you to give me twenty pounds this time. Because . . ."

"Yes yes yes," Robin interrupted, pulling two bulging pouches from his belt, sighing. "Everything has gotten more expensive. John and I have already heard it."

For a moment the smile disappeared, but returned immediately. Almost gently, she explained, "No, Robert, don't think you're paying me too much. Lately I've been pondering long and hard. And I know now how to relieve you of all your discomfort."

"You mean . . . ?"

"Yes, Robert." She clasped her hands together. "And such a cure comes at a price."

Fiercely, John squeezed his friend's arm. "If it's true," he murmured, "then I'll pay ten pounds more on top of that."

"Reverend Aunt," Robin said frankly. "In all of England, you are the best healer."

"I know." The tall figure straightened. "Now come, Robert! It is time. We'll begin with a physic and bloodletting." She pointed up to the top of the tower. "The top room is prepared for you. Just below the sky." She asked the giant for patience. "The medicine needs time to take effect. Also, the care of the wound will certainly take longer this time. Allow yourself to rest and enjoy our beautiful garden! The fruit is ripe."

John objected. "Better to stay with Robin. All those stairs. I'll take him up."

"No!" In the next instant, her tone lost its edge again. Quietly, she continued. "Though I don't appear to, I do have strength enough to carry my nephew up myself."

"Enough!" Determinedly, Robin hobbled to the gate. "Neither of you will help me." He swung his leg onto the first step. "Now come, Aunt! What are you waiting for?"

John stood back and folded his arms. *Fine.*

A light-filled room. In the middle, a raised straw bed, covered with gray linen. A rope, fresh cloths, and bandages lay carefully arranged over a stool. In the blood bowl on the floor gleamed the fleam, the silver instrument for opening the vein.

"A moment, Aunt!" Breathing heavily, Robin stepped to the window. He drew in the air. His gaze ran along the monastery wall, wandered through the cut meadows, across the river, and on to the distant edge of the forest. "How still everything lies."

"Give me your weapons!" demanded the voice at his back. Robin unfastened his sword belt, slipped quiver and bow from his shoulder.

"The tunic, too, nephew," she urged.

Robin obeyed. "How good the land smells." He breathed deep.

Mathilda stepped up beside him. "Drink this, Robert!"

With the small bottle in his hand, he pointed out the window. "Even up here, I can still smell the hay."

Her lips quivered. He did not perceive it. She pulled on his arm. "Drink, nephew!"

Robin emptied the vial in one gulp. He contorted his face briefly at the taste, shook himself. "I'd prefer a sip of malmsey," he said.

"The bitter always comes before the sweet." Her voice wavered slightly.

Robin looked to the far edge of the forest, "How wise you are. I have been fighting all my life. And at last, I prevailed. But my happiness did not last. You have forgotten one thing, venerable aunt. The fight goes on. As long as there is injustice, the sweetness is followed by bitterness. It comes around again . . . like . . ." Robin struggled to hold the thought. "Like summer . . ." He broke off, wiping his brow. "My eyes? I see . . ."

Mathilda grabbed his arm. "What, Robert? What do you see?"

"The . . . meadows. They're blurring into the river."

"It's all right, nephew. The medicine is working." She led him away from the window. His step became more sluggish, his muscles almost failing. Mathilda held him until he stretched out on the bed.

All at once, his pale face contorted again. "You must—" He coughed, trying to speak louder. "If you mean to . . ." His voice faded to a whisper.

"It's all right, Robert." Quickly, she laid the rope, cloths, and bandages beside him, sat on the stool, and pulled his left arm straight. She pushed the loose fabric of his shirt up to his armpit. Mathilda did not hesitate. She took the thin fleam and set its silver rose thorn against his skin. Her finger struck down on its end. Dark blood welled from the vein. Matilda's eyes flinched. Her finger struck a second time, harder, a third time. Bright blood spurted. The jet splashed against the whitewashed stones. In bursts, new jets followed, again and again.

Robin lifted his head with difficulty, trying to see. "Red?" he whispered. "Is that my blood? There on the wall?"

"It's all right, Robert." With a hard grip, she held his arm. "You have a strong heart. That's why the blood leaps like that." Only when the flow weakened did she place a cloth over the opened veins. She rose swiftly, laying his arm on the stool. Under the linen, the blood continued to pulse steadily.

Robin looked up at the tall figure. For a moment, the veil lifted from his eyes. “My blood has stained you, venerable Aunt.” He smiled faintly. “On your breast.”

“It’s fine, Robert.” She strode to the door. “I’ll wash it off.” Mathilda left the room. She locked the door firmly, hiding the key behind a stone.

The prioress stepped out of the gate. In the shadow of the tower, Little John leaned against the wall. Indecisive at first, she walked quickly over to him. “Did you know Gamwell?” Her voice was brittle, so brittle. “My nephew?”

John was startled. His gaze lingered on the bloodstains; he dared not look into her face. “Will Scarlet? Yes, he used to be with us.”

“I loved him.” She turned and hurried away.

John looked after the prioress. The white-clad figure strode between the flower gardens toward the nuns’ residence.

By Dunstan. Why did she ask me that? We don’t talk about Gamwell, Robin said.

Robin? The giant stared up at the tower. Saw the blood on the nun’s robe again. Robin? It was going to take longer this time. Her words repeated in his head. *And she’s leaving? So soon? Surely she can’t leave him alone while he’ s being bled!*

“Robin!” John cried out.

Panic drove him forward. He rushed into the tower, running up the twisting stairs. “Robin!” His heart beat wildly. His roar echoed, rushed before him.

He did even try the door—with all his might, he threw his giant body against it. Wood splintered. John froze. There was blood on the wall. Robin lay still on the bed. So still.

He fell to his knees beside him. Gently stroked his forehead. “Robin?”

His eyes opened. “Yes, John. I hear you.” He spoke softly, struggling for each word. “My limbs . . . are heavy as iron.” With an effort, he sucked in his breath. “But that’s good, Mathilda said.”

John saw the blood-soaked cloth, saw the great dark pool on the floor. His fist gripped Robin's left arm, squeezing closed the flesh over the open veins. "She wants to kill you. Kill you!"

"She has . . . she has already done it."

"She can't," John stammered. His voice roared. "I'll burn the convent. And the nun! And all of them! Till there's nothing left!"

"Enough!" Softly, yet it was an order. Robin groped with his right hand for John's big fist. "We don't kill defenseless people. Remember that, John!"

"Because of Gamwell. And for that baron. That's why she did this."

"No one stays blameless. Tell Roderick that, too." He brushed his fingertips over John's hand. "Let the blood flow! It's over, my friend. She gave me poison. Mathilda has already won the fight." All at once, light returned to the gray eyes. "Quickly. The bow. Choose a good arrow!"

John nodded. He held them out to his friend.

"I can't do it alone. Help me!"

And the giant sat down behind him, pulling Robin up to his chest. Robin's weak hand wrapped around the bow. John clasped it tightly. He nocked the feathered shaft, guided Robin's fingers to the string. John lent him his strength. The arrow sped out through the open window.

"A good shot." Robin groaned, falling back against John's broad chest. "Where you find the arrow. That's where I want to lie."

He held on to the bow. "It's a shame, John."

He was silent too long.

"What, Robin?" John lightly squeezed the hand in his. "Tell me. What?"

"Our little condition. Now . . . now you have to dance with her." His head sank back.

John wept. Trembling shook his wide shoulders. As if afraid to wake him, John gently curled over Robin, burying his face in his friend's hair.

The abbey bell rang out. The noon chime called the giant back into the world. He carried Robin in his arms down the stairs and stepped out of the dark confines. The light stung.

With great haste, the gate was opened for him.

John strode through it and out across the shorn meadows. He followed the arrow's flight without stopping.

And he found the arrow.